Shadows of Doubt

A Novel

Herb Brown

DONALD I. FINE, INC.
New York

Library of Congress Catalogue Card Number: 93-74478

ISBN: 1-55611-394-3

Manufactured in the United States of America

10 9 8 7 6 5 4 3 2 1

Designed by Irving Perkins Associates

For Beverly

For suggestions on incidents described in the story I am indebted to Don Fine, Beverly Brown, Susan Cohen, Virginia Tsipas, Tom Brandt, Norton Girault, Delmer Norris, Marcia Mengel, Colleen Palazzo, Terry Perkins, Dr. Maurice Rusoff, Barbara Terzian, Dr. Judith Westman and Craig Wright.

I
Kathleen

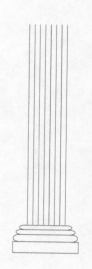

This shaking keeps me steady. I should know.
What falls away is always. And is near.
I wake to sleep, and take my waking slow.
I learn by going where I have to go.

— THEODORE ROETHKE

Chapter 1

THE CHARGE WAS **Murder One** and the red light above the
locked door meant that the jury, after two days, had still not
reached a verdict. Kathleen Sullivan felt that she, like her client,
was awaiting judgment. The defendant, her client, was also her
half-sister.

It was a little past ten on a Saturday night. The green light
hadn't come on since the jury asked for supper. Food was taken
to the jurors at six and since then the red light had been on
constantly. When the red light went off and the green came on it
would mean that the jury had done something or wanted something. It could be the verdict. They could have a question or want
a part of the testimony reread. Or it could mean they wanted to
recess for the night.

She was staring at the light the way she once stared at Jesus on
the cross when, as a little girl, her parents took her to mass. Jesus
had never revealed his secrets. But when the light above the jury
room door changed from red to green and the jurors brought in
the verdict there would be answers; her life would be changed
and so, of course, would her sister's.

For Kathleen, the hardest part of a trial had always been the
wait for a verdict. She looked at the two rows of empty chairs and
the door at the rear of the jury box. Behind the locked door with

the red light above it, the twelve were exercising their God-like power.

When the jurors left their chairs to enter the deliberation room, there was nothing a lawyer could do but wait. You thought of the decisions you had made during the trial, the questions you —or in this case, your colleague—shouldn't have asked, what might have been said by the witness you decided not to call, the argument you forgot to make in your summation. You saw the face of the lady in chair number nine; the lady who had folded her arms across her chest and averted her eyes as you made your plea. You remembered your intuition during voir dire examination. You should have challenged her, removed her from the panel. Now she was behind the locked door and you prayed she wouldn't be elected forelady.

In any trial the wait was tense. Kathleen had been trying cases for more than ten years. But those were civil cases. A civil case could also change lives. When the green light came on and the jurors brought in the verdict, it could tell a quadriplegic who had suffered injury in a coal mine whether he would receive medical care and over a million dollars in damages or be turned away because the accident was caused by his misuse of the equipment.

But she had never felt as she did waiting in the half-lit, nearly empty courtroom on that Saturday night. It was the first criminal trial she had had anything to do with; a first-degree murder, no less.

Because of the bond that had developed between them, as well as her own conviction, Kathleen strongly recommended that her sister reject the state's plea bargain. "The best deal I ever offered in a murder case," was the way Socko Bender, the state's attorney, had put it.

"You must stand trial," Kathleen had insisted. "You *aren't* guilty and it will destroy your life if you give in. Even if you admit to involuntary manslaughter it means jail time." Kathleen had taken responsibility for, in effect, deciding for her sister. And if she was wrong, then what—fifteen years in the penitentiary?

Waiting for the green light and the verdict, she was rethinking all that had happened, going back to the night of the killing. That night, after she met her sister Deb Garrison at Central Police Headquarters and did the protective procedures that had to be done there, she had driven to the scene.

Lights were still flashing on cruisers parked outside the Garrison house, which had been secured with yellow crime-scene tape. Detectives in plainclothes and uniformed officers were everywhere.

They would not let her go inside. Then the body came out, on a stretcher and covered by a green canvas sheet. The policeman on the front end of the stretcher was talking to a man in plainclothes who walked beside him.

"You ever see one like this?" the cop asked. "You think death was instantaneous?"

"Maybe," said the plainclothesman. His head was down and he seemed to be thinking of something else, little interested in the cop's chatter.

"It's open-and-shut," the cop said.

The plainclothesman grunted his agreement.

Light came from every room in the house. Detectives and policemen could be seen as they passed the upstairs windows. Kathleen recognized Socko Bender's Oldsmobile parked in the driveway between two of the cruisers with flashing lights. The assistant county prosecutor had come to the scene of this crime. If the case were so open-and-shut, a lot of people were working to make sure it stayed that way.

"The only out," said the cop, "would be insanity. And this woman's no psycho. Unless frying your husband makes you a psycho."

The plainclothesman, as if reminded of something, turned and ran back into the house . . .

"Open-and-shut." The cliché, spoken by the cop who had carried the stretcher nine months before, rang in Kathleen's mind as she waited on this Saturday night, her eye on the red light above the locked jury room door. Had the relationship with her sister persuaded her that there was a way out? It was too late to be asking the question, but she did anyway.

There was the old saying Kathleen first heard during her freshman year at Harvard: "The lawyer who represents himself has a fool for a client." Well, she wasn't representing herself, wasn't even, in the usual sense, the lawyer of record. But didn't the rule apply here nonetheless? And hadn't she violated it? Wasn't this as much *her* case as it would have been if she had stood in the well and asked all the questions herself? She had put the defense together, made it fit the law. She had been the main witness for the defense. It was her credibility the jury was weighing as they deliberated behind the locked door and the red light.

My God, she thought. What if the jurors come out stony-faced and looking at their feet? What if the verdict is Guilty as Charged?

Usually Kathleen felt relief as well as tension after a jury went into deliberation. She thought about decisions and mistakes but she knew nothing could be done. It was a release of sorts not to be watching reactions—from the judge, witnesses, your client, the jurors. You were rid of the burden of thinking that everything you did could cause the case to be won or lost. You talked to the bailiff, had tea with the judge in his chambers, tried to worm a prediction out of the court stenographer, read the newspaper, went down to the cafeteria and left word where you could be reached if anything happened. You went into the preparation room and made telephone calls.

This case was different. The verdict depended more on what she had done than in any case she had actually tried. And the charge was murder. And the defendant was her recently discovered half-sister, with whom she had formed an instant bond.

She recognized the verdict to come as one of the dividing marks in her life—like when she discovered she had been adopted, like when she, for reasons she dared not even try to understand then, was punished in school and not allowed to carry the statue of Mary in the festival of the Blessed Virgin, like the afternoon she had opened the letter telling her she had been admitted to Harvard Law School, like the morning she had gotten her bar examination result, like the night she first had intercourse, like the time she had worked late in the office with Tony and then gone back to her house in German Village to fantasize about him and masturbate, like the day she had been called into Managing Partner Si Wallace's office to be told they had made her a partner in Latham, Fuller and Richards, like the decision she had made to try cases for clients other than doctors, hospitals, insurance carriers and Fortune 500 companies.

As she waited she sat on the defense counsel table in the well of the half-lit courtroom, one foot dangling and the other on the parquet floor. Ellen Sharkey, the reporter for the Columbus *Post,* had been steadily looking at her, searching for reactions. On the other side of the well the prosecutor Socko Bender was swapping stories with Junior Fultz, the bailiff. The lights had been turned off above the raised bench, leaving the flags at either end and the chair from which Judge Conklin had presided in shadows. Shadows . . . this case was full of them.

She was listening to her associate Tony, he seated behind the counsel table, and she twisted to look at him while she kept the red light at the rim of her vision. Her sister's case had brought her and Tony together. Close together.

The clock on the wall above the bailiff's desk burped and the minute hand bounced forward. It was 10:53. The red light went off and the green one came on above the door to the jury room.

Kathleen immediately got up from the table and watched Bailiff Junior Fultz approach the door with his key. He would go in, find out whether the green light meant a verdict, another question or recess for the night.

The green light, as she stared at it, seemed to glitter. It did not quiet her to know that it was probably no more than a request to break for the night and that the wait would take up again in the morning.

Tony had also stood. He had come around the counsel table to stand beside her. She reached for his hand. It was as cold and clammy as hers.

Chapter 2

ALITTLE OVER a year before the murder trial, Kathleen had been working late, in her office on the twenty-third floor of the Capitol Tower building, rehearsing the argument she would make the next morning in the Ohio supreme court. It was twenty to eleven. She walked to her window and looked down on the lighted statehouse, the deserted capitol grounds and the streets of Columbus. She was trying to think what questions a justice might ask that would surprise her.

It was the most important case of her career up to that point. The issue was whether Ohio should recognize a "Wrongful Life" cause of action. Kathleen's client, Dr. David Whitney, had failed to perform a tubal ligation. As a result the mother gave birth to a baby boy she couldn't afford to support. Should she be able to make the doctor pay for the expense of raising the child? Most states did not allow it but some did and Ohio had not decided the point.

Kathleen's case was being watched by insurance companies, doctors and hospitals. Those people, their lawyers, board members and executives had questions about whether she (a woman, thirteen years out of Harvard Law School, a relatively young partner in Latham, Fuller) shouldn't have given way to a heavy hitter. Some wanted to bring in the attorney who'd won a similar case in the Pennsylvania supreme court.

She felt the anticipation in her stomach, the tension that came the night before an argument or the start of a jury trial. It was nothing like what she would later feel during the murder trial. No lawyer who hadn't been there could understand what it did to your body when you became convinced of a defendant's innocence, got personally involved with the defendant, then risked yourself and the defendant to the judgment of a jury in a murder trial.

The "Wrongful Life" case would be Kathleen's fourth argument in the state's highest court. Someday one of her cases might go up to the U.S. Supreme Court. She loved the appellate practice, the battle for supremacy in the briefs, using the oral argument to expose an opponent's weakness, the challenge in distinguishing the case authorities, the give-and-take of questions from the bench.

It was quiet in the law offices of Latham, Fuller and Richards this late at night. Two or three partners might be working at their desks and a few associates would be doing research in the two story library that occupied the central space on the twenty-first and twenty-second floors. Kathleen didn't anticipate interruption but she'd closed her door to forestall the possibility.

Kathleen loved her office. It was more home than the house she'd purchased in German Village. It was a corner office with a window view of the capitol building and statehouse grounds. She could look south along High Street to the City Center Mall and the Franklin County Hall of Justice. Si Wallace, the managing partner, had insisted she take the corner office when Howard Fuller III died two years ago. The office, as much as her success each year when partnership shares were reevaluated, established how far she had come at Latham, Fuller since joining the firm as an associate twelve years ago.

The shelves and walls held her life as a lawyer, going back to *Black's Law Dictionary* which had been her first purchase from the Co-op, the bookstore at Harvard. Her certificates and Dickens prints were hung. The engraved gavel she'd won during the Cooley Moot Court competition was on her desk.

In her office, especially late at night, she was above the city, removed, secure. Across Broad Street from the floodlit capitol building, she could see the State Office Tower. Lights were on in several windows, including two on the third floor. She wondered if one of the justices or maybe law clerks might be studying the briefs in the case she would argue at ten the next morning. As she stood at the window she could hear the tick of the grandfather clock in the far corner.

The tension she felt wasn't fear. She'd proved herself in the firm, had become a player in cases with millions of dollars at stake. The legal system was the heart of the deserted city below and when the city came to life in the morning, she would be ready.

In her office, in this city, in her firm, in her practice, in the law, she was legitimate. Cardozo, Holmes, Blackstone, Lincoln, Clarence Darrow and Daniel Webster were her forebears. She was cousin to Nizer and Nader, F. Lee Bailey, Edward Bennet Williams, Kunstler, Scalia and Sandra Day O'Connor. She belonged. The law had not adopted her. She had chosen it.

When you were adopted, Kathleen guessed, you never got far away from wondering what that meant. The case she would argue in the morning was in a way about adoption. The mother had admitted on deposition that she loved her baby, wanted to keep him. If the mother had truly wanted to avoid the cost of another child, Kathleen had argued in her brief, the mother could have placed the baby for adoption.

That's what Kathleen's mother had done. Why? All she knew was that her mother had been nineteen, from a good family, intelligent and healthy. Her birth parents were college students. Kathleen didn't want to know more. Actually she did. But not at the cost of making a search and inquiring of the agency that handled the adoption. She was curious about her roots but dreaded the thought that those roots could become part of her life.

Kathleen had fantasies, explanations to herself of how it might have happened. She used to think of herself as being like Jesus, who just materialized in the manger for Mary and Joseph. In none of her fantasies did she see herself as having lost better parents than Dan and Erin Sullivan. Maybe she was different. She'd read about adopted children and their searches. Many imagined wonderful mothers who would treat them better; some believed their true parents to be famous people, royalty even.

Standing on the twenty-third floor of the Capitol Tower building, looking down on the lights of the deserted city, she wondered. If the laws had been different thirty-seven years ago, would she be here? "The mother could have aborted her pregnancy if the economic well-being and education of her existing children were of paramount concern," she had written in her brief.

She could go for weeks and not think about her adoption. Then something would happen, a dream, someone looking at her strangely or making a chance remark—like in the doctor's office when the nurse asked about ages and diseases of her parents when taking the history prior to her annual physical. Well, maybe she did anticipate that just before the question was asked but it was still unexpected in that it was not something she thought about on the way to the doctor, not anything she'd been wondering how to cope with.

She'd been ten and it was at her daddy's St. Patrick's Day party that she'd felt what it meant that Dan and Erin Sullivan weren't her real parents.

She could, twenty-seven years later, see Daddy and Uncle Johnnie, hear their voices. Daddy was standing on the deck, at the house on the hill overlooking the river, the same house he and her mother still lived in and had for forty years. Daddy's arm was across Uncle Johnnie's shoulders. They had mugs filled with green beer, daddy's resting on the railing. Both men were short but Daddy was slim, handsome, dapper in his green blazer. Uncle Johnnie was a barrel. They were looking down on the flagstone patio, their backs to the doorway into the dining room where Kathleen stood. Beyond the patio the lawn, still browned from winter, broke in a gentle slope down to the tree line. Through bare limbs you could see boats on the river taking advantage of a balmy mid-March day.

Some of the guests were refilling mugs from two kegs just beyond the fringe of the flagstone. They, like Daddy, Uncle Johnnie and those who'd formed a circle on the patio, were watching the girl. The girl was step-dancing. She was Kelly Sullivan, Uncle Johnnie's second youngest, Kathleen's cousin. To an accordion and two fiddles, Kelly's heels clacked on the stone while grownups and kids clapped to the rhythm of Kelly's clogs.

Kathleen opened the French doors. She was finding Daddy to deliver Mother's message that Grandma and Grandpa Daugherty needed to be picked up. Kathleen felt good, having sung "Danny Boy," a surprise she and Mother had rehearsed for St. Patrick's Day a year before, a performance she would repeat in two weeks at Dan Sullivan's St. Patrick's Day bash. In two weeks her father's eyes would mist over for the twenty-ninth time and Kathleen, too, wouldn't get through it without her handkerchief. Her father would tell her she got better every year, that it was almost more than his heart could stand. Her father wouldn't hug her, though, as he'd done when she was ten. Her father was the sort of man who thought it was fine to hug a little girl but wrong when she started to be a woman.

What froze Kathleen as she stood in the doorway on St. Patrick's day twenty-seven years ago, what made that minute stick in her memory, was the conversation.

"She's prettier than her mother," Uncle Johnnie said, looking down at Kelly. "In four years no one will touch her for Rose of Tralee."

Daddy punched Uncle Johnnie in the shoulder. "She's an Irish sweetheart," he said, raising his mug and taking a swig of the green beer.

"Pardon me braggin'," said Uncle Johnnie, "but isn't she the prettiest colleen to ever step the dance? Just look. Have you ever seen such an Irish stunner?"

"You swell-headed, ugly bastard," said Daddy. "It's Irish genes all right, but the girl got her looks from Eileen."

Uncle Johnnie went down the balcony steps to hug Kelly. Kathleen came out on the deck. "Time to pick up Grandma and Grandpa," she said.

Daddy pulled her into his arms. "You'll come with me, won't you, sweet-pie?" he asked.

With his arm around her, he held her next to him as he backed the Mercedes out of the garage. "Are you having a good day?" he asked.

"St. Patrick's is my favorite day," she said. It was. It was better than the Fourth of July, even Christmas. He looked at her as if he appreciated the truth of what she'd said. "Just look at this weather," he said. "It's a great day for the Irish."

She nodded, looking out the side window to see what people on the patio were doing as Daddy turned the car, then drove out the twisting gravel lane.

"The best part," he said, kissing the top of her head, "was your 'Danny Boy.' You're Daddy's princess."

She snuggled closer to him. She silently promised to make up for what she wasn't. It was a promise she thought she had kept.

She was no Irish stunner, never had been and never would be. Even her name—Kathleen Sullivan—was a fraud. There was an Irish look. She could spot it instantly. She had studied herself in the mirror. No part of her was Irish. Her grandparents, her aunts, uncles and all those cousins weren't really relatives.

"You are an attractive girl," Mother had often told her. Kathleen guessed she was, in an ordinary sort of way. She'd never been fat. She had black hair which she now wore in a short cut, groomed, with sideburns. It was her best feature. But she had small breasts and her legs were too long. She wasn't petite like her mother. "Stilts Sullivan," she'd been called in high school.

She had known she was adopted from the time she could remember. "We are so lucky to have found you," her mother explained. "We chose you. We wanted a little girl so badly. We kept praying and God gave you to us." Not once could she remember her parents showing their disappointment. She could see Dad's eyes when the graduation processional at Harvard Law School passed where they were sitting and she stepped out of the line to kiss him on the cheek. Like herself, Dad was a lawyer. He'd worked nights and weekends, but he'd been there when her team played, every time she won an award on school-prize day.

Her parents, though, had always seemed uncomfortable talking about the adoption. They'd never said—and though she was thirty-seven, Kathleen was still unable to ask—why they hadn't conceived a child of their own. What her parents did tell her sounded like advice from a book. "Make her feel wanted, special; give her a good sense of her worth and build her self-esteem," she could imagine them having read in a manual. Not when she was ten, but later and in her memory of the early years, she could see how hard they'd tried.

Like saying her birth mother loved her but wasn't able to give her the life she deserved and so had placed her with the agency. "She gave you up because she loved you," her mother said. But how could you be so loved when your birth mother only saw you a few times at the hospital? She knew that much, that Erin and

Dan brought her home from Columbus General when she was three days old.

As a little girl, she'd worried about her birth parents showing up, taking her away. It was irrational, but she'd always been sure those people would find her. But she'd had no intuition that when it happened they would draw her into a first-degree murder trial; that she, her sister and her birth mother would one night be together on the ninth floor of the Hall of Justice, waiting while a jury deliberated behind a locked door with a red light above it.

The grandfather clock chimed eleven and Kathleen turned away from the window. She willed an end to the questions about her adoption, questions she knew would come again, questions that could never be answered. She wanted to look again at the opinion the other side would use against her tomorrow.

There was a knock at her door. Irritated, she shouted, "Come in." You had to shout to be heard through solid cherry.

It was Tony. If it weren't for the argument in the morning, she would have been happy to see Tony Biviano. Tony was thirty, seven years younger, an associate at Latham, Fuller, long on personality, clothes, dark Italian good looks; short on academic excellence. But in the last year she'd been seeing that grades weren't an accurate measure of Tony's intelligence. Tony had a fierce ambition to make partner and knew it would be a struggle, that he would have to outwork his peers and tie himself to a mentor with clout.

Three years ago, to Kathleen's chagrin, he'd latched on to her. Slowly, he'd won her over. No task was too mundane, menial. He put aside weekend plans to meet emergencies. He'd startled her with his ability to tell when a witness was lying.

He had staked his future in the firm on her. He'd told her, "You're the best damn trial lawyer in the city and I want to learn." She thought he believed it when he said, "I'd crawl across town on my belly to try cases with you." There was this sweetness about Tony. You couldn't dislike him even when he was flattering you outrageously. She was, after all, human.

In a way it was his very difference from the other buttoned-down types . . . all right, his earthiness . . . that had attracted her, made her believe that something could happen. For the past year, she'd imagined him taking her, making love with him. When she stimulated herself, Tony rolled down her panties, sucked her before spreading her thighs and entering her. Before they were to go out of town together to take depositions, she would imagine the way it might happen. Later, she would see her missed opportunities, where she had hesitated and let the moment pass. She reimagined those scenes, made the move she had failed to make, resolved to act next time.

There had been her bad experience with Greg Meeker during her junior year at Denison. She hated to remember it . . . his hands all over her, refusing to hear *no* when she said it over and over. Since then she had just not gotten involved. Fantasy and masturbation were safer. With Tony, though, it could be different . . .

So if it hadn't been for the argument in the supreme court, she would have welcomed the surprise of having Tony knock on her door at eleven o'clock.

"Brace yourself, Kathleen," he said, sliding into the wingback chair she had placed to the side of her desk for one-on-one conversations with clients.

He slouched, hooking a leg over the arm of the chair, ignoring her frown which should have told him she had no time for chit-chat.

"I heard some bad news," he said.

Chapter 3

"HEAR YE! Hear ye! Everyone rise."

As the marshal called the opening of the Ohio supreme court, there were a handful of spectators in the gallery along with lawyers who were waiting to argue cases. A reporter for the Columbus *Post* was in the front row. To cover my case? Kathleen wondered.

The seven justices, robed in black, paraded in across the raised granite dais. They stood behind high-backed chairs, beneath the chrome-and-crystal seal of the Great State of Ohio, which was mounted on the paneled wall above the bench.

The "bad news" was taking the chair between the Chief and Justice Clara Wilkins-Brady. He was Judge Sam Roberts, "Union Sam," the lawyers called him. He sat on the Franklin County Court of Appeals and Kathleen had tangled with him before.

She remembered her first case in that court. In her brief she'd cited a case from Arizona, not an important case, but one that had been overruled.

"Where did you go to law school?" Roberts had asked.

"Harvard."

"Ms. Sullivan, did they teach you how to use Shepard's Citator at Harvard?"

Humiliated, she'd apologized, but he'd kept hammering her,

looking for reasons to decide against her. The clients Kathleen's firm often represented (doctors, insurance carriers, manufacturers, banks and corporations) were, to Roberts, enemies of the people.

And now she was stuck with him on the biggest case of her career. There he sat, a fidgety little man with a pencil mustache, eager to "shape the law" and make the most of his opportunity to substitute for a day on the state's highest court. He was replacing Justice Wilson, whose vote she had counted on but who was attending a judicial seminar in Hawaii.

Roberts was watching her, smiling in anticipation, it seemed, as she took papers out of her briefcase and arranged them on the counsel table. He would have to wait for his crack at her since her opponent, Max Sindell, would speak first.

Her uneasiness grew as Sindell made his argument. Kathleen reminded herself that she was prepared, had a strong case; that the substitution of judges was beyond her control. She was glad, though, that she'd asked Tony to come. She wouldn't be alone when Judge Roberts ripped into her.

Sindell finished his argument, reserving two minutes for rebuttal.

Kathleen stood behind the lectern and tried to establish eye contact with each of the justices. "May it please the Court," she began. Roberts smiled and leaned forward over the granite bench as if she were a fish to be unhooked, cleaned, filleted and panfried.

Holding both sides of the lectern, she stood erect. Though five-ten, she was wearing three-inch heels. Since the fourth grade, when she was the tallest in her class, she had heard the voice of her father. "Stand up, Kathleen. Be *proud* of your height." Not so easy when boys her own age often only came to her navel.

On top of the lectern a clock was bedded in the wood. It was 9:20 and she would watch the clock to make sure that questions didn't consume her fifteen minutes before she made her three main points. On the rim of the lectern, visible to the lawyer and to the justices, there were two lights—one white and one red. The white light would come on when she had two minutes to go. The marshal would switch on the red one when she had to stop. Unless she was answering a question from the bench, the red light was absolute. Chief Justice Cook had cut lawyers off in mid-sentence.

"The pivotal issue in the case," she began, "is—"

"Ms. Sullivan," Roberts interrupted. "In your brief . . ." He paused to pick up a thick sheaf of papers, bound together and bearing a beige cover. He licked a finger and turned about half of those pages under. "You say public policy is against recognizing the wrongful-life cause of action. I guess your argument is that the psyche of the child can be damaged when he is older and learns that his mother didn't want him?"

"That's right," said Kathleen. "We should not make the child an emotional bastard."

"Very colorful." Roberts rocked back in his chair. He held the upper hand. He could be nasty, unfair, but the lawyer always had to act respectful. You couldn't risk alienating the other justices. "Don't parents have a legitimate right to limit the size of their family?" Roberts, though smiling, was not looking at her. She was sure he had addressed himself to the mother. Sindell had ushered June Snell into the courtroom, seated her in the first row of the gallery as the chief justice was calling the case.

"Judge Roberts," she said. "I suspect that Ms. Snell changed her mind after she became pregnant."

"Where do you find that in the record?" Roberts scowled at her. "I've studied this record pretty thoroughly."

"If Ms. Snell hadn't changed her mind," said Kathleen, "she could have placed the child for adoption or had an abortion."

"Ms. Sullivan." Justice Wilkins-Brady had spoken from the other end of the bench.

"Please," said Judge Roberts, glancing at Wilkins-Brady. "Might I be allowed to finish?" Kathleen noticed that Tony, at counsel table, was scribbling on his yellow pad.

"Let's suppose along with you," said Roberts, "that June Snell decided to have an abortion."

"I could never do that." The voice from the gallery, not loud, had to be June Snell's. Kathleen did not turn, though all of the justices were looking towards where the voice had come from.

"Let's further suppose," said Roberts, "that the doctor negligently failed to get the abortion done. And let's suppose a child was born." Roberts leaned back, pleased with his hypothetical though the likelihood of such a happening was remote. The gallery had filled, and Mrs. Snell's blurted reaction (assuming it had been her) was providing the dramatic background Justice Roberts wanted. "Any damages against that doctor?" Roberts asked.

Tony had gotten up from his chair, was sliding a note in front of her. Four minutes of her time had expired and she had not begun her argument. She glanced at the note. WILKINS-BRADY IS A CONSERVATIVE CATHOLIC had been printed in capital letters.

"I would never *require* a mother to have an abortion," she said. "But the child could have been placed for adoption."

"I take it you don't want to answer my question," said Roberts. "And I further take it that you are abandoning the abortion argument you made in your brief." Roberts raised his hand to silence her as she started to respond. "Let's pursue your fall-back position," he said. "That June Snell should have given her baby up for adoption."

"Your Honor, I didn't say *should* have. I said Ms. Snell could have if she did not want to raise a child. There is great demand for adoptable babies."

"Yes," said Judge Roberts. "Back when I served on the domestic-relations bench, we saw those. They do not always work out quite as neatly as you seem to believe. Adopted children frequently have problems in coming to terms with their lack of roots. Many never overcome a feeling of abandonment." Roberts lowered his voice and glanced again at a place in the gallery from which the voice had come. "Might not a child who had been given away," he said, "feel like—to use your phrase, Ms. Sullivan—an emotional bastard?"

She grasped the sides of the lectern. The argument was being taken away from her. "I know about the feelings of adopted children," she said. "Judge Roberts, I am adopted." Her answer hung in the quiet courtroom. Roberts, for the moment, had been thrown off stride.

"No child could have finer parents than mine," she said.

Roberts leaned back in his high-backed chair. "Justice Wilkins-Brady?" asked Kathleen. "Did you have a question?"

"You have covered my issue," said Wilkins-Brady.

"The central point," said Kathleen, "is that a child is not property. We cannot apply traditional measures of damage when the claimed injury is a healthy child." She glanced down at her outline. She had seven more minutes to defend Dr. David Whitney from the charge of a mother suing because he had allegedly botched a tubal ligation and allowed her to give birth against her will when she could not afford more children—the so-called Wrongful Life.

"Ms. Sullivan." It was Roberts again. She fought to stay calm. The man was determined to keep her from making her argument. "Isn't that precisely what we do," asked Roberts, "when someone is killed in an automobile accident? Don't we place a value on that life—whether it be adult or child?

"We do, but—"

"Excuse me, Ms. Sullivan. You don't suggest that turns the person into . . . a piece of property?"

"No, Your Honor." Her fingers, where she'd been clutching the lectern, had turned white. But her voice remained steady. "When the law allows damage," she said, "it also allows an offset for benefits."

"Ms. Sullivan, I don't believe we are communicating."

"In these cases the benefits can't be measured," she said. "Can we put a value on a baby's smile? The first time the little boy says daddy? Who knows? This child may turn out to be a millionaire, a doctor, a president. Even," she paused, "an erudite judge who may someday sit on the Ohio supreme court."

The justices laughed, as did the spectators in the gallery.

The white light came on, and seconds later, it seemed, the red. The other justices, preempted by Roberts, had used her last minutes to get in questions. Tonight in bed, she knew she would think of better answers.

Tony had the bag. She stuffed in the outline she had removed from the lectern and followed Tony out to the lobby. Behind her, the chief justice was calling the next case on the docket.

In the lobby, she was surrounded by people waiting to congratulate her. There were attorneys who had come to the argument because of their interest in the issue. The executive director of the Ohio Hospital Association and the president of the Academy of Medicine wanted her to do articles for their publications. Dr. David Whitney treated her as if she had saved his life. She hoped it didn't show, but as she accepted their praise, she felt the cramp in her stomach and as if her whole body were trembling.

When the others left she said, "Tony, let's have a beer and

early lunch." They went to get her green Corvette, which was parked in the garage beneath the statehouse.

"You were terrific," Tony said as she buckled herself into her 'Vette. She leaned to kiss him on the cheek. "Thank God you warned me last night," she said. "I would have frozen when I saw Roberts in Wilson's seat."

They drove north on the freeway, to Hunan Gardens, her favorite Chinese restaurant, where they'd not likely see anyone they knew. She put the pedal down, passing cars on I–71.

At the Hunan Gardens they got a booth and ordered beers. "I'm queasy," she said.

"Jeez, Kathleen, you've got a winner. I'll lay a month's salary on Wilkins-Brady. She hated it when Roberts monopolized the questions. I think they all did. They loved that line about growing up to be an erudite judge. I mean, Roberts isn't even a regular member of the court."

"I knew Wilkins-Brady was Catholic, but how do you know she's conservative?" Kathleen had assumed that, like herself, Wilkins-Brady wasn't much interested in the Church.

Tony snapped his fingers. "She goes to my parish," he said. "Hey, you got her when you told that bastard you were adopted. Dynamite." Tony kept shaking his head, repeating the word, his dark eyes on her.

"I missed things, though." She was remembering what she had wanted to say about public policy.

"But you hit the main points. And, oh man, the way Roberts was eating up your time. You kept your cool."

She smiled. "Grade-card day at a strict Catholic girls' school is good practice." She was feeling much better.

They ordered another round. She told him about grade-card day, how in junior high school each girl stood, one by one, to receive her grades and evaluations. "Some nuns were really mean, would throw your card on the floor if you had less than a B, make you pick it up before they lectured you."

Tony was smiling. "I bet you never got anything but A's."

"I was terrified," she said. "I got lectured on pride, feeling superior instead of grateful to God for my so-called intelligence." She told him about the time she got the B in biology, how she'd been unable to eat supper with her parents, cried herself to sleep, then threw up her breakfast on the way to school.

It was one-thirty when they got back to the office. Connie Englewood, her secretary, presented her with a sheaf of pink call-back slips. Soon there would be a parade of interested partners and associates coming to hear about the argument. It was a ritual, after a trial or an important argument. This would be an afternoon to waste, to believe you were as good as everyone made you feel.

She thumbed through the call-backs. They could wait, all except managing partner Si Wallace. Rather than telephone, she decided to go down to Si's office. It was on the twenty-second floor, directly below hers. She wondered why the managing partner's request had been marked 'Urgent.'

"Kathleen, I've been hearing nothing but raves about your argument." Wallace gestured to the corner of his office where a bay window was built out on the High Street side. "Sit down and tell me about it," he said, following her to a pair of wingback chairs in the bay. He used the telephone on the table next to his chair to request coffee, remembering that Kathleen took hers black.

Simon Wallace was fifty-five, a securities lawyer who had the ability to say no and still be liked, who for eight years had been the managing partner at Latham, Fuller, who made the effort to call each of the seventy-two associates by first name and held the respect of all factions and age groups in the partnership. An energetic-looking man who wore tailored three-piece suits, Wallace smiled at Kathleen and wiped his glasses with his handkerchief.

Wallace prompted her with graceful questions, allowing her to claim her triumphs without appearing to boast.

"The word on how you handled Judge Roberts spreads fast," said Wallace. "Columbus General wants to retain us in a major malpractice case." Wallace smiled. "Provided you are available as lead counsel."

Kathleen sipped her coffee as Wallace identified the parties and described the case. "This is important business," he said. "We've never done Columbus General's work." Behind those wire-rim glasses his gray eyes seemed to dance. "They have bond issues," he said.

For an instant, Kathleen had wondered why the hospital hadn't called her directly. The answer was obvious. Columbus General was a major client of Howland and Beck, her father's firm.

"There is a complication." Wallace eyed her, as if he knew she had been withholding curiosity about where her dad's firm fit in. "Dan Sullivan has been retained to represent the doctor," said Wallace. Because of the conflict, he couldn't represent the hospital. Nor could anyone in his firm.

"The hospital administrator wants to see you at nine tomorrow morning," said Wallace.

"I'd like to talk with Dad."

Wallace said he would have suggested that if she hadn't. At the door, Wallace looked at her with a question in his eyes. He seemed uncertain whether to ask it.

"What?" she asked.

Wallace smiled. He closed the door and retreated. She followed him. "If we take this case," he said, "you'll need help. We need to do a job for Columbus General. They'll be measuring our work against Howland and Beck's."

She nodded. She'd seen that from the beginning.

"I suggest you use Jay Melnik and Laura Redding."

Kathleen nodded again, still puzzled. Melnik and Redding were the best associates in litigation. If Wallace could free them, that was terrific.

"I thought you might want to use Tony Biviano," said Wallace.

"You think this case is too much for Tony?"

"I think Tony needs to work with some of your other partners." Wallace was still smiling. "This case calls for a major time commitment and it might not be fair to Tony."

"You heard something?" She was piqued, despite her liking for Wallace, who had sponsored her in the firm.

"Tony has been on the bubble since he came to the firm," said Wallace. "He's made something of a turnaround in the work he's done for you. But other partners are skeptical, wondering if he hasn't adopted you as his ticket to partnership."

"Who?" She had gone from piqued to pissed.

"Relax, Kathleen." Wallace put his hand on her arm. He was one of the few who could touch without offending, but she pulled away. "It's not your problem," he said. "The point is simply this. The next year is critical for Tony. He needs exposure to other partners."

"I see," said Kathleen. But she didn't. Wallace wasn't telling everything. She resolved to keep her ears open, to ask Marty Fleck about the rumors concerning Tony Biviano. Marty was a partner, Kathleen's contemporary, her friend. Marty knew everything.

Back in her office, Kathleen called her dad. He had heard that Columbus General wanted to retain her, was thrilled, wanted to have lunch tomorrow.

"They'd like to see me in the morning," she said.

"Go ahead," Dad said. "There's no real conflict between the hospital and the doctor. We'll defend this case shoulder to shoulder."

"Our firms are competitors," she said. "Columbus General pays a lot in legal fees."

"Oh, hell." Dad laughed and she could imagine it being heard two offices down the hall from his. "That doesn't mean anything," he said. "Not when you and I have the chance to do this together."

She agreed to meet him at the Columbus Club for lunch. Then she settled into the pleasant occupation of receiving well-wishers for what remained of the afternoon. Her question nagged, though. What had Si Wallace heard?

"Ready to celebrate?" Marty Fleck flounced into Kathleen's office, shucked off her pumps and put her stocking feet on Kathleen's desk. As relaxed as if she'd just come back from one of her vacations where she spent her days in the sun reading crime novels, Marty shooed the last two associates out, saying she and Kathleen had to "discuss a confidential matter."

Kathleen and Marty found a table in the dark, at the rear of the Pewter Mug and away from the antique bar. The table was next to a leaded, stained-glass window. The dim glow of a London pub had been achieved by lighting in the space between the windows and a concrete block wall. Sawdust covered the floor and a guitarist was perched on a stool between the bar and the front door. It was Wednesday night and there were empty tables. On Fridays you had to arrive before five or wait in a line that stretched down the concourse and around the corner past the Kwik Kopy Shop.

Marty left to get a half-pitcher of beer and glasses from the bar. Two lawyers, from Howland and Beck, Kathleen thought, approached Marty at the bar. One was admiring Marty and it looked like the other was asking her to join their table. Marty laughed and said something, causing both lawyers to look back to where Kathleen was sitting. She waved them bye-bye.

"What couldn't you tell me in the office?" Marty asked, pouring beer into the glass she placed in front of Kathleen. "Did Si Wallace tell you something juicy? Good God, you were with him for an hour."

"What do you do?" asked Kathleen. "Have your secretary keep a log on who sees Si Wallace?"

"What did you find out?" Marty leaned forward.

Marty and Kathleen had come to the firm during the same week. They became instant friends, partly because both admitted to insecurity. "I get the feeling," Marty had said, "that a lot of back-stabbing goes on around here." No one had said anything to Kathleen, but she'd picked up the impression that some associates thought she was too eager, too anxious to please. Kathleen and Marty made a pact. "For our self-preservation," Marty had said. They would tell each other everything.

They had been united by starting on the bottom. But they were different. Kathleen couldn't really handle the way Marty flirted her way into the center of attention at partnership dinner meetings—leaving Kathleen feeling like she wasn't at the table. "I undo an extra button on my blouse when I go in to see Si Wallace," Marty confided. Kathleen thought that was more than a bit much but didn't say so. Marty, who liked to describe herself as "a recovering Catholic," accused Kathleen of still living in dread of the nuns.

"Have you heard rumors about Tony B?" Kathleen asked.

Marty, about to drink from her beer, put it down. "You aren't letting that character snow you?" Kathleen felt her face redden. "I mean," said Marty, "I know he's working for you. I know he brings you a few clients. I assume his work isn't the disaster it was and I know he's busting his ass. But Jesus, Kathleen . . . you aren't getting involved?"

Kathleen nudged her glass toward the center of the table. She put her hands on her lap. Her fingers were shaking and Marty had noticed. "Oh, Kathleen, honey . . . we need to have a long talk."

Kathleen was furious, mostly with herself, but she let Marty run on, saying how Tony was seven years younger, an opportunist, would hurt her. "I could tell you some horror stories," said Marty. "He fucked Laura Redding the first year he was here because he spotted her as a winner."

Marty's eyebrows knitted. "I'm breaking promises," she said. "But that man . . . boy, really . . . is all charm. He's known what to do in the backseat of a car since he was thirteen."

Kathleen's face felt hot. Marty talked on, mistaking Kathleen's silence for agreement. Kathleen was afraid to speak for fear Marty would counter her denials, find more confirmation.

Suddenly Marty stopped talking. She stared at Kathleen. "I've offended you, haven't I?"

"I guess," said Kathleen. She pushed her chair back. Her beer was untouched.

"I'm sorry," said Marty. "But, well, what's a friend for?"

Kathleen managed to extract herself from Marty's apologies. She said she was exhausted from staying up to work on her argument, that she wasn't herself.

"Well, what *did* you want to tell me?" Marty asked.

"It doesn't amount to anything," said Kathleen. "Maybe I'll catch you tomorrow."

She stood at the base of the escalator, still on the concourse level, questioning her decision to go back to her office. She did have work to do. On Monday she was scheduled to take the deposition of a metallurgical engineer in a products liability case. Two piles of material—drawings, summaries of witness statements, treatises and literature—were stacked in the corner. With Columbus General usurping the next morning, she doubted if the weekend would leave enough time to prepare. There were the call-backs she hadn't made, other cases that needed attention. She got on the escalator.

On the main floor, waiting in front of the elevator bank, she turned and went back down the escalator, through the tunnel to the underground garage. She couldn't face the office. Tony would be there.

He'd told her that after hoops (his team had a five o'clock game in the league at the athletic club) he'd look in, see if she wanted to get a bite to eat. Others who were working late would stop to chat about her argument. She wasn't up to them. The image of Union Sam choking on his smile after she got off the erudite judge line was still with her but it gave no pleasure. How had she been so suddenly and completely swallowed by a mood that made her feel the way she had on that day she had been disqualified from carrying the Blessed Virgin's statue in the May festival? Why did a stupid assumption by Marty Fleck flatten her, shame her the way she'd been shamed by Father Hogan and Sister Marguerite twenty-five years ago at St. Catherine's?

Chapter 4

K ATHLEEN, IN THE sixth grade at St. Catherine's School for Girls, was the tallest and smartest in her class. She'd been chosen by Father Hogan to carry the statue of Mary in the ceremony of the Blessed Virgin which was held each year at the end of May.

The procession would start in the chapel and wind out through the garden to a small grotto back in the trees. The honored child, always a sixth grader, would be dressed in white and wear a floral crown as she led the other children, then placed the statue she was carrying beside the larger one in the grotto. The other children carried flowers, laid them on the floor of the grotto around the two Marys.

Kathleen expected to be chosen. Father Hogan, since she came into his religious education classes in the fourth grade, had taken an interest in her. "You may have a vocation," he told her. He had invited her to his study, selected readings to develop her spiritual growth.

A week before the ceremony of the Blessed Virgin, Kathleen was excused from class to spend time with Father Hogan in preparation for her duties. She went to his study wearing the thin white dress the nuns had altered so that it would scrape the top of her shoes as she walked.

On previous occasions Father Hogan had kissed her cheek after blessing her. He had asked her to sit on his lap the time he read the story of St. Theresa, the little flower, to her. She had raised five dollars for her "pagan baby" in Ethiopia and had picked Theresa as her name for the pagan baby. She adored Father Hogan. He was much kinder than Sister Marguerite.

Father Hogan closed the door and suggested that she sit on his lap while he explained the significance of the ceremony in which she was to play the main part. His study was roomy, with stained-glass windows through which the sun cast a yellow light, dark upholstered furniture, bookshelves on two walls, the smell of incense mingling with must from old books and papers. She remembered how hot it was, how the thin dress stuck to her. She could feel his moist hand, lifting the dress and touching her skin as he positioned her on his lap.

She remembered how uncomfortable she became as she sat on his lap and listened. She had stared at the solid oak door, wanting to run, open it, get out as soon as he released her. When he told her they would continue her preparation the next day and every day until the ceremony, she'd blurted out, "I don't want to." Beyond that she couldn't remember. She was sure nothing terrible had happened, that her reaction had been childishly inappropriate, offensive to Father Hogan. But she couldn't stand his touching.

Suddenly Father Hogan changed. She was standing in the center of his study. He was looking down at her. "You don't deserve the trust I've placed in you," he said. "You will not carry the Blessed Virgin." He lectured her on pride, humility and disobedience; told her that the good marks she'd received did not make her superior in God's eyes. She was terrified. She wasn't sure how he would punish her but he now seemed meaner than the most severe nun. Sister Marguerite came to Father Hogan's study to get her. There was a lot she couldn't remember, and years later, she couldn't separate memory from imagination. Like Sister Marguerite told her, she did have an evil imagination.

Mary Grace Cohagen carried the statue in the procession to celebrate the Blessed Virgin. Kathleen stayed home, sick with the flu.

Naturally, Kathleen's parents had questions. "I don't know," she told them. "Father Hogan just thought Mary Grace was more . . . deserving."

She prayed—harder than she'd ever prayed for anything—that her mother wouldn't talk to Sister Marguerite or Father Hogan. She prayed that neither Sister nor Father would call her parents in for a conference. Getting sick had been an answer to her prayers. Her parents saw how the questions upset her and stopped asking.

In the seventh and eighth grades, when Father Hogan saw her he acted as if she were a child he didn't know. Much later, when she was in high school, and her dad was helping her apply for a National Merit Scholarship, he had said, "Kathleen, you'll never know—until you have a child of your own—how proud I am of what you've done." Then he said, "I can tell you now, I am very relieved you gave up the notion of a vocation. Do you remember how disappointed you were when they changed their minds about your carrying the statue of the Blessed Virgin?"

She felt the nausea, the same as back then. After five years, was he going to ask questions?

But he didn't. "That may have been a blessing," he said. "After that disappointment we never again heard you talk about wanting to be a nun . . ."

And so many years later, she was feeling the old fear and nausea because of Marty. What were people saying about her and Tony?

Three years after Kathleen made partner in Latham, Fuller she bought a house in German Village. It was a narrow two-story brick on a cobblestone alley four blocks across the bridge from the Franklin County Hall of Justice. In warm weather she walked to her office. She lived alone, had converted one of the three bedrooms to a study, restored the fireplaces in the sitting room and master bedroom. She put the floor-to-ceiling sliding doors in working order. Only in her resolve to keep a small garden in the stockade-fence enclosed backyard had she failed.

The floorboards in the old house creaked as she went to the kitchen to scare up something for supper. Her thoughts skittered between Tony, Si Wallace, Father Hogan, Marty, Sister Marguerite and the argument in the supreme court (which seemed long ago and not so likely to produce a decision in her favor). She ground enough coffee to brew four cups, put a frozen dinner in the microwave. Except for breakfast, usually a bowl of bran flakes topped by a sliced banana, she almost always ate out.

She forced down a tasteless veal cutlet, green beans and lumps of mashed potatoes while berating herself for not bringing home the material she needed to prepare for her depositions.

She had no idea what might be on television on a Wednesday night and no desire to find out. Maybe she would read the new Anne Tyler novel, a Christmas gift from her cousin Kelly. In school, and during the first two years at the firm, she'd liked nothing better than to snuggle into her fuzzy sleeper, crawl in bed with a good novel and a cup of coffee, identify with the characters as they confronted conflict and pain. Or escape into a courtroom thriller. She filled her thermal carafe and took it, along with Anne Tyler, up to her bedroom.

Propped against the headboard, she sipped hot coffee, reading the blurb, which told her she was holding Tyler's "most accomplished work to date." Kathleen put the book on her nightstand. She warmed her half-empty cup from the carafe.

She felt as if Marty, maybe Si Wallace, maybe everyone knew she had a crush on Tony. But that shouldn't affect her decision to support him. He should be told at year-end that he was on track to make partner. She could cite work in a dozen cases, offer testimonial from difficult clients. She shouldn't be worrying about how others would look on her support for Tony. But she was, and it humiliated her to realize it.

If they thought she'd been snowed by Tony, they were wrong. Wrong about him, about her. True, from the time Tony arrived as a summer clerk she had been skeptical. She was remembering now the tennis tournament that year. She could feel her face flush, not because of what had happened but because she'd confessed her anger to Marty.

At the tournament Tony had been paired with Jay Melnik, a first-year associate. Melnik, a nerd from his baggy three-piece suits to his penguin walk to his thick-lensed glasses—which he taped to his head and protected with Plexiglas ski goggles when he entered tennis competition—was destined to be a star in the law firm. You could see that from the day he arrived wearing his Phi Beta Kappa key across his vest and put his certificate as former editor of the Harvard Law Review on his wall. Melnik was quick and smart, fought over by partners, the sort that people in the business of making money liked to have do their legal work.

But Melnik was no star of anything athletic. He'd been paired with Tony because Tony was an outstanding tennis player. Tony and Jay, in the upper bracket, advanced toward the showdown with Kathleen and Chip Drucker, who were sweeping through the lower bracket. Kathleen, though not an athlete in Tony's class, had been a standout in high school girls hockey, a member of the track and cross-country teams. She was a pretty good tennis player, and she and Drucker played well together.

The finals were held on a Sunday afternoon in mid-August at the compound on Si Wallace's 600–acre horse farm. With most everyone in the firm there (and spouses), the speculation was whether two capable players could beat a hot shot paired with Jay Melnik. Ordinarily the whiz and the klutz would lose, but in the preliminary rounds Melnik, who'd skipped the tourney during his summer clerk year, had shown an amazing ability to get to the ball, put his racket on it and send it back in a high lob that descended deep in his opponents' court. Tony played the net, relying on Melnik to retrieve half the balls that got by. Tony was putting away more than were getting by. It was a winning strategy. The flaw was Melnik's serve, a guaranteed loss every fourth game.

Kathleen and Chip took the first set 6–3. Miraculously, it seemed, Melnik discovered that if he removed the Plexiglas wraparounds, he could get his serve in. Athletic recognition was a new and heady incentive to Melnik, who decided that having his name engraved on the trophy was worth breaking his glasses for. Jay and Tony took the second set in a tiebreaker, with Tony egging Jay on, complimenting each feeble serve, clenching his fist in admiration for the graceless lobs, slapping Melnik on the back when they won a game.

In the second game of the third set Tony saw that Kathleen was annoyed. The situation was aggravated by spectators, most of whom were backing the Melnik—Biviano team and giving loud approval to each point Melnik saved. Tony modified his antics but by then Melnik was hitting a new level. It ended 6–1 with Tony and Jay accepting the trophy, Tony pouring a pitcher of beer on Melnik's head. Melnik giggled and whooped.

Later Kathleen would look back, happy that Jay Melnik had

SHADOWS OF DOUBT   *33*

been office doubles champion. It probably was the best day of his life. She liked Jay and could imagine what it must have been like for him as a kid, before his brain made him someone to admire.

But at the time, after the trophy ceremony, Kathleen wanted to skip the lawn buffet, get in her car and go home where she could take a hot shower and get control of herself. "Hey, Kathleen." It was Tony calling from across the lawn. A can of Coors in hand, he was bearing down on her as she tried to slip through the shrubbery to her car. "Let's you, Chip, Jay and me find ourselves a spot in the shade to wet our lips before we chow down."

She nodded and followed him. She was betraying her feelings but as Tony hailed her she saw it would really be bad form to sulk off. She was, after all, a partner.

The four sat cross-legged on needle-thatched grass under tall pines that had been shorn of limbs up to twenty feet. As partners, associates, summer clerks and wives came to offer congratulations, Tony exuded charm, cracked jokes, kept Jay Melnik on his cloud.

In the buffet line, Tony followed Kathleen. "Kathleen, you've got great legs . . ." The effect was as if he'd pulled the collar of her shirt to pour ice water down her back. She held herself in, took a step forward, took a shrimp from the ice bed with a toothpick, dipped it in sauce, put it on her paper plate. She thought she had survived—he struck again. "No kidding," he said, "I loved watching them during the match. It's your secret weapon." He laughed.

She turned to face him. *"Thank you.* I don't get compliments like *that* very often."

Maybe not politically correct, but she still considered it one of her best moments, still couldn't believe how effectively she had masked her rage. For her that was important. Exposing such an emotion was cross-grained to what the nuns had required in her. And by the way, she did not regard her legs as so great. Slender and strong, maybe, but not sexy. Because she rarely wore shorts and considered lying in the sun a slow death from boredom, her skin was white as talc. If he hadn't been trying so hard to get an offer from the firm, she would have been sure he was just being sarcastic. Maybe he was, anyway.

Later, when she'd confided the story to Marty Fleck, Marty had made some crack about Kathleen and nuns, refused to support

Kathleen's opposition to making Tony an offer to join the firm as an associate.

"The partners on the hiring committee think he's going to be a rainmaker," said Marty. "And I agree with them."

"Not a chance," Kathleen had said.

In his first year, Tony came close to fulfilling her negative expectation. Working mostly with Chip Drucker in the Workers' Compensation Group, Tony screwed up pleadings, took too long to complete assignments and seemed unable to grasp the statutory scheme that governed workers' comp claims—occupational disease, temporary disability, permanent disability, permanent partial, temporary total, safety violations and so on. At the end of his second year, he was told he was "in trouble."

Tony petitioned to be transferred to a different group. No one wanted him. If you couldn't cut it in workers' comp, what *could* you handle? Still, the firm prided itself on giving associates every chance, and so Tony was moved to one of the litigation sections. Kathleen's. She was not happy. Her group was already shorthanded and Tony, after exhausting his second chance, would be told to start looking at year's end.

Kathleen started him on a dog, a subrogation case in which the insurance company was trying to recover money it had paid on a fire loss. They needed to prove that the fire was caused by a negligently installed conveyor belt. Big money was at stake but proof of causation and damages would be hard to come by.

Tony came through. He spent hours in the foundry where the fire occurred, demonstrated a talent for loosening the tongues of closemouthed factory workers. The evidence he collected forced a settlement. Kathleen's client was ecstatic.

"Tony," she told him. "That was good work. I'm going to let people around here know about it."

He was sitting across the desk from her in the office she'd occupied before being given the corner one on the twenty-third floor. She closed the door. They talked about Tony's problems in the firm, their conversation ending two hours later in the Pewter Mug.

"I'm scared," Tony admitted. "I've been scared since I came here as a summer clerk. The people here—they all knocked law school dead. I'm not in that class, no pun intended."

And then Tony proceeded to tell her about himself. He was the

fifth of nine kids. They lived above his father's grocery on a corner in South Philadelphia. Tony's great-grandfather had opened
the store in 1886. In high school Tony realized the store would go
to his older brother Chris, the one in Tony's generation who'd
shown the most aptitude for taking charge. Tony would not have
gone to college except for the athletic scholarship to Penn State.
At Penn State, though, he discovered that by planning his time
and working harder than anyone he knew he could have academic success—a solid B average. His dad was proud but thought
the idea of going to law school a crazy dream. "Dad couldn't pay
and Dad has more pride than anyone," he said.

Since getting the call to Latham, Fuller and Richards for the
summer, Tony's dream had been to make partner. "I don't dare
fail," he said. "But sometimes I'm sure it's only a matter of time."

Since that afternoon, Kathleen had come to rely on Tony, see
his potential. He had an instinct for cross-examination. The mistake had been assigning him to the Workers' Compensation
Group. He'd tried but no amount of effort could overcome lack
of interest. And who, Kathleen had to admit, became a lawyer to
do Workers' Comp cases?

It was about a year and a half ago that Tony had become the
object of her fantasies. She began to invent scenes when she used
her vibrator. She unzipped his fly to give him blow jobs in her
office. She let him take her from the rear, asked him to go down
on her and give her a long juicy one. Nobody, of course, would
guess that she, whose life was tied to her career and who demonstrated no interest in sex, harbored such fantasies. Nancy Friday's
book, *Women's Sexual Fantasies,* was not as ridiculous as she first
thought. Some in the firm, she knew, suspected she was a closet
lesbian. They figured she had the hots for Marty Fleck because
the two went to plays, the symphony and movies together. What a
joke. The nuns were right, she lacked the strength to resist. She
satisfied herself so easily and in such bizarre ways that she would
never find a normal relationship.

The exception, though it was hardly normal, had been Greg
Meeker. She met Greg at a Theta lawn party. Social mixers with
fraternities was not part of the social life at Denison that she
enjoyed. She liked eating with the girls and had made friends in
her sorority, but she didn't feel she belonged. If her mother

hadn't been a Theta, if the sorority hadn't wanted her four-point to help the house GPA, she wouldn't have been asked to join.

The sisters got dates for her and sometimes she would even be interested, go out a few times until a kind of . . . awkwardness came up and the guy stopped calling.

She noticed Greg Meeker checking her out as she made trips between the house and the lawn, bringing out trays stacked with finger sandwiches for the serving table. It was the weekend after spring break and back then she valued a tan.

When Greg walked toward the table she knew he was going to ask her to sit with him on the lawn. He was tall, like herself. He had muscular shoulders and was better-looking than she would have expected in someone who'd shown an unarranged interest in her. He had green eyes, she remembered.

He was a critic of fraternity life. "Why are you a member?" she asked, amused and suspicious of the claims boys made to make themselves seem interesting.

"Gathering material," he said.

That should have been her warning. But he was easy to talk to, more comfortable than any boy she'd dated. He was an English major, already working on a novel.

They talked about literature. He admired her interpretation of *To the Lighthouse*. The conversations weren't phony—she had been in enough of those to pick up the first whiff. He wanted her —something she had never *felt*.

The next week they studied in the library, went to a Dustin Hoffman movie in Newark, had dinner at the Granville Inn on Saturday night. They held hands, snuggled. But he put no moves on her. It was all natural to her feelings. She became comfortable. He called at odd times to read something "good" from Evelyn Waugh. She dreaded being separated during the summer when Greg lined up a construction job working on a pipeline in Alaska.

He wanted to make love, she was sure. They would lie on a blanket beside Ebaugh's Pond, stroke each other, hold long, deep kisses. She yearned for him to confirm her feeling—that he wanted her so much he would *have* to have her.

It happened almost as naturally as the first kiss. Her stomach tensed when his hand moved up her thigh, slid under her panties. She protested but he kept on, sure of himself, taking control in spite of her objections. They were on a blanket beside the pond, at their place. It was shielded by spruce trees, the place where they read, listened to music on his portable radio. It was a clear, warm night.

Afterward, she lay beside him looking up at the May sky. She felt giddy-happy. Not that intercourse had been so wonderful. It was less a turn-on than kissing or feeling his hands on her body. But she had done it! She was, as they said, a woman.

She had chosen the right man. They cared for each other. It was right, whether or not they decided to get married. She was glad he'd been strong enough to override her objections. The nuns were wrong, sex could be good and make you come alive. Next time she would be more relaxed, feel him inside her, let herself go.

There was no next time. In fact there were only two further dates, both awkward. He saw much less significance than she did in what they'd done and became evasive as she talked about her feelings. Three weeks later a sorority sister told her he was seeing a Tri Delt.

"You're better off," another Theta told her. She smiled, agreed and volunteered no details. She had learned something about herself, something she hadn't realized when he slipped his hand under her panties. She had wanted to be cared for, lusted after, adored, loved, nurtured, taken by a man who would never let her down. She was a twit. She was to blame and she was paying the price. No one knew how badly it hurt . . .

As she sat propped in bed, sipping hot coffee, abandoning her intent to start the Anne Tyler novel, she saw another reason why she had reacted so strongly to the comments by Si Wallace and Marty. The notion of seducing Tony was as absurd as her belief that Greg Meeker was Prince Charming.

Her seniority to Tony in the firm, the situation that made her fantasy possible, could not be exploited. She couldn't live with the gossip, being an object of ridicule, the hard-up, thirty-seven-year-old loser.

She took two sleeping pills. Eight hours ought to improve her outlook, and it did. She awoke the next morning eager to be at work, to get into the Columbus General case. Sometime during the day she would find Marty Fleck, patch up the misunderstanding.

Tony was waiting, sitting in her favored-client chair when she got to her office at 8:15. He put his coffee cup on the table and folded the newspaper he had been reading. "Kathleen," he said, "you aren't mad at me?"

"Why should I be?" Whom had he talked to? What had he been told? He remained in a slouch, one leg extended.

"Tell me about Columbus General," he said. "I hear they decided to retain you after someone caught your argument yesterday."

"Where did you hear that?"

"Last night at the club, after basketball. Word spreads, Kathleen. You're a hot ticket. Every lawyer in town is talking about how you put it to Union Sam. I want in on this one," he said.

She nodded.

"Is there a problem?"

She was trying to avoid showing her concern. Damn Marty for running off at the mouth. Tony's earlier grin dissolved. There was that ability of his to read people.

"I'd like you to help me," she said. "The group from the hospital will be here at nine."

II
Jill and
Deb

What in us really wants truth?
—NIETZSCHE

Chapter 5

THE HOSPITAL room was bright and cheery with its pastel colors, the lovely Renoir girls, flowers on the low sill beneath high, spotlessly sparkling windows. The scent of roses seemed to float on the medicinal air. Here there were no germs. Here Jill Donahey, birth mother of Kathleen, was safe from herself, though she could assure them—whether they believed her or not —that the need to protect her from herself no longer existed.

Jill stared at the bandages on her wrist. There was an ache but the bandages were clean. She didn't remember how she got there, whether her husband Harrison had driven her or she'd been brought by the emergency squad. Obviously she'd fainted before she had a chance to cut the other wrist. She did remember being in the bathroom, that Harrison had been downstairs watching C-Span on cable, glued to coverage of the campaign work prior to Super Tuesday, the next and critical stage in the presidential primary season. Harrison, a poli-sci professor, had been making notes on sheets attached to his clipboard.

Jill remembered the sight of her blood mixing in the basin with cold water from the tap. She remembered how confidently she'd drawn one of Harrison's blades across her wrist, the first slash. She had no doubts, though the idea of suicide hadn't been in her mind when she left Harrison with his C-Span, his clipboard and his politics. Her thought then had been her failure to tell him, her fear of how he and the girls would take the news of her disease. The disease was genetic; it would change all of their lives. I must tell them tomorrow, she decided, saying she was tired and wanted to go to bed. "Be quiet when you come upstairs," she said.

She remembered how detached she felt in the bathroom, watching her blood swirl down the drain. No sorrow, no guilt. It had been an act that suddenly had to be done. And now she knew she shouldn't have.

She could hardly bear to see Harrison, let alone the girls. Harrison would be sympathetic but he would be hurt. Her girls would be angry—for sure Debbie would be. Fortunately Denise was in California. Debbie, though, was here and Debbie was pregnant, just got the news a week ago. And what about her other daughter, the one born thirty-seven years ago, the one her husband Harrison, her daughters Debbie and Denise knew nothing about?

Though waiting for Harrison to come and dreading the confrontation with Debbie, Jill couldn't avoid thinking about her *other* daughter. All morning, both before and after the psychiatrist came to see her, Jill had been reliving the months of her thirty-seven-year-old pregnancy. She'd thought she'd never have to endure anything like that again. But in this cheery room, the future looked as bleak and hopeless as it had thirty-seven years before in the Alice Webster Shelter for unwed mothers.

Jill remembered the Alice Webster Shelter, the gray walls in the high-ceilinged room she had occupied for eighteen weeks. Years before Jill came, gray paint had been applied to the chest with drawers that lacked handles and were swollen so you had to pry them open. The windows had been paint-sealed. The matron wore gray, was sarcastic and cold, as gray as her uniform and the walls.

She was there because of her mother, because she'd been too shamed to make decisions, to resist the family disgrace she had brought on by being raped. She doubted if her mother believed her. Maybe Billy Joe and Dad didn't either. The decision to place the child with an agency was Mother's. She accepted the decision, at the time relieved that someone was taking over. Really, there was no option. The first time she questioned the choice was when she was signing the papers.

The hospital, though better maintained, was no improvement

on the shelter. She felt judged by the doctors, the nurses, everyone at Columbus General. She didn't try to explain. They wouldn't believe her. By then she scarcely believed herself.

She went into the delivery room defeated. When her water broke the nurse called her a *pig*. As punishment—or maybe it would have been that way anyhow—she'd gone without anesthesia for the delivery.

The baby was whisked away. Unlike the other mothers on the maternity floor, she made no trips to the glass to see her baby. She understood that if you were giving up a baby it was better not to get attached. She wouldn't swear to it but she thought she wasn't told until three days after delivery, during the half-hour counseling session that preceded the paper-signing, that her baby was a girl.

The surrender papers were a blur. "I pledge myself not to interfere with the custody or management of said child or allow anyone else to do so." She remembered that part. A grim, elderly bitch witnessed her signature. "For the sum of one dollar ($1) and other valuable consideration," the document read.

Then the feeling hit. That night she dreamed she killed her baby. Had she been screaming? She awakened to find Mother in her bedroom. The next morning Mother and Dad were afraid she would change her mind, try to get the baby back. They took her in for counseling.

"It will hurt for a little while. Then you will forget," the therapist told her.

She didn't forget, though she tried to console herself by imagining her baby girl's new home. The home had been nonspecifically represented as "well to do," the adopting parents as ideal.

She enrolled at Miami the next fall. Step two in her mother's plan. Dad could afford the tuition. They wished she'd gone there in the first place instead of following her high school crowd to Ohio State. At Miami, she made a new start, the depression lifted, she met Harrison, a young instructor who taught a class in political science as well as the one Jill took, "The United States As a World Power."

But even after she started dating Harrison, the nightmares continued. She killed her baby a hundred times, stabbed her, suffocated her, abandoned her in a garbage dump, lost her in an automobile accident. The most frequent was the drowning dream, in which Jill reached into the water, then reached lower, just missing the baby's raised arm as the baby sank.

The dream disappeared when she learned she was pregnant with Denise. In the end the therapist was right. Almost. The hurting lost its edge—except on birthdays. Jill had yet to get by the ninth of November without being drawn back to the shelter, the hospital, the surrender papers, the wondering. What had become of her baby girl?

One other worry persisted. It hit her when the telephone rang or when she heard the door chimes but was not expecting company. She had been searched for and found. The girl had come to ask questions, to pay her back. And now, with this disease, the reason for the suicide attempt, would she be forced to find the girl who'd been born thirty-seven years ago on a November ninth? Did that girl have children? Could she be pregnant? Was there any need to tell her? No—that was asking too much. She didn't even know if the girl—girl? She'd be a woman of thirty-seven—was alive. Harrison would never understand why she'd kept that kind of secret.

Harrison was coming, would be there within the hour. The nurse had removed the lunch tray and wondered if there were anything more she could do. "Would you like help with your hair?" Jill did not. Leave me alone, she wanted to shout. Harrison had gotten her a private room but what good was that when people were flitting in and out, making her feel like a teen getting ready to impress Mr. Wonderful.

After all, she and Harrison had been married for thirty-two years, had raised two daughters, had two grandchildren and the one more on the way. Jill was fifty-seven. She and Harrison had become comfortable enough with each other to host Harrison's college students and provide a stimulating evening when she and Harrison were in the middle of a fight and wouldn't speak to each other until the first student arrived; would resume hostilities as soon as the last left.

She had concealed her disease for four years. She had known before cutting her wrist that Harrison had to be told; he, Debbie and Denise. About her father and her brother she was less sure. Maybe they already knew. They had as much reason as she—or did they? Jill wondered if the impulse to kill herself might have been a way to get the telling done.

She had Huntington's disease. She had read everything she could these past four years. Dr. Calder had answered her questions. She knew the disease had been identified in 1872 by George Huntington, an Ohio GP, that it was sometimes called Huntington's Chorea, that folk singer Woody Guthrie was its best-known victim, that the disease was genetic, that if either parent had the gene the child had a fifty percent chance of receiving it, that the disease rarely manifested itself before middle life, that it could not skip a generation, that after onset it came on gradually but surely, increasing by degrees and often taking years in the development until the sufferer became a quivering wreck of her former self, that the gene was dominant and had not yet been located despite years of research, that it might soon be discovered but even if it were there was no cure and death was the inevitable outcome, on average sixteen years after the onset. There was also the tendency to insanity.

Now Debbie and Denise would have to live with the risk she had been trying to shield them from, praying it wouldn't be necessary to tell them even as she became sure the prayers were failing.

What about her own future? The inevitable institution, maybe a nursing home like the one in which they'd put her mother. How much did Billy Joe and Dad know about Mother? Jill could remember visits to that gloomy room, her father wheeling Mother out on the terrace and the two of them talking to Mother, watching Mother struggle to swallow, not sure if Mother was trying to respond or just breathe, not sure if Mother understood anything. No one diagnosed Mother—her condition had been thought to be mental.

Dr. Malcolm Calder had diagnosed Jill four years ago. But he left the door open, said he could be wrong. Two years ago he closed the door. She had been sure from the first time Dr. Calder asked, "What do you know about Huntington's disease?" The prayers, the delusion that she might not have it, had been her way of living with her secret, protecting her life and sparing her daughters. She had come close to telling Harrison. There were times when the compulsion got overwhelming.

Even so she had resisted Dr. Calder yesterday, on her last visit to his office. She arrived at the Medical Science building promptly at ten. Dr. Calder came to his reception area, escorted her back himself—not to one of the examining rooms but to his study.

"Jill, I've blocked out the rest of my morning," he said, confessing that worry about seeing her had disrupted his sleep. He directed her to a mammoth leather chair.

"Did my tests show anything new?" she asked.

"No," he said. He sat on the corner of his desk, crossed his legs and was bobbing one foot. He'd tossed his white jacket over the back of the swivel chair behind the desk. He loosened his tie. She'd not seen him like this, nervous, unprofessional. If he hadn't been her doctor for thirty-two years she would have questioned the wisdom of coming to him. Dr. Malcolm Calder had been Harrison's doctor, acquired by her in the marriage. But she had felt close to him, especially during the last four years when he'd been the only person to know about her disease. He had treated Denise and Debbie, was still Debbie's GP. He was probably older than Harrison, maybe close to seventy, a small man, completely bald with a ruddy face. He looked like a doctor, all competence, with keen blue eyes. But he was not himself as he sat facing her, fidgeting with his tie.

"You must tell Harrison and your girls," he said.

She nodded. He'd been urging her to do so for two years, always, however, adding that it was her choice. He couldn't put himself in her place, couldn't really appreciate how hard the telling might be. Nor had he offered a medical reason to support his suggestion. There was no cure for HD. So nothing could be done for Denise or Debbie. They were at risk but probably would not notice symptoms for years. Jill had not until she was over fifty and the late onset of the disease, as well as the disease itself, tended to be hereditary. Why spoil her daughters good years? Besides, fifty-fifty meant a fifty percent chance they'd never endure the pain she was going through. You could lose sight of that.

"What's kept me awake," said Dr. Calder, "is that I'm not sure what my responsibility is if you continue to keep this secret from your family."

"Are you threatening me?" He was. The sleepless night, the greeting out in the reception area, the morning free from other patients, this conversation in his study without the usual history-taking ritual by his nurse—it all came clear. If she did not tell

Harrison, Dr. Calder would. In an instant, years of medical trust were snuffed out.

"I'm not sure what my ethical obligation is," he said. "I've consulted with colleagues—in a hypothetical way, of course. There is no clear line." He forced a smile. "My hope is that we can come to an understanding, that I won't be required to make a decision that seems wrong whatever I do."

"I'm listening," she said.

He glanced beyond her shoulder to a mini-fridge on top of a credenza. "Would you like a soft drink?" he asked. "I've got beer too."

She shook her head, not commenting on the inanity of the offer. Maybe he wanted a beer, maybe something stronger. "You see," he said, "I'm not only your physician. I'm Harrison's. I have a duty there. Debbie is also a patient, though of course she's under the care of her OB just now."

"You've already told them?" She had not mentioned Debbie's pregnancy to Dr. Calder. She was sure she hadn't.

"Dr. Weingard requested Deb's records." The frozen smile had not changed.

"Why are you pressuring me?" she asked.

He told her about the test again. If enough blood samples could be obtained from family members, it was possible to predict with ninety-eight percent certainty whether someone at risk for HD actually had the gene. The test had been discovered in 1983. Jill hadn't considered it. She knew she had the gene. Testing would make her affliction known, turn her into an object to be pitied by Harrison, her family, her friends. With pity came rejection. She knew that from watching her mother, though she hadn't known the cause of her mother's disintegration. People turned away from the ugly, the diseased, the unfortunate. She didn't want to be like the homeless beggars she refused to look at when she went downtown. Not one day before she had to.

Dr. Calder explained that Debbie might decide to be tested. Even if she didn't she might want to test her fetus. That could be done without Debbie having to be told whether she herself had the gene. If the fetus had the gene, Debbie was early in her pregnancy, might consider an abortion and conceive again. The odds were in favor of Debbie's fetus, only twenty-five percent that the gene was being carried. The same for Denise's two children. Debbie and Denise had the right to make choices, to know they were at risk. With Debbie's pregnancy, her choices became urgent.

"So that's it. You think Debbie should have an abortion." Jill saw it clearly. If Jill had known, she would not have wanted children.

"No," Dr. Calder said. "That's a choice Debbie and her husband should make."

Another point that concerned Dr. Calder came from his conversation two days earlier with a research physician working on Huntington's disease at Johns Hopkins in Maryland. "There's no guarantee, of course," said Dr. Calder, "but geneticists are locating new genes every day and may be close to finding the HD gene. The possibility that a cure will be found can't be ignored."

Jill felt her stomach tighten, her hands turn moist and cold. It was too cruel, holding out the possibility of escape from a fate she knew to be inevitable. Dr. Calder had never been optimistic, had downplayed Jill's inquiries into whether science might find a cure.

"We can't know for sure what science will discover," Dr. Calder said. "Suppose, though, that something happens to me. If your girls don't know they are at risk, they might not seek treatment when the cure is found."

Jill nodded. She felt like she might faint. In all the hours she'd spent asking herself questions, she'd missed arguments that seemed so obvious. Dr. Calder stopped talking, sat facing her, waiting for her to collect herself.

"You're right," she said. Already she was thinking of how to tell them, how hard it would be. Debbie, especially, would not forgive her for keeping the four-year-old secret. Harrison would be hurt. Would Debbie want an abortion? You couldn't know (Dr. Calder couldn't, she couldn't, no one could) the consequence of her disease. It was like the state lottery cards she bought at the deli—the ones where you rubbed off the surface to see whether you won or lost. She felt sure the decision she was being pushed to make would lead to tragedy, that the tragedy was already in place and waiting to be revealed . . .

A year later, when she would be on the ninth floor of the Hall of Justice waiting with Kathleen for a jury to return a verdict on a charge of first-degree murder against her daughter Deb, she would think back to that moment in Dr. Calder's office—and wonder what more would come from the gene she'd inherited . . .

"I don't mean to rush you," Dr. Calder was saying. "I thought we'd talk, that you might have questions, that you might want to reflect on our conversation."

At that moment she could have killed him, she hated the small red-faced man whose face blatantly advertised the pity to which she'd known she would be condemned. He was only the first.

"If you like," he said, "I can be with you when you talk to Harrison."

"I don't need you to talk to my husband," she said.

"I'm sorry," he said. "I'd give anything not to be having this conversation—"

"I'm sure." She checked herself, kept from adding, "How would you like to trade genes?" At the moment it was as if *he* had afflicted her with the gene, as if *he* were the cause of her pain.

He walked her to the passageway that connected the office building and the garage. In her car, she sat behind the steering wheel with the seat belt buckled, numb.

When she got home the house was empty. Harrison had gone to meet his one o'clock class. She was having trouble walking, had staggered coming up the ninety-three steps from the bottom of the ravine. In the house, it felt as if she were making her way across a shallow river on slippery, teetering rocks. Her symptoms had never been so severe.

When Dr. Calder came in to see her in the hospital she said, "I didn't tell Harrison, I underestimated how hard it would be."

Now she wondered if Harrison had talked to Dr. Calder. She couldn't remember how that had been left. It would be better, when Harrison came, if he knew.

"What is it?" The nurse was back, the young snit with "Cindy" on her name tag, the one who chewed gum, turned up the television and chattered as if she'd lived her life in a world created by Disney.

"Thought you might like an extra chair," said Cindy. "When Harrison comes it might be good to be out of bed."

"Bring it in," she said. "Then please, leave me alone until my husband comes."

"How would this be, honey?" Cindy placed two chairs in front of the window, close enough to suggest intimacy, angled so the sunlight wouldn't strike either occupant in the eyes.

She swallowed, trying to find her voice. Under the sheet the insides of her body were in turmoil.

"Fine. Now *please,* leave me alone," she said. Why tell the girl that her husband was a professor at Ohio State, held the John W. Bricker Chair in Political Science, that he was Dr. Donahey and not "Harrison," that she didn't appreciate being *honeyed, sweetied* and *Jilled.*

When Cindy left, Jill was exhausted, drained. She got out of bed, steadying herself on the frame. Stiff-legged and spreading her feet, she extended her arms to avoid falling backward as she made her way to the closet. The nurse had hung up the dresses Harrison had sent, put her cosmetics in the bathroom and most of the things from her suitcase in the chest of drawers.

She felt shaky. She wondered if she would have to ask for help to put on a dress. How could she have deteriorated so rapidly? The symptoms she'd been looking for were surely here. But the disease was supposed to develop slowly, over years. It was as if the disease had been held in check by her concealment.

She got the dress on, the green one with patched flowers. She forced herself to keep going, to apply lipstick, line her eyes, brush her hair. She reached one of the chairs by the window just as the nurse opened the door. Had she been spying? Was the room equipped with a two-way mirror? They would justify that by the need to monitor her symptoms. Or maybe it was because of the suicide attempt. What ward was she in? What floor was she on? How did she know this was Columbus General Hospital?

"You look wonderful, Jill." The girl was smiling at her, innocent as Jesus. "Harrison is in the waiting area."

Jill nodded.

When Harrison opened the door Jill began to cry. She couldn't help herself. And she couldn't even reach the box of tissues on the swing table beside her bed.

Harrison got them for her, then moved the flowers he'd sent, making a space for himself on the sill and closer to her than he could have gotten in the other chair. With his long legs pulled in, his bony knees were outlined beneath thin slacks. He was slender, angular, handsome with white hair and distinguished sideburns. He was sixty-four, seven years older than Jill, but age, people said, was kinder to men. He seemed relaxed, as comfortable in his turtleneck and tweed jacket as if holding a seminar with a handful of his honor students.

He fed her tissues, resting a hand on her knee, patient in letting her pull herself together. Patience. That was Harrison.

"Jilly Bean," he said. "I had a long talk with Dr. Calder." He'd called her Jilly Bean when he was an instructor and she a student at Miami of Ohio in Oxford, when they started going together. He was the only person who called her that. She needed more tissues.

"You've gone through hell." He reached for her hand. She wadded her tissue into her fist. He closed his hands around hers. Though her wrist ached beneath the bandage, his fingers felt healing.

She nodded.

"I knew something was wrong," he said. "For a long time, but . . ."

"Dr. Calder told you?" She studied his eyes. Behind the shell-rimmed glasses they were gray, unflinching, kindly.

He nodded. "Until this morning I hadn't even heard of Huntington's disease. Now I'm an authority."

He was making it easy. She could feel the inner twitching subside. It wasn't as hard to swallow, to talk. But what was he really thinking?

He hadn't mentioned the suicide attempt. Was he avoiding it? No, he had deliberately put his fingers on her bandage. "Did you find me in the bathroom?" she asked.

He nodded.

"I won't do it again," she said. She wanted him to look at her, to see he could trust her. But he was reaching into his jacket pocket, for his pipe she was sure, though he withdrew his hand. Of course he couldn't smoke here in the hospital.

"I talked to Debbie and Denise," he said. "Denise is flying in from California." Had he picked up her fear of telling the girls? They were that way with each other. Usually Harrison *seemed* detached, almost not there. Then unexpectedly he would say something that made her believe they communicated at an unconscious level, that the dialog went on when there seemed to be nothing between them on the surface.

"How did the girls take it?" She made herself look at him but she could hardly bear to hear his answer.

"They know you cut your wrist," he said. "I want Dr. Calder to talk to them."

"Then they . . . they . . ." She was struggling to swallow, unable to speak. "They don't know," she blurted.

Then there would be Debbie's husband, Buzz, the state senator and politician, in the midst of a bitter campaign to be the democratic candidate for Congress in the Fifteenth District. Buzz Garrison could be obsessed with appearances. Anything Buzz or Debbie did—the Ford Taurus and the Chevrolet they drove, the vacation they took to Russia, the Columbus Symphony concerts, their work rehabbing slum houses, the groups they joined, their membership in Broad Street Presbyterian—everything eventually was evaluated by Buzz as a political plus or minus. He didn't like to be seen riding in Jill's Honda, though the car had been manufactured in Ohio. Did Buzz expect them to buy cars from someone other than Trader Bill, the agency started by her father, now run by her brother Billy Joe?

Where, on the political scale, would Buzz Garrison rate a mother-in-law with Huntington's disease, a wife and soon-to-be child who were at risk? A plus, maybe, Jill thought maliciously. Buzz could get involved in the Huntington's Disease Society, work his concern into political commercials, the "up close and personal" series. But a suicide attempt—no way would that be a plus.

Cindy opened the door. "Just wondering if I should order a tray for Harrison," she said. "If you two want to have supper together."

"Get out!" Jill shouted.

"Jilly?" said Harrison.

"I'm sorry," said Jill. "Yes, that would be nice."

"Get me out of here," she said after Cindy left. "I don't need to be in a hospital."

"Let me see what I can do." he said.

As soon as she spoke, Jill had second thoughts. She wanted to be home. But this might be the place to see Debbie and Denise. The hospital was also a haven from starting the life she dreaded, being seen by her friends as some kind of freak.

Denise and Debbie, like her, would now start watching themselves for symptoms. Though not yet afflicted, they would start thinking of themselves as *different.* They would blame her for putting their children at risk. Hadn't she cursed her own mother . . . ?

Jill had cried for her mother too. Some of the worst times had come when she remembered how hard the end had been for Mother. It wasn't Mother's fault. Jill's grandfather had supposedly died of "heart troubles" but there had always been a mystery about that. Had the compulsion to hide, like the HD gene, been passed from generation to generation? Jill wasn't sure what her mother knew, or her father, or Billy Joe. Maybe that's why Billy Joe didn't have children. Maybe each had been keeping a secret. Did it make any difference, really, what anyone had known? God, how would Debbie take this?

Harrison was staring at her. How long was it since either one had spoken? Harrison said he'd studied the disease. If so, he knew the tendency to insanity. So why would he believe she wouldn't try again? She would be under his microscope. He would watch her as she had been watching herself. He would be looking for irregular spasmodic movement in her legs, arms, face, muscles. He'd monitor her moods, her crankiness, her difficulty in thinking logically. He would pay attention to the way she ate and swallowed, the way she talked.

An attendant, not Cindy, wheeled in a cart with two trays. Harrison moved from the sill to the chair. The attendant put the trays on their laps and took away the heat-retaining covers.

As they ate—spaghetti and meat sauce, coleslaw, Jello—Harrison found himself babbling, describing ideas for the television commercials in Deb's husband, Buzz Garrison's campaign for Congress. Why had Harrison changed the subject? What had he seen, staring at her while she was off in the endless, unanswerable questions?

Politics was safe ground for Harrison. And no aspect of politics so enthralled him as his son-in-law's campaign. It was heady stuff, an opportunity to be closely associated with a practical expression of his otherwise academic life. "Buzz has a very attractive concept," said Harrison. "Buzz Garrison is fed up with mealy-mouthed politicians who are afraid to say what they believe if, indeed, they *believe* anything. That's the theme and it will be delivered by a voice-over while the graphic shows a chameleon changing color to blend with different backgrounds. Buzz comes in. The camera zooms, stops at a head-and-shoulder shot with the stars and stripes as backdrop. 'Here's what I stand for,' Buzz says. He'll do ten, hitting the ten issues that concern voters most according to our polling. The use of the flag is a bit corny, I admit, but good causes need to use all the tools."

"Harrison," she said, "do we have to talk about the campaign?"

"No . . ."

"I'm sorry, it's just that when you talk about Buzz I can't help thinking about Debbie. I feel terrible, hitting her with this a week after she's found out she's pregnant. She was so happy. Buzz too."

Harrison put his tray on the sill. He slid out of his chair. His sixty-four-year-old knees creaked as he knelt on the floor. "Bean," he said, leaning his head against her legs and putting his arm around them, "Debbie will understand."

"She can still have an abortion. It's early enough."

"Jill, you're letting your imagination torture you."

"Debbie will hate me."

"Jilly Bean, this isn't your fault." He wanted to take her pain away. He couldn't.

He squeezed her legs. Suddenly she was overcome by love for him. How many times had he rescued her, starting back in college. She hugged his head. She kissed the small bald spot.

He fought back tears.

Chapter 6

THE ROOM was cozy with a fireplace, a hooked rug, pine furniture, latticed windows overlooking the pond. Outside, March gusts pounded the shutters and clanged through the wind chimes. Deb had a fire started and it was warm and snug inside. Except for the chill between herself and Buzz.

"Damn it, Deb. What's the point of the test? You *do* want an abortion. I'm afraid you haven't been telling me the truth." Buzz had been on his way out to a candidate's night sponsored by the Hilltop Federation of Democratic Women. He'd thrown his suit coat over the back of the couch, but he was still standing, making an effort to hide his anger.

"Honey, let's talk later," said Deb. The doctors said she could find out if her fetus was carrying the HD gene. If it was . . . she might want an abortion. She could get pregnant again. She wanted time to think. As her OB said, "You shouldn't decide on the spot. There is no harm in having the test. They can test the fetus without telling you whether or not you have the gene—if that is your preference. You and Buzz can have more children. Talk to Buzz, think this through."

She wanted Buzz to leave. Maybe when he came home after his meeting she could tell him, Honey, you were right. But it was her decision. He had no right to press her, to assume that only his view counted.

He had shocked her by his reaction. Shocked her because she'd known in her very soul that Buzz would be with her whatever she decided. Shocked her because, after all, he was committed to *Roe* v. *Wade,* had the endorsement of NOW, had given speeches on the need for tough laws against sexual harassment, had aligned himself with the feminist groups. It confused and angered her that he would campaign for the rights of women but deny her hers.

"Buzz," she said, "we can't get anywhere when you're thinking about a speech."

"I thought there was some urgency," he said. "Isn't that what the doctors told you?"

"There is," she said. "But it doesn't have to be decided tonight." Since Dad called to report Mom's attempted suicide, Deb hadn't gotten a quiet minute. She didn't trust herself. She had spent the morning at the hospital with her mother. In the afternoon she saw Dr. Calder and Dr. Weingard. Tomorrow morning at six she had to be at Port Columbus to meet her elder sister Denise, who was flying in from Los Angeles on the Red Eye. The guest room had to be made ready. Two Tylenols had not relieved a murderous headache.

Buzz walked around the couch. He hovered over her, all six and a half feet of him, waiting for her to explain the inconsistency between wanting the test and saying she hadn't decided to have an abortion.

"I can't sort out my feelings with people picking at me, with you standing over me like that."

He turned away. "Sort out your feelings," he said, repeating her words as if they were so much jargon. He picked up his coat. On the steps going up to the center hall, he turned. He was standing under the ox yoke they'd bought on their first vacation after the honeymoon. Deb had spotted the yoke in the corner of a stable where they'd rented horses. "Do you think you might get your feelings sorted out before your sister moves in on our life?" Not waiting for her answer, he disappeared into the hall.

She heard the garage door go up, the start of the engine in his Taurus. She felt cold. She tended the fire, reshaping it, adding logs. She wrapped herself in a quilt, returned to her chair.

She wanted the child she was carrying. She had dreamed about a child since she could remember. But did she want a child with an incurable disease? No. She told herself to relax. She was assuming she had the gene even before the test. But she did. Somehow she knew she did.

Deb was still looking at the space he had occupied, on the steps beneath the ox yoke. Only three years ago Buzz had spent fourteen days refinishing the yoke. He had scraped off the grime and green paint, sanded, restored the metal pins, refinished the wood as carefully as a cabinet maker. Every night for two weeks and all of the weekend between it took him. He'd worked in the basement, often calling up the stairs for Deb to come down and see his progress.

Deb's best friend from college, Judy, who'd gotten married in her senior year and who later was Deb's maid of honor, told Deb on the day before Deb got married, "The first year is something you have to live through. Then it gets better." How many times had Deb thought how wrong Judy was. The first year with Buzz, in fact the first two years—they'd been the best of Deb's life. There wasn't anything they didn't tell each other. They liked each other, wanted to be together. So much that old friends had dropped away. Deb and Buzz jogged, loved to ride, spent lavishly on long meals at restaurants they discovered, talked often about the family they wanted (four children, spaced two years apart). Sex had stayed exciting.

When politics became the big part of the dream for Buzz, it became hers too. They plunged into the first campaign together, going door-to-door in the district, staying up nights to put labels on mailers, laughing as they wrote up the press releases they got the suburban weeklies to run.

When Buzz won election to the state senate Deb felt like she had won too. "Thank God we don't have to go through that again for four years," Buzz said. But after a month Deb was missing the campaign and working with Buzz until late into the night. Buzz talked her into doing an eight-week seminar for Dad's political-science students—"Practical Politics," it was called. She, Dad and Buzz led the class.

The next winter Wylie Ferguson, the eight-term congressman from the Fifteenth District, announced that he was going to retire. "I have as good a shot as anyone," Buzz had told her at

Rigsby's restaurant. They were celebrating their third anniversary, halfway through a bottle of Pinot Noir, about to order.

Through dinner and while lingering for an hour afterward, the dream expanded. Buzz was only thirty-two, loved politics, had discovered he was good at it. Government was exciting, provided a chance to be part of "something that matters, not just making money as a lawyer." Deb thought again how lucky she was, how lucky *they* were.

Congress, statewide office, maybe governor, maybe U.S. senator; the dream had intoxicating possibilities. "Who knows," he said. "There's so much luck involved, nothing is impossible." Both at the moment dared to think of the White House, what a presidential campaign might be like, how it would feel to be First Lady and President. He laughed first, then she, as they recognized what the other was thinking, and the absurdity of it.

Across the table, she mouthed the words, "You're my hero." She'd been teasing, but he really was. He was her stringbean lawyer who bragged about his college basketball days. "I could have played in the NBA if I wanted to pay the price." Deb loved his optimism. Like Tigger in the *Winnie the Pooh* stories she once begged her mother to read at bedtime, Buzz Garrison could do anything.

After the anniversary dinner they went home to make love. It was quick, explosive—for him. Then she played with him, felt his stiffness come back. "Fuck me again, Mr. Congressman," she said, nibbling his ear.

"This time let's try for a baby."

"Yes," she agreed as she rolled on top of him and smothered him with kisses.

Three months later, Buzz left the partnership he had formed with two of his law-school classmates. He joined a medium-sized firm, Kasich and Levy. They had a labor practice, represented unions. The United Auto Workers became the client Buzz spent most of his time on. He was building support for a congressional campaign.

"The money's better," he said. "We've got to think of more than you and me now." He kissed her and patted her stomach. She wasn't pregnant, had momentarily felt what he said as a criticism—then convinced herself she was being unfair. But God, she hoped they wouldn't have to go through the stuff some couples did in order to conceive . . .

Now she was looking back, wondering if she had been deceiving herself. Jarred by his surprising reaction to the fetus test, she was seeing how much she had always submitted to his plans. She dieted, exercised to stay cute and perky. He loved it at a political gathering—one of those intimate dinners attended by two hundred "good people" who pretended to be best friends—when Buzz could be admired for having the best-looking, most charming woman. "How did you get such a doll?" was the question he liked and always passed on to her. Almost by habit, in spite of what had happened between them, she would still be there for him again tomorrow night, be his "doll" at the state Democratic party dinner. She was active in Buckeye Boys Ranch, the Broad Street Presbyterian Church ("It's worth the drive and puts us in contact with an important slice of the community"), the Urban League and, of course, the Federation of Democratic Women. Politics had become her life as well as his.

There were all the things she had accepted as the price of political progress . . . She had tolerated the pawing from Sam Roberts, the court-of-appeals judge who knew everything and who had spotted Buzz as a comer, and whose alcoholic wife was twenty years older than Deb. The judge and his wife were one of the few couples she and Buzz still went out to dinner with.

A change had taken place without her knowing . . . or maybe she *had* known but hadn't been able or willing to face it. She didn't dare to be moody, critical (except concerning her mother or when she and Buzz were by themselves) or, heaven forbid, sick. Sick? God, she was heading for *incurable* sick. Huntington's disease.

Buzz had held her, been with her as the Buzz she knew when they got the call from Dad. "Sweetie, this is dreadful," he had said. He'd canceled his campaign event and they'd talked until after midnight. This morning he'd dropped her off at the hospital to visit her mother. He would come when she finished her visit. "You and Mother Jill will be more comfortable if I don't butt in," he had said.

After the visit she called him, reached him through his pager. In the car, still on the hospital parking lot, he held her, stroked her hair as she told him more about the disease. She was sure she had the gene. God, what now . . . ?

"Sweetie," he said, "it's horrible but there's as good a chance you don't." He asked if she wanted him to go with her to see the doctors. "I can cancel my appointments real easy," he said, reaching for the cellular phone that was mounted between them.

She kissed him, said she could manage the doctors. He pulled her close again, stroked her, cradled her. Not until he let her off at Lake in the Woods did she realize her disappointment. Shouldn't he have dropped what he was doing until, at least, she recovered from the shock? She had been so careful to protect her mother. She needed Buzz to be there when she fell apart, as she vented her unseemly rage against her mother, as she tried to decide whether she could bear giving up the baby she'd thought about ever since she was told she was pregnant, and years before that.

She would have supported her mother, even if Dad hadn't lectured her (*Look at this objectively . . . She was trying to protect you . . . It isn't her fault . . . She has the disease, you don't*). She would have seen how much her mother needed her the instant she walked into the room on the seventh floor at Columbus General.

Mom got out of the chair by the window. Small, brittle movements of Mom's hands made Deb feel Mom would splinter if she fell. Mom stopped, a step from the chair, to regain her balance. Fear was in Mom's eyes.

They hugged, then sat in the chairs by the window. "I'd give my life in a second," Mom said, "if I knew you and Denise wouldn't get the gene."

Deb hadn't meant to look at the bandage. But Mom saw that she had and that activated her spasms. "It's all right," Deb said.

She waited, then listened as her mother recited the family history, told how Deb's great-grandfather had died mysteriously, how Grandmother Eichorn might not have known what she had, how Grandmother Eichorn had been difficult for Pops, had spent her last three years in a nursing home. Grandmother Eichorn died when Deb was two. If they'd taken Deb to the nursing home she couldn't remember. Mom didn't know what Pops or Uncle B knew.

"Has Pops been in?" asked Deb.

Mom shook her head. "Uncle B and Pops are coming tonight," she said.

After the first hour Deb had to force her sympathy. She was thinking about her baby. She saw her mother's purpose . . . to convince her that she was facing the fate of Grandmother Eichorn, to earn forgiveness for keeping her secret.

But full anger hadn't come until she was in Dr. Calder's office, didn't fully hit until her OB, Dr. Weingard, joined the consultation.

The three were in Dr. Calder's study on the fourth floor of the Medical Science building. Dr. Weingard, who was seated on the arm of the couch, had questions about the test procedure. "How long does it take to get a result?" Dr. Weingard asked.

"It can be done in two weeks. Usually it takes longer. Usually there's an extended period of counseling." Dr. Calder glanced at Deb. He had a file folder, thick with reprints of studies and articles from medical journals. Deb, seated in a leather chair that swallowed her like a child, held a duplicate set on her lap. The file containing copies for Dr. Weingard was on the couch beside him. Dr. Calder pulled a medical journal reprint he had marked with a green highlighter.

"Despite the availability of the test," said Dr. Calder, "most people who are at risk don't take it."

As the doctors spoke she wavered, thinking one moment she would, the next—no way.

Dr. Calder was telling her obstetrician about a survey that indicated that sixty-five percent would have their pregnancies terminated if the test were positive for the fetus.

"If you elect to be tested," said Dr. Calder, turning to her, "you can change your mind at any time. When they have a result they ask if you want to hear more. Then they'll tell you whether a prediction can be made. If one can, you still have choice. You can decide you don't want to hear it."

Dr. Weingard said she should read the materials, talk to Buzz, be sure of her decision. Because of her pregnancy she shouldn't delay the process. "But you shouldn't decide anything until you've thought it through. You've had a lot sprung on you in the last two days."

If she was to be tested she needed blood samples from close relatives, including someone diagnosed with HD. That would be

Mother. To have a good chance at a prediction there should be six to eight samples. The determination relied on genetic markers.

She wondered how Denise would react. She wanted to talk with her sister.

"There are practical considerations," Dr. Calder said. "If either the test for you or the fetus is positive, you can prepare for the expense, buy insurance. A trust fund can be set up for the baby." Buzz would want to know these things, she thought.

That was when the doubts crept in. How secure was her marriage now? Would Buzz come to see her as a liability? Based on the last year or so, she had to wonder if his decision to start their family was part of his plan to capture a seat in Congress and go on from there. Her doubts were irrational, she told herself . . . she was taking out on Buzz the anger she felt toward her mother. But anger didn't go away as Dr. Weingard and Dr. Calder kept talking. It didn't go away until she decided she should at least have the test. She just couldn't live with the uncertainty.

Would there be enough blood samples? Besides her mother and Denise, there were Pops, Dad and Uncle B. "Do Denise's children count?" she asked.

Dr. Calder looked through his materials. The answer wasn't there. He would make calls. What if Denise refused? "Could Denise give a blood sample if she didn't want to be tested?" she asked.

"Of course," said Dr. Calder. In fact he thought samples should be collected at once, in case anyone in the family wanted to be tested.

Buzz came home early. "Let's go out," he suggested.

"No," she said. "I've already taken two pickerel filets out of the freezer."

He sat on a stool in the kitchen, listening, asking questions about HD while she pan-fried the filets, tossed a salad and put two Idahos in the microwave.

"In addition to the test for me," she said, "there's a test for the fetus."

"Fetus? Are we talking about our baby?"

"Yes," she said. "They can test the fetus."

"I don't suppose I have any say in what you're doing," he said.

"Well, it's my body," she said. "I'm the one who's at risk." She had been trying to avoid this, even as his questions convinced her they couldn't dodge a bad argument. She knew she was reeling—from her mother, from the disease itself, from the surprising reaction by Buzz, from her reconstructed view of the past year.

"Well, it's our baby, sweetheart, and we've got some talking to do." When he said *sweetheart* in that tone of voice it was like a fist in the stomach.

He got up from the table. Neither had eaten. "I've got to change and shave," he said.

"Don't forget," she said. "Denise gets in at six tomorrow morning. I'll have to set the alarm for four."

"Jesus," he said. "This really comes at a rotten time. Tomorrow night is the state Democratic party dinner and—"

"That reminds me," she said. "You aren't expecting me to go?"

He looked at her. "All right, sweetheart, if that's the way you want it. I'm out of here."

She had struck a low blow, she decided. He had counted on her at the state dinner. They would go around to the tables together, shaking hands with fifteen hundred people. He was especially looking forward to this one. "Judge Sam," as Buzz called him, had wangled two minutes for Buzz on the podium. Buzz thought it would give him a considerable leg-up going into the last month before the primary. It was unthinkable that she wouldn't be at his side, standing up with Buzz in the crossed spots when introductions were made. She had told her mother they'd be at the state dinner on Saturday night. Through the afternoon-long session with her doctors she'd not thought of canceling.

She ran out of the kitchen, caught him on the stairway. "I'm sorry," she said. "I'll go to the dinner." She pushed herself into his arms.

"Honey, we need to talk," he said. "I don't have to be at the meeting this early."

They went back into the kitchen. They ate the pickerel. The conversation was civil, but both seemed guarded. He feared losing her for the state dinner and she was afraid of polarizing his opposition to testing their fetus. Why couldn't he see? As Dr. Calder said, there was only a twenty-five percent chance that the baby she was carrying had the gene. The test didn't hurt anybody.

And if the baby was clean, as was most likely, they'd be saved a lifetime of uncertainty.

They were eating the lemon tarts she'd microwaved for dessert when the telephone rang.

"What?" she asked. From his end of the conversation she had seen he was upset.

"They're screwing with our television buy." he said. "Trying to cut me out of six news adjacencies."

"Who is?"

"It's a long story but I've got to catch Socko before the meeting and straighten this out."

"We'll talk when you get home." She was thinking of building a fire, sitting in the family room and trying to find a compromise while he was gone.

"It could be late," he said.

"I'll be up."

He seemed to relax, to be thinking of having a cup of coffee with her, letting Socko Bender handle the crisis in television commercials. "This'll work out. I sort of went crazy when I realized you wanted an abortion." His voice, like his eyes, had turned soft.

"All I know is I want the test." She felt a cramp in her stomach. Her body tightened.

"But why the rush?"

"I don't see the advantage to waiting," she said.

"Not even until after May fourth?" It was the date of the primary. That upset her. What was at issue here? A diseased baby? An election?

She temporized. "Buzz, I don't know what I want." She couldn't discuss this when he was angry and had Socko Bender, TV commercials, the Hilltop Federation of Democratic Women and the campaign on his mind. "Let's talk later," she said.

He agreed, went upstairs to change and shave. She'd gone into the family room to build the fire. She had it started when he came in on the way out. It seemed he couldn't let it go. The argument broke out again, worse than before . . .

Now she was alone. The fire was going strong, crackling, popping, the flame licking the top of the fireplace. She felt betrayed, what else? The political dream was after all, his, not theirs. At least that was what it had become. It was more important than they were, then she was. She mattered if she played her part.

Otherwise . . . "You're just upset," she cautioned herself, "you're being unfair to Buzz." It helped a little . . . she tried to think back, picture them in the good times. But mostly she saw Buzz at the lectern, impressing the Hilltop Women, delivering his line—"I guarantee you. Buzz Garrison will be the first person in Congress to fight anyone who so much as hints at a law or regulation that deprives a woman of her constitutional right to choice."

Chapter 7

DENISE LOOKED smashing, slim and tan in a yellow dress as she came off the Red Eye from Los Angeles. She did not look like she had been buckled into a cramped seat for five hours. She and Deb went directly to the hospital. Mostly Denise listened as Deb reported Mom's condition, described HD and the test.

Denise was marvelous, giving love, transforming Mom as Deb watched. They talked about Denise's children. Mom promised to visit California in the summer. They planned what they'd do, how much fun Mother would have going with Kiefer and Lance to Disneyland. Over the two hours Mom's difficulty in swallowing disappeared. The fidgety movements quieted and she was talking easily but animated.

"Mom did exactly right," Denise told Deb as they were leaving the hospital. "She kept her life together as long as she could. She protected us."

"I guess I don't see it that way," Deb said. But they didn't argue. Nor did Deb suggest that it was easier to be so nurturing and supportive when you could go back to California.

Denise wanted no part of testing. "Why would I want to know?" she said. "No one in the family has been stricken before fifty. That's twenty years. By then my boys will be adults and better able to handle it, if they must."

* * *

Buzz met them for lunch. He was charming, called Deb *little mother* and *sweetie,* remembered that Denise was missing Kiefer's birthday, asked how Keith made out trying to negotiate with L.A. Tool and Die. "Stephens," said Buzz. "He was the prick lawyer who was causing trouble, wasn't he?" Buzz was phenomenal with names and obscure facts that made people think he cared about them.

"It would probably bore you," said Buzz, "but I lined up an extra ticket for the state Democratic party dinner tonight. You could sit at our table, Denise."

Denise was eager to go, quickly fell in with the campaign, said she found it fascinating.

When Buzz learned that Denise wouldn't hear of being tested, his generosity expanded. "You must stay until May fourth," he insisted. "There'll be one hell of a party on election night."

Denise was tempted, said she wished she could, looked at Buzz in her sincere fashion.

"It would be great for the little mother to have you." Buzz glanced at Deb, a signal to gush agreement. It was so transparent. Buzz obviously thought sister-in-law Denise would be a good influence, do his work with Deb. "If you stay it would be wonderful for Mother Jill," Buzz said. Mother Jill had gone home from Columbus General the day after Denise arrived.

Denise, after staying two weeks, finally went home. Deb was relieved to see her go, then inexplicably sad returning from the airport to Lake in the Woods. The burden of Buzz, and the test, had closed in.

Denise did supply blood, and got samples from Kiefer and Lance, even Keith. "I don't want to know," Denise said. "But I see how badly you do. Maybe I'd feel different if I were pregnant."

Denise had been curious. "You aren't considering an abortion?" Denise looked shocked when she said it. Deb's answers had been vague. She wasn't sure what she wanted. She'd never tell Denise but she was thinking about abortion all the time; rejecting the possibility, then realizing that might be because she was afraid of Buzz, that if he were supporting her she'd probably do it. Diseased or not, she was no longer enthusiastic about starting their family. She wished she were not pregnant, that they'd waited . . .

Deb met her dad at the Faculty Club. They got a window table, with a view of Mirror Lake. It was mid-April, quite warm, the grass green and the shrubbery sprouting early buds, the Ohio State campus coming into its season.

"How are you doing?" Dad asked.

"Scared," she said. At one-thirty, after lunch, they would meet Dr. Calder and Dr. Weingard at University Hospital. A doctor and a psychologist, members of the team from the Department of Medical Genetics at Indiana University, would also be there— with the test results. It was a requirement that the person being tested be accompanied. Buzz knew she was having the test but she didn't want him there. She and Buzz couldn't talk about their dispute anymore. Though they'd backed off to a silent truce, that had not happened until she had declared herself, and the argument had pushed Buzz close to violence.

"I believe in the right to choose," Buzz had said. He sounded like he meant it. "But abortion is a choice I can't make. And I'm really, *really* disappointed to find out you could."

"So that gives you the right to make my decision."

"Isn't it my decision too?"

That was the problem. Buzz . . . maybe it was being a politician . . . knew how to compromise, about everything. She had thought there was no problem the two of them couldn't work out. But how do you compromise on this? Compromise was no more possible than Solomon's offer to let the two women who claimed to be its mother cut the baby in half.

"There's a difference between having the right to choose," he said, "and deciding what choice—if you have to make it—is the moral one for you."

"Wouldn't your women's-lib backers like to know that the right to choice doesn't include your wife?" she said. He'd grabbed hold of her, then scared her, came close, she felt, to hitting her.

He had backed off but his voice had been as cold as his eyes. "I can't stop you," he said. "But if you do this, Deb, we're through. I mean it."

"Buzz," she said. "I just haven't decided. I'm not sure I want to even if the test is bad." But she was sure, or at least almost sure. She didn't dare go beyond that with him . . . In the last three and a half weeks she had discovered a different man than the one she'd married. Very different.

"I want . . . I'm not sure . . . I haven't decided." Buzz shot back her words. He hadn't heard her. "What happened to *us?*" he said. "Why is it suddenly I—I—I? Do you *want* a divorce? Is that it?"

"I don't know what I want. I'm just really, really hurting. Why can't you see . . . ?"

"Why can't *you?*" His voice held a menacing edge. She stepped back. "This disease doesn't hit till middle age. Who are you to decide whether my child gets a chance to live thirty or more years of healthy life? What would my child decide if you weren't murdering him?"

"You're a damn phony." She was yelling now. "You're a closet right-to-lifer. Why don't you be honest about that . . . ?"

Without answering he walked out of the kitchen and she grabbed the countertop to steady herself . . .

But hadn't she been manipulating him? She'd known that a threat to expose him as a political phony was at least one way to stop the argument.

Now about to get the test results, she wondered if they could have avoided their fight. No, she decided. The crisis had forced her to see some unpleasant truths. She'd surrendered her life to Buzz, and she wanted it back. Since they'd started dating she'd made it so easy for him. Could he stay in a relationship where *she* made a decision? About herself, her baby?

The night she had told Buzz she was going to have the test he'd come home from a schedule that started with the St. Agatha Men's Club breakfast, included a luncheon speech to the North-west Lions and ended with a four-hour session taping new TV commercials.

There was no fight. "Fine," he had said. "Let's pray for the best." He went on to bed, saying he was "absolutely bushed." He was taking it, she thought, as a defeat, as her assertion of her will. Well, he was right. The change had come so unexpectedly that she thought it wasn't real. But it was. She had even considered divorce, no matter what the test showed.

That night, a week ago, was the last time until this morning that HD or the test had been mentioned. This morning he had asked her to call as soon as she got the result. The result, he was probably hoping, would solve their problem. She didn't think so.

"Shouldn't we be going?" Dad was asking now. It was such a nice day, they decided to walk to the hospital, about fifteen minutes away. They walked slowly. "I don't want to wait in there for half an hour," she said.

"Buzz tells me the latest polling shows him with a three-point margin," Dad said as they walked across the campus. Dad thought it would help to talk about the campaign. He was with her because she'd told him Buzz couldn't escape a campaign commitment. "The margin for error is plus or minus four," she said knowledgeably. How could she not be knowledgeable?

The receptionist in the Department of Genetics was looking for them, took them at once to a small conference room. There was a table with four chairs on each side, a blackboard and x-ray box mounted at one end, a movie screen at the other. No one was there. "Sit anywhere," the receptionist said. They turned down an offer of coffee or a soft drink.

It was 1:17. Thirteen minutes to wait, or longer if the doctors were behind schedule. God, she thought, do I really want to know? In her handbag she carried the picture taken of her baby by ultrasound. At first, she had strained to see a baby. But now she could, a little person hardly more than an inch tall. A baby was wiggling around in there. She couldn't keep her resolve to think of her baby as a fetus. Mom cried because the disease might pass to her and Denise. Deb felt like crying when she looked at the ultrasound picture.

At precisely 1:30 the receptionist came in to ask if she was ready for the team. Did she and her father want a few more minutes?

"No," she said.

The team came in, Dr. Calder, Dr. Weingard and the other four. Who was the woman? Which was the geneticist and which the psychologist? She got none of their names. The woman was the geneticist and the extra doctor was from the staff at University Hospital.

"We have expedited this process," said the psychologist. "The usual counseling has been omitted."

She nodded her understanding.

The woman asked the question. "Do you want to hear what we have learned?"

She nodded. Without reading it, she signed a paper described to her as "a waiver and a consent." She was certain her news was bad. If not, why these precautions and signings? If not, surely they would just blurt out the happy news.

"At this time we are unable to reach a conclusion," the woman said.

"Why? You had seven samples."

The explanation followed. Since the HD gene could not be located, testing depended upon genetic markers. The primary marker was G–8 on the tip of chromosome 4. Depending on the markers found in the samples provided, a result could sometimes be predicted with as few as three samples. Conversely, in a rare case, ten samples might not be enough. "It depends on luck." The samples from Keith and from Denise's two children meant nothing. She'd heard most of it before. Why had this team been assembled, the main players brought from Indiana, to tell her nothing?

"New markers are constantly being discovered," the woman said. "The gene may soon be located. We'll keep your test open, under review."

"What about the fetus test?" Maybe she hadn't heard that part.

"As I said, that was also inconclusive." The psychologist assured her of their interest. Her material could help in the search to find a cure for the disease.

She and Dad walked back across the campus. Students were lying on the grass, tossing Frisbees, reading, soaking up sun, hurrying for three o'clock classes. "I hope Buzz got his endorsement from the FOP," she said.

"Don't be too hard on him," Dad said. "This isn't his fault. Buzz is under pressure," he said. "The last weeks in a congressional campaign are murderous."

She was afraid to respond. If she did, Dad would see through her. She couldn't tell him about their fight, that it was probably irreparable. Dad and Buzz still talked almost every night after the eleven o'clock news, evaluating issues and developments, planning campaign strategy. "You're the only person whose advice I trust," Buzz had told Dad. At least twice a week the two met for a six o'clock breakfast at the Bob Evans on Olentangy. Divorce would kill Dad. The thought of explaining was more than she could bear.

They walked on without talking. She was thinking irrationally again . . . Suddenly she was blaming Mom for destroying her marriage. It was her body, not Mom's. If Mom had told her this could have happened, she would not have gotten pregnant . . .

She drove around the subdivision, not wanting to go home. Her house seemed alien, his ally. She hadn't tried to call him on his pager as he had asked.

When she activated the garage door opener she saw his Taurus. He met her at the door. "Are you all right?"

She nodded, let him hold her.

"What about our baby? Does our baby have the gene too?"

Deb shook her head. "They don't know what anyone has," she said.

He walked her into the family room, asked if she wanted a drink. She did. "When you didn't call," he said, "I panicked. I canceled a meeting with the big-bucks people who might pay for extra commercials."

"That's too bad," she said.

He ignored it or didn't get it. "Well, what does this mean?" Which apparently was what really concerned him.

"It means I'm like Mom and Denise. I won't *know* until it hits me."

"Listen," he said. Did he look relieved? "We need to get away, Deb, find what we've lost." He proceeded to apologize for not having time to communicate with her during the campaign. "I should be able to free up a week at the end of May," he said. "What say we line up a condo at Sanibel? Just the two of us?"

She said that sounded nice but the way she felt it was hard to think about vacations.

He asked if she wanted to talk about it. Was there anything he could do?

She shook her head.

He wondered if it would be all right if he slipped back downtown for a few minutes to catch Socko Bender. "No problem," she said. "I'd like to take a nap."

"Don't let this get you down," he said. "I've got this strong feeling you don't have the gene. Our baby doesn't. And look at the worst case. If by remote chance you do . . . well, the odds are they'll discover the cure before you ever get the disease."

His words, sounding forced to her, made her feel as if she were a blackboard and he was scratching his fingernails across her. He thought he'd won, that with a little coddling he'd have her back as she'd been before the disease came between them and screwed up her pretty little head.

She waited until his car left the drive, poured herself a Jack Daniels, drank it and poured herself another.

She had fallen asleep in the chair by the fireplace when his call awakened her. He wanted to know how she was doing. "Fine," she said, being careful with her words because she didn't want him to notice slurred speech.

"One of my cases blew up," he said. He could repair the damage between now and the time he was due at a candidates' night in Dublin but he would come home if she needed him. She said no, she was still groggy from her nap, not really hungry and thought she'd go to bed.

She sat then, staring blankly at the telephone.

Chapter 8

O<small>N ELECTION NIGHT</small>, Jill and Harrison went to Buzz Garrison's victory celebration in the ballroom at the Hyatt on Capitol Square. Early returns kept the crowd tense until ten o'clock when it became apparent his margin would exceed the forecast from the last poll.

"Mother Jill, you and Harrison come on up here with me and Deb," Buzz shouted from the platform. His voice was hoarse from campaigning. As supporters cheered, he put his arm around Debbie. Debbie and Buzz raised their free arms. Flashbulbs exploded as amateurs joined the media in photographing the couple on the night of their triumph. Jill, holding onto Harrison, managed to mount the steps and walk down the platform without noticeable faltering.

"Stand beside the mother," Buzz croaked into the microphone, smiling at Debbie, gesturing Jill and Harrison to their places. Harrison pressed Jill closer to Debbie. Jill began to feel herself tremble. Squeezed between Harrison and Debbie, Jill's arms were dangling, with no place to go. She looked at her hand. To her surprise, her fingers were steady.

Could it be in her mind? Whatever, Jill felt Debbie's anger, and the blame for the non-informative test.

Buzz spotted Judge Sam Roberts. "Come on up," Buzz

shouted. He grasped the microphone and leaned into it. "Judge Roberts, a people's judge." The crowd roared. "In two years there'll be an open seat and we've got to get him on the Ohio supreme court."

The judge, now on the platform, jammed both fists into the air, looked to his right, then his left, playfully punched one of the helium balloons.

As Buzz continued to speak, touching his themes—jobs and progress, women's rights, equal opportunity, cleaning the environment, supporting the American worker, making the streets safe by going after the cause of the disease rather than slapping a band-aid on the symptoms—Jill felt Debbie trying to pull away.

Then Buzz was looking at Jill, easing Debbie to the side, pulling Jill close to him. "This campaign will require courage," he said, holding Jill. "You have demonstrated the will to fight, to hang tough in the teeth of those early polls. But our fight will get harder." Jill felt like a rag doll, clutched by Buzz as he spoke. "Drew Dawson," said Buzz, "is a puppet of the establishment. Dawson believes in negative politics. He will not debate the issues as have my honorable opponents in the primary."

Buzz paid tribute to the two he had beaten in the primary, inviting support from "those who in good conscience believed in their candidacies." It was a startling departure from the conversations Jill had heard between Buzz and Harrison. Why was she being made a part of this message?

Buzz leaned down, still holding her. The force of his grip had lifted her onto her toes. "This dear lady, our mother," he said, "is going to be my model as I walk the minefield between now and November."

Her legs felt like jelly. Buzz tightened his grip to keep her from falling. "This great lady doesn't want me to do this," he said. "And don't worry, Mother, I'm not going to break my promise. But I want you folks to know the tremendous inner strength it takes for this lady to be with us tonight."

Buzz eased her down but kept supporting her. The speech ended. More helium balloons descended from holders on the ceiling. A band, playing the Ohio State fight song, could barely be heard over the cheering. Socko Bender helped her to a seat on the platform. As people pressed forward, crowding against the platform, she saw tears in their eyes. They wondered what tragedy had called for the tribute to her courage. At least Buzz hadn't mentioned the disease. She didn't think he had. He'd promised Debbie he wouldn't.

Reporters had Buzz surrounded at the end of the platform, where he stood on the steps under klieg lights as the three channels recorded answers to questions. Harrison sought out Judge Roberts. They talked, halfway between Jill and Buzz. Socko Bender took Debbie to accommodate an interview request by a student reporter from the Ohio State *Lantern.*

Jill saw Pops and Billy Joe making their way through the crowd. She had not seen them enter the ballroom. Nor had she expected them. Her dad was a straight-ticket Republican. Long ago he and Harrison had come to an understanding. Politics was not a topic for discussion. Her brother had no interest in politics.

She dreaded seeing Pops. A week ago he had asked her, "Have you thought about contacting the adoption agency?"

Yes, she had. Not an hour passed without reconsidering her position. Deb needed another blood sample.

"Damn, if this isn't something else," said Billy Joe. He and Pops had wedged into a space on the floor, next to the platform and directly below her. "I'll write Buzz a check for five grand," said Billy Joe. Pops, the straight-ticketer, didn't argue.

Jill liked her older brother. He would not press her. Billy Joe, or Trader Bill, as he did business, knew two things: selling cars and making money. "I'm breaking my rule," Billy Joe said. "I never gave a dime to a politician. Never thought who's in and who's out had the first damn thing to do with the way I live or the way I do business."

Billy Joe had caught the bug while standing in the crowd, watching "my nephew and favorite niece. . . . Buzz is sharp," said Billy Joe. "He presents himself. He's competing with assholes. He could go a long way."

Jill had seen the phenomenon in Harrison's students. In Harrison, for that matter. It was the first intoxication that could lead to addiction. Why people worked endless hours for nothing, got on their telephones, went door to door with literature, gave more money than they'd donate to church or the United Way—she didn't understand. Nor could Harrison explain it.

Pops was gawking at the crowd. He was eighty-three, had built the agency as a Chrysler-Plymouth dealership. In the seventies, Billy Joe got the jump on the trend, switched to Japanese cars, elevated an already strong dealership to the largest in the Midwest, spent a fortune in advertising and had made himself a guitar-strumming television celebrity.

Jill was looking for Debbie, hoping Billy Joe and Pops would leave, maybe seek out Buzz, who had finished answering questions and was accepting handshakes, hugs, slaps on the back. A dishy blonde on tiptoe pushed her boobs into his chest and opened her mouth to plant one on him. Buzz handled her well, without encouragement or rejection.

Debbie was returning to the platform, and Socko Bender's smile indicated she'd done well in the interview. Buzz disengaged from well-wishers to join them. Harrison and Judge Roberts came over.

"Buzz," said Judge Roberts, "I've got to leave. You're arguing the case for the auto workers, aren't you?"

Buzz nodded, smiling. He said he felt guilty about neglecting preparation.

"The issue means a lot to labor," said Roberts.

Buzz nodded soberly.

"Call me tomorrow," said Roberts. "Your brief missed the best argument." Roberts left.

"What was that about?" asked Pops. His eyes had snapped into focus at the mention of auto workers.

"I've got an argument in the court of appeals." Buzz laughed. "I've let my practice go to hell."

Pops frowned. "Will Roberts sit on your case?" he asked.

"Don't get the wrong idea," said Buzz. "He only wants to talk about a procedural matter."

Pops wasn't convinced, but he let it go. He, like Jill, had seen Debbie's expression and Socko Bender's smile when Buzz said *procedural matter.*

"How's the little mother doing?" Buzz asked, sidestepping to Debbie, putting his arm around her.

"She's your best asset," said Socko Bender. "We have to think of ways to keep her in the campaign without putting too much of a load on her."

Debbie said this had been a great night but she was tired, wondered if someone could drive her home.

"I'll run you out and come back," said Socko Bender. "Tell me again. When's the due date?"

"November twenty-third." Debbie's enthusiasm seemed forced.

Harrison went to wait with Debbie at the hotel entrance while Socko got the car. Watching Debbie, knowing what she must be feeling . . . It broke Jill's heart.

A week later Jill waited until Harrison left to meet his one o'clock class, then drove out to West Jefferson, to the five hundred acres known to anybody who watched television as Trader Bill's. Lights were on in the suite Billy Joe had created for Pops. It was in the circular, mostly glass building you came to on the entrance boulevard, where the road divided into Trader Bill North and Trader Bill South. She drove around the building to park in back. She hadn't come to see Pops.

"Have you driven the new Eclipse?" Billy Joe asked.

She shook her head.

"It's a dream," he said. "Let's take a spin."

The idea of a drive pleased her. They could talk without interruption, especially from Pops. The Eclipse was fire red, solid, luxurious, with the new-car smell Jill had loved since she was a little girl riding with her daddy. Pops, like Billy Joe, drove new models, sold them after two months.

"I can't go on without telling Debbie about the adoption," she said. She was looking at him, twisted in the passenger seat with her back and shoulder against the door post. She was wedged and belted, braced to hear his verdict.

He drove, not fast, with both hands on the wheel, keeping his attention on the winding, hilly road he'd turned off on a few miles back. "Sis, I feel so damn guilty," he said.

She gasped.

"I'm sixty," he said. "And no indications. So I assume I'm clean."

"I thought you were going to tell me you had fathered a child," she said.

He looked at her sharply, then relaxed, smiled, returned his attention to the road. "No chance," he said. "It's that one of us had to get the gene and you drew the unlucky number."

"It doesn't work that way," she said. "The chance is fifty-fifty but we both could have gotten it, we both could have been skipped."

"That's not the way it feels."

"Billy Joe, just listen." She talked for the next twenty miles, until they slowed to come into the town of Cedarville. She explained why she hadn't been able to tell Harrison, her fear of his reaction.

As she talked, Billy Joe kept his eyes on the road. She couldn't tell whether any of it made sense to him. "The separation between Debbie and me is worse than the disease," she said.

Billy Joe nodded. He was maneuvering the Eclipse on an aimless course through the sleepy streets of Cedarville. "There might be a way to notify the agency," he finally said. "Maybe the girl you gave up for adoption could be told about her medical history. If she's alive. Maybe blood samples could be exchanged. Maybe no one needs to be identified."

"Let's go home," Jill said. They spoke little on the way back. It was difficult to see herself as fifty-seven and Billy Joe as sixty. They were children, sister and brother.

When he pulled into Trader Bill's, she kissed him. "I'm going to tell Debbie first," she said. "Then Harrison and Denise." Debbie was nearing the end of her first term. There wasn't time to try Billy Joe's way.

It was nine o'clock. Buzz would be out of the house and Debbie should still be there. Jill had thought of telephoning before driving over. She couldn't. She was afraid of the conversation, that her resolve would weaken.

Last night she had decided. Harrison would be at the university, participating in an all-day symposium, "Invasion of a Candidate's Private Life vs. the Public's Right to Know."

She looked at herself in the car mirror. The twitching she felt inside was evident at the ends of her mouth and in the tiny muscles under her eyes.

She drove slowly, the car fighting her all the way out to Lake in the Woods. There would come a time when she would have to give up driving. When? A year, two, ten? Would she make the decision or would Harrison make it for her? Would Harrison be there? After today, anything could happen.

Debbie was wearing no makeup, hadn't dressed, was in a silky, cream-colored robe and slippers. Debbie looked alarmed. "What happened?" she asked.

"Can I come in?" To steady herself, Jill grasped the top of the wrought-iron porch rail. Debbie walked her to their family room, helped her into one of the chairs next to the fireplace.

"Debbie, there's something I must tell you," Jill said, ignoring the offer of coffee. She was shaking. She had to swallow to get the sentence out. Debbie stood, not three feet away, staring down at her.

Debbie didn't move the whole time. When Jill stopped talking, Debbie sat in the chair on the other side of the hearth. They stared into the fireplace. Like a metronome measuring their silence, a clock ticked at them from the corner.

"You told me so I could get a test result." Debbie's voice startled her.

"I told you for a lot of reasons," Jill said.

Debbie kept staring into the fireplace as if she were considering whether to build a fire. "Yesterday I thought I felt life. I'm not sure, though." Debbie's voice was flat.

"That's wonderful," said Jill.

Debbie spoke to the empty fireplace, not looking at Jill as she described the argument she'd had with Buzz before Jill came. He had gotten angry over breakfast when she questioned a telephone call from Judge Roberts. "Why don't you tell Drew Dawson?" he asked. "Give Dawson a gun to shoot me with."

"I don't care about Dawson, this campaign, whether we go to Washington *or* Judge Roberts," Debbie had said.

"Oh, great. That's just great. All you care about is yourself."

"Thank you. And you?"

"Don't push me, Deb. I've let you put too much on me. Okay, you've been upset about your mom and the disease. But that's not my fault and I'm tired of taking the blame. I've just about had it."

"And what are you going to do about it?"

Buzz had glared at her. Debbie had thought he might hit her.

"Has he ever?" Jill asked when Debbie told her this.

Debbie shook her head. "Last night," she said, "when I told him I thought I felt life, he said, 'That's *neat,*' and rubbed my stomach. He sat beside me on the couch, patting my stomach. 'My God, Deb, how could you think about an abortion?' he asked."

She had taken his hand off her stomach. He hadn't said anything but he got up. On the way out he'd said he had to call Socko Bender about some glitch in getting the union bug on bumper stickers.

"I wanted to kill him." Debbie turned from the fireplace, looked at Jill. "I don't want my baby to come into the family we've . . ." Her voice trailed off. She turned back to the fireplace. "I think I really hate him," she murmured. "It's hard to believe he's the same man I married, or thought I'd married . . ."

Jill said nothing. They listened to the clock.

"You won't tell Dad," said Debbie. "Promise me you won't. I just don't know what I'm going to do and I don't think I could stand it if Dad gets involved."

Jill promised.

"Do you have any idea where my half-sister is?"

Jill said she knew nothing except the name of the agency that had made the placement.

"Can we go to the agency?" Debbie asked.

"Right now?"

Debbie nodded. "I've got to know," she said.

"I haven't told your dad yet."

Debbie looked at her. Had there been a coming-together? "We can go to the agency if you want," said Jill.

"Why do you wish to make contact?" The woman had introduced herself as Ms. Letitia Silbernagle. She sat across from them at a table in a cubicle partitioned off by carpet-covered beige dividers. Ms. Silbernagle blinked her eyes, giving the impression of one who was often put upon and had a nose for trouble.

"The reason is medical," said Jill. Though the agency looked not at all familiar once she stepped inside, the memory of her earlier mistreatment filled her with loathing for this social bureaucrat who played God in awarding babies, deciding what a mother could know about her daughter or vice versa, who judged the "best interest" of all who came before her.

Jill related her medical history, the failure of Debbie to secure a test result for lack of blood samples. "The daughter placed for adoption also has a right to know the significant medical facts," said Jill. She used the arguments thrown at her by Dr. Malcolm Calder. Debbie, alert, listened as Jill took the lead. Ms. Silbernagle made notes. I may get Dr. Calder involved, Jill was thinking.

"I see the need for exchange of medical data," said Ms. Silbernagle. "What isn't clear is the reason for a contact." She had checked the file, verified the status with the probate court by telephone. No release of the confidentiality privilege, as required by Ohio law, had been filed by the adoptee.

"Is she alive?" asked Jill. "Do you know where she is?"

Ms. Silbernagle smiled. "No death is recorded," she said. "That's as much as I am permitted to tell you." Perhaps not meaning to sound cold or harsh, she added that Jill's daughter had found a "wonderful situation," that the last reports indicated she was quite well adjusted, excelling in school, had no health problems. Jill was again being treated like an incorrigible teen, as one not sufficiently responsible to have a child.

But weren't there advantages to a simple exchange of medical data? If it could be done quickly, wouldn't that serve everyone's needs? Maybe—with Debbie's support—it might not be necessary to tell Harrison.

"This is outrageous." Until then, Debbie had not spoken. The force of her intervention momentarily ruffled the social worker. "I don't believe I understand," said Ms. Silbernagle. Neither did Jill.

"I have a sister," said Debbie. *"I want to see her."*

"I understand the feeling," said Ms. Silbernagle, now back under control. "But she has as much right as you. This agency's reputation is built upon respect for the best interest of everyone whose lives we touch."

"And what if she refuses to provide a blood sample?" Debbie's hands clutched the edge of the table.

"Let's cross that bridge if and when we come to it," said Ms. Silbernagle.

"I am three months pregnant." Debbie had raised her voice, causing the social worker to look on the other side of the partition to see if anyone were using the adjoining cubicle. "The child I'm carrying may have a genetic disease that is incurable, hideous and terminal. There is no time to waste on your stupid procedures."

"Believe me, I understand," said Ms. Silbernagle. She promised to become personally involved, to "expedite the red tape." She would take a consent from Mrs. Donahey. She would try to locate and advise the adoptee. Perhaps the adoptee would respond with a consent. They might be making a problem where none existed.

Debbie was having none of it. She had nearly lost control, was threatening a lawsuit. Notwithstanding what she'd said about Buzz that morning, she brought him into the threat, told Ms. Silbernagle that his campaign manager, Socko Bender, was an assistant county prosecutor. The agency had better rethink its policies or there would be a scandal.

Nervous as she was, Jill still took satisfaction in watching the current spokesperson for her old oppressor squirm.

"Let's all reconsider our position," said Ms. Silbernagle. "I will talk to our legal counsel. Surely we can find a solution acceptable to everyone."

"How *soon*?" said Debbie.

"Let's talk tomorrow morning at nine."

Debbie had driven to the agency. They'd left Jill's car at Lake in the Woods. On the way back Jill said, "I must tell Harrison tonight."

"Mom," said Debbie, "I'm glad you found the courage to do this."

"Jilly Bean, I've known since before our marriage." Harrison's amazing admission couldn't be trusted. The fights they'd had, the angry things they'd said. If he'd known, it would have come out.

"Your mother told me," he said. "The Sunday afternoon before we got engaged. She was convinced that sooner or later I'd find out, that it could wreck our marriage."

"But you said nothing," Jill protested. "Nothing when you found out I have HD. Nothing when Debbie's test failed."

"I couldn't," he said. "Your mother was wrong to tell me. I thought it should be your choice."

Debbie picked Jill up in the morning. "Did you tell Dad?" Debbie asked.

"He took it . . ."

The fight was still on, however. It had broken out late the previous night. Since then, she and Harrison hadn't spoken. This morning she had left Harrison in his study, working on the fourth revision, updating his widely used text, *Understanding the American Political Process*. His habit was to rise at five, work on the manuscript between six and nine. Except on the mornings when he had breakfast with Buzz.

It seemed to Jill as if she had not slept. The relief she felt on hearing his admission that he knew had soon led to questions. He should have told her. "I decided it was your choice" sounded infuriatingly self-righteous. And she had suffered. Suffered because she'd been afraid of losing him. Maybe he'd wanted her to suffer. At first she said none of this. Then came the anger. When she thought what her mother had done. Save the marriage, her mother had told Harrison. That woman had been trying to *stop* the marriage.

Jill and Harrison got into their argument about an hour before the eleven o'clock news. He had been so full of himself, the magnanimous husband, feeling relief that the secret was out, taking credit for his . . . what? Chivalry? Then he wanted to tell her about his performance in the seminar, win approval for small victories. He had picked up some negative material on Drew Dawson from a *Post* reporter who was on the panel. It seemed he couldn't wait to call Buzz.

"Buzz is an s.o.b.," said Jill. *"And* a lousy husband."

"Jill, Jill . . ." He tried to placate her, to change the subject. But it had begun and neither could keep it from escalating. Jill's complaint about his keeping the secret came out.

"I can see why you don't feel so good about yourself, over the adoption," he said. "But that's no reason to take it out on poor Buzz—"

"Why shouldn't I feel so good about myself?"

"I don't want to fight," he said.

"Fine. I'm going to bed."

She had pretended to be asleep when he came upstairs. He pretended that he believed it . . .

"Dad's incredible," Debbie said, waiting at a traffic light.

"Yes," said Jill.

"I called Dr. Calder. If we need him, he'll help with the agency."

"How did Buzz react?" Jill asked.

"I didn't tell him. He'd . . . I don't know what he'd do," said Debbie.

Ms. Letitia Silbernagle, morning fresh in a powder-blue jacket, white blouse and perky bowtie, greeted them as if they were guests she had been hoping to entertain for months. "We have good news," she said as they assembled in the same beige upholstered cubicle.

Jill couldn't quiet her hands. She cleared her throat, trying to swallow. "Would you like a glass of water?" Ms. Silbernagle asked. Jill nodded. Debbie slid her chair close, put her arm across Jill's shoulders. Jill got the first swallow down. "I'm all right," she said. She wanted out of here, to be home by herself. The baby girl she'd given up was going to find her. She wasn't prepared for that.

"We now have consents in the file from all parties," Ms. Silbernagle said. "You are free—and she is free—to make such contact as you or she choose."

"She knows the reason?" Debbie asked.

Ms. Silbernagle nodded. "It was the basis that made this expedited response possible." Ms. Silbernagle reached across the table for Jill's hand. "I think," said Ms. Silbernagle, "you will be very, *very* pleased to see how well things have turned out. Your daughter is here in Columbus, a successful lawyer." Had the reason they needed to open the file made no impression on Ms. Silbernagle, Jill wondered.

"How do we make contact?" asked Debbie.

"That, I'm afraid, will be up to you," said Ms. Silbernagle. She withdrew her hand to remove a three-by-five-inch card from the file. She gave it to Jill. The name, address and telephone number had been neatly printed in green ink.

Kathleen Sullivan
668 City Park
Columbus, Ohio 43206
(614) 221-8253 (r)
(614) 464-9000 (o)

III
No Way
Out

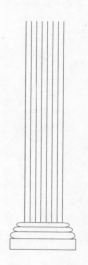

This is the Hour of Lead—
Remembered, if outlived,
As Freezing persons, recollect the snow—
First—Chill—then Stupor—then the letting go—
                              —EMILY DICKINSON

Chapter 9

KATHLEEN WAS ON Tony Biviano's mind as he stood naked in the locker room at the Athletic Club dusting his body with talcum. He was showered and scented, energized by four-on-one roundball. His team had won the division championship. Maybe she would tell him the cause of her strange behavior the last five days. Thank God she seemed more herself today, had even suggested supper after his game.

In the shower he'd thought about her tall graceful body, felt himself stiffening and, not wanting to be seen as stimulated by showering players, quickly turned to face the tile.

Last week he'd been on the verge of confessing how smitten he was. It was a verge he'd approached several times since she had invited him to her dad's St. Patrick's Day party. But then he'd retreat, decide she was a woman he should leave alone. He could jeopardize his partnership. If he told her how he felt she might well think he was using her. He hadn't forgotten her reaction during the clerkship summer. He remembered the looks he caught when he was seeing Laura Redding.

He also remembered St. Patrick's Day. "Since you're working with Dad on Columbus General, would you like to come to his party?" Kathleen had asked him the day before.

At the party he'd noticed Kelly James, Kathleen's cousin. Kelly was a woman everyone stopped to visit with and wanted to be noticed by. "What do you make of her?" Kathleen asked.

"She advertises herself," he said.

Kathleen laughed. "You'll be good in the courtroom," she said. "You read people."

"I can't read you," he said, smiling.

"What do you want to know? I might tell you."

He let that go. She was a partner, his chance to make it in the firm. Caution took over. But he still wanted to know if she had any of the feeling for him that he had for her. He wanted to ask why she had invited him to the party. He wanted to know what the deal with Marty Fleck was. He wanted to know why she seemed so skittish about men. He wanted to say he'd like to know her better and in a different way, that, to be blunt, she was giving him an ache in the groin.

He was waiting for her to take the initiative, at the same time feeling she was a woman who wouldn't. Two months later he was still waiting. But hadn't she invited him to the party? Hadn't she said, ask your questions, I may answer them?

Five days ago they had been going over records in the Columbus General case, working in the small, windowless conference room on the twenty-third floor, getting set to prepare the nursing supervisor for a deposition. Documents were stacked on the table and along the base of the bookcase wall.

When they broke for lunch she told him about the previous night's partnership meeting. It was great news. Si Wallace had called her aside, told her he'd heard favorable reports about Tony from several partners, including Chip Drucker.

Kathleen suggested dessert, talking him into hot apple pie with cinnamon ice cream. He loved looking across the table at her clear eyes, fair skin, the clean line of her neck. Her black hair, cut in a neatly groomed pageboy, had wisps over her ears and across her forehead. He watched the way her mouth formed around her words.

Laughing, they returned to the office. She would join him as soon as she checked with her secretary. When the telephone rang, it was Kathleen. "Something came up," she said.

"Anything I can do?"

There wasn't. She sounded all business in telling him to call the hospital administrator, move the meeting with the nursing supervisor to the next morning.

In mid-afternoon he took a break, walked by her office. The door was closed. When he checked again at 4:30 she was gone, hadn't told her secretary where. He worked until eleven, calling the night operator several times to make sure there were no messages.

When he came in the next morning, she was at her desk, studying one of the red volumes to Page's Ohio Revised Code. She closed the book and slid it under the keyhole. Her hair seemed in disarray. There were pouches under her eyes. "What happened?" he asked.

"It doesn't concern you." Then softening, she said, "I'll tell you later. We've got to get our nursing supervisor prepared."

She didn't explain later. Not a hint in five days. She didn't come to the office over the weekend. *It does concern me,* he decided.

Then she appeared in the doorway to his office, smiling, still looking tired, but with some playfulness back in her eyes. "Can I buy supper?" she asked.

He almost decided to skip the basketball game, probably would have if it hadn't been the division championship. "I'll wait," she'd said. "We can eat late."

She'd made a reservation at Christopher's. "What's the occasion?" he asked as the hostess led them to a candlelit table in the corner twenty stories above the night city.

"I'm sorry, Tony," she said. She'd started to reach for his hand, at least he thought she had. "I've been exhausted," she said. "I've had to force myself to come to work. I really appreciate the way you covered on Columbus General," she said.

The waiter came to see if they wanted a drink before ordering. "Do you like Beaujolais?" she asked.

"Sounds terrific."

She asked the waiter for a recommendation.

"I'm treating," she said when the waiter left to get the wine. "You don't have to be back—I mean, I know there's always work, but you don't *have* to be back?"

He noticed the green in her eyes which were mostly dark brown. They were wonderful eyes. She was a woman who didn't look away when she talked to you. She didn't require a candlelit table and a night city below to give clear-eyed attention. She gave it to everyone, looked at people as if what they had to say mattered. But it wasn't normal for her to take a wine recommendation without checking cost. She checked even when they went to a pricey restaurant on a client's tab. When they took depositions out of state she flew first class, but she never boarded an airline without assurance that her frequent-flyer points were being credited. She wanted to know the cost when a waiter described "specials" that were not listed on the menu.

"You're going to tell me why we're celebrating," he said.

"Before that, I want to explain. I got a call from the adoption agency last Thursday," she said. "My birth mother is *alive,* she lives here in Columbus! And I have *two* half-sisters."

"Is that what you did over the weekend? See your . . . your birth mother?"

She shook her head. "I'm to meet my sister on Saturday, but I haven't told Mom and Dad yet." She seemed nervous. He remembered how tense she had been during the deposition of the nursing supervisor, that she'd declined her dad's offer of dinner at the Columbus Club when the deposition ended at six.

"I told Marty Fleck," she said. "No one else knows."

She was trusting him. Good. But why wouldn't she tell her parents? She'd just discovered sisters. Her birth mother! She was thirty-seven. It would be like solving a mystery—having questions answered where you'd thought there could never be answers. He wished she'd talk more about her adoption, how it had been for her as a little girl. But whenever he tried, she turned quiet, uneasy.

"The reason we're celebrating," she was saying, "is that we settled the burn case."

"We did?"

She raised her wine glass and extended it, waiting for his. "The plaintiff took our offer," she said. "It was the deposition we took in Chicago. The plaintiff was staring at a directed verdict. They thought our offer might come off the table." She smiled, sipping her wine. "I feel like I've been given a month I didn't have," she said. The waiter had been eyeing them from between the pillars at the rear of the dining room. Kathleen motioned for him to take their orders.

When the waiter left she said, "The last few months have been a killer, Tony. I never felt like I was in a rat race before."

"You ought to drop everything," he said. "You missed your ski week. Just take off. Like you said, we've been given a free month."

She looked at him oddly, a question in her eyes. But only for an instant. She smiled and said, "Too bad it doesn't work that way."

He knew what she meant. A trial lawyer had to settle cases to survive.

Brightening, she said, "But you could. When was your last vacation?"

"Couple of years," he said. "Maybe next year . . . hey, I'm not complaining." He wasn't. With her help, partnership looked closer. "If I were to cut out," he said, "it wouldn't be for ice and cold and wind."

She laughed. "Where?"

"Between college and law school, then after my first year at Pitt, I worked in Bermuda. My baseball coach knew the owner, got me the job."

"That's where you'd go?"

He nodded. "I'd live on the beach, let the sun bake out the files I'm worried about."

"Lying in the sun is boring," she said.

"That's because you haven't seen Bermuda. It isn't hot and sticky. Hey, you can exercise, jog, ride bikes and you don't feel wilted."

"What kind of a job did you have?"

"Cottage boy at Kensington Gardens." He'd stocked the cottages with supplies, served tea in the afternoons and breakfast in the mornings. "You'd love snorkeling," he said. "Or just walk the beach, feel the wind, look out at blue-green coral water."

"It does sound awfully nice," she said.

"We could both go. I'd love to show you around . . ."

"Are you serious?"

"Kathleen, would you consider it?"

She was embarrassed, her face coloring. *She wants to,* he thought. "We'd have a terrific week," he said. "On a clear night you can lie on the beach under a blanket, see more stars than you thought there were, listen to the waves. It takes you away from everything."

She emptied her wine glass and he refilled it. She *was* interested. He told her about cozy restaurants, motor-scootering with a picnic lunch, exploring beaches. He told her about the secluded place in the gardens where she could sneak away to read, how fresh and sweet everything smelled following an afternoon rain.

They talked into a round of stingers after dinner. "If I weren't half-smashed I wouldn't be listening," she said.

"That sounds like my clue to order another round." He motioned to the waiter.

"I'll think about it," she said as he walked her to her car in the underground garage. When they reached her car he kissed her. She kissed him back. And no embarrassment in it.

Chapter 10

SHE COULDN'T SLEEP and didn't want to sleep. Bermuda with Tony. What did she have to lose? After dinner she'd felt herself and Tony coming together. She could hardly believe it was happening, so suddenly easy. In Bermuda it could keep going, without the pressure of law practice, without worrying about Si Wallace, Marty Fleck and the firm.

None of them understood Tony. They hadn't seen that he could be a trial lawyer, a contributor to the firm. They, like she in the beginning, saw him as good-looking, slick, dependent on charm. They were wrong. Since St. Patrick's Day she'd seen more of the real man. Come down to it, he could be as different as she had been. She was getting to trust him . . . she might even tell him about Greg Meeker and the priest and the ceremony of the Blessed Virgin.

The taste and feel of his kiss was still with her. She still felt the press of his body. She had even been wrong about his height, he was actually an inch taller than she . . .

She woke up early, with doubts. God, what had possessed her to think of confiding, letting him see how needy she was? It had been the wine and the stingers. She had a hangover. Bermuda was out of the question. He would agree, they couldn't just take off when his partnership was at stake.

More than any of that, she was bothered by her dishonesty, by not telling him she was at risk for Huntington's disease. Oddly, the disease itself didn't scare her. Her health was excellent, the disease seemed remote. But how would Tony react? Would he still have suggested Bermuda? If he wanted children, they would be at risk. Did he want children? Did she? She was being a twit again, no wiser than when she had made love with Greg Meeker. She had no basis for thinking she and Tony had reached the point where children were an issue. She dreaded seeing him again. At best, this morning would be awkward.

He was waiting for her, slouched in her favored-client chair. "Look at your calendar," he said. "We'll pick a date. I'll call and get a cottage on the ocean—"

"Oh, Tony, I don't know." She stood there in her raincoat, feeling as foolish and pathetic as she probably looked.

He got up, closed the door and told her to sit. She sat in the chair facing her desk, the one Connie used to take dictation.

"Look," he said. "It's scary. There are always reasons not to. Second thoughts."

She smiled. She wished it were that easy, that there was no firm, no life beyond him and her and the next month.

"We don't have to call today," he said. "Think it over, Kathleen. It's what we should do."

"Let's talk later," she said. Time was what she needed. Time to find a way out of the mess she'd created.

Then he nailed her, like when he had complimented her legs at the tennis party. "I wanted to kiss you for a whole year," he said. "I'm smitten. Corny but true." He stood and walked to the door. Turning, he said, "I just wanted you to know." He blew her a kiss and left.

On Saturday morning, she got to Tommy's Diner first. Deb had suggested Tommy's, a blue-collar restaurant on West Broad Street. "They have home-cooked breakfasts, and we won't see anyone."

It had been only ten days since the agency lawyer called, though it seemed longer. The agency lawyer came to the office, and after he left, Kathleen called Dr. David Whitney.

"Did we win?" Whitney asked, sure the call was to announce a ruling from the supreme court.

"No," she said, "this is personal."

What he told her sent her to the Ohio State Medical School library. She stayed until it closed at eleven, reading Folstein's *Huntington's Disease*. Then she wondered if the agency would contact her parents. She called the agency lawyer, got him out of bed. They hadn't. They wouldn't. She agreed to have her birth records unsealed.

After Deb called, Kathleen went to University Hospital and gave a blood sample. Then she and Deb had agreed to meet.

At Tommy's Diner she took a booth by the window to watch for Deb. They'd described themselves over the phone, Kathleen identifying herself as tall with black hair cut in a kind of pageboy with a few strands over each ear. The waitress brought a cup of coffee. She interested herself in the art deco posters. The one with Bogart, Elvis, Marilyn Monroe and James Dean was titled "Boulevard of Broken Dreams" and made her think of Greg Meeker, the hollowness of lust for its own sake.

"I'm Deb, you must be Kathleen."

Kathleen got up to shake hands. She hadn't seen the woman until she was approaching the booth.

"You were the only one in here that looked like a lawyer," said Deb. They laughed as they slid into opposite sides of the booth.

"I'm nervous," Deb said.

"Me too." She instantly liked this woman with the friendly face. Woman, hell. Sister. Then she noticed the bruise under Deb's eye. Deb had plastered makeup over it. Still, Deb was prettier than she'd described herself, had a figure that made Kathleen think of her cousin Kelly.

The waitress put a cup of coffee in front of Deb, warmed Kathleen's and left padded menus with laminated coverings. "Have you thought about taking the test for HD?" Deb asked.

"Not really." Nothing could be done so why get tested?

"That's what my . . ." Deb hesitated. "Denise . . . our sister, I don't know what to call her."

Kathleen smiled.

"Anyhow," said Deb, "Denise thinks the test is a mistake. I guess I look at it differently because I'm pregnant."

"When do you get the results?" asked Kathleen.

"Monday."

"God," said Kathleen. "How can you stand the wait?"

"Not very well. I still don't know if they can make a prediction. They're real finicky about the way they do this. Sometimes I think I won't make it till Monday."

"Do you wish you hadn't been told?"

Deb shook her head, frowning. "That's a problem between me and Mom," she said. "I know Mom meant well, but I keep thinking. It's my body, my choices. How could she do that to me?"

"Tell me more about her."

"She knows we're meeting. Do you want to see her?"

"What does she want?"

"I don't think she wants to see you," said Deb. "But you've got as much say as she does."

"Do you know who my father is?"

"No, but . . ."

"But what?"

"I really don't know. I shouldn't have . . ."

Kathleen reached across the table for Deb's hand. It surprised her how drawn she was to this person who was her half-sister. "I want to know what you heard," she said.

"Mom's not too reliable . . . I mean, she didn't tell us, see . . . not till after the disease forced her . . . not even Dad. She feels so guilty and I wouldn't . . . but anyway, I think it might have been some sort of date rape."

"Rape?" God, Kathleen had thought her interest was clinical. She wasn't prepared for the feeling that seized her stomach, left her staring at Deb, unable to add to the one-word reaction she'd blurted. She felt her face coloring. She was embarrassed to be embarrassed over what had taken place way back then—something, after all, she had no responsibility for.

"Listen," said Deb. "I really don't know what happened. You should talk to Mom. You've got questions. You must have had them for years." Deb was squeezing Kathleen's hand with both of her hers.

They sat looking at each other, not speaking, tears forming in their eyes. Deb looked so vulnerable, as if *she* were somehow responsible. Kathleen still wasn't able to talk. If she did, she'd make a scene. She hated being like this.

"It's not urgent. I would never have tried to find her." Kathleen's voice sounded strange to herself, like some mechanical talking doll.

Deb winced.

"I'm not blaming you," Kathleen said. "But I was abandoned. I'd never do that, even if I had been raped. Sorry . . . I didn't expect to be drowned in feelings this way."

"I know," said Deb.

"Not after thirty years." Kathleen withdrew her hand, wiped her eyes with her handkerchief. As the waitress came to refill their coffees Kathleen was regaining control. But she knew this wouldn't be the last of it. At night, at times when she didn't expect it and wasn't prepared—she'd be sucked back into the questions.

"I know Mom is glad the placement worked out," Deb said. "But she can't forgive herself. She thinks you'll blame her. That's what gets me. Mom's had such horrible stuff happen. I feel like a shit, I mean, resenting her. Denise does much better."

"I'll probably see her sometime," said Kathleen.

"Listen," Deb said. "I have an idea." Deb offered to take her mom shopping, tell Kathleen where. Maybe they would eat at a restaurant in the mall. Kathleen could watch without the need of a meeting. "Mom wouldn't even know."

Kathleen wondered. Could one of the women at the counter, or the lady chain-smoking in the back booth, be her birth mother? If Deb would do that for her, why not the other way around? No, Deb wouldn't. There was a feeling between Deb and herself, a feeling she could trust.

After the waitress took the plates and poured a fourth cup of coffee, Kathleen needed to use the restroom. It was clean with a scent of pine from an aerosol can. When she came back, Deb put her fingers on the bruise. "Surely you noticed," she said.

"It's none of my business," said Kathleen.

"Buzz, my husband, hit me last night. It was the first time. I thought he might have a violent side but he never touched me . . ."

Kathleen thought she believed that.

"The argument started because of Judge Sam Roberts," said Deb. "I'm sure you know who he is."

Kathleen nodded, checked the impulse to smile.

Deb told her about Roberts, his nastiness, the charm when it suited his purpose, the touchy-feely incidents that stopped short of justifying a complaint.

"That's disgusting," said Kathleen.

"That isn't a problem," said Deb. "I can handle it. The thing is, he's been calling the past couple of weeks about a case Buzz is set to argue."

"In the court of appeals?"

Deb thought it was. Roberts had called last night, said he'd been trying to reach Buzz all day. Deb promised to have Buzz call when he got home. " 'Maybe Garrison doesn't care about his practice,' Roberts told me." Deb repeated her promise to have Buzz call. "Forget it," Roberts said. "I'm through messing with you and Garrison."

"When Buzz came in it was nearly midnight," said Deb. "I told him I was sick of Roberts. Buzz was giving me the look he knows intimidates me. 'What do you mean?' he said. I told him among other things I didn't like the way he talked to me. I also didn't think Judge Roberts should be calling about cases. 'Stop being a pain in the ass,' Buzz had said. Well, that escalated it. I said that the next time that slimeball called or put his paws on me he might be reading about himself in the *Post*."

Which was when Buzz hit her. With his fist, hard enough to knock her down. Almost immediately he turned contrite, went for a washcloth, made an ice pack, pleaded with her to forgive him. "He's terrified of what I could do." Deb, as she stared at Kathleen, looked terrified herself. "You won't repeat any of this? My God, we've just met and here I am spilling my life to you. Sorry . . ."

"No, I won't repeat this, and please don't be sorry."

"I shouldn't have told you, but I feel like, long-lost sister or not, you're a person I can trust."

Kathleen nodded, smiled encouragement.

"Maybe it's getting my results on Monday," said Deb. "Thinking about that drives me crazy. It's going to be bad. I can feel it." Kathleen could barely hear her. "I'm going to have an abortion, Kathleen, but I haven't told anyone."

Kathleen nodded. She wanted to support Deb, yet at the moment all she could do was listen.

"Are you thinking of divorce?"

"Yes. I wouldn't until after the election. You don't really get to know someone . . . not till something like this comes up. No matter how much you think you do."

As Deb talked, Kathleen had to think about Tony. How well did she really know him . . . ?

"I told Buzz about my first test," said Deb. "But he doesn't know I'm going on Monday." Deb's hands were unsteady now. "I'm sorry," she said. "I needed to unload." She seemed calmer, telling how she'd gone to the bathroom to look at her eye last night and heard Buzz on the telephone, *apologizing* to Judge Roberts for calling so late.

"Roberts is a disgrace," said Kathleen. "He shouldn't be a judge."

"You won't do anything?" Deb seemed terrified.

"I promised you I wouldn't."

People were coming into the diner for lunch. It was eleven-thirty. She and Deb had been talking in the booth by the window for three hours. "I feel better," Deb said. "Even the test doesn't scare me as much."

They had parked next to each other on the lot next to the diner. Kathleen was backing out, watching for the lamppost behind her, when she heard Deb pounding on the window. Kathleen rolled the window down.

"Could you go with me on Monday?" Deb asked. "I have to be accompanied."

Kathleen tried to remember. Was there anything she couldn't get out of? "Of course," she said. "What time?"

"One."

Deb leaned in to kiss her. "I didn't mean to lay so much on you," she said. "Dad went last time, but I don't want him to see this." She touched her bruise.

Kathleen asked if Deb didn't want to go someplace for lunch. Deb said she'd be fine, had grocery shopping to do. She was looking forward to the night at home. "At least with this bruise he won't want me to go to the Franklin County Jefferson-Jackson Day dinner," she said.

"Call if you need me." Kathleen gave Deb the number that rang on the third line in her office, a number she'd given only to her parents, her buddy Marty Fleck, and Tony.

"I'm glad I found you," Deb said. "You're everything I'd like to be . . ."

You're everything I'd like to be. Deb's words stuck with Kathleen all weekend. Thirty-seven, needing the firm to feel worthwhile, an old maid who couldn't form a relationship, approaching the end of her childbearing age, at risk for Huntington's disease, maybe blowing her last chance at a man who according to some was using her to get into the partnership. A whole lot there to envy.

Deb had said she would feel better after their morning in Tommy's Diner, but Kathleen felt as if *her* life had been scrambled. She was, though, very glad she'd found Deb.

On Monday morning Kathleen told Connie to hold her calls. A stack of files needed attention. At five after ten her intercom buzzed. "I think you'll want this one," said Connie.

It was from the clerk's office, the Ohio supreme court. The decision in *Snell* v. *Whitney,* her wrongful-life case, was being announced.

"Read me the last line," said Kathleen, bracing herself for the worst.

"Let's see," said the nasal voice on the phone. "There's so many footnotes. Yes, here's what you want. Judgment affirmed."

"We won," she yelled to Connie. "Call Tony."

She paced between the door, her desk and her window, waiting for him.

"Walk with me to the court to pick up a copy of the opinion," she said when he came.

In the court's public information office they took two copies off the pile. The opinion ran sixty-three pages, including the dissent by Judge Roberts. They took their copies to the cafeteria in the basement of the state office tower, got coffee and started to read. It was total victory with the majority lifting much of its "analysis" from her brief.

"Let's cut out, celebrate at Spagio's," he said.

"I wish I could."

His eyes questioned her but he didn't ask. It was eleven-thirty. She gave him instructions for Connie, asked him to make calls reporting the decision. "All except Dr. Whitney," she said. "I'll call David."

"This gives us one more reason to take the Bermuda trip." He looked at her. "You *are* still considering that?"

"Yes."

"Well?"

"I need more time to think, Tony."

She met Deb at University Hospital. "This is the same room," Deb said when the receptionist showed them to a small conference room set up for seminars with a built-in blackboard, a movie screen, an x-ray box. The wait was affecting Kathleen. It felt as if she were about to have her future revealed. "How do you feel?" she asked.

"This is worse than last time. It's because I've felt the baby."

The medical team came in, introduced themselves. Deb nodded when asked if she still wanted to go forward. Deb signed the forms, her hand shaky.

"We have a result," the woman said. "For both you and your fetus."

"I want to know the results," Deb said. She signed another form.

"The chance is ninety-eight percent that you have the gene, but ninety-eight percent that your *fetus* does not." The woman sounded cold, but maybe it couldn't be otherwise.

Deb cried and hugged Kathleen, then the doctors. "I'm so *relieved* . . ."

They stood and talked in front of the hospital, Deb still excited. "I'm going to the lobby," she said. "I want to call Buzz. Forget everything I said on Saturday. I just haven't been myself. Buzz . . . I know Buzz will be so thrilled."

On her way back to the office, Kathleen wondered. Deb was only twenty-seven. The onset of the disease would be years away if the family pattern held. There could be a cure by then. If not, Deb's child would be raised and out of the house. Her child wouldn't get the disease. But wouldn't there be a reaction when Deb realized she had the disease? Wouldn't it be harder to watch her mother go down? Maybe not. Maybe having an unaffected child would make the knowing bearable.

But she couldn't make sense of Deb saying, "Buzz will be so thrilled." How could he be when his wife had been diagnosed?

She worked late at the office. She couldn't forget Deb. Nor

could she ignore the other thought. If they could predict for Deb, didn't they have everything they needed to do the same for her?

At ten, she called Dr. Malcolm Calder at his home. "I was with Deb Garrison this afternoon," she said.

"Yes," he said. "I remember."

She apologized for the call but he assured her it was all right. She asked her questions.

"I'm not sure," he said. "You have a different father and they did use the blood sample from Deb's father." On the other hand, Deb's case was unusual, and ordinarily not so many samples were required.

"I saw none of the studies," he said, "so I really don't know whether they can make a prediction on you." He suggested that she contact the geneticist from University Hospital. "Don't expect a quick response," he said. "You aren't pregnant and don't have the same urgency. You'll have to go through counseling."

On Friday at five she agreed to have a beer with Tony. "I won't bug you," he said, "but are we any closer to Bermuda?"

"No," she said, smiling, changing the subject to pass on a compliment about Tony's work that she had heard from Si Wallace. It didn't seem to cheer him.

The next Monday she called Dad to see if he was free for lunch.

They were given his regular table at the Columbus Club, in the corner by the window and to the side of the fireplace. His partner, H. Roger Howland III, was eating alone in the opposite corner. On the way to his table Dad had asked Howland if he was still up to his ears in music, music, music. Howland had nodded and grimaced a little.

"What was that all about?" Kathleen asked.

Dad laughed. "You can't believe how proud Roger is of being general counsel to the Columbus Symphony. It makes him a man of the arts."

But in the last month Howland had gotten in the middle of a dispute with the symphony's principal horn player. The horn player, though gay, had been given a foster child by the Children's Services Board. No adoptive parents could be found because the child was born with a drug dependency. After three years the horn player had bonded with his little boy and wanted to adopt. The Franklin County Children's Services Board decided to oppose, citing the horn player's sexual preference. The horn player, who shared an apartment with a travel agent, decided to fight. Other players in the orchestra were supporting him. A petition had been circulated. "Things had reached this point," said Dad, "when Roger and the board decided that publicity could hurt the fund drive, aggravate the symphony's financial crisis." The horn player was told his contract would not be renewed.

"The horn player then got hold of this zealot who's out to punish bigots and reform the world. They're making Roger dance. The musicians' guild is filing an unfair labor practice charge."

Kathleen frowned. "Well, I think the whole story stinks," she said. "Why shouldn't the musician be able to adopt? Has he got AIDS? Even that shouldn't matter. Who thinks an institution is better for the little boy?"

She sipped her lobster bisque. This was spoiling the mood for telling him what she had been putting off.

"Calm down, Kathleen," he said. "Tell me why you invited yourself to lunch."

She put down her spoon.

"I assume it's about our case," he said.

"No," she said. "But that reminds me. Tony found an opinion from the New York court of appeals. It sets a lower standard for psychiatrists than for other doctors in malpractice cases."

Dad leaned forward, alert. Obviously the person assigned to research at Howland and Beck had missed the case.

"I'll send you Tony's memo," she said.

"Kathleen, the chance to work with you is nicer than you could imagine," said Dad. "I wish we could have practiced together." Howland and Beck had a no-nepotism rule, though it didn't apply to Roger and others who'd been grandfathered in.

"It's great for me too," she said. "Dad . . . I need your help."
"What?"

"Especially with Mom. I've been putting off telling you something. I shouldn't have and . . . oh . . . I don't know where to begin."

He looked alarmed.

"I found my birth certificate." She finally got it out, and the rest of the story. "The risk of Huntington's disease doesn't really worry me," she said. "Maybe it should, but I'm healthy, I can't believe I have it. They may be close to locating the gene and in ten years they'll probably find a cure."

He nodded uneasily.

"I didn't tell you when I was with you right after I found out," she said. "I've been afraid of how you and Mom will feel. Especially Mom."

"I'll take care of Mother," he said. She saw that he meant it.

"No," she said. "I'm going to drive out as soon as we leave here. But she and I are so guarded, afraid of saying the wrong thing. I know she feels left out. You and I have the law. So I want to see her, just her and me. But could you help her see that I love you two more than anyone in the world, that I'm not worried about the disease . . . About the disease," she said. "No one but you knows that. Marty and Tony only know I found my birth mother."

"You're serious about Tony, aren't you?"

"I don't know what we are." She said it so there would be no more questions.

She found her mom pruning rosebushes, retying vines to a trellis. "What a pleasant surprise," Mom said. "But I look a mess."

"I should have called but Dad told me you were home." Kathleen kissed her.

"Let's go up on the deck," said Mom. "Should I break out a bottle of champagne?" God, Mom thought she'd come to announce her engagement.

"There's nothing to celebrate, Mom."

Alarm chased the smile. "Then what?"

"The agency opened my file . . . I know who my birth mother is." This wasn't the way she had planned it. Her mother did a double-take, then recovered quickly.

"What is she like?"

"I don't know," said Kathleen. "I haven't decided to make contact."

Mom was no porcelain doll. "I'm grateful for your sensitivity," she said, "but I want you to have a relationship with your birth mother, if that's your choice." She was trying to make it easier, while Kathleen had been worrying how to tell her about Huntington's disease.

"Mom," she said, "I do worry about hurting you. But you're just like you've always been . . . when we talk about my adoption you do tend to disappear. That's why I worry about hurting you."

A flash of anger, then hurt. Erin Sullivan didn't look away. "That's what I've done," she said. "Kathleen, I've never been sure how it feels to you, but I ache every time I think of you having to live with the knowledge of being abandoned. I'm doing the best I can not to let my own fears add to that pain. If it comes out sounding false, it's because I can't stand hurting you. And yes, I'm afraid of losing you."

"Mom, I'm thirty-seven!"

"Honey, do you think that means I'm not threatened? Since the day we brought you home from the hospital and the adoption was only on probation, I've been afraid of losing you. In a way it's gotten worse."

"But you must know, no one could take your place."

"I don't know that. If you get together with this person, you may discover a closeness we haven't had since you were ten."

Kathleen stood behind her, wrapped her arms around her. "We've kept each other at a distance," she said. "But it hasn't been because I don't love you. I *know* you've tried to protect me. I owe everything to you and Dad."

"Well, sit *down*. I'm no good at scenes like this."

"Me neither," said Kathleen. "They opened my file at the agency because my birth mother has Huntington's disease. It's a disease that's inherited genetically." There, she'd gotten it out.

"Disease! Kathleen, what do you have?"

Kathleen told her about it, that she had a fifty-percent chance of having the gene, that there was a test but she didn't want to take it, at least not yet. Even if she had the gene, the disease wouldn't affect her for years and a cure might be found before she even had any symptoms.

Her mother searched her eyes, trying to make sure. She was *there* in a way she hadn't been when Kathleen told about the file having been opened.

When she left, her mother took her hand, walked with her to the car. They hugged, staying in the embrace, clinging to each other. It had, unpredictably, brought them closer than ever before.

Chapter 11

D EB WAS DRYING her hair, hurrying so she would have time to do her nails. Buzz was in the Jacuzzi reading a newspaper. He kept up with about fifteen each day. She and Buzz spent as much time together, it seemed, in their living-room-size bathroom as in their den or kitchen.

Before they went to dinner or a political event, Buzz liked to relax in the Jacuzzi, read newspapers, maybe sharpen the text of the speech he would be giving. Sometimes he practiced, asking her for evaluations. That was impossible with the hair dryer going. "Can you turn that thing off a second," Buzz would shout when he came to a phrase that he wanted to test out.

The bathroom was the showplace of the house, the feature—next to being in an advantageous district—that had prompted them to buy. The Jacuzzi was huge, a luxury model with sixteen nozzles, sculpted so you could read in comfort or lie flat and immerse yourself. An attachment held books and newspapers for reading. Swing it out of the way and you could watch a thirty-inch television.

His-and-her vanities faced each other on an island between the Jacuzzi and a tanning bed. The commode and shower stall were screened behind a folding partition lacquered with Japanese drawings. Deb pruned the ferns and the three rubber trees, kept a close watch on the tropical flowers, made sure everything was fresh and watered, kept the bubble top skylight clean.

They were getting ready for the big fundraiser in his campaign. Vice-President Arden Boggs had been lured as an attraction. Boggs would be flying in from Washington and over a thousand people had each shelled out $200 for a ticket.

Buzz, she thought, was still annoyed and she didn't care. She could not forgive him. It had been nearly a week since she had come home from University Hospital and gotten him on his cellular phone to deliver the good news about their baby.

"You what?" he said on the phone. "You had a test without telling me?"

"I didn't want to fight you," she said. "But now . . . I couldn't wait to tell you. Do you understand, Buzz? We're going to have a normal, healthy baby."

"I hear you," he said. "I mean, that's great, but I'm just floored . . . where are you?"

"University Hospital. In the lobby."

"Well, listen," he said. "I've got to stop at the office. Then I'll come home. We'll celebrate."

"Buzz," she said. "What's wrong?"

"No, no, this is great, Deb. It's just that . . . well, I guess I'm just caught a little off guard. I guess it maybe bothers me a little that you didn't tell me you were getting the test—"

"I'm sorry, I should have, but—"

"We'll talk when I get home."

She was hurt, too hurt to keep talking.

Had it been his tone even more than what he said? Or that he hadn't even asked what the result was for *her?* As if a trapdoor had opened under her, she was plunged into the dismal certainty that there really could be no future with him, that the pain that had hardened during the last month couldn't just be kissed away by a healthy baby. The joy had been taken out of the incredible miracle she'd felt when the doctors gave her the news.

On the drive home she thought about her baby. Her healthy baby. She touched her stomach. She had her baby. No matter what happened between her and Buzz, she was going to be a mother. She'd make her life with this child who'd broken the awful genetic chain.

She went into the family room and sat by the cold fireplace, forcing herself to make plans. Would a house or an apartment be best? Would there be money enough?

She heard Buzz come into the drive. He ran through the kitchen and into the family room. "What did you find out about yourself?" he blurted out.

"I've got the gene." She didn't get up.

He hit the sides of his head with the palms of his hands. "Oh God, I'm sorry," he said. "I was just so shocked . . . then you'd called from the hospital lobby, I couldn't call back . . . my God, how do you feel?"

"Like I've been given new life," she said. "Like I've been smothered and then given a chance to breathe."

He came to lift her and put his arms around her. She slid out of the chair, away from him.

"Are you mad at me?" he asked.

"No."

"Yes you are," he said. "Deb, I just wasn't thinking." He stepped toward her and she retreated. But she was listening. She wanted it to be all right, for him to say the words that would change her feelings. He was saying he cared and wanted to support her in this. He apologized again, but it ended, as usual, with him blaming her. "I made a mistake, but, honey, if you'd been honest with me—I mean, if you'd trusted me . . . your call came out of the blue. And then you sounded so happy, our baby and all. I mean . . . I just didn't . . . Deb, it just wasn't fair to get the second test without telling me." He stopped talking and looked at her, waiting for a response.

"Well?" he said.

"It isn't just you not asking about me."

"I know. God . . . you've got the gene. Don't you think you ought to see someone? Maybe get counseling?"

"I'll be fine."

"But what are you thinking? Don't you see that we both made mistakes?"

"Yes."

"Good God, Deb." He stepped back. He was staring at her as if he'd just made a discovery. "Was I wrong?" he asked. "You *are* happy that our baby doesn't have the gene?"

"I can't take this, you actually think I don't want . . ." She turned and ran from the room.

He followed her. "You told me the truth about that, didn't you? I mean about the baby not having the gene?"

She faced him. "You can *check* with the hospital," she said, ran up the stairs and locked the bedroom door behind her.

Through the door she heard him. "Deb, I'm going to give you time to work this through. But I'll be here when you want to talk."

The next week she tried to avoid being alone with him, which wasn't difficult. He was campaigning hard, working at the office in between to keep his practice going. She would help him get elected, then file for divorce. All week she had been thinking of finding an apartment, living with her baby, raising her child. With the help of the dream she could stick it out until November fourth. By sticking it out she would pay her debt, what she owed him. She worried about him contesting her over custody, though . . .

"You look lovely," he was saying as he got out of the Jacuzzi and began rubbing himself with a Turkish towel. She had finished drying her hair, was seated at her vanity doing her nails. "I'll pop in the shower, put on my suit and we'll be off."

He looked handsome, the thin black stripes in a dark blue suit making him look even taller. His eyes had the softness she remembered. And for an instant she felt hope. There had been many of those instants in the last month, she realized, but they were always turned around on her. Buzz, a man of moods and appearances, hadn't really changed. Her perception of him had. Finally . . .

The fundraiser went off without a hitch. Judge Roberts, master of ceremonies, introduced the dignitaries. Buzz attacked his opponent as a "product of the privileged class who is utterly insensitive to the idea that women are entitled to full citizenship, to make choices with dignity."

Vice-President Boggs brought the crowd to its feet with a plea to elect Democrats "if we are to reverse the trend toward a police state; the intolerance which is taking over the Republican Party." Boggs praised Buzz in words that made the election a matter of national survival. Socko Bender estimated that after expenses the fundraiser would net $150,000.

On the way home, Buzz put his arm around Deb. "I know there are unfinished things between us," he said, "but our love is strong enough to survive all that." He smiled. And once, not so long ago, it would have been enough.

The next morning they went to church at Broad Street Presbyterian. As usual Buzz guided her to the third pew, on the aisle, directly in front of the pulpit. They stayed for an hour after the service, having coffee, working the crowd. It was another political event. Well, going to church had not been a family activity when she was growing up so this didn't really bother her. Buzz felt the same way.

So it came as a surprise when on the way home Buzz took one hand off the steering wheel and reached for hers. "I felt God's presence during the silent prayer," he said.

"You did?" She hadn't meant to sound skeptical. A peculiar expression came over his face.

"It may sound crazy, honey, but God spoke to me. Oh, not in words. I didn't hear a voice. It was more a direct knowing . . . He was squeezing her hand, had slowed the car to a crawl. "God has given us a sign," he said.

She stared at him, trying to decide if he actually believed what he was saying. "First came the election. There was a time when I thought we had no chance to win the primary. Then—and this is the big one—you get the test that shows we're going to have a healthy baby." He pulled over to the curb, took both of her hands. "God wants us to stay together," he said. "God wants to use us to do his work."

He did believe it. No question. And whether or not God had spoken to him, there was, she supposed, a kind of logic in what he said. She had tried to convince herself of the same thing when she was alone, full of anger, arguing with her feelings, trying to see things from his side. But for her it was more fate or serendipity than some sort of divine intervention. Still, she was trying to believe this, she did hope that they could go back where they were in those first few days after she learned she was pregnant.

Her argument with herself didn't work. Her feelings might not be the voice of God, but they were real, too real. She sat in the car, hoping he would start driving, seeing his eyes kindly as a saint's, knowing he wasn't trying to dissemble, knowing he believed the words he'd spoken. Which made matters scarier.

In a way she felt sympathy for him, along with the upset and anger. It would make it easier to postpone telling him until after the election, to help him get his seat in Congress. And she wanted to have her baby before she faced a showdown. If she knew Buzz at all, and that knowledge was dispersing all the time, he would make extravagant promises. There would be grief and pain—maybe beyond what she'd already felt—before he would accept the divorce . . .

In the afternoon she visited her parents. Her mother was apathetic, impossible to interest in conversation. Deb told her about the amniocentesis that would let her know whether the baby was a boy or a girl. She told stories Vice-President Boggs had confided to her when he sat next to her at the dinner. She showed her pictures of Kathleen and the clippings, including the one about the case Kathleen had won in the supreme court. Jill had asked for pictures the last time Deb came, but now they aroused no response.

"It may be the new medicine," her dad explained when he and Deb drove to the supermarket to get ice cream. "Dr. Calder put her on Haldol. It's helped the jerky movements and she has better balance when she walks. But she's lethargic, doesn't seem to care about anything."

"I feel closer to her since I found out," she said. And it was true. Her mother now seemed someone who shared a curse, less the person who had given it.

"Did I make a mistake?" she asked. "Giving her the pictures of Kathleen?"

"I don't know," her dad said. He seemed low himself. He was not the same person as in the weeks following Jill's attempted suicide. Then Deb could feel their need for each other, and her dad had seemed almost desperate for her to forgive, to understand her mother.

Now it was as if he had become the caretaker, wondering how he was going to manage if it went ten, fifteen, even twenty years. The change in her mom's symptoms didn't really account for her dad. Good and bad spells had followed the attempted suicide.

The disease didn't progress that rapidly. A month ago she had urged her dad not to martyr himself. Now she was seeing the other side. Without his support—what would happen to her mother?

The three sat on the screened porch overlooking the ravine, sharing butter-pecan ice cream. Deb couldn't tell them she would be getting a divorce. She doubted her mother would be shocked. But her dad's reaction, he was so wrapped up in Buzz's political career—that was part of what she wanted to postpone until after the election and the birth of her baby. She promised to come back on Wednesday, take Jill shopping and to lunch.

At ten on Wednesday morning Deb thought she might be coming down with the flu. She felt faint, headachy. She had cramps. Her forehead was burning. She called Jill, had to cancel shopping and lunch, took two Tylenols and went into the bedroom. A nap might help. Buzz wanted her with him that night for a church supper at Mountview Baptist. "Those folks like it when the wife comes," he had said. She was determined to help with the campaign . . . it made her feel better about the decisions she'd made.

At noon she felt so weak she decided to call Dr. Weingard. She never made the call. When she got out of bed she felt a contraction. The next one ripped her stomach. When she looked she saw blood on her underpants. God . . . she was in labor. The contractions came violently. A fist-sized blob came out. She got down on her knees, retrieved the bloody tissue and flushed it down the toilet. She scrubbed the carpeting.

She made it back to bed and collapsed. The contractions weren't as fierce but they hadn't stopped. She was bleeding. Now she did call Dr. Weingard.

"Can someone bring you to the emergency room?" he asked. She didn't know. Buzz? Dad? Who? "I think I can drive," she said. He told her not to try, he would send an ambulance.

In the emergency room they left her on a gurney. People came, did things, examined her. "Sweetheart, you're going to be fine," she was told by a man in a washed-out green cap and matching jacket. "I've notified Dr. Weingard and you're scheduled for a D and C. Just a clean-up procedure. We want to make sure you're set for your next baby—that this won't give you a problem when you get pregnant again." He patted her knee through the sheet, asked if she had questions.

She shook her head. She felt numb. She wanted to be left alone, to sleep, escape . . .

She was in a hospital room and it was dark outside when she woke up. Buzz was sitting on the sill. "I've been here for an hour," he said. "I didn't want to wake you."

She saw that a curtain was drawn on the side of her bed opposite to the window. "You have a roommate," he said.

"Buzz," she said. "I had a miscarriage . . ."

The only light in the room came from a table lamp beyond the foot of her bed. But she would never, never forget his face. Pure, scary loathing. "They told me," he said, speaking quietly as if the woman on the other side of the curtain might be trying to sleep. The voice and the expression didn't match.

She wanted him to leave. She wanted to go back to sleep. She wanted this waking nightmare to end.

A nurse came in and flicked on a switch, flooding the room in bright, fluorescent light. Was she ready for some food? Buzz introduced himself and they discussed how well Deb seemed to be doing, as if no one were on the other side of the drawn curtain, as if he had never shown his true feelings a moment earlier.

"I peeked at her chart," Buzz confessed with a winning grin. The nurse smiled back as though that sort of rule-bending was what she would expect from a devoted, concerned young husband. A handsome one, too.

Buzz put his hands on the frame at the foot of the bed. He bent forward, looking at her. His long body seemed to extend halfway up the bed. "Hon, I'll stay as long as you like," he said. "It's totally up to you. Just say the word and I'll make a couple of calls." He twisted toward the nurse, explained that he was in a campaign where twenty-four-hour days didn't give him half enough time to meet the demands made of him. But of course *none* of that was important now.

"I'm fine," she said. "You go on. Really. I'd feel better if you did."

He kissed her, said he'd be there in the morning.

After he left, the nurse told her how lucky she was. The nurse was a Republican but Frederick "Buzz" Garrison was one Democrat she would cross lines to vote for in November.

She had no clear memory before she went into the operating room, the anesthetic had kicked in. But when she came out and was back in the same room, he was there. "Doc Weingard told me you can have as many kids as you want," he said. He looked at her as if laying down a challenge. She listened, wanting to blurt out that she would never let him make love to her again.

At home he was excited about the debate on Saturday night sponsored by the Columbus Metropolitan Club. Dinner would precede the debate. "I don't want to push you," he said, "but it would mean a lot if you could be there." Drew Dawson's wife would be at the head table. "I'm worried about this one," he said. "Dawson's a slasher. He's quick and he's good."

She promised she would be there, told him she was confident he could handle Dawson. And hoped she could handle herself. "You know the issues," she said quietly.

He smiled. "If you don't feel so hot on Saturday just let me know." She said it was okay. "It's totally your choice," he said.

The "totally your choice" clicked. "Totally up to you," he had said in the hospital. She could see his face, feel the . . . *hate.* Yes, that was the word. He blamed *her* for the miscarriage. There was an edge beneath everything he'd said and done since. She hadn't told him she wanted a divorce but he must have sensed it. And he knew—or thought he knew—what that would do to his dreams of higher office. Oh, he was making an effort to hide what he felt, but the blinkers were off her eyes. Maybe he was hiding his feelings to prevent damage to the campaign, but his control was thin, she'd *felt* what happened when it broke, and she was afraid of him, afraid it would happen again . . .

She did feel better on Saturday, a little stronger. She was at her vanity drying her hair and he was in the Jacuzzi again, whistling the Ohio State fight song. With the water churning, jetting against him, he was whistling and reading a dossier. Issues and answers, she guessed, that might come up during the debate or in questions from the panel of journalists.

"Deb," he shouted. "Turn that thing off a second. I want your reaction to this."

She snapped the dryer off. "I'm trying to get ready," she said. "What is it?"

"Aw, *forget* it," he said. "And fuck you."

She turned the dryer back on.

"You don't give a damn about me or anyone but yourself," he suddenly shouted.

She tried to ignore it, kept blowing her hair.

"Don't think you fool me," he shouted over the whir of the dryer. "I know you *think* you want a divorce. And I know what you *did*. We can *pretend* a miscarriage but we both *know*. It was an induced abortion, you just couldn't stand to have my child so you killed it . . ."

She took a step toward him. The same loathing she'd seen in the hospital was there. "Goddamn you."

Hands clasped behind his neck, he repeated it: "You killed my child." His eyes were so cold . . .

She threw the dryer down on him. It hit the gurgling water and crackled as it flashed. His "ahh . . . ahhhg . . ." was snuffed as his body jerked, stiffened and fell back into the still bubbling water.

In shock, she pulled the plug, bent to lift his head. He was limp, not breathing.

She let his body slide back into the churning water. She turned the Jacuzzi off. His face was under a layer of water. She had killed him. But she felt . . . what? Nothing . . . no. Fear? No. *Relief?* . . . No, no. But maybe yes . . . Oh God, she didn't know, she couldn't believe what had happened . . . She sat on the floor, breathing hard, unable to think straight, to sort out her jumbled thoughts . . .

She wasn't sure how long she sat before she went to the telephone. There were two of them in the bathroom, one mounted within reach of the Jacuzzi. But she couldn't make the call there. She went into the bedroom. She dialed 911.

"I just killed my husband." Her voice was flat. The operator took her name and address.

She called her parents. She had to tell them what had happened. Dad answered. "I don't *know*" was all the answer she could give to his first shocked questions.

She heard the siren in the distance. "The police," she said, and hung up.

She got to the door as two policemen with revolvers drawn came up the walk. She led them to the bathroom, pointed to the Jacuzzi. She started to try to talk but the older policeman held up his hand as the younger one read from a card he took from his billfold.

She had the right to remain silent. Why should she? It was obvious what she had done. She had the right to a lawyer. A lawyer? Kathleen was a lawyer . . . yes, Kathleen, she needed to talk to Kathleen . . .

The younger policeman went with her as she got her handbag. She found the folded slip of paper. What time was it? Nearly six-thirty on a Saturday night. Would Kathleen be there?

Kathleen answered on the first ring. "The police are here," Deb said. "I need a lawyer, I—"

"Don't say another word," Kathleen said. "Not about *anything*. Not about how you feel. Not about the weather. Not anything. Do you understand me?"

"Yes."

"Can you do that? Can you keep from talking until I get there?"

"Yes."

Kathleen wanted to speak to the officer. Deb handed the phone to him. She didn't listen to his side of the conversation. The officer handed the phone back to her. "She wants to tell you something," the officer said.

"They are taking you to Central Headquarters," Kathleen said. "I'll meet you there. They are not allowed to ask questions until I see you. Do not say one word to them."

IV
Looking
for the
Way Out

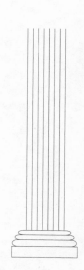

Often a lawyer is asked to assist the client in developing evidence relevant to the state of mind of the client at a particular time. The lawyer may properly assist the client in the development and preservation of evidence of existing motive, intent, or desire; obviously, the lawyer may not do anything furthering the creation or preservation of false evidence. In many cases the lawyer may not be certain as to the state of mind of the client, and in those situations the lawyer should resolve reasonable doubts in favor of the client.

—FROM EC 7–6; CODE OF PROFESSIONAL RESPONSIBILITY

Chapter 12

KATHLEEN HAD never tried a criminal case, much less a murder. At Harvard and earlier as an undergrad at Denison she had read a few courtroom thrillers and watched the movies and TV shows. In high school she raced through the Perry Mason books, setting her sights on a legal career. She had seen herself as the defender who sprang the innocent, who broke the lying witness on cross-examination, who risked danger to uncover corruption. But this was different. This was reality. Unknown territory, really.

Assistant County Prosecutor Socko Bender, the late Buzz Garrison's campaign manager, was heading the prosecution team. At least the state was not seeking the death penalty, figuring they would not get a jury to send Deb to the chair. But even without a capital specification, the indictment was serious enough.

Deb had been released on bond and was living at Lake in the Woods. She was refusing interviews, scrupulously following Kathleen's order that she talk to no one about the case.

Still, Kathleen figured her secret would come out. The prosecution surely knew about HD. They had not leaked it to the newspapers but maybe they wanted to avoid building sympathy for Deb, who was taking a pounding in the press.

Every time Kathleen picked up the newspaper she expected

punishment for not leveling with Tony. Maybe he knew, had figured it out. She had told him that Deb was her sister.

He also knew that Buzz and Deb had argued about aborting a diseased fetus; that tests showed the fetus was okay; that Deb had been devastated by her miscarriage; that Garrison had nevertheless perversely accused her of inducing an abortion. Tony needed these facts to do the legal research.

On Sunday afternoon, a week after the indictment, Tony reported the results of his research. Kathleen, wearing jeans, was sitting on the edge of her desk. "There are four ways we can defend." Tony, also wearing jeans, was standing—as if making an argument in the court of appeals. "The first is accident."

Kathleen interrupted. "Deb admitted to killing him. To the nine-one-one operator and probably, though we don't know just what she said, to the policemen when they arrived." The admissions to the police might be suppressed because of *Miranda,* but not the statement to the 911 operator.

"Killing isn't murder," said Tony. "You kill a jaywalker when he runs in front of your car but it's not . . ."

"Go on to the next one." She had considered the claim of "accident" while she'd been tracking down witnesses, having the scale model made of the Garrison bathroom and talking to an accident-reconstruction expert. The dryer could not have fallen in the Jacuzzi if Deb had still been standing at her vanity. Deb had been angry. It wasn't clear what Deb had done but her action had been a response to being accused of killing her baby. Socko Bender would eat Deb alive on cross-examination—with or without the 911 operator's testimony.

"The case law on insanity isn't bad," said Tony. In Ohio, no distinction was made between insanity and temporary insanity. It was all Not Guilty by Reason of Insanity (NGRI). The test was whether Deb knew right from wrong when she dropped the dryer. If the jury bought the defense, Deb would be sent to the Central Ohio Psychiatric Hospital. She would be released when a judge decided that her disorder presented no threat to herself or others. That wouldn't be long, Kathleen thought. The "if" was whether a jury could be sold on Deb's momentary loss of sanity. There was no chance without the support of a psychiatrist.

Kathleen had retained Dr. Lance Westphal. The problem, Dr. Westphal said, was Deb's history—nothing to suggest a momentary derangement. Kathleen had consulted two of the best criminal defense lawyers in town. Both were generous with their time, maybe responding to her confession of being in over her head, maybe believing she would bring another lawyer into the case at "nutcracking time," as one put it. The result of her self-education was to wound what she thought might be the best defense. Temporary insanity sometimes worked in the movies. But unlike in fiction, insanity—even with a psychiatrist's support—would be a hard sell to a central Ohio jury.

The thickest of Tony's memoranda concerned the "battered-wife syndrome." Ohio had adopted the rule. If a history of past beatings caused the wife to believe herself in danger, it could be used to show she was acting in self-defense. The trouble, of course, was the stretch required to make dropping a dryer into a Jacuzzi an act of defense. A second problem was that no real history of physical abuse could be proved. Just the one time. Nevertheless, Kathleen wanted to see every case in the country where the battered-wife defense had been attempted. Could the abuse be purely psychological?

"No court has gone that far," he said. "The wife must believe she's in danger."

She didn't want to give up. An instruction to the jury on battered wife could help sell the insanity defense. Deb had mentioned Garrison's dark side, the violence beneath the surface.

"Keep digging," she told Tony. "Look for assault cases, not just the homicides."

He shrugged. He thought it wheel-spinning but wasn't saying so.

"Our fourth option is complicated," he said. "The law is inconsistent. Even the opinions from our supreme court."

"No!" she said, smiling. He laughed with her.

"Let's go down to the kitchen and get a soda," he suggested. They talked as they got on the elevator.

"If you intend to kill it's murder," he said. "But if you're provoked, act in justifiable passion, it's voluntary manslaughter."

"Like a husband finding his wife in the sack with another man?" She remembered a case like that from law school. The so-called crime of passion.

He nodded. "The case law isn't clear on what constitutes a reasonable provocation," he said. "Second, who has the burden of proof? The law is confusing where there's an affirmative defense that turns on the defendant's intent."

No one was in the kitchen, a hall-like room on the nineteenth floor where associates and employees of the firm could bring lunch, store food in the refrigerators, use the microwaves, get things from a bank of vending machines. Partners had access to a formal dining room and the service of a full-time cook—though the unwritten rule was to use that facility only when hosting a client. Tony ran two bills through the changer, got himself a Pepsi, a ginger ale for her. They sat on the edges of Formica-topped tables, facing each other.

"At worst," he said, "this is a crime of passion. Manslaughter. It gives us a fall-back. The sentence would be much lighter."

She didn't respond. She was thinking, not about what Tony had said, but about forming a theory that kept alive each of the defenses. In any trial, she looked for a theory of defense. It should be simple. You couldn't ride two horses. But she was thinking about riding four. Or was she? The case law might have developed in four compartments, but as applied to Deb Garrison, weren't there four ways of seeing the one event?

Tony was looking at her, awaiting her reaction. "I don't want a manslaughter verdict," she said. "And a jury won't acquit her. I want to sell temporary insanity."

"Naturally, but—"

"I won't settle for manslaughter."

"Kathleen, I'm not against you."

She apologized. She said he had started her thinking.

He was enthusiastic, offering arguments suggested by the cases he had read. He wanted to "hit the books again."

Riding the elevator back to her office, she admitted her weariness. "This case won't let go," she said. "It's with me at night, when I'm eating, when I'm working on other stuff. We've let Columbus General slip."

"I guess we won't make it to Bermuda," he said.

She nodded.

"Tell me," he said. "Would we have gone?"

"I wanted to," she said. Her weariness was also related to her inability to level with him, her failure to respond. They had worked together as if the kiss in the underground garage hadn't happened, as if he hadn't said he was smitten. But he had said it, and not a day passed without her wondering what he really meant.

When they got back to the office, he stopped abruptly. "You wanted to," he said. "What does that mean?"

"What does what mean?" Of course, she knew what he was asking. She didn't know the answer.

"What are your feelings about me?"

In the instant it took to form an answer, she censured everything. This was not the time to mention HD. She felt stupid, standing with her hip pushed against the edge of her desk.

"Sometimes," he said, "I believe it could happen. Then I think we'll never be more than buddies. Maybe partners. Kathleen, half the time I want you and the other half I'm afraid of you. I've never been in a deal like this."

Why had he picked this time? She was due to see Deb at Lake in the Woods at six. Then back to the office, work until after midnight, trying to keep too many balls in the air.

He was not going to let her off. He made no move to sit. He just stood there in the middle of her office, waiting for her answer.

"It's complicated," she said.

He softened a little, his shoulders seeming to drop. "All I'm asking, Kathleen, is what you feel about me. About us."

"I like you, Tony—"

"Like?"

"There's the firm, there's your partnership. There's . . . there's . . . like I said, it's complicated. It's mostly me. I just don't know if it's possible . . ."

He took her hands. "What might be possible?"

She wanted to look away, to avoid his eyes. She didn't. When she was confronted she didn't look away. "I'm scared, Tony," she said.

He kissed her. They held each other.

"I want us to be more than buddies, friends, colleagues," she said. It felt and sounded as if someone else, a ventriloquist, had spoken for her.

He let go to close the door, then kissed her again. He said he wanted to go with her to see Deb.

How could she take him? That wasn't the way to tell him she was at risk for HD.

"You do need to meet Deb . . ."

"You know what they say. A lawyer who represents herself has a fool for a client. That applies to a relative, too. You're putting too much into this case."

"I know, but—"

"Let me talk with Deb," he said. "Maybe she isn't as vulnerable to cross-examination as you think."

She begged off, relying on half of the truth. "I haven't had the desire," she said, "or the courage—call it what you like, to see my birth mother. But I have to. She could be a witness."

He nodded. "Deb's father, too."

"I'm seeing Deb to talk about the best way to approach my birth mother," she said. "She doesn't want contact. It's a long story but it involves the guilt she apparently still feels over giving me up."

He finally accepted that "this particular time" she wouldn't be comfortable if he were there. "But come back as soon as you finish," he said.

She said she would.

On the way back from Deb's she had decided she really couldn't pull it off. Tony should hear about HD from her. She owed him an explanation for her avoidances. She was close to falling apart. Tomorrow she would see her birth mother. The visit would be a surprise. "If you do it any other way," Deb said, "anything's possible. She tried suicide once."

Kathleen found Tony in the library. Jay Melnik and six other associates were also spending Sunday night on the books. "How was Deb?" he asked on the way to her office.

"As you'd imagine. And now she's worried about paying us." Garrison had left no estate other than the house at Lake in the Woods, which carried a $1,500 per month mortgage. Both cars were financed. Visa and MasterCard accounts were near the limit. Garrison was heavily insured, but on Friday Deb got a registered letter telling her about the clause that voided the policy where the intentional act of the beneficiary caused the death of the insured.

"Deb wants to plead guilty," Kathleen said. "She keeps saying,

'I did it. What's for a jury to decide?' I spent the time bucking Deb up, telling her she can win."

"What about your birth mother?" he asked.

"I'll see her tomorrow. Listen, Tony, can we go to my place and talk?"

She got there ahead of him, started coffee, checked her refrigerator. The six-pack of Amstel Light she kept for emergencies was there.

"I've never been in your house without company," he said as they took their beers into the sitting room. He slipped his arm around her waist, leading her to the couch.

She veered away, took a wing-back chair. "I have things to tell you," she said.

He sat on the couch. "I'm listening," he said.

She didn't know where to begin. When she mentioned the disease he would assume she was thinking about marriage. Didn't that make her pathetic?

"I want you to know why my adoption records got unsealed," she said. "It was for medical reasons." She felt a little relief. Now it couldn't be taken back.

He didn't interrupt as she told him what she knew about Huntington's disease, of her fifty percent risk.

"Are you going to be tested?" he asked.

"I don't think so," she said.

"God," he said. "I don't know what I'd do." He was still sitting on the couch. Just looking at her. Then he did something that almost made her cry. He slid off the couch and came across the floor. He pulled her down with him. He stroked her hair as she buried her face against him.

"We make stuff too complicated," he said. "All I know is I'm so crazy about you I don't care about anything else."

She took a deep breath. "Well," she said. "Are we going to do anything about it?" A ventriloquist had spoken for her again.

He put his hands on the side of her face and held it in front of his. "I'm going to make love to you, lady, ready or not."

He stayed the night, and it was nothing to be explained or decided. They had orange juice, coffee and bran cereal for breakfast. Bright sunlight streamed through the latticed window and two jays squawked on the feeder just beyond. The glare of day was taking her away from the lovely, loving night and into the harsh need to figure out meanings. She dreaded going to the office, thought about staying home until she went to see her birth mother.

What had they done? No, what did it mean to her? For them? Answers to the question came in questions. Could they work together as before? What did she tell Marty, Si Wallace about them? Would Tony's partnership be affected by their personal relationship? Where did they go from here? What did he expect tonight? What did *she?* And the darker one . . . HD did give him an escape, whenever he wanted. After he made partner . . . ?

Stop . . . stop . . . stop being a damn killjoy. Accept the pleasure. Try. She could feel his hands on her body, she was deliciously sore.

They sat across the kitchen table, watching each other eat. "It'll be hard to be a lawyer today," he said. "But we have to get used to this. At least I hope we do."

Don't feel *guilty,* she told herself again. Tony isn't Greg Meeker. I'm not who I was yesterday. Good. Too good. Was her punishment to come later? *Stop it . . .*

In her office she made a list of calls she had neglected, files that needed attention. List-making was what she did when she faced more work than she could manage. She started working her way through the list by calling the hospital administrator at Columbus General to assemble the psychiatric team for a conference on Friday.

Deb called. "I need to see you," Deb said. "This house is getting to me. I can't go in there where . . . you know. But it might take a year to sell and—"

"Deb," she interrupted. Deb had told her these things before. "I'll come out to Lake in the Woods right after I see Jill . . ." Jill . . . it felt awkward, strange saying Jill. But Jill wasn't her mother, and "my birth mother" felt no better.

Chapter 13

JILL ROLLED to look at the clock on the nightstand. It was 3:20. It felt as if she hadn't slept. But the last time she looked, it had been a few minutes past one. Harrison was awake too. His breathing lacked the rhythm of sleep. She hoped he wouldn't ask if she wanted to talk.

Since taking Debbie's call, just as they were ready to leave the house to attend the debate at the Metropolitan Club, Harrison hadn't left home except to shop, to meet his classes and to visit Debbie. He cooked the meals, sat with Jill on the sofa and held her hand while they watched television. Like herself, he just couldn't accept that Debbie was going to be tried for murder.

Jill blamed Malcolm Calder. She wanted to screech her rage. She should not have let him browbeat her. If she'd kept her secret, Debbie wouldn't be facing a murder trial and a future worse than HD. Debbie would have gone full term, delivered a baby. The genetic chain had been broken. Jill's grandchild wouldn't have been born with the gene.

"I won't be forced to look again at that man's face," she told Harrison.

"I understand, Jilly. I really do."

He was probably afraid she'd try to kill herself again. She

wouldn't. She resisted not because she looked forward to any-thing, but because of Harrison and Debbie.

When she woke up in the middle of the night, which was every night, it was worry about Debbie. Debbie, alone in her house at Lake in the Woods. Jill prayed that nothing worse would happen. But like the old prayers against the HD gene, these seemed empty. Why wouldn't Debbie leave that house, come stay with them?

The next morning the telephone rang at eleven-thirty. Harrison was in his study, working to meet the deadline for revisions to his manuscript.

"My name is Kathleen Sullivan," the voice said. Jill had so often imagined the call. "Yes . . ." she said.

"I need to see you," the voice said. "I was going to just come, but decided it would not be right to surprise you." The voice sounded polished, like someone who was sure of herself, certainly a person of greater strength than herself.

"When?" she asked.

"This is awkward," said the voice. "I have some feelings about it too, so I'm sure you must. The polished voice did not seem possessed of feelings. "It's difficult to explain on the telephone," said the voice. "I am free to come now."

The voice was having another effect on her. This was her *daughter*. "I can see you," she said, then suggested waiting until after twelve-thirty when Harrison left to meet his one o'clock class. The voice said that would work out perfectly.

The voice became Kathleen.

"I have your address," said Kathleen. "Two eighty-eight Iuka. Deb says Iuka runs through a ravine north of the university."

Jill gave directions, told her where to park. "The house is one of the big old ones on top of the ravine," she said. "There are ninety-three uneven steps. Be careful because the concrete is crumbling and hasn't been cleared of vines this year."

She stared at the telephone, now silent in front of her, as if it were Kathleen. She went to the library, pulled the drawer where she kept the pictures. Kathleen Sullivan. There were also clip-pings, reporting that Kathleen was representing Debbie, the story about the decision in the supreme court, the one showing her sitting as a judge of moot court competition at the law school and another about her selection by the junior chamber of commerce as one of the outstanding young citizens of the year.

Studying the pictures, she had detected family resemblances, the same nose as Denise, Debbie's arch at the end of her eyebrow. London Bates was there too. But hearing the voice made a difference. She tried to put the pictures with the voice. She was looking at a different woman than when she'd looked at the pictures before.

She slid the pictures and clippings back into the drawer. There was something she had to do. She knocked on the closed door to Harrison's study. Rarely did she interrupt his work. "Come in," he called out, louder than necessary to carry through the closed door.

"Kathleen Sullivan called," she said. "She's coming at twelve-thirty."

Harrison looked upset. "Is that what you want? Do you want me to cancel my class?"

"No," she said. "I just wanted you to know." She didn't tell Harrison her other feelings, that Kathleen was not coming to blame her for HD or to unload a thirty-seven-year-old resentment.

From the screened porch she watched through the new green on the trees as Kathleen parked her Corvette, got out, looked up, reached back into the car for a briefcase and started up the steps. There was energy in the way the young woman climbed the old, crumbling steps. She was wearing a summer suit, pale blue.

When Kathleen was halfway up the ravine, Jill lost her nerve. She found the arm of one of the wicker chairs and sat. She could hear Kathleen approach the house. The chimes rang but she didn't move. The chimes rang again. She pushed herself up from the wicker chair.

"Just a minute," she called. She'd done that without choking or stuttering. She went to the end of the porch where she could look down, see Kathleen standing on the stoop. "I'm up here," Jill called down. "I'll be right there."

Kathleen looked up.

Going down the stairs, Jill grasped the handrail. She was taking forever. She should have left the door unlocked, asked Kathleen to let herself in and come up to the porch.

Through lace-covered side panels she could see Kathleen standing erect, so tall and poised, her arms at her sides. I am a miserable sight, Jill thought as she got the latch turned and opened the door.

Kathleen's smile vanished. Oh God, Jill thought. She could see the revulsion—

Kathleen caught her before she fell. She tried to speak but couldn't. She couldn't explain that her symptoms flared when she got tense, that she would be all right in a minute.

Kathleen held her with strong, capable arms—like the nurses at Columbus General. Kathleen's scent was cool, fresh. Everything inside Jill's body seemed to be in motion.

"This is why we avoided meeting," Kathleen said.

Looking up, Jill saw only the side of Kathleen's face, the attractive cut of her black hair and the tiny pearl earring. "These things hit me when I'm under stress," she said.

Kathleen picked up her briefcase and offered Jill her other arm. "I have a pitcher of iced tea and glasses on the porch," Jill said. "I thought that would be a nice place to visit."

"This house is huge," said Kathleen, trying to recover. "Is it four stories?"

"Too much," said Jill. "We'll move when Harrison retires. I hope I can manage those steps until then." The house seemed to fascinate Kathleen. They walked through the library and out onto the porch.

"I'm nervous too," said Kathleen, forcing a smile. She poured iced tea, got Jill seated in one of the wicker chairs and placed the other so the two could converse. The girl had the clearest skin, alert bright eyes. She looked almost regal, like a princess, Kathleen thought. "I feel I'm about to find out who I am," Kathleen said, "though that is an awkward way to put it."

Jill nodded, felt rude the way she was staring at this young woman. Her daughter . . .

"We have to talk about Deb's case," Kathleen said. "But, well, I want to know about you, about your parents, your life—everything."

"Yes," said Jill. She felt the same. How had the baby in the hospital become this elegant young woman? The pictures Deb had provided were no preparation.

"Isn't it cruel," said Jill. "I mean, what forced us to meet."

"Yes, but I'm glad it happened." Kathleen put out her hand. "I mean, being able to meet."

Jill felt warmth in the hand. Kathleen had kept her from falling, helped her up the steps and into the chair, but this was the first that Jill had felt her touch.

"I liked Deb the minute I saw her," Kathleen said. *"Cruel* doesn't describe what she's suffering."

Jill pulled her hand away. The words had hit like a kick in the stomach. Kathleen kept talking. Jill saw that she was talking about Buzz Garrison's death and the murder charge, not the disease or anything Jill had done.

"I was thinking about the disease," Jill said. "That's the cause of everything. That's why they unsealed the files."

"I'm not sure what to call you," Kathleen said. "Mother feels awkward. But I can't call you Mrs. Donahey." Kathleen was smiling, looking at Jill. "What about just Jill?"

"That's fine."

"Well, Jill, none of us had a choice about the genes we inherited."

"It doesn't feel that way," Jill said. Then the word registered. *Choice.* Had that slipped out? There might be no choice about HD but what about the other choice, the choice she had made thirty-seven years ago, the choice they hadn't talked about.

Kathleen was saying she understood why Jill had kept her condition a secret. But that didn't help . . . *choice.* The word refused to let go. *Choice. Choice.* "You must want to know about the adoption," Jill said.

Kathleen nodded. Waited.

"Your father played football at Ohio State," Jill began. "His sophomore year he started at defensive end, made AP All Big 10 honorable mention. His last two seasons he was an academic All-American. But that was after. I didn't really know him. I met him on a blind date arranged by my big sister in the sorority. His name was London Bates."

"Bates? Was he Irish?"

"I don't think so."

Kathleen looked almost wistful. "I've been raised by Irish Catholics," she said. "When I heard your name was Donahey I wondered."

"I'm an Eichorn," Jill said.

Kathleen listened, never shifting her intent dark eyes, giving no clue—other than great interest—to how she was being affected.

"Today what happened to me would be called date rape," Jill said. She was doing better talking, actually feeling relief. "I was what they used to call a party girl." She smiled at that. Spring practice had ended the Saturday before and there was a spread at the Gordon farm. Les Gordon was a multimillionaire, owner of racehorses, backer of Ohio State athletics who showered largesse on the players. Jill was eager to go, although it was only her third date with London Bates.

Jill said she had downed four or five orange blossoms. She and Bates wandered off, got into heavy petting. When they went back to the Beta Sig house, she'd gone up to the third floor with him. That's where he lost control and she hadn't been able to stop him.

"I never told my parents his name," Jill said.

"Did he know you were pregnant?" Kathleen asked.

Jill shook her head. "That night was the last time I saw him."

Kathleen was still looking at her, but behind the dark eyes Kathleen didn't seem to be there, seemed to be thinking about something else, someone else . . . ?

Jill went on to tell about dropping out of school, the five months at Alice Webster, the delivery. She could see pain now in Kathleen's eyes.

"I thought nothing worse could happen," Jill said. "Then they made me sign the papers."

Kathleen moved her chair closer. She took both of Jill's hands.

"I was so damn weak," Jill said. "I let my mother make my decisions."

Did Kathleen understand? Maybe she did, Jill told herself. Her hands felt warm. Forgiving?

"There's more I need to tell you," Jill said. She tried to explain the nightmare, her shame, why she had kept everything from her husband Harrison. She had, to tell the truth, dreaded Kathleen's call, but was so relieved to know that things had turned out well for her. "Only I thought of you as Laura," she said. "I would have called you Laura."

"Do you know where London Bates is?" Kathleen asked.

Jill didn't. After that night, she avoided reading the sports pages, hated even hearing or seeing his name. She did know he'd tried professional football but wasn't fast enough.

"I don't think my sorority sisters knew why I dropped out of Ohio State," she said. "Summer vacation came at a convenient time. I've kept it from everyone. Everyone except you."

Kathleen looked away. It was the first time since they'd come to the porch. Kathleen had turned at the mention of sorority sisters.

"We need to talk about Deb," Kathleen said. "I need to hear what you and your husband know."

"That was a tragic accident."

"Accident?"

"She didn't intend to kill him. Debbie told Harrison she didn't. You have to make people believe," she said. "The newspaper has it all wrong."

"Tell me about Deb's marriage," Kathleen said.

"It was a mistake. I didn't really see it until the campaign but it was wrong from the beginning. Debbie had good reason to hate him, that's why her reaction is so confused. But what happened was an *accident.*"

Kathleen leaned closer. "What did you see? I mean, about her feelings as you describe them?"

"Well, I'm afraid Debbie has a lot of anger. I think she's angry at me for giving her HD and for keeping it a secret, and then for telling. If it hadn't been for me she wouldn't have had the miscarriage. And the accident wouldn't have happened."

"She told you all this?"

"Not in so many words. But it's what she believes."

"I still want to know what you saw that made you say Deb actually hated Buzz."

Kathleen was smart, she missed nothing. She must be a good lawyer. She had changed the moment the conversation turned to Debbie. Did she dare trust her? If she told Kathleen about the morning she saw Debbie after the argument with Buzz, what would happen? *I wanted to kill him.* She hadn't forgotten Debbie's words. She wasn't going to get trapped into giving testimony against her own daughter in court. She should not have used the word *hate,* she told herself.

"I don't know," she said. "Talk to Harrison. He's spent more time with Debbie."

Kathleen put her attaché case on her lap. It was expensive-looking, cordovan leather with brass fittings. Kathleen turned it to unsnap the catches and Jill saw the embossed initials, K.A.S. "Mind if I take notes?" Kathleen asked.

Jill shook her head. "What's the *A* for?" she asked.

Kathleen looked puzzled.

"On your case."

"Oh," said Kathleen. "Anne."

"Kathleen Anne." Yes, the name seemed to fit.

"How did Harrison get along with Buzz?" Kathleen asked.

"Harrison thought the world of Buzz Garrison," said Jill. "They talked on the phone almost every night. They went to the Democratic National Convention in Atlanta, met Dukakis. 'Best time I ever had,' Harrison said. They attended seminars together, published a joint article in the *Journal of Political Science.* Harrison couldn't keep from crying when he told me . . . Harrison can be childishly sentimental . . . that Buzz promised to name the baby Harrison if it was a boy. 'They'll call him Harry, after Harry Truman and me,' Harrison said. And now his own daughter . . ." Tears came to her eyes.

"Harrison must have been shocked."

"He couldn't believe it when Debbie called. We drove out to Lake in the Woods, but Debbie had been taken to police headquarters. There was police tape across the door, policemen and investigators everywhere."

"Did you talk to anyone?" Kathleen looked worried.

"No."

"What about Harrison?"

"At the police station, my symptoms made it impossible for me to go in. But Harrison did and Debbie told him you'd already been there and didn't want her to talk about the accident. So we didn't think we should . . ."

"Wait a minute," said Kathleen. "Did Debbie ever actually use the word *accident?*"

"Well, that's what it was."

"But did *she* use the word?"

"I can't remember."

Kathleen was scribbling rapidly on a yellow legal pad. She had a peculiar way of writing, her pen pointed out and backward as she held it between scrunched fingers.

"That's what . . . ?" Kathleen was looking at her expectantly. "You were about to tell me something when I interrupted."

"Bender called the next day. It was in the afternoon. I told him we didn't want to discuss the matter with him."

"He accepted that?"

" 'You'll have to sooner or later,' " is what he said.

"Have you talked to anyone else?"

"No. We've been very careful. Of course I don't go out much. I've given up Faculty Wives and Eastern Star."

Kathleen said she felt guilty for not calling sooner. "The lawyer I'm working with reminded me yesterday that a lawyer who represents herself has a fool for a client. I'm Deb's half-sister, after all."

"Debbie knows how good you are."

Jill thought she heard Harrison. She got up, went to the screen. He was partway up the steps. "Come on up," she called down. "We have company."

Kathleen had also gotten up. They looked down as Harrison paused on the steps, holding the iron railing as he caught his breath.

Kathleen put her arm around Jill's waist and walked her away from the screen. "I'm sorry to barge in with questions after our earlier conversation," said Kathleen.

"Harrison will be more help," Jill said.

"But before he gets here," said Kathleen, "I want you to understand. There is much more I want to know about you. I keep wanting to interrupt, even when we're talking about Deb. I hope we can get to know each other, that you'll want to tell me about yourself."

"I want that very much, I'm so proud of you." She opened her arms and Kathleen turned into them.

"My girl," Jill said quietly.

Harrison insisted that Kathleen stay for supper. He suggested they eat on the brick patio beneath the porch, with an adjoining deck that cantilevered out over the ravine. "I'll get the grill going," he said.

During supper Kathleen kept up the questions. She wanted to see pictures of Buzz, of Buzz and Debbie. She asked about the seminars, the trip to the convention in Atlanta. She had questions about the wedding, the campaign for state senator and the one for Congress. "Exact words as close as you can remember," she said when Harrison was telling about going with Debbie to get the results from the first HD test.

"Did Deb tell either of you that Buzz accused her of inducing the miscarriage?" Kathleen asked.

Harrison shook his head. Jill tried to remember. Kathleen had asked the same question before Harrison got home. Had Debbie said anything like that? The accident was a subject Debbie didn't want to talk about . . . Harrison said she had not, even on the night it happened.

After supper they went into the library and the questions and answers went on. Kathleen was nearly through her second legal pad. Jill remained fascinated, as she had been while they were eating and during the afternoon, just watching Kathleen. Kathleen sat in the library with her legs angled gracefully to the side. She had long, gorgeous legs. Her posture suggested training as a dancer. Jill marveled that she had produced this person. But why wasn't Kathleen married?

"It's after ten," said Kathleen. "We don't have to cover everything tonight." She tore a piece of paper from her tablet and wrote out the name *Tony Biviano,* along with two telephone numbers. She said Tony might be talking to them, he was in her law firm.

"When will the trial be?" Harrison asked.

"The state must try Deb within two hundred seventy days of the indictment. It will probably be after the first of next year."

"I don't believe the state will try Debbie," Harrison said when he came back from walking Kathleen to her car.

"Did Kathleen say that?" Jill asked.

"No, no. Nothing like that. She's doing her job, running scared, preparing for the worst."

"Then what? What do you mean?"

"I've talked to some people . . ."

"Who? No one but Debbie and me is what you told Kathleen."

"It's best you not be bothered by details," said Harrison, "and I don't think it's advisable for Kathleen to be involved either. There are political considerations. I know a little about the prosecuting attorney and his ambitions, why he's handling this the way he is."

"What political considerations?" She was trying to stay calm, to keep her anger from showing.

"Buzz was high profile, Jill. They have to make a show. But after a thorough investigation I doubt they'll find enough to proceed against Debbie. They must know it was an accident. Anyway, I did my best to make sure of that. Naturally, they can't drop the investigation until the story cools."

Harrison was pacing in front of the fireplace in the library. He was remarkably nervous, Jill thought. Why? Was this another of Harrison's never-ceasing ploys to make her feel better? When he did that he usually made her feel worse, and this time was no exception. "I'm glad Kathleen is involved," she said, and deeply meant it.

"Jilly Bean, don't let this upset you." Harrison stopped his pacing, sat beside her on the sofa. "I'm really pretty sure it will never get into the courtroom." He put his hand on top of her leg. "I've received some assurances," he said. "But this *must* stay between you and me. If it leaks out and the prosecutor gets embarrassed . . . Bean, that wouldn't help Debbie at all."

Chapter 14

TONY AND KATHLEEN were sitting on their new beanbag chairs in the parlor, each holding a small dish of vanilla ice cream, Kathleen's ritual fix.

"Something about the professor doesn't sit right," Tony said. He had questioned the professor, he had flown to California to see Deb's sister Denise, he had met with the grandfather and Billy Joe, the uncle. And he had spent time at Lake in the Woods.

"He and Jill want to help," said Kathleen. "But they weren't there. None of those people can do much for us from the witness stand."

"It's more the professor than Jill," he said. "He knows something . . ."

Kathleen was licking her ice cream bowl. "That's gross," he once told her. In fact it was sort of erotic, he thought but didn't say. He doubted she would do that in front of anyone else, and that pleased him.

Kathleen put her licked-clean bowl on the floor. "I think Deb probably said something to her dad after she got the results of the first test. Something he thinks would hurt her defense."

Tony considered the possibility. Maybe, he thought. In any case the prosecution would soon confront the professor. They had not needed to do it to get an indictment, but at some point the professor would have a choice. Tell what he knew or lie.

"When you get to court," Kathleen said, "you've got to be careful with Harrison. If you decide to use him."

"What?"

She was smiling. "You'll do fine," she said. "Once the case is prepared, putting it on stage is the easy part."

That was bull and they both knew it.

"I have to testify," said Kathleen. "No one else saw the bruise. I can support all of Deb's story, tell the jury how the fight over abortion changed to the point where Deb was living for her baby. Deb desperately needs corroboration and I'm the only one who can give it."

"But if you testify, doesn't that knock me out too?" The canons of ethics precluded a lawyer from testifying in a case where the lawyer represented one of the parties.

"Bender has agreed that you can try the case," she said.

"Damn it, Kathleen, I don't know." This was homicide. He thought she'd ask him to take some of the witnesses, divide the summation, maybe do the opening statement. "Is it fair to Deb? Shouldn't we turn the case over to a criminal defense lawyer? Maybe Jack Harter?"

She was smiling as she shook her head. "We know the case," she said. "We can do it better than anyone."

She had caught him utterly unprepared. But if she had that much confidence in him he didn't want to disappoint her. He couldn't. But what if he lost? She should have given him warning, not spring it like this on a Wednesday at midnight. Why had she talked to the assistant prosecutor first?

"I'm going to see Si Wallace in the morning," she said. "Maybe he'll agree to give us Jay Melnik. There should be two lawyers at counsel table."

"You didn't just think of this."

"I'm sorry," she said. "I had to be sure the prosecutor wouldn't object to you. I talked to Socko Bender late this afternoon. Even then . . . it kills me to give this up . . . but tonight I realized there simply is no other way."

"Who calls the shots? Me? Melnik? You?"

"You don't think I'd ask you to take the lead and then second-guess you?"

It sounded okay in *theory,* but he already felt the burden. As someone had said, the space between first and second chair in a major trial might be inches but the difference was miles. And why was Bender being so cooperative? It was obvious—Bender wanted an inexperienced opponent, one he figured he could eat for lunch.

"Come on." She was standing over him, pulling him out of the beanbag chair. "It's late," she said. "There's a long time between now and trial."

He got up and she shoved herself against him. "I'm horny," she said without embarrassment.

God, she had surely changed since the night he'd first slept with her. And what she liked to do—it was unbelievable, and wonderful. She was in a way more a mystery to him than ever. Did the change really go beyond her attitude toward sex? He just couldn't shake the feeling that one day, for reasons he'd never know, she'd run.

At ten Tony was trying to finish research Chip Drucker had wanted the previous Friday when his secretary told him, "Mr. Wallace would like to see you."

Tony knocked on the closed door, was told to come in. Kathleen was standing, Wallace seated behind his desk. "Mr. Wallace thinks I'm being unfair to you," said Kathleen, and it was apparent the conversation preceding Tony's arrival had been chilly.

"Sit down, Tony," said Wallace. "Kathleen is upset. A candid discussion is the best way to stop a small problem from becoming divisive." Wallace smiled. If he was also angry, he was concealing it. He was the presiding partner, on his turf, ready to apply a dab of oil to squeaking parts in the firm's machinery.

"Let me be very direct," said Wallace. Two olive-drab, clothbound notebooks lay open on his desk. Tony recognized them, felt a clutch in his stomach. The books contained the sheets logging his and Kathleen's billable hours. When the managing partner called you in to account for billable hours you were in trouble. "I've run the numbers for July," said Wallace. "Two-thirds of your time is charged to 'Debora Garrison—criminal.' Kathleen tells me the firm obtained a retainer of ten thousand and that the prospect of getting more is slim."

Tony nodded. The ten thousand came from Deb's grandfather, who was also supporting Deb. Kathleen had been gracious, telling Deb ten thousand should cover the tab. It wouldn't cover the time spent in July. Some would go to expenses—travel, the psychiatrist, demonstrative evidence, witness fees for Dr. Calder and Dr. Weingard. But Deb was a relative. Kathleen said there would be no problem with the firm.

"The representation was undertaken without going through the screening committee," said Wallace. "Kathleen acknowledges the mistake."

Kathleen sat in one of Wallace's captain's chairs. She turned to look out the bay window. "I thought the representation fit the exception," she said, talking to the window. The exception was "work for immediate family." Everything else went through the screening committee to be checked for conflict of interest, whether the prospective fee justified the probable time commitment, whether the client was solvent, whether the case might lead to future business, would it embarrass the firm or another client. Often the review was routine, but defense of a murder charge would undergo severe examination. We do all types of work except criminal and domestic, partners were fond of saying. Of course we would handle a divorce or personal matter for a valued client, they usually added.

"I suggested that we refer Mrs. Garrison to someone specializing in criminal practice," Wallace said. "Kathleen doesn't want to do that. We'll back Kathleen. Her judgment is not quite what I would expect were she not personally involved. But Latham, Fuller stands behind its partners."

Wallace proceeded to lecture Tony . . . too much of his time was being spent on Kathleen's work, he needed exposure to other partners, if he stayed on the Garrison case it made a difficult situation more difficult. "Kathleen agrees it should be your choice."

Choice? Tony glanced at Kathleen, who was still turned away. "I couldn't quit now," he said. "This is our case."

"Kathleen and I expected you might react that way," said Wallace. "Let's establish some ground rules."

Without assuring him that Latham, Fuller stood behind its associates when they made ill-advised choices, Wallace proceeded to the ground rules. First, Jay Melnik was out of the question. So was everyone else. "No additional manpower can be committed to this effort." Second, Tony would do much of the work on his own time, be expected to show thirty-five billable hours a week on other work. Third, he would accept no more assignments from Kathleen. Fourth, Chip Drucker would be his mentor. "I want you to report at least once each week to Chip, review the work you are doing for the firm." Finally, he needed to understand "though this should not affect your long-term prospects at Latham, Fuller, you may not advance as quickly as you might have hoped."

"Goddamn him," Kathleen said as she and Tony left Wallace's office. "I'm ready to tell them to go screw themselves." Though she'd kept quiet during the conference, she was nearly out of control now. "Let's get out of here," she said.

She drove her 'Vette like a maniac, not speaking, her knuckles white as she strangled the steering wheel. She parked diagonally across two spaces in the Hunan Gardens parking lot.

"No," she said, when he asked if she wanted a beer. "I can't do this to you. I can't ruin your chances with the firm. I *know* them."

"Hold on," he said. "Didn't you tell me a good trial lawyer got even, not mad?"

"You only heard part of it," she said. "People are bending Wallace's ear because they don't like our being together. They've got it in for you."

"You aren't serious."

"How's this for serious? Wallace says, 'Some of the partners wonder if it isn't time for the firm to consider a no-nepotism rule.' No hires for kids of partners. If partners marry, one must—" She stopped talking. She was blushing. In her rage she'd failed to hide what she was thinking and he felt like climbing across the table to hug her.

She picked up her napkin, on the verge of tears, it seemed.

"Kathleen," he said. "We're in this together."

She nodded.

"I've never been so happy as during the two months we've been living together," he said. "I love working with you. Being with you. I want us to last forever."

"I don't know what I want," she said.

"That's what scares me," he said.

Her eyes were especially beautiful. "I wish to hell I could *trust,*" she said.

The office of Dr. Lance Westphal was on the third floor of a glass-and-stainless-steel building along the outerbelt. The windows looked out on a pond, lined with white pebbles, surrounded by a manicured lawn and shrubbery. The water had been dyed to a crystalline blue.

Dr. Westphal always allowed Tony to select his chair. There were two, on either side of a table with a grass-skin cover, a lamp, an ashtray and a vase containing a spray of dried flowers. As before, Tony chose the chair that put his back to the window.

"I can say that Debora was incapable of distinguishing right from wrong at the moment she acted." Dr. Westphal smiled, aware that this was the answer Tony had been seeking. "It was a brief reactive psychosis. The mechanism that triggered the psychosis was the accusation of aborting her fetus," said Dr. Westphal. "The underlying condition that contributed to the manifestation of the psychosis was a post-partum depression. The stress placed on her by her husband converted the depression into a temporary psychosis, a detachment from reality."

"That's fine, doctor." Tony was taking notes. He didn't want a written report. A report would have to be given to Socko Bender. The doctor would be stuck with his words at trial, and as Dr. Westphal put it, his opinion was based "in no small part" on hypothetical facts.

"I am assuming you can prove the assumptions you ask me to make," he said. "Quite frankly, those assumptions go beyond the history I obtained during my sessions with Debora herself."

"Is that a problem?" Tony asked. Since Kathleen had retained Dr. Westphal, he had shown a frustrating tendency to offer opinions, then waffle.

"No." Dr. Westphal smiled and lit his pipe. At their first session, Tony had assured him that his smoking was not offensive. "With a patient such as Debora," said the doctor, "one expects a substantial underlay of repressed material."

It looked as if Westphal had reached a firm position, and if he had, his testimony would force Judge Conklin to submit the question of insanity to the jury. But Tony hid his pleasure. Westphal had required much work, kept demanding additions to the necessary hypothetical facts.

"Quite frankly"—the doctor liked to introduce his opinions in those words—"the dream work Debora and I have done is helpful to my diagnosis and findings. The collective tends to underestimate the messages sent to us from the unconscious. I'm not sure how strongly you'll want to stress this aspect with the jury."

Quite frankly, Tony was nervous about his witness. How would the tweed-jacketed, effete-looking puffer of pipes hold up on cross-examination?

The dream that intrigued Dr. Westphal was one in which Deb and Garrison were out in a boat, taking along a picnic lunch. Suddenly Deb was drawn underwater and into a struggle with a scaly monster. "It demonstrates that Debora has not come to terms with the monster aspect constellated by her husband," Dr. Westphal said. "Archetypal and unconscious psychotic forces took control of her ego. The impact is significant, given the history of her dispute with Buzz and the peculiar combination of circumstances that confronted her that night."

"That's impressive," said Tony, at least it sounded impressive. It was nearing the end of their hour. The doctor scheduled Tony as he did patients.

Tony left the office, satisfied that the critical element for the defense was in place. Tomorrow, he would find out a great deal more about the prosecution's case. Judge Martin P. Conklin had scheduled a pre-trial conference at one in the Hall of Justice. The prosecution would be required to identify their witnesses, furnish statements, exculpatory material and investigating reports—the so-called Brady materials. The defense would seek permission to add the Not Guilty by Reason of Insanity plea. That would give the prosecutor access to Deb and to her medical records.

It was late September, two months since Si Wallace had laid down his ground rules. In that time Tony had worked harder on the case than before. If they made him wait an extra year for partnership, so be it. His view of the partnership had undergone a change, starting at the Hunan Gardens during lunch with Kathleen.

"Tony," she had said, "I don't know what they'll do. Wallace didn't like it when I brought you into Columbus General. But whatever happens, you and I will be working together." She meant it and had repeated the promise. They'd talked about options. They could open an office, hang up their shingle in German Village. That would be a sacrifice for Kathleen. Without Latham, Fuller she would have a lesser, duller practice. "We could go as a package in a lateral move," she said. "The Cleveland firms are short on litigators in their Columbus offices."

She had renewed her promise just last night after he told her about Chip Drucker's shot: "Have fun diddling with your shrink tomorrow," Drucker had said with a prick-smile at their nine o'clock meeting.

Beyond the working relationship Tony was less sure where he and Kathleen stood. He was still living in her house, sharing expenses. They spent more time together than most married couples, and there was no less electricity when they were naked and sweating.

But something held her back. He didn't think it was HD. "Who knows what could happen in fifteen years?" he'd told her. "That's half of my life." Maybe the age difference bothered her more than him. Maybe she thought it would in time create problems. "I have to be sure," she kept saying. There were times when he thought he should be getting out of a bad deal. But the moods didn't last. He adored his screwed-up brainy woman.

She reacted like a giggly kid when he told her the news from Dr. Lance Westphal. "This case will make a name for you," she said. Actually it made him nervous when she got this optimistic. All he could think was *What if I lose.* It was being first chair. Before, he'd always seen the strength of the case he worked on.

She wanted to celebrate, have dinner at Spagio's though that would mean a late night at the office. "We have to talk about the pre-trial anyway," she said. She was still working hard on the defense, would go with him to the Hall of Justice tomorrow. The ethical canon precluded her only from trying the case.

In the middle of dinner—he wasn't sure exactly what he'd said or even what they'd been talking about—she put down her fork and leaned forward. "Do you remember the tennis party when you were a summer clerk? When you told me I had good legs?"

"And you got furious but pretended to be cool."

She actually blushed. "Did you mean it?" she asked.

"Are you serious?"

She nodded.

"Your legs are sensational," he said.

She looked puzzled.

"Don't tell me you aren't aware of how the men in the firm look at you when you walk away from them."

She was blushing extravagantly as she reached across the table, squeezed his hand. "I'm crazy about you," she said, and added to herself, God help me.

Judge Martin P. Conklin sat at his desk with counsel arrayed around him. Tony and Kathleen had the couch. The walls in Judge Conklin's chambers were covered with pictures and awards, including his certificate of appreciation for speaking to the Downtown Kiwanians and plaques for lecturing at continuing legal education seminars. The pictures showed him with George Bush, Henry Kissinger, Arnold Schwarzenegger, Ronald Reagan, Jesse Helms, Dan Quayle, Richard Nixon, Newt Gingrich, Gerry Ford, Bob Dole, Nelson Rockefeller, Lee Greenwood, Governor Voinovich and Gen. H. Norman Schwarzkopf. All had inscriptions like "My best to Judge Martin P. Conklin," and signed "Your good friend Stormin' Norman," etc. Those were the prominently displayed ones. There were many more and the judge arranged them according to current value. William C. Westmoreland, now partly obscured by a four-tier file cabinet in the corner, had once occupied the place of General Schwarzkopf.

Directly behind and above the desk, a portrait of the Great Emancipator, Abraham Lincoln, presided from its gilded frame over Judge Conklin and the assembled attorneys.

"The trial date will be March 9th." Judge Conklin, a wiry man with thinning brown hair, looked at each of the lawyers over half rims. Did anyone have a conflict? All understood that a later attempt to postpone the assignment would provoke judicial wrath and succeed only upon the direst grounds.

Judge Conklin, though affable enough at bar outings and when campaigning, ran his courtroom like a strict high school principal. He insisted on punctuality and was proud to move the heaviest docket in the state.

Kathleen liked the draw. "Conklin can't be back-doored by Socko Bender," she had said. "He'll make the prosecution turn over the Brady materials in time for us to use them. Conklin couldn't have been a fan of Liberal Buzz."

"I see Ms. Sullivan is to be a witness for the defense." Judge Conklin, arching an eye, looked at Bender. "Any objection to a member of her firm trying the case?"

"No, Your Honor. Not so long as Mr. Biviano doesn't testify himself."

"Very well." The judge made a notation on his checklist. "Will there be any amendment to the indictment or plea?" he asked.

Tony said the defendant wanted to plead NGRI, to raise battered wife, insanity and provocation to passion. He offered a confidential brief. "It contains authority that may help the court understand the theory the defense will be urging," he said.

"Any objection?" The judge looked at Bender.

"Well, Your Honor," Bender said, "this comes awfully late and as a surprise. I think we should be copied with any arguments—"

"That's nonsense." Conklin then told Bender he too could submit a confidential brief if he wished. "The court appreciates your effort to make the trial go smoothly," said Conklin, looking at Tony with a tight smile. "You can be more frank with the court if you are not required to divulge strategy to your opponent."

The judge turned to Bender. "This case has had coverage," he said. "Too much publicity, in my opinion. You will not turn this trial into a circus."

"Of course not, Your Honor."

"All right. We're ready for the Brady materials." Judge Conklin excused himself to attend other matters. "I'll be back in twenty minutes to deal with problems," he said. He offered the continued use of his chambers. "Joyce has coffee and a kitty," he said. "The usual contribution is a quarter a cup."

Socko Bender pulled the material from two box-sized briefcases. He removed Judge Conklin's judicial magazines from the coffee table and divided the materials into two stacks. He and his assistants helped themselves to coffee and stood, watching for reactions as Tony and Kathleen started through the material. The purpose of this review was to scan, see if everything they expected was there, see if the material suggested documents that hadn't been produced.

Tony felt his fingers go cold. It would be hard to conceal his shock. He was looking at a stapled, four-sheet statement taken under oath and signed, "Harrison J. Donahey." Deb's father!

The statement had been taken on June 15th, the second morning after the death. There was no mention of the abortion dispute or of the accusation that Deb had induced a miscarriage. Deb was quoted as having told her dad, "I don't know how it happened. We were getting ready to go out, talking in the bathroom. I turned and the dryer slipped. It was just an accident. I didn't mean to kill him. We hadn't even been arguing."

Without unduly lingering, Tony tried to decide what it meant. If the defense were to be accident, Harrison's statement would be exculpatory. But it was a huge problem if they went with insanity, the battered-wife syndrome and provocation to passion. The strange twist to the fight about abortion was the key to Dr. Westphal's opinion. Donahey's statement made Deb look like a liar and the multiple defenses a desperate attempt to avoid a murder conviction. To revert to a straight defense of accident would put Deb in the position of having to lie or not testify. Jesus . . . "We weren't arguing," the statement quoted Deb as having said. The prosecution would clobber them with that. Harrison Donahey, in trying to help his daughter, had driven a spike into the heart of their defense. Why hadn't Harrison told them he'd given a statement?

Scarier yet, it was obvious the prosecution knew more than was revealed in the Brady materials. They had probably anticipated the plan to plead NGRI. It explained Bender's relatively mild opposition to the plea.

Tony exchanged his stack with the one Kathleen had been reviewing. When Judge Conklin came back, the judge asked if there were problems.

"I don't see any." Kathleen answered quickly, not allowing Tony the chance. "Of course," she added, "we haven't had an opportunity to study the material in depth."

"Do that in the next two days," said Judge Conklin. "Objections with a supporting brief no later than ten days from today." He favored Socko Bender with the tight smile. "Copies of that brief to be furnished to the prosecution." He then asked if there would be a plea bargain.

SHADOWS OF DOUBT   *153*

"A negotiated plea is always a possibility," said Bender. "But that has not yet been explored."

"The court has allowed two weeks for trial," said Judge Conklin. "If there is to be a plea, it need not be made on the eve of trial. That wastes everyone's time."

The judge said he was ten minutes behind for his next pre-trial and invited counsel to use his courtroom to explore the possibility of a plea.

An empty courtroom, like a cathedral on a weekday morning, was a lifeless place. The raised bench, the chairs in the jury box, the heavy railings, the counsel tables and the pews in the gallery sat like so much lugubrious furniture, surrounded by walnut walls. Only a few lights, recessed in the domed ceiling, had been turned on.

Socko Bender hiked his rear end onto the corner of one of the counsel tables. A short, thick man with black hair parted in the center, he had a wrestler's neck that bowed in the back. "We're going to give the defendant a break." Bender spoke in a deep bass. "It's a lay-down murder, but we don't think she's a threat to society." He minced the words *threat to society,* indicating what he thought of such bullshit. "We've got to have some jail time," he said. "There's been too much publicity."

"I wonder why," Kathleen said.

Bender ignored her. Because the prosecutor had been "politically close" to Buzz Garrison, Bender claimed that it put them in an awkward position. "I was his campaign manager," said Bender. "As close to Buzz as anyone. In this trial, everyone has something to lose."

"Why didn't you let one of the other assistants take the case?" Kathleen asked.

Bender looked at her like a linebacker crouched to make a hit. "Two reasons," he said. "I owe this to Buzz. If we go into the courtroom, I'm not going to let you smear his reputation. Buzz has a lot of friends. They go back to when he was playing ball for Cap. They'll be looking over my shoulder."

"You said two reasons." Kathleen could be as blunt as Bender. But Tony was wondering about her promises. Was this his case or hers?

"The second reason," said Bender, "is that I want to see a plea. I'm in a position to get that done."

"How so?" Kathleen asked.

"That, Ms. Sullivan, is none of your business."

"Give us your proposition." Kathleen wanted to go to war.

Bender laid out his deal. Voluntary manslaughter. A two-year sentence with eighteen months suspended. Assurance that Deb would serve the six months working at a library in a minimum-security facility.

It was a bright, crisp, early fall day. Tony and Kathleen had walked the five blocks from their office to the Hall of Justice. On the way back he said, "It's a better offer than I expected."

Kathleen stopped walking. They were in the seedy section of High Street, on the sidewalk in front of the Gentlemen's Book Store. "Get a little backbone," she said. "You can't try cases on a Jello stomach."

"Hey," he said, "take it *easy.*"

"Deb's *not guilty.* We're not pleading her guilty to *anything.*" She started walking, striding out with her long legs, making him hurry to keep up, and at the moment wondering if he wanted to.

Chapter 15

T HEY WERE WORKING together, but with tension. She wanted to make up. Tony seemed to be holding out. He tried to pretend he was over his feelings but she saw through him. She did feel sorry for the way she'd gone after him following the pre-trial. At the time she'd taken out on him her anger from discovery of the statement Deb's father Harrison Donahey had innocently, but damagingly for her, given to the prosecution. Working in her office, she would look forward to seeing Tony, imagine herself apologizing, having a beer in the parlor and laughing at how childish they'd both been.

But it hadn't happened.

She was glad she'd driven to work separately. She would be going to Lake in the Woods at six to have supper, go over the Brady materials with Deb. "I think it would be better if I went alone," she'd suggested.

"Probably," he said.

"How is it going?" she asked Deb, and immediately was sorry for such a fatuous question. But Deb seemed to ride right over it.

"I got good news this afternoon," said Deb. "The broker sold the house. The closing is in a month."

Talk about looking for silver linings, Kathleen thought. Her half-sister was still fighting; not giving up.

"I could look at apartments with you," Kathleen said, scoring another ten, she felt, on the baloney scale.

"God, will I be glad to get out of here," said Deb. "I mean . . . it's got his stuff, his clothes, his . . . I don't use that bathroom. Let's eat," Deb said quickly. "I made shrimp salad."

As they ate, Kathleen talked about the prosecution witnesses. No surprise about BCI people who had done the forensics, the sergeant who had stayed two weeks at Lake in the Woods, the 911 operator. The Franklin County Democratic party chairman, among others, would testify to Garrison's commitment to women's rights—a sure indication that the state knew more than Kathleen had suspected. Deb thought Buzz might have confided in Bender when she was defying him. Several statements attested to what a considerate husband Buzz had been.

"Even after our fights started, Buzz treated me nicely in front of other people," Deb said.

Some of the witnesses might not be called, could have been shown by Bender on the build-a-haystack-to-hide-the-needle theory. Actually, the state's case would rest mainly on the physical facts. Aside from the experts, they might not call many witnesses, Kathleen said.

She also told Deb that state-appointed psychiatrists would examine her. "We'll prepare you when we get notification of the time and place." That would be crucial. The insanity defense made it impossible to conceal Deb's claim that Buzz accused her of aborting the baby. What Deb told the psychiatrists could be used at trial.

Aside from Harrison, the Brady materials contained two surprises. Grace Jaeger was the patient sharing Deb's room at the hospital, on the other side of the curtain, when Buzz visited. Ivy Phillips was the nurse whose vote Buzz had won. They would have to be interviewed.

Kathleen had decided not to reveal that Deb's father was listed as a prosecution witness. He was, she felt, a naïve meddler. He might be trying to help but that only increased the danger. Kathleen resolved to say nothing that could be repeated to Harrison and kindle a second effort to "help." Still, there were questions that had to be answered. "What have you told your dad?" she asked.

"You said not to talk about it. And I haven't. Even though I see Dad almost every day. He's been . . . well, without him and you, I'd . . ."

Deb didn't finish and Kathleen had to wonder . . . though she'd said she'd never take the easy way out. "What Mom did was cruel," Deb had said. "I couldn't do that to Dad." Still, according to Dr. Westphal, Deb was clinically depressed . . .

"On the night it happened," Kathleen went on, "you saw your dad at police headquarters. What did you tell him?"

"I really don't remember." Deb got up. "I almost forgot," she said. "I brewed fresh coffee." She went to the counter.

Kathleen followed her. "Deb, I really need to know. Did you tell your father what Buzz said just before you dropped the dryer?"

"He didn't believe me." Deb refused to look at her.

"Did he blame you?"

Deb turned. Her eyes were swollen and red. "He convinced himself it was an accident. He can't accept the truth."

Kathleen could not retreat. She had to probe the wound. A murder charge was at stake. "Why?" she asked.

"That night he couldn't understand why I'd been arrested . . . I hardly remember what I said, but . . . I mean, he kept saying it didn't make sense, talking about the great marriage Buzz and I had, that we didn't argue, treated each other so well . . . that I must be in shock, confused. He said he could understand that. I wanted to plug my ears . . . I mean, it was all I could do not to scream at him." Then, very softly, Deb said, "I might have told him I hated Buzz, that he wanted to control everything I did . . . that he'd accused me of murder . . . that I was glad he was dead . . ."

"But, Deb, you didn't intend to kill him."

"I don't know what I intended . . . I must have . . . intended to put the dryer in the water . . ." Her voice conveyed no feeling. She sat and slumped forward in her chair, as if waiting for Kathleen to bring a whip down across her back.

Kathleen pulled a chair up beside Deb's. She put her arm around her. Deb turned, grabbed Kathleen's arms and held on as if her life depended on her grip.

"Deb, you are *not* a murderer," Kathleen said. "You've got to stop blaming yourself. Even if you wanted to hurt Buzz when you dropped the dryer—"

Deb pulled away. She was looking at Kathleen, looking with an expression Kathleen hadn't seen. She was trying to tell whether Kathleen meant what she'd just said or was offering comfort.

"Why can't *you* try the case?" Deb asked. "Why does it have to be someone else?"

Kathleen explained—though she'd done so at least three times before. "I must testify, so I can't try it. Look, I'll be with you after court recesses—every day. I'll help you prepare to testify. I can be with you more than if I had to try the case."

"You are the only person who understands," Deb said.

"We can make Tony understand."

Deb seemed to be considering the possibility. "I like Tony," she said. "He's nuts about you, you know. You're making a mistake if you let him get away."

Kathleen ignored that, got up, poured herself a cup of coffee. She didn't criticize Deb for having lied to her and Tony, didn't give the lecture on how hard it was to help a client who didn't trust her lawyers. Kathleen was seeing the problems . . . they couldn't win if Deb didn't testify, and yet if Deb did—the way she was talking, on cross-examination she'd convict herself.

They cleared the table, put the dishes in the washer. They took fresh cups of coffee into the family room. "I could make a fire," Deb said. That sounded good. It was chilly and damp, raining outside with water beating on the window.

"It's weird," Deb said abruptly, "but I find myself thinking about him . . . Buzz . . . it's like he's still here . . ."

Kathleen didn't respond to that. How could she? She certainly had lost her objectivity, which was bad for a trial lawyer. She thought Buzz had deserved what he got. Her job was to make a supposedly impartial jury see that, and clear Deb.

"There are still memories, not all bad . . . I can't lose them. And it shouldn't have happened to us: At the same time I hate him for what he did to us, my life . . ."

"Deb," Kathleen said, trying to bring her back to the case, "after you got the test on your baby, you were happy, running back in to call Buzz, tell him how you felt . . ."

Deb nodded. They'd gone over this so many times.

"The question keeps coming back," said Kathleen. "How, after that, could Buzz have thought you wanted an abortion?"

"I think about that all the time. I just don't know. From the day we heard about Mom . . . he was someone I just couldn't figure. Maybe he thought I wasn't telling the truth. Maybe he thought, the way we weren't getting along, I was going to get an abortion anyway and pretend it was a miscarriage."

Kathleen nodded, although it was pretty vague, speculative, and Deb could tell that was her reaction.

"I can tell you what Dr. Westphal thinks," Deb said.

"What?"

"He calls it a projection. Buzz projected his own capacity for destructiveness onto me. He wanted control, total. Dr. Westphal says he's convinced Buzz would even have sacrificed a baby to maintain control, so he believed I was doing that."

Kathleen thought that was pretty farfetched too, but she listened.

"The control issue . . . Dr. Westphal says that started when I first made up my mind to have the test. That ate at Buzz . . . he was worried about the effect of anything on his campaign . . . until he created his own reality."

Kathleen cut through it. "Deb, they're offering you a plea, a way to avoid the trial."

"What?"

Kathleen explained the proposition.

"I could be out by April . . ."

"Deb, you can't plead guilty to anything. You're not guilty."

But Deb seemed not to hear . . . "I could go to California in May." Denise had offered to find her a job. "What's to prove, Kathleen? I killed him. What difference does it make if a jury says I didn't know what I was doing?"

She obviously did not believe that would happen, or she wouldn't have said it, Kathleen thought. "When we were in the kitchen, you told me I was the one who understood."

"Yes."

"Then please trust me. You can't plead guilty, not to anything. You've got to stand up for yourself, Deb. That's the only prayer you have of starting a new life. You're *entitled* to that. It's my job, and Tony's, to see that you get it."

"But if I lose?"

Kathleen had to tell her it could be fifteen years, at best parole after five. "But if we handle this right—"

"And if they find me insane, how long do I stay in the psycho hospital?"

"Don't think of it as insane." Kathleen had gone over this repeatedly. "That's only the legal term. We have to put what happened in terms that fit the law," she said. "The test is whether you knew right from wrong at the moment you dropped the dryer. Period."

"But how long in the hospital?" Deb persisted.

"Not long." Kathleen realized she just didn't know . . . Deb *should* be released right away, but trial publicity could affect the willingness of a judge to apply the law. If the public saw a murderer, even if innocent in the eyes of the law, being turned loose too soon for their comfort . . . you couldn't answer Deb's question until after the trial.

Finally, Deb did agree. "But I'm not doing this because of your arguments," she said. "I'm doing it because of *you.*"

Kathleen blanched at that, realizing the enormous responsibility she was taking on. Well, she'd asked for it. Now step up to it.

"But don't take what I told you the wrong way," said Deb, seeing Kathleen's expression. "It's still my choice."

Tony wasn't home when she got there. She considered calling him at the office, decided not to. She had fallen asleep in one of the beanbag chairs when she heard the door open at one-fifteen.

"Tony, I've been a bitch," she said.

He kissed her.

"On top of us," she said, "I botched it with Deb on the plea bargain. Coming home, I couldn't stand myself."

"What happened?"

"You should have gone to see Deb. I think you've been right all along. I'm too involved, it's like Deb and I are merged. Same person. Fool for a lawyer, like you said."

He suggested they get coffee. With their coffees, they sat in the beanbag chairs and he listened.

"You did good, Kathleen," he said after she had finished. "You were the right person to talk to Deb. You're the one who can get Deb ready for trial."

"Did you hear what I told you about Harrison Donahey? He thinks he's helping but it could be worse than the statement, worse than Deb admitted."

"Do you think we should confront Donahey?" asked Tony.

"I just don't know," she said. "Harrison lied to us. I'm afraid of what he might do."

They talked for an hour, came to no solution. "This is a bitch of a case to try," she said. "I've been putting you in a bind." Him and maybe Deb as well, she silently added.

During October and November Kathleen met her mom for lunch, once a week if possible. She kept hoping for the closeness she had felt after she'd told her the agency file had been opened. But their luncheons were strained, aggravated by Mom's incessant questions about how things were going with Tony. After each lunch Kathleen saw how she could have done better, next time she would take the risk, and ask *her* questions. Was Mom suffering as she and Dad went about their separate lives? Did Mom have regrets? Why no children of their own? She sensed that Mom had a piece of the answer to what kept her from giving her trust to Tony.

She wondered how Mom and Dad had felt before they got married. Had Dad excited Mom the way Tony did her? Would marriage spoil what she and Tony had?

She knew what she wanted, or thought she did. To be insatiably desired by another individual. To be loved by him through everything, no matter what. But did marriage insure that? Did Tony want her enough? Was it even possible for him to want her enough for her to trust? Was it reasonable to expect it?

It seemed to her they were using Deb's case—and the good sex —to avoid such questions. And her practice was thriving . . . Columbus General wanted her to represent them in two more cases, new work had come in as a result of the supreme court decision, which had been featured in the magazine For the Defense. Si Wallace took note.

"When we make new group assignments at year end," he said, "we're going to get you more help." He took her to the Columbus Club for lunch. "You've become a rainmaker, Kathleen. Your practice has moved to a new level. The key is no longer a simple matter of how well you do the work. It's how you handle the client and your ability to delegate."

Ms. Wonderful.

But for Kathleen the long hours had become exhausting. In six fast months she felt herself on the way to becoming a burnt-out case. The products liability and medical malpractice suits, though complex and interesting, were about saving money for corporations and insurance companies.

The defense of Deb, her sister, *mattered.*

Maybe she would return to so-called normal after Deb's trial, but she doubted it. She wished she could try Deb's case in court. She envied Tony. She also worried about him. The Si Wallace luncheon indicated she had been restored to grace, but would they hold Deb's case against Tony? Tony was averaging forty-five billable hours per week on work for other partners. On two of his files she'd helped do the research, told him to bill her time as his. Associates at Latham, Fuller got evaluated in December.

She invited Marty Fleck to dinner, and said flat out she was in love. "Tony's made me see myself, *feel* myself, as a different woman. But because we're living together and he's working on a case that won't bring in a decent fee, well, I'm afraid he's going to be hurt, Marty."

Marty took her cue. She named the partners who could be a problem, promised to do what she could to turn them. "I hope you can forget my foot-in-the-mouth act at the Pewter Mug last March," Marty said.

"I got mad," said Kathleen, "because I had some of your same feelings. At the time . . ."

"This is do-able," said Marty as she left. She got halfway down the front walk, turned and came back. Kathleen was still standing in the open doorway. Marty kissed her. "I'm really happy for you," Marty said.

The next morning Kathleen wondered if she had made a mistake. Had she made herself a hopeless item of juicy gossip? A laughing-stock in the firm?

She still had not told Marty that she was at risk for HD. Except for Tony, no one at the firm knew. But after Deb's trial, someone would put the facts together, and she dreaded that prospect.

The risk, though, didn't seem to bother Tony at all. But did she really *know* what he thought? They had never talked about children. Had he thought of that part of the risk?

There was an obvious answer. She should be tested.

Kathleen picked Deb up at her new apartment in Grandview. "I think I'm as nervous as when I went to get my own results," Deb said.

"It hit me in the shower this morning," said Kathleen. What she was going to hear could change her life. Then she remembered . . . Deb didn't get a firm prediction the first time. Would it be necessary to find London Bates, her birth father, a man who might refuse to believe he'd fathered a child thirty-eight years ago?

University Hospital was decorated with plastic spruce stringers and Christmas lights. A fifteen-foot tree with white lights stood in the waiting area surrounded by neatly wrapped packages, no doubt empty boxes. Christmas was ten days away.

The same two doctors from Indiana University were seated at the table in the same small conference room. Also present were the geneticist from Ohio State and the psychologist who had counseled her. How will you prepare if you definitely have Huntington, she had been asked. She shouldn't make drastic changes, she'd been told. She was perfectly healthy. But there were things to consider. "If you decide to marry, you and your husband might want to think about adoption or, perhaps, elect not to have children."

The two sessions had been miserable. The psychologist had not pressed but knew she was keeping secrets from her childhood, was not being forthcoming about how being adopted had affected her. She got drawn into telling about Tony, revealing her fear of discussing children with him. She came across as one so needy that to some extent she was inventing the relationship. "I'm not sure I want children," she had said. "I just turned thirty-eight. My practice is coming into its prime." Why couldn't they give you a result without torturing you? She could still see the look in the psychologist's eyes. That woman, about her age, was now sitting across the table, looking at her as she had during the counseling sessions. *You're pathetic* seemed written in the woman's eyes.

"Do you still want to go forward?" The question came from Dr. Gaithers, the geneticist from Indiana.

"I want to know," she said. She signed the papers.

"It's good news. There is a ninety-eight percent probability that you do not have the Huntington gene."

Deb screamed. Jumping up, she grabbed Kathleen.

"Are you certain? Are you really sure?" Kathleen kept asking.

"After our time together," the woman psychologist said, "I know how much this means."

"I feel guilty," Kathleen said as she and Deb drove back to Deb's apartment.

"Don't," said Deb. "I couldn't have stood it if you had tested positive."

She called her office from Deb's apartment. She asked Connie to find Tony. She hadn't told Tony about the test. Just as Deb had not told Buzz about the test of her fetus . . .

"What is it?" Tony sounded out of breath.

"I'm clean," she said. "I had the test."

They had dinner at Spagio's to celebrate. "When did you change your mind?" he asked.

"I just couldn't tell you, Tony. I don't know what I would have done if the test had gone the other way. Can you understand?"

Under the table, he reached for her hand. His was warmer than hers. "Did you change your mind because of us?" he asked.

She nodded. "There's so much I need to tell you," she said. "There're things that make it hard for me to trust you." He looked like she'd slapped his face. "It's *not* you," she said quickly. "It goes way back. Please, Tony, could we put this talk off until after the trial?"

She could feel his disappointment, though he squeezed her hand and kept looking at her.

"You're still not sure," he said.

"I'm sure I want to be," she said. "Can we leave it at that?"

He grinned. What else, after all, could he do . . . except walk away. And that was the last thing he wanted to do.

*   *   *

The firm Christmas party was to be held on Friday night. At eleven-thirty on Friday morning five senior associates, including Laura Redding and Jay Melnik, assembled in Si Wallace's office to be given the news they'd dreamed of hearing for six years. They would become partners in Latham, Fuller and Richards commencing January first.

After the short meeting and a glass of sherry with Wallace, a memo was dispatched to all partners and associates. The elected five went down to the Pewter Mug to receive congratulations. The firm furnished the beer, ordered a buffet table of food and paid for the exclusive use of the café. It was a firm tradition. Partners and associates would drift down, offer congratulations until it was time to change into tuxedos and go to the Christmas party. Black tie for the party was another firm tradition.

"Next year it will be you," Kathleen said as she and Tony went down to the celebration.

"I'm not counting on it," he said. He was apprehensive about his meeting with Chip Drucker and the Group Evaluating Committee that was set for Monday at ten.

The party had been going on for over two hours when she and Tony arrived. Laura Redding stood on top of a table with her shoes off, taking swallows as beer mugs were handed up. Two more tables were being pushed through the crowd, shoved against Laura's table.

"Get them all up there," shouted Chip Drucker. Laura kept one of the beer mugs she'd been handed and emptied it on Jay Melnik's head as he climbed up. Soon all five were drenched. Laura had taken off her jacket and her lacy bra could be seen beneath a clinging white blouse. Kathleen shook her head, remembering how she'd endured the ritual seven years ago and hated it.

Si Wallace stood at the back of the cafe, smiling tightly, not participating. When Laura Redding hiked her skirt and extended her leg so an associate could kiss her stocking-clad toes in mock-servitude to the new partner, Wallace moved in, banged an empty mug on one of the tables, waggled the mug, inviting Chip Drucker to fill it from the pitcher Chip was carrying. "I have a toast," Wallace said, lifting his mug. "To the future of Latham, Fuller and Richards. And to these five upon whom the brightness of the future depends."

Wallace extended his hand, offering Laura Redding assistance in getting down from the table. Kathleen admired Wallace's ability at least to nip an incident before it happened.

She and Tony then made the rounds, congratulating each of the five. In Tony's position, as one of those next in line to be considered, he had to stay. But Kathleen left as soon as she had done her duty.

On Monday, after Tony received his year-end evaluation, he and Kathleen drove out to Hunan Gardens for lunch. "Next year isn't out of the question," he said, "but I think they'll make me wait."

"We'll see," she said. With Marty Fleck's help, at least progress had been made.

"They told me this is the most important year for me since I joined the firm," he said. "There are still doubters and it's up to me to convince them. They told me who the doubters are. Each one is to give me a project." The doubters were the ones Kathleen and Marty had identified.

"They want to see a more goal-oriented work effort," Tony said. " 'Convince us you want to make money—for yourself and for the firm,' Chip Drucker said. Lloyd Arthur told me, 'The best partners are greedy sons of bitches.' They thought it was a real hoot."

"It's a survival year," she said. "You grovel, I'll help you do it."

"I don't know," he said. "Maybe it's living with you. I know Deb's case has affected me. Partnership in Latham, Fuller isn't exactly the trophy I once thought. *You* aren't a greedy son of a bitch. And there's no stronger partner in the firm."

"Look at it this way," she said, putting aside her recent feelings about Latham, Fuller. "This is a great firm. After you get in, you have more flexibility—to pick your work and whom you work with."

"Maybe," he said. "Hey, maybe I want it so bad I'm easing the pressure by making excuses in advance."

But he didn't think so.

* * *

On Tuesday, the week after New Year's Day, Laura Redding came into Kathleen's office and closed the door. "Have you got a minute? Marty urged me to come directly to you."

"I have time," said Kathleen, although she didn't.

Laura sat in Kathleen's favored-client chair. "It's about Tony Biviano," she said.

"I guessed."

"I can't see Tony as a partner."

"Why?"

Laura was losing some of her poise, fiddling with the sleeve of her blouse. She couldn't meet Kathleen's stare. "It's been four years, and I thought it was over, that I wouldn't say anything. I guess being made partner has given me more confidence. Guts. Whatever." Laura talked in the singsong cadence of yuppie-speak. She looked at Kathleen, as though expecting permission to go on. Kathleen wasn't giving it. She was on her own.

"This is painful, Kathleen. I made the mistake of letting Tony snow me . . . and we had an affair for a year. I admit it takes two to tango. But . . . well, I thought he really cared about me." She went on to say she had cut the relationship off when she found out he was having one-night stands with Chip Drucker's secretary, which came out when the secretary's husband caught them and called Drucker. "After Tony and I split, some others, you know, came forward, told me their stories . . ."

Kathleen had heard none of this, at least not the specifics.

Laura, seeing Kathleen's face turn red, rushed on to say she wanted to be *fair*. She'd heard no rumors in the past three years, "but I have misgivings," she said. "I mean, you're a big girl, Kathleen, but how will Tony treat the younger women when and if he's a partner?"

Kathleen wanted to scream, tell her to get the hell out of her office. Instead she smiled sweetly and said, "This took a great deal of courage, Laura. I'm glad you came to me. I really am."

Somehow she got Laura out of her office, then called Marty Fleck. "I've been waiting for your call," Marty said. "I'll be right up."

"Laura's an unhappy, frustrated woman, dredging up ancient

history," Marty said. "She's jealous. What she says tells more about her than Tony . . ."

Marty had wanted to tell Kathleen about Drucker's secretary back in March at the Pewter Mug, "but then when I saw what was happening between you and Tony, I was damn glad I didn't."

Kathleen was furious. More at the women trying to protect her, if that's what it was, than at Tony's previous affairs. Still . . .

"It can be managed," said Marty. "I carry more weight than Laura Redding, especially on a woman's issue. I think I can convince Miss Roundheels that bad-mouthing Tony could hurt her more than him."

After Marty left, Kathleen sat at her desk, unable to concentrate on any work. When she imagined the gossip in the firm, herself and Tony the juice of that gossip, she felt like having no more to do with *any* of them.

And what of this did she tell Tony? Nothing, she decided. Not a damn thing.

She had invited Tony to spend Christmas with her and her parents at the big house on the river. All day she had watched him handle her mom. Incredibly, her mom, the devout churchgoer, hadn't once criticized her decision to let Tony move in with her. Mom, she decided, thought she needed help and wasn't really capable of attracting and holding an eligible man. Maybe that was a harsh judgment, but it did seem that way.

Christmas night she and Tony had exchanged presents. He gave her a pearl necklace, she gave him an attaché case. "I want something from me on your table during the trial," she had said.

Tony was not the man Laura Redding thought or implied. Like Marty said, "He stopped playing around when he fell for you." During January and February, as the trial date neared, she kept reassuring herself with that.

The night before trial she couldn't sleep. Tony in bed beside her was rolling from one side to the other, making a shambles of the covers. This was more difficult than if she were going into the courtroom. She'd spent hours and hours working on Deb, and Deb still wasn't ready to withstand cross-examination. "She will be by the time she takes the oath," Kathleen had promised Tony.

What kind of juror would be best? Working women, they'd

decided. Catholics and right-to-lifers could go either way, would have to be carefully evaluated. Who should be avoided? She thought blue-collar housewives; he would boot "any man who wouldn't let his wife have her own checking account."

They drove separate cars to the Hall of Justice, Kathleen taking Deb, who had moved into their spare bedroom on Friday night. They got to the courtroom at eight, an hour before court would open. Tony picked the counsel table that faced the jury box. Kathleen got Deb settled in a small room adjacent to the courtroom. It was the one reserved for defense counsel and the defendant.

"I'll stay with Deb until court opens," said Kathleen. Socko Bender had filed for a separation of witnesses, so she would not be allowed in the courtroom except when she testified.

Kathleen was intensely aware of the risks now. If the jury found Deb not guilty by reason of insanity, might not Deb be held for months or longer in the Central Ohio Psychiatric Hospital? What if a judge, facing an election, decided Deb wasn't "fit to rejoin society?"

Kathleen knew Deb must be thinking the same or worse. Fifteen years, with HD, could be all the life Deb had left.

V
The Trial

In criminal law and as a defense to an accusation of crime, insanity means such a perverted and deranged condition of the mental and moral faculties as to render the person incapable of distinguishing between right and wrong, or to render (her) at the time unconscious of the nature of the act (she) is committing, or such that, though (she) may be conscious of it and also of its normal quality, so as to know that the act in question is wrong, yet (her) will or volition has been—otherwise than voluntarily—so completely destroyed that (her) actions are not subject to it but are beyond (her) control. Or, as otherwise stated, insanity is such a state of mental derangement that the subject is incompetent of having a criminal intent, or incapable of so controlling his will as to avoid doing the act in question.

—BLACK'S LAW DICTIONARY

Chapter 16

I<small>T WAS TUESDAY</small> morning, the second day of trial. Voir dire was finished; a jury of eight women and four men had been sworn in. Two alternates were seated outside and next to the jury box. Tony had never felt more alone. He was aware of Deb beside him at counsel table, could hear her breathe and move as she adjusted herself in her chair. Except for Deb and himself, it seemed, everyone in gallery-packed Courtroom 9A knew what they were supposed to be doing.

In the center of the pit the court reporter's fingers played on her stenotype machine as mechanically as if the case involved a tenant eviction. Junior Fultz, Judge Conklin's seventy-five-year-old bailiff, who had been bored and working a crossword during the voir dire, was sitting jauntily erect behind his small desk as he auditioned Socko Bender's opening statement.

Bender stood at the jury box, his arms spread, his hands resting on the rail. He was confiding to the jurors in a rumbling voice that could be heard at the back of the gallery but that excluded everyone except the twelve in the box and the two alternates. At Bender's side was a cardboard mock-up of the vanity island, the floor and the Jacuzzi section of the Garrison bathroom. A red circle was drawn around the electrical outlet on the Jacuzzi side of the vanity and about halfway between the floor and the countertop.

"This is murder." Bender held the 1,500–watt hair dryer in his hand. "She had to take a step, bend and deliberately drop this into the water."

Tony considered an objection. Argument was improper during opening statements. But jurors were craning forward, eager to watch the demonstration. They might think he was trying to keep them from understanding. What would Kathleen have done? He wished there were a lawyer, any lawyer, at his side. With two, maybe he wouldn't feel that he didn't belong in a murder trial.

"The cord was seven feet long." Bender held the dryer up, letting the plug end scrape the floor. "If the defendant had not acted deliberately . . ." Bender inserted the plug in the outlet ". . . even if she had thrown the dryer in anger . . ." He paused, pointed with his free hand to the tub and then to the outlet. "If she hadn't known exactly what she wanted to do, the plug would have pulled out.

"Or, if this dryer had slipped out of her hand when she was standing at the vanity," said Bender, "it could not have fallen in the Jacuzzi. So this was no accident." He demonstrated, stopping short of releasing the dryer from his hand.

"The evidence will show that the defendant had decided to divorce Buzz. She wasn't honest enough to tell him, but she wanted to be rid of him. She was biding her time. Now, we don't say she planned this murder days in advance. But we do say that when the opportunity came, the rage she had suppressed took over and she seized it."

Bender stepped back from the rail. "The physical facts," he said, "tell us everything. Witnesses can have faulty memories. The defendant may give you a different story if she is brazen enough to take the stand."

"Object." Tony rose from his chair as he spoke.

"The facts will stop her if she tries to tell you she meant no harm to her husband." Bender had shouted the words over Tony's objection and the rap of Judge Conklin's gavel.

Judge Conklin was angry. He declared a recess, asked the jury to stay in place and summoned counsel to his chambers. In chambers, he remained standing. "Do you want a mistrial?" he asked Tony.

"Your Honor," said Bender. "May I be heard?"

"You may not," snapped Judge Conklin. "You have flagrantly —and I'm sure deliberately—violated the defendant's Fifth Amendment right to remain silent."

"Mr. Biviano has indicated that she will testify. She has entered a plea of NGRI." Bender wasn't one to let a judge browbeat him.

"She has not testified yet," said the judge. "The right to remain silent has not been waived and you know it." The judge turned to Tony.

What should he do? If he took a mistrial, could he argue double jeopardy? Usually a mistrial was good for the defendant— the evidence grew colder. But this wasn't a usual case. Also, a postponement would be hard for Deb, maybe unbearable. What would Kathleen do?

"May I have a recess to confer with my client and examine the law?" he asked.

"No," said the judge. "I've blocked two weeks on my calendar for this trial and I expect to meet that deadline."

There was another consideration. In two weeks, Conklin might start him on an ulcer, but Conklin would keep Bender in line. Bender had worked the criminal courtrooms for twenty years. Tony also remembered Deb's remark, that Buzz Garrison thought he'd taken a screwing every time he tried a case in Conklin's courtroom. On a second trial, they couldn't draw a more favorable judge.

Then there was the jury. Despite the attention they were giving Bender, Tony liked the panel. "We don't want a mistrial," he said. "But the jury should be instructed to disregard Mr. Bender's argument."

"I intend to do that." Conklin was on his way into the courtroom. Behind the judge's back, Bender was grinning.

As Judge Conklin announced his ruling and gave the curative instruction, Tony realized he should have demanded that the court stenographer make a record on the refusal to let him consult with his client. Without a record, the error was lost for appeal.

"Here's the question the defense can't answer." Bender was winding up his opening statement. It was nearly noon and he wanted the jury to think about what he'd told them as they ate lunch. "Who," Bender asked, "heard the defendant say she had been accused of abortion by her husband? Her mother? Her father? Any of her friends? Her OB-GYN? Her family doctor?

"None of them." Bender thundered the answer. "Isn't it strange? The defendant won't be supported by any of the people you'd expect." Bender lowered his voice to a husky whisper. "The only one," he said as he turned away from the jury and pointed at Tony, "is that man's partner. Ladies and gentlemen, it's not much of a case when one of the lawyers has to supply the evidence that no one else saw or heard." Bender returned to his table as Judge Conklin gaveled the noon recess. And Tony saw, very clearly, why Bender wanted Tony to be the trial counsel in a case that would turn on the credibility of Kathleen's testimony.

"This case is about a state of mind," Tony began. He was playing it straight, standing behind the movable lectern three feet in front of the jury box. He couldn't beat Bender at dramatics, but he could be the frightened young lawyer struggling to get out the truth and see that his client was treated fairly.

"Try to put yourselves in Deb Garrison's shoes," he said as he neared the end of his statement. The jurors were giving him the same close attention they had paid to Bender.

"Deb Garrison has lost her baby. You're going to hear—not just from her but from her doctors—how badly she wanted that baby. Yes, she and her husband had fought over whether it would be right to abort a diseased fetus. But Deb's baby did *not* have a genetic disease and she wanted that baby more than anything—so much that it could not diminish her joy to hear that she herself had the fatal disease.

"When she tells her husband about the test and the good news about their baby, he can't hear what she's telling him because he's so upset that she had the test. He's so upset that he forgets to ask Deb whether she has the HD gene. Then he misinterprets her, suspects that she is lying to him about wanting the baby.

"He was, of course, wrong about that. Tragically wrong. The evidence will prove that beyond any possible doubt.

"Buzz Garrison's suspicions eat at him. He thinks he knows the reason—he has guessed that Deb will divorce him; he thinks she no longer wants the baby. He thinks his future in politics is in jeopardy. Worse than that, there is nothing he can do about it.

"He just didn't get it—hadn't since he and Deb learned about the risk of Huntington's disease. He didn't understand that it was his obsession to control Deb utterly that drove her to the realization that divorce was inevitable.

"He is consumed by his campaign and the need to keep up with his law practice. As his suspicions fester, he convinces himself that Deb is trying to sabotage his campaign. He has no sensitivity to the hurt she feels at having lost her baby. He doesn't appreciate the sacrifice she is making to get him elected.

"How does he repay her for helping to get him elected? Oh, he's nice enough when other people are looking. But at home he's something else. He *threatens* Deb. He *smashes* her face, *bruises* her. Deb was *terrified*. You will hear evidence of just how frightened. You will understand why she decided on divorce to save herself, and why she was afraid to tell him of her intentions in the middle of his campaign for Congress.

"So, let's move to the night of June thirteenth, the night when tragedy caught up with this couple. Deb is suffering from a clinical postpartum depression because she has lost a baby that meant more to her than life. She is struggling to go out, fix herself up, get on the campaign trail and look good for her husband. She'll do it even though he has given her no support—considered it 'bad timing' for his campaign when Deb's mother tried suicide, when Deb herself was diagnosed with Huntington's disease.

"But she's getting herself ready, trying to please him, trying to forget the loss of her baby. Then he unloads on her with what he's been brooding about. *He accuses her of killing her baby.*"

The jury was with him. He could feel the response as he explained Dr. Westphal's expected testimony; that the accusation had triggered a reactive psychosis.

"Deb herself—and you will hear her testify—hardly knows what she did. She reacted without any conscious mental process. She reacted to, in effect, a knife that had been stuck in her stomach a week before, a knife that had been twisted until she was in so much pain she didn't know what she was doing. Then he stabs her again. The worst cut of all. Her reaction was a reflex. Temporary insanity, self-defense. Both together. *But it was not murder.*"

Tony felt drained but satisfied as he walked back to counsel table, took out his handkerchief and wiped his forehead.

"Call your first witness." Judge Conklin looked at Bender. Tony had expected a recess, wanted to telephone Kathleen. There was no time to rethink his opening statement, to indulge his feeling that the case could be won if Deb, Dr. Westphal and Kathleen came through.

Bender led with the 911 operator, followed with the investigator from the Bureau of Criminal Investigation who had constructed the model. The coroner pronounced the cause of death as heart failure secondary to receipt of an electrical shock. A police sergeant testified that no physical change had taken place in the bathroom from his arrival on the scene until the completion of the investigation two weeks later. A fingerprint man from the BCI put Deb's prints on the dryer. It was marked State Exhibit A.

Bender called an electrical engineer. "When the dryer hit the water, Mr. Garrison's body became part of the circuit. It was not grounded and one hundred ten volts surged through his body. It's much different than the jolt you might get if you put your finger into a socket. There you might be grounded on carpet. But in water—it's almost like putting someone in the electric chair."

"What then," asked Bender, "would be the natural and probable consequence of putting a live appliance into a Jacuzzi when someone is immersed?"

"Death by electrocution."

Tony had conducted no cross-examination. He couldn't impeach the electrical engineer and questions would reinforce the grisly impression. The other witnesses had nothing to do with his defense.

Judge Conklin recessed court for the day. He was pleased with progress. In chambers, he ruled against Bender's proffer of the "confession the defendant made to the police when they arrived on the scene."

"*Miranda,*" the judge said. He didn't want to see the brief Kathleen had prepared. Though expected, the ruling was still a relief. In a Bender prosecution you worried about a cop claiming Deb said, "I killed the bastard, finally got the chance I'd been waiting for."

* * *

They had dropped Deb at the house, stopped by a Chinese carry-out and gone to the office. Kathleen wasn't saying so, but she saw the mistake in not making a record in chambers.

"The way Bender seems to be trying the case," said Kathleen, "Harrison Donahey's testimony could kill us. Still, he doesn't want to hurt Deb. I think we should go see him."

"I don't know," said Tony. "Won't it look worse if he changes his story?"

"I thought so," said Kathleen, "but maybe we can figure a way to cross-examine him."

Jill answered the door. Her hands shook worse than Tony remembered. "Harrison is in his study," she said. "You go up. I don't feel like climbing stairs."

"I'll be there in a minute," said Kathleen. "I want to talk to Jill." . . .

Harrison Donahey took books off a battered armchair to make a place where Tony could sit.

"I know why you're here," Deb's father said. "Let me make it easy. I am not going to testify against Debbie. They can put me in jail but they can't put me on the witness stand."

"Do you still think it was an accident?" Tony asked, deciding to wait for Kathleen before reacting to Donahey's threat to disobey the state's subpoena.

"I do," said Donahey. "But I can see you want to try the case differently. I can see where my testimony could work against Debbie. I won't do it."

"Didn't Deb tell you her husband had accused her of aborting the baby?"

"She may have." Donahey flipped his hand, scattering papers on his desk.

"You knew they'd been arguing?"

Donahey, in the process of reassembling his paperwork, looked up. "I thought she was hysterical, didn't know what she was saying."

"You could admit that, say you were just trying to protect her."

Tony waited, giving Donahey time to consider the escape he'd been offered.

"No," Donahey finally said. "I'm not going to testify. I'll end up making it worse."

Maybe he was right. Donahey was looking over Tony's shoulder as Kathleen came in.

"Dr. Donahey is going to refuse the state's subpoena," said Tony.

"I'll spend my life in prison first," said Donahey.

"Does the prosecutor know?" asked Kathleen.

"Of course, he does." Donahey's answer caught Tony by surprise. He had assumed from Bender's demeanor in court that Bender did not know.

"What was Bender's reaction?" asked Kathleen.

" 'If you prefer jail, that's your privilege' is what he said. That was after his threats, after he saw I wouldn't budge. Bender is not a nice person. To put it mildly."

"Right," said Tony. "Double right."

"I never realized when he was running the campaign," Donahey said. "You understand I would *never* have given the man a statement if he hadn't promised that Debbie wouldn't be tried for murder. After the investigation and the furor died down, the charges were supposed to be dropped. Bender said he needed my statement to support a decision not to press the charge."

"Have you confronted him about it?" Tony asked.

"He says he agreed to drop the charge but you refused."

"Because he insisted on pleading to voluntary manslaughter and jail time," Kathleen said.

"I know. The man never told me that part." Narrowing his eyes, Donahey fixed them on Kathleen like a professor grilling an unprepared student. "Are you certain it wasn't a mistake to reject Bender's proposition?"

"In a trial, nothing is certain, but Deb is not guilty. A plea could ruin her life . . ."

"Well, that's over the dam," said Donahey. "And I can tell you I am not going to testify."

On the way back to the office Kathleen was quiet. Donahey probably had her second-guessing herself again. Bender might still offer the plea—it wasn't necessarily over the dam, as Donahey had said. But there was no time for a postmortem on plea bargaining. It was already after ten. Tony needed to prepare to cross-examine the nurse from Deb's miscarriage and the patient on the other side of the curtain. When court recessed, he had seen the nurse waiting in the back corridor.

Wednesday was not a good day. It surprised Tony when Bender called the patient ahead of the nurse. Grace Jaeger was a young blonde with an innocent face. Several jurors nodded as she testified. Stung, Tony attacked her on cross. "You only saw Buzz Garrison in the hospital," he said. "How would you know if he accused Deb of having an abortion at some other time?" He knew better. You never asked a hostile witness the *why* question.

Grace Jaeger smiled and looked at the jury, all sincerity. "I know because he was the kindest, most understanding husband you could imagine," she said. "I was there right after the miscarriage and anyone who says he thought she induced an abortion is lying."

It was outrageous, but the jury seemed to be buying it. That should have taught him. But he did worse with the nurse.

"You promised Mr. Garrison your vote," he'd said. "Wouldn't you describe Mr. Garrison as a candidate trying to make a good impression?" It was a clumsy question, a point better left for summation. But he was trying to recover from Grace Jaeger.

"If you're saying Mr. Garrison was trying to impress me," said nurse Ivy Phillips, "you couldn't be more wrong. I paused in the doorway before I entered the room. It was so sweet, the way Mr. Garrison was with his wife. He couldn't have known I was listening."

Then Ted Gill, the Democratic county chairman, testified, and it was a tribute to Buzz as a husband and human being. "Buzz realized his wife wanted a divorce," said Gill. "He thought I should know in case I heard rumors. He also thought they could solve their problems after the campaign."

If Wednesday was bad, Thursday got worse. The state's alienist, Dr. Ryne Durenberg, had credentials that would have impressed Freud. With Dr. Westphal's help, Tony had planned a cross based on questions Westphal said would "pin Durenberg to the wall." The questions served as opportunities for Durenberg to conduct mini-seminars for the jury on the theory of psychosis.

Using a blackboard, Durenberg had listed the "episodes" he considered "therapeutically significant." After presenting each episode, the doctor concluded, "This convinces me, beyond all question, that Mrs. Garrison was able to delineate right from wrong. There was no psychosis, brief or otherwise."

But the worst was yet to come. After recess for the day, Bender asked Judge Conklin if he "could be heard in chambers on a procedural matter."

The judge was relaxed, pleased with the number of witnesses that had been called. The trial would meet his schedule. He tossed his robe on the sofa, suggested that his secretary bring coffee. The judge, instead of sitting behind his desk, took one of the chairs in front, joining a circle formed by the lawyers and the court reporter. "Be my guest," he'd said with a wave of his hand when Bender requested permission to make a record.

"Harrison Donahey refused the subpoena of the court," Bender began.

The transformation of Judge Conklin's personality was instantaneous. In short, angry questions, Conklin elicited the facts. He directed his bailiff to summon a deputy sheriff. "Send out a cruiser," he told the deputy. "Bring the man in and hold him overnight in the lockup."

The deputy dispatched, Conklin turned his reddened face on Tony. "What do you know about this?"

"We saw the witness on Tuesday night, but—"

"We? Who is *we?*"

"Myself and Ms. Sullivan."

"All right." The judge glared at Bender. "I want this investigated."

"Certainly, Your Honor," said Bender.

"The court is considering several possibilities." Conklin fixed Tony with a vindictive stare. "One is referral to the board of discipline and grievances. A second is whether Ms. Sullivan will be permitted to testify."

"Kathleen, it was a bloodbath," said Tony. They were in her office, Tony slouched in her favored-client chair.

"It's never as bad as you think," she said, but without much conviction.

"I think we should see if the plea bargain is still on the table," Tony said.

"No," she said. "You don't settle when the case has taken a torpedo. You wait for a turn. There's always a turn. If we have to negotiate we'll do it after Dr. Westphal testifies."

"I'm telling you, Kathleen, I think the judge is after our ass too."

"We haven't violated any canon," she said. "Cool it and see what happens tomorrow." . . .

When they got home Deb was in a serious funk, worried that she couldn't go through with the trial. "That Dr. Durenberg was right," she said. "I knew what I was doing."

Just what Tony needed to hear.

The night's sleep apparently did not improve Judge Conklin's mood. "No one will put himself above this court of law," he announced to open the discussion. "Now. Where is Ms. Sullivan?" he asked, looking at Tony.

"I'm sorry, Your Honor. I hadn't understood that you—"

"I told you to have her here this morning."

He hadn't, but Tony apologized, said he would make a call. "Do that right here so we can listen." The judge pointed to the phone on his desk.

Kathleen got there in ten minutes.

"All right," said Judge Conklin. "Bring in the witness."

The professor, handcuffed, was escorted into chambers by a deputy. He had not shaved and appeared to have slept little during his night in the lockup.

Judge Conklin proceeded to lecture the professor. Frequently using the phrase "you lib professors who think you are above the law," Conklin described what was in store. It would be the county jail for starters, until the end of the term. "I wonder," said the judge, "if you lib professors know how it is in the county jail when you get no favors."

Harrison would not be intimidated, even when the judge told him he would beg for a second chance after the third night. As Harrison stood his ground, Judge Conklin's face grew redder.

"This is judicial brutality," said Harrison.

"No one is above the law," Conklin said. "This jury is entitled to know what you saw and heard."

"I further want it recorded that I've made my own decision," said Harrison. "The defense lawyers had nothing to do with it. In fact, they didn't know until after I'd talked to Mr. Bender." Harrison looked at Bender as if he were an untouchable. Bender smiled.

"All right," said the judge, "we've wasted forty-five minutes. We're going into the courtroom."

"I will say nothing in the courtroom," said Harrison.

"Take the cuffs off," said Judge Conklin.

Harrison refused to budge from the chair in which he had been placed. He sat surrounded by lawyers, the robed judge, Bailiff Fultz and two deputies.

"Put the cuffs back on," Judge Conklin ordered. "Put him in the witness box. When you have him in place, bring in the jury."

"With all due respect," said Tony, "this deprives my client of a fair trial."

The judge looked at him. "Your client does not have a right to prevent the jury from hearing material testimony," he said, and proceeded out to the courtroom.

The jury came in, the bailiff convened court. Tony walked across the well toward the court stenographer. "Counsel, take your seat," said the judge.

"I'm going to make my record," said Tony. "If you prefer, I'll do it from counsel table."

Conklin glared at him, then swiveled, turning his back as Tony bent to whisper to the reporter. In open court the stenographer would record everything said. Conklin knew it was not the place to retaliate.

"Swear the witness," Judge Conklin told Bailiff Junior Fultz when Tony returned to counsel table.

Though Harrison was unable to raise his hand, the oath was read to him. Harrison did not nod or blink. "Let the record reflect that the witness has been duly sworn," said Judge Conklin. "You may proceed, Mr. Bender."

"Did you have a conversation with your daughter on the night of June thirteenth of last year?" Bender was standing behind the jury box so he could watch the jury and force the professor to look at the jurors.

Harrison stared at Bender but didn't move his lips.

"Your Honor," said Bender. "Request permission to treat the witness as hostile."

"Without objection, so ordered."

Tony let it pass. He was in enough trouble and objection on the point would mean little.

"Are you taking the Fifth Amendment?" asked Bender.

Harrison stared at Bender.

"Aren't you really of the opinion that your daughter committed murder but tried to put a less damaging face on it in your statement—?"

Tony stood to object.

"Sit down," said Judge Conklin.

Tony sat. "I object," he said loud enough to be heard out in the lobby.

"Well?" Bender looked at Donahey as if he would wait all morning for an answer. Harrison kept staring.

"It's all right," Deb blurted. "Dad, you can answer his questions."

Tony didn't need that, the defendant practically confessing. Deb still didn't seem to understand what could happen to her. She still felt she did mean to kill Buzz, or at least wasn't sure she didn't.

Harrison shook his head. "The jury is instructed to disregard the defendant's comment, she was not under oath," Judge Conklin told the jury.

Bender walked slowly around the jury box, past the witness and back to his counsel table. He picked up Harrison's signed statement. He asked the stenographer to mark it as State Exhibit R. He folded the first three pages under and held the fourth in front of Harrison's face. Harrison refused to look at it. "Is this your signature, given under oath?" Bender asked.

Harrison held himself rigidly, not moving his head.

"Your Honor," said Bender. "We can prove attestation. Subject to doing that, may I read the statement to the witness?"

"You may."

"Tell us, Mr. Donahey, if any part of this is not what you swore to."

"Object." Tony spoke as he rose. "There is no basis in the law for putting this before the jury."

"Mr. Bender," said Judge Conklin, "you should move for admission before you read the statement."

"The state moves the admission of State Exhibit R."

"Mr. Donahey," said the judge. "You have been shown your statement. Do you wish to change it in any way?"

Harrison refused to look at the judge. "Very well," said Conklin. "It will be admitted, subject to proof of attestation." Conklin looked at Tony. "Does the defense contest attestation?"

"No," said Tony. "But we strenuously object."

"The jury may take the statement with them when they retire for deliberation," Judge Conklin ruled. "Mr. Bender, do you want to read it to the jury now?"

"If I may, Your Honor."

Tony endured as jurors glanced at him and Deb during the reading. They stared at Deb when Bender, who obviously had practiced and was getting the most out of what Harrison had signed, read—"She told me it was an accident, that there had been no argument. She was getting ready to go out and turned to answer a question Buzz asked. The hair dryer slipped out of her hand. She wasn't sure, thought maybe her hands were wet."

The mail carrier, juror number five, was looking at Tony. His look asked the question—Why did you lie to us in your opening statement? You said she was not guilty by reason of insanity, now it's an accident? You can't have it both ways.

Bender returned to counsel table, held a whispered conference with his assistants. "The state rests," he announced, obviously pleased. The defendant's own father had just contradicted her defense.

Judge Conklin nodded. "Defendant's motions for judgment of acquittal will all be overruled," he said. "Mr. Biviano, call your first witness."

"Your Honor," said Tony. "May we have a recess? We anticipated that Mr. Bender would call additional witnesses." There had been eight more names on Bender's list. Tony had also counted on motions being presented in chambers before Judge Conklin overruled them.

"Call your witness," said the judge.

"We have a procedural matter," said Tony. "It should be addressed in chambers." He was desperate. Though Harrison had signed the statement—there was no doubt about his signature—

Tony wished he'd forced the State to prove attestation. It would at least have given the defense time.

Tony started toward the bench, trying to come up with a request that might stand a chance. Judge Conklin waved him back. "We will consider your procedural matter during the morning recess," he said.

In the small doorway to the side of the bench, the one used by Bailiff Fultz, Kathleen was waving her hand. She was mouthing the name *Calder*.

"The defense calls Dr. Malcolm Calder," Tony announced. Junior Fultz roused himself, shuffled back through the gallery and out the doors leading into the lobby. He called the name. Dr. Malcolm Calder came through the doors, down the center aisle, opened the gate to the bar, stepped into the pit and raised his hand to be sworn.

Kathleen had sized up the situation, gotten on the telephone.

Calder testified impressively and in great detail, describing the HD test—first for Deb, then for her fetus. Tony followed each answer with clarifying questions.

"Is all of this necessary?" Judge Conklin asked.

"Yes, Your Honor. It is vital to the defense."

After the morning break, Tony asked Dr. Calder to describe the first and second conferences between Deb and the team of geneticists. Maybe Kathleen had briefed the doctor, or maybe he saw what Tony was doing. The doctor was enlarging his answers, reporting everything said by every person who'd attended those conferences. Tony made it to the lunch break.

In the afternoon he followed the same tactic with Dr. Weingard, Deb's OB-GYN. Enduring the withering looks from Judge Conklin, he consumed the afternoon. Fortunately it was Friday and the judge didn't want to keep the jury late.

Kathleen was waiting at the car when he and Deb got to the Hall of Justice garage. They would need every minute of the weekend to consider changes in the defense, repair the damage from Harrison's statement, made naïvely to help Deb and, as used by Bender, doing the opposite. And they had to get Deb ready to testify.

Deb, without speaking to Kathleen, climbed into the back seat.

"I came to the garage," said Kathleen. "It seemed best not to be seen near the courtroom." She and Tony stood outside the car.

"God," said Tony. "We can't take another day like this one."

"How did the doctors do?" asked Kathleen.

"Bender couldn't touch either one on cross. He really didn't try very hard."

"Good," said Kathleen. "Those were important witnesses." She looked in the car window. Deb was slumped against the door, her eyes closed. "Is she all right?" Kathleen asked quietly.

"During the morning recess she told me she would never accept a plea bargain from Bender after what he did to her dad."

Kathleen kissed him. "You did good," she said.

"Yeah. Real good. I sat there and watched the case go down the tubes—"

"No, no. You hung in there, took a beating from the judge. That's the mark of a real lawyer."

"Harrison could cost us the case," he said.

"Maybe not . . . this may work out better than if Harrison had actually testified. He was, after all, a problem either way. We've known that."

"Kathleen, you weren't there."

"Sometimes jurors don't like it when the judge seems unfair."

"But they didn't see the worst he did."

"Well, letting that statement in is at least grounds for reversal . . ."

"Kathleen," he said, "if you hadn't been thinking . . . if you hadn't gotten Calder there, he'd have made me put Deb on the stand."

"Come on." She opened the passenger door. "The weekend will be gone before we know it. We've got to get Deb ready. If the jury believes Deb *and* if Deb holds up . . ."

She didn't finish. She didn't have to. *If, if* . . . maybe it at least would no longer be a lock on losing.

Chapter 17

"I WANT TO stay with Mom tonight." Deb, in the back seat, had not spoken as Tony was giving Kathleen a detailed account of what Judge Conklin had done to Harrison Donahey. They were pulling into Kathleen's driveway in German Village.

"Deb," said Kathleen, "you are the next witness. We're going to work with you all weekend—every hour that you aren't eating or sleeping."

Deb did not answer. She had been reduced to a ten-year-old, pouting, her head turned to watch three joggers laugh as they came up the City Park sidewalk at an easy gait.

Deb, ready or not, had to testify on Monday morning. "We must know what she says in court before you put Dr. Westphal on the stand," Kathleen had told Tony a month earlier. It was the only way to make sure Deb did not contradict the assumptions the psychiatrist would be given when he was asked to render his opinion.

If Deb were stronger it would be better to call her as the last witness. They certainly did not want to end with the psychiatrist. So it was decided that Kathleen would be the anchor. The responsibility would be hers to support Deb's story, give the defense an emotional charge just before final arguments and deliberation.

In the garage, Deb stayed in the car. Kathleen opened the door. "Let's get something to eat before we go to work." Deb didn't answer.

What should they do? Pull her out of the car? What if she decided she didn't want to testify? That was a defendant's right, and the court would support her. It was ironic, Kathleen thought, remembering cases she'd heard about where the defendant had insisted on testifying—against the lawyer's recommendation—and gone to jail for the insistence. But in this case, you couldn't win *without* Deb—especially after the jury had heard Harrison Donahey's statement. If Deb balked, she would need to bring her toiletries on the last day of trial.

"Okay, we'll take you to Jill's," said Kathleen. "But, Deb, you must promise to be ready when we come to get you at seven tomorrow morning." She'd made the decision without consulting Tony. Deb was *her* responsibility. But God, would Deb accept the bargain? Would Deb, after a night with Jill, be any more receptive tomorrow morning?

They climbed the steps to Jill's house and rang the chimes. Jill did not answer. Using Deb's key, they let themselves in. They found Jill fully dressed, in the bedroom. "I thought it was another reporter." Jill was having trouble talking. She took a drink from the glass of water on her bureau. "I've stopped answering the phone."

Deb hugged her mom. The two sat on the bed, holding each other. "You must . . ." Jill lost her voice. Deb got the water glass; Jill gulped a swallow. ". . . do something about Harrison." Jill hadn't talked to him, but knew from reporters' calls that he was in the county jail.

Kathleen promised. It was another thing to do tonight, but like yielding to Deb, it could be critical to getting Deb on the witness stand come Monday morning.

Kathleen and Tony went straight to the firm. She wasn't hungry, maybe later she'd get something from one of the machines on the nineteenth floor.

Tony went to his office to work on his outline for the direct examination of Deb—make the changes required after Donahey's statement, take advantage of the best answers obtained from Dr. Weingard and Dr. Calder.

Kathleen called her dad. "Are you and Tony in trouble with the judge?" he asked. "I didn't like what I heard on the six o'clock news."

"Did the judge publicly criticize us?"

"No, but I have a bad feeling. The reporter said the defense had been dealt a crippling below and indicated that there could be an investigation of misconduct."

"Well, we didn't do anything wrong. Listen, Dad, I called to ask a favor."

"Don't take the prosecuting attorney lightly. Or Judge Conklin. I'm going to do some checking, see what's going on. If there's trouble it's important to get right on it."

"Thanks. But I need more than that. I hate to ask, but could you see about getting Harrison Donahey released on bond?" She told him it was a long story but she felt uncomfortable asking anyone at Latham, Fuller.

"I think the Civil Liberties Union is already involved," he said. "It's Dave Goldberg from the Ohio State law faculty, according to the six o'clock news."

"But could you check? Make sure everything possible is being done?"

"I'll do it as soon as we hang up. You and Tony can't be worrying with this." Her father was nearly seventy but he hadn't lost the ability to make a client feel that nothing was more important than the client's crisis—even on a Friday night.

She went down to the library to look for cases to support her conviction that Judge Conklin had committed reversible error. The research might boost Tony's confidence. Better, it might have an effect on Judge Conklin. When the judge calmed down, he might reverse the ruling on Harrison's statement. If not, he might bend over backward on the critical evidentiary rulings to come. He might be persuaded to give a more favorable charge. Conklin, like any judge, detested it when one of his cases got reversed by the court of appeals.

By midnight Kathleen had pulled together enough authority to worry Judge Conklin. She found Tony in his office. He was working on proposed jury instructions. "Let's go home," she said. "I'll go over the instructions while Dr. Westphal is on the stand."

When she and Tony got home there was a full load of messages on the machine. Two calls had to be returned.

"Goldberg's on top of everything," her dad reported. "Judge

Davis will see him in the morning at nine." Goldberg said he was sure that Davis, a court of appeals judge, would issue a writ releasing Donahey on bond. "Goldberg thought Davis would have done it tonight except for not wanting to offend Conklin."

So Harrison would spend another night in jail but would be out the next day. His rights would be competently asserted. Goldberg was fascinated by the legal issues, had a Fifth Amendment theory based on misprision of felony. "But Donahey may ultimately serve some time," her dad said. "He did disobey a subpoena."

"Tell me about that later." Kathleen wanted to return Jill's call.

The phone rang seventeen times. "I'll have to drive over," Kathleen told Tony.

"I'll go with you."

Deb, still dressed in black as she had been for court, let them in, and Kathleen delivered the news on Harrison, promising that Harrison would be released and be home tomorrow and have nothing to worry about.

Back home, Kathleen turned off the light and kissed Tony. "I think Deb will be better in the morning," she said. But she couldn't sleep. She was wondering what else could come undone. Tony, on his back next to her, had his hands clasped behind his head. She didn't need to ask what was keeping him awake.

Deb was wearing the same black dress when Kathleen and Tony picked her up. Maybe she had no change of clothes at her parents' house. She had eaten breakfast, was ready to leave. Jill, stuttering worse than on the night before, wrapped her arms around Deb. She'd be fine, she said, Deb shouldn't worry about her. Nobody was reassured, no surprises.

Tony had reserved the mock courtroom on the twenty-third floor for the weekend. Though smaller than those at the Hall of Justice, it had counsel tables, a witness box, a raised judicial bench, even seats for a jury of six. Litigators at Latham, Fuller used the facility to rehearse appellate arguments and for trial preparation. Kathleen, sitting as judge, administered the oath to Deb, whose face was a mask.

"Tell us who you are and how you met Buzz Garrison," Tony began.

"Buzz was the Ohio advance man for Walter Mondale's presidential campaign. I was a senior at Miami University and trying to get an interview with Mondale for the school newspaper . . ."

For the entire morning Tony asked background questions. "The jury has to get to know Deb," Kathleen had said. "We want them on her side when you take her into the disease, the arguments, the night Garrison was killed."

So far Deb was doing better than Kathleen had dared expect. You identified with her every time she faltered, took time to compose herself when the question forced her to remember the good times—like the night before she and Buzz took the ski week at Boyne.

"We'd been going together for several months. Buzz was building his law practice and I had my job in the travel department at the bank. It was my first year out of college. Neither of us was seeing anyone else . . . we knew . . . or at least I did . . . that we were going to get married, probably in another year.

"Mom and Dad invited Buzz for dinner the week before we left for Boyne. Nothing was said but I could feel . . . and Buzz said he did too . . . my mom . . . I mean, she'd married an older man, her instructor . . . but she wasn't comfortable with us driving up to Boyne, spending the week together. Dad liked Buzz but they didn't really know each other back then. I was twenty-two and a twenty-eight-year-old lawyer seemed . . . well, I guess Mom thought maybe I was being used.

"On the night before we were to leave, Buzz and I went shopping . . . to get last-minute stuff. We decided to have a late dinner at Lazarus after we finished shopping. We were in the Chintz Room, had just given our order when Buzz pulled out the small box, handed it across the table and asked me to marry him."

Deb had a box of tissues on the shelf in front of her. She stopped talking, wiped her eyes. "I'm sorry," she said. "It may sound crazy now, but back then . . ."

Tony nodded and waited, didn't come in with a prompting question. Kathleen made a note to tell Tony, when they took a break, that he could skip some of the background questions. The impression Deb was making, if she did the same in the courtroom, was exactly right. But there was a risk of losing spontaneity.

"I'm sorry," Deb said again. "I'll do better in the courtroom."

"Go ahead," said Tony.

"We left the restaurant and drove out to tell Mom and Dad. They were shocked . . . I think more upset than Mom had been about me running off on a ski week. But we were in love . . . I mean, I was flabbergasted but I knew as soon as he slid the box across the table what my answer was . . . I knew why he'd done it too . . . I mean, not why he decided to get married because that would have happened later anyway . . . he did it that night because . . ." Deb couldn't finish the sentence. Kathleen guessed it was the first night they would be intimate.

"Let's take a recess." Kathleen rapped the gavel on her bench. It was ten-thirty. "You're doing fine," Kathleen told Deb. "Tony and I need to make some telephone calls. We'll do that in my office, be back in a few minutes."

Deb nodded, said she'd like a cup of coffee. Obviously she was relieved to be left alone.

Kathleen and Tony went down the hall and around the corner. "Listen," she said, "Deb is perfect on the background questions. Let's move on to the harder stuff. Then I'll take a crack at her on cross."

Kathleen did make a call to her dad and learned that Harrison Donahey had been released on bond. Deb hugged Kathleen, perking up some for the first time.

At noon they had a pizza brought in. "The key," Kathleen said as they washed down pizza with Diet Pepsi, "is that you *did not know*. You *can't* say what your intent was when you dropped the dryer. Yes, you were angry. But you did *not* plan to kill him."

"That's the truth," said Deb. "Haven't I always said that?"

"Right," said Kathleen. "Whenever you get stuck, the answer is 'I don't know.' Like you've been saying—everything after he accused you of killing your baby is a blur."

Deb nodded. Since the morning break, Kathleen had seen the concentration in Deb's eyes. Deb was making a great effort to answer questions without admitting her horror. She had wanted to hurt Buzz, probably thought that if she'd had a gun she would have pulled the trigger. It wasn't that they were putting words in Deb's mouth, telling her what her intentions had been. It was, Kathleen felt, that Deb was so conflicted in her memory, tortured by guilt, by the anger and hate . . . yes, hate . . . and who could blame her? . . .

Maybe—probably—no one, including Deb, especially Deb,

knew what had triggered the impulse to drop the dryer. Though Deb had, on occasion, virtually acknowledged an intent to kill, she didn't know what her intent was—not in terms of the law's insanity defense. The challenge was to resolve the ambiguity in favor of Deb, to help Deb present her state of mind to the jury in the most favorable way. The challenge was to project that ambiguity into the minds of the twelve in the jury box; to make the twelve receptive to the testimony that would come later from Dr. Lance Westphal and finally Kathleen . . .

After lunch Kathleen began the practice cross-examination. It would last the afternoon, go on until eleven that night and take all of Sunday.

In the beginning Kathleen came on soft, testing Deb's claim that she wanted a baby and had been happy with the HD results, faulting Deb for her "dishonesty" in not telling Buzz she wanted a divorce, pretending disbelief when Deb explained her reasons for waiting until the campaign was over. Kathleen worked to trip Deb on the details of the arguments with Buzz. On the one following the call from Judge Roberts, the plan was to avoid mentioning the judge by name unless Bender insisted. Kathleen was not trying to embarrass the judge and she was afraid Judge Conklin might let Roberts testify to rebut the claim. She didn't want a court-of-appeals judge to appear as a witness for the prosecution.

As the afternoon wore on Deb got stronger. This was ground on which she apparently felt solid. She was even becoming rather animated, adding to her answers—"Maybe I should have confronted Buzz but I was afraid . . . I mean physically afraid, and I got more afraid every day. I didn't know what he'd do if I told him I wanted a divorce in the middle of the campaign. Then when he hit me . . . the second before . . . I mean, from the look in his eyes . . . I thought he might really hurt me . . . or worse. And then . . . you might not believe this, but I wanted him to get elected. It got to where I thought that was the only chance for us to separate without tearing each other apart . . ."

"Perfect," said Kathleen. "Let's take our afternoon recess." Deb's spirits were up. They drank coffee as Kathleen praised Deb. "You're handling this better than I imagined possible, I'm really proud of you . . ." But she knew too well that it could come unraveled in a minute in court.

On Saturday night Kathleen moved the questions to the night of June 13th. For three and a half hours her questions had but one purpose—to elicit the answer "I don't know, I can't explain how it happened." Keep the target that narrow and Bender, though he might snarl, provoke, get sarcastic, would be hard put to score a knockout.

Kathleen's questions were straightforward: "What were you thinking when you dropped the dryer?" "Weren't you angry, wanting to hurt him?" "Didn't you realize what happens when a live electrical appliance falls into water?" "Didn't you admit to the nine-one-one operator that you intended to kill him?" And there were variations on variations.

As she saw Deb improve in questioning, Kathleen made the questions tougher. It could be—it was Kathleen's *hope*—that Deb was somehow forging a new consciousness, a way of looking back at the night of June 13th, that the new consciousness was hardening and would withstand Bender's attack.

"She did really well today," Tony said as he turned off the light and kissed Kathleen goodnight.

Kathleen agreed. But underneath, Kathleen knew, there was the guilt Deb felt, the blame she put on herself that no amount of assurance could erase. And Deb hadn't truly been tested yet. That would happen tomorrow when Kathleen did a slash-and-burn cross-examination. It had to be harsh, tough, even cruel, or it wouldn't prepare Deb. Kathleen could only hope the result would not be to undermine the progress they'd already made.

At least one thing was clear. Whether to please Kathleen, to save herself or to retaliate for the way Bender and the judge had humiliated her father—Deb *wanted* to do well. Compared to the day before when Kathleen had wondered if Deb might refuse to testify, this had been a good day. But as you climbed the ladder and got closer to the top, the fear of falling increased as well.

Sunday morning they were back in the mock courtroom. The task was to explain the statement given by Harrison. Deb was as convincing as she had been when Kathleen forced the truth out of her at Lake in the Woods—just after the disclosure of the Brady materials. The answer was simple and Deb had mastered it against every angle of attack presented. "Dad didn't hear me, he was trying to protect me."

In two days the windowless mock courtroom had become a separate world inhabited by Kathleen, Deb and Tony. The landscape of the world was the bench behind which Tony now sat, the witness box, the counsel tables, the small pit where Kathleen had been standing as she asked her questions. It was a world bounded by the oil portraits of the four Latham, Fuller partners who had gone on to become judges. There was no reality outside those walls. Not for these three.

Following the Sunday afternoon "recess," Kathleen and Deb were alone, and what followed was for real. No more "mock." There was only the action between Kathleen and Deb. It was combat. Kathleen was trying her best to break Deb, watching every twitch, every stumble, every time Deb cut her eyes away; watching the pauses when Deb hid behind a tissue. Kathleen was using what she saw, shooting out unfair questions, deliberately misinterpreting Deb's answers. But at the same time Kathleen's fear was that she would *succeed,* that Deb would crumble. The practice cross-examination had become a kind of verbal and emotional dance of death.

Kathleen, always one to look for problems when she thought things were going well, discovered a new worry. Was this artificial world giving Deb more assurance than she would feel in Courtroom 9A at the Hall of Justice with twelve jurors staring at her and Socko Bender barking the questions? No matter how harsh her interrogation, Kathleen was a friend, a *sister,* someone Deb trusted. What a situation . . . Kathleen needed to put on an Oscar-winning performance.

"I want to try something else," Kathleen said at eight o'clock on Sunday night. She took a chair and put it on top of one of the counsel tables, helped Deb climb onto the table, told her to sit in the chair. Kathleen would walk around the table, fire questions from behind Deb's back.

"We've watched you use your tissues." Kathleen was standing behind Deb, making Deb turn in the chair and twist her head. "We've seen how broken up you are when you think back about the wonderful good times with Buzz. Tell us, Mrs. Garrison, did you also cry when you saw that you had *electrocuted* your husband?"

"I was stunned—"

"Did you cry when you called the nine-one-one operator? When the police came?"

"I don't think so, it was a terrible shock—"

"A terrible shock? Any other feelings?"

Deb shook her head.

"No grief? For your dead husband horribly killed?"

"I was too stunned."

Kathleen came around, got in Deb's face. "There's no way that what happened could be an accident, is there?" As Harrison had said in his damaging statement.

"I'm not sure what it was."

"After accidents, don't people usually experience grief?"

Deb didn't answer.

"You said you didn't tell your father it was an accident. Isn't that because it wasn't an accident?"

"I'm not sure just how it happened."

"Did you tell the nine-one-one operator it was an accident?"

"No."

"How about the police?"

"No."

"Well, which was it? Did you drop the dryer accidentally or intentionally?

"I was angry, but I'm not sure."

"I guess you don't want to answer."

"I just don't know."

Pleased, Kathleen pressed on. "Let's go back. I thought we'd agreed that it wasn't an accident."

Deb nodded.

"So what else is there? If it wasn't an accident what was your intent?"

"It seems like it just happened."

"Mrs. Garrison, you wanted a divorce?"

"Yes."

"You were afraid of your husband?"

"Yes."

"And you wanted to get rid of him?"

"No. I didn't murder him."

"Well, you sure did get rid of him. And you didn't shed that first tear."

Deb sat, silent, her shoulders trembling.

"Those tears are an act for the courtroom, aren't they? Tell us the *truth,* Mrs. Garrison. Weren't you *glad* when you saw that he was dead?"

Deb started to answer and choked. She went to her tissue box but before she could use the tissues she was sobbing, bent over with her head in her hands. Tony, from behind the bench, was looking at Kathleen, hoping she would ease off.

"It's a little late for this crocodile boo-hooing." Kathleen kept her face within inches of Deb's. "Do you think if you cry long enough and loud enough that you'll be excused from frying your husband?"

Deb shook her head without looking up.

"Do you really expect us to believe your tears when you had none after you killed your husband?"

"Stop it, I can't *take* anymore. Why are you saying this?"

"I'll answer *that* when you tell me what you intended when you dropped that live electrical appliance in the Jacuzzi."

"I don't know how to answer."

"Okay," said Kathleen, realizing she'd gone as far as she could for now. More would be counter-productive. "Let's quit here." She helped Deb out of the chair and down off the table.

Deb didn't want to be held or comforted—didn't want Kathleen even to touch her. She sat in one of the chairs beside the counsel table—stunned, as if in shock. Kathleen waved Tony back as he came up to Deb. "Let her have a few minutes," she said.

A new wave of convulsive crying. The old complete trust had been destroyed, which Kathleen had to accept. No matter what happened in the trial, or later between her and Deb, they would never, she believed, re-form the bond that had started in the diner when they met and which had become stronger than if they had been full sisters.

Well, it was the price Kathleen knew she was paying for getting Deb ready to face Bender in the courtroom. The old adage about a lawyer who represented herself having a fool for a client was ringing in her head. So were Tony's warnings about her involvement in the case. You couldn't do your job as a lawyer without sacrificing the relationship. She'd been forced to choose and she'd chosen advocacy, to save her sister.

"Deb," she said. "I'm very proud of you."

Deb's distress increased.

"You feel destroyed, but you haven't given yourself up."

Deb looked at her, a puzzled expression on her swollen face.

"What *matters* is that you didn't crack on the basic point. *You just don't know how it happened.*"

"You're saying that because you want to win. You don't believe me. You know what really happened, you know I wanted to kill him."

Kathleen took Deb by the shoulders. "I *don't* think that. I absolutely believe you are innocent. I believe that more than you do yourself."

When Kathleen let go, Deb began crying again. Trembling, she sat with her arms wrapped across her chest. "I don't care what happens tomorrow," she said.

"*I* care, Deb. And not just to win. I care because of you. I love you, damn it. If that jury finds you guilty I don't think I'll be able to . . ."

Deb looked up. Obviously she wanted to believe. She let Kathleen take her hand.

Kathleen and Tony spent another hour with Deb in the mock courtroom, then an hour in the parlor of her house. Deb was still in pain, hadn't really forgiven her, but she had *listened.* Had she convinced Deb that she didn't believe she was responsible for killing Buzz? Was Deb still blaming herself? She couldn't answer those questions.

There was, though, some life in Deb's eyes when she turned as she was going up the stairway. Kathleen had been following her to the guest bedroom. "Don't worry," Deb said, "I'll do the best I can to testify the way you want me to . . ."

Wonderful. Not exactly a great reassurance.

Kathleen went back downstairs to be with Tony, felt drained, miserable, needing someone to tell *her* to stop blaming herself.

"Jesus, Kathleen, you were scary during that last hour of cross-examination," Tony said.

She came into his arms. "I feel godawful," she said.

He held her tight. "You had to do it," he said. "I think Deb's going to come through." Did he really, she silently asked herself.

"Just shut up and hold me," she said.

Deb was wearing a plain but stylish navy-blue dress. She had taken care with makeup. She was, as Kathleen had recognized many times before, quite a beautiful woman.

At the Hall of Justice Kathleen went with Deb to the cubicle assigned to the defense. Tony wanted to be in Judge Conklin's chambers before the judge got there. He was armed with photocopies of the authorities Kathleen had found on Friday night, the pertinent parts highlighted with a green marker.

The Harrison Donahey problem seemed relatively distant to Kathleen after the intense preparation of Deb and concern for how Deb would do when she got on the stand. But it wasn't really distant. Judge Conklin had to be faced and Tony had been nervous on the drive to the Hall of Justice. "Should I give him the cases this morning or see whether he's still angry? Maybe it would be better to wait."

"You'll have to play that by ear," Kathleen had said.

Sitting in the small cubicle adjacent to the courtroom, Deb seemed alarmingly composed. It was as if the testimony she was about to give were of no concern to her. She certainly didn't appear to be a defendant fighting for survival.

"I know you're going to do well," said Kathleen.

Deb nodded. She didn't want to talk. She turned her head toward the bookcase wall. But she didn't seem angry. Her lips moved. Was she going back over the questions Kathleen had asked, thinking through the answers she would give?

When Tony opened the door it surprised them both. "The bastard is mercurial," he said. Conklin had come in, flush from the attention that had been given to his rulings. "He loved it that the Civil Liberties Union is involved. It amused him that students at Ohio State are circulating a petition to impeach him."

"He's reading it right," said Kathleen. "The publicity translates into votes at his next election."

"Anyway, he took our cases, said he'd study them, asked Bender to submit material."

Deb didn't appear to be paying attention to the conversation. Tony looked at her. "Are you okay?" he asked.

"I'm fine."

"We'd better go in then," Tony said. "We need to be at counsel table when the jury is brought in."

Kathleen gave Deb a hug, held her hands. "Good luck." To both of us, she silently added.

Deb pulled away to follow Tony. Her hands had felt like ice.

Kathleen went around to the rear corridor and stood outside the bailiff's door until she heard Judge Conklin say, "Call your first witness," and Tony respond, "The defense calls Debora Garrison."

Kathleen went back to the small cubicle. She doubted if there would be anything she could do, but she wanted to be there when the court recessed for the morning, lunch and afternoon breaks.

She had done the best she could, but she felt depressed and scared. It was as though she had just been to Deb's funeral. Her *sister's* funeral. At the same time she felt so jumpy she knew she'd get no work done if she went back to the office. It wouldn't be so bad if she could have been in there with Deb . . . She knew that no amount of training, of preparation, could prepare anyone for the first time she faced enemy fire in a courtroom.

Chapter 18

H ER VOICE, naturally soft, was hard to hear and jurors were leaning forward. Answering the first question, Deb had not taken her eyes off Tony's. He got up from the counsel table, crossed the well and took a position at the back of the jury box midway between the two ends. He wanted to force Deb to look at the jurors.

"Try to keep your voice up," he said quietly.

"I'm sorry." Deb glanced up at Judge Conklin, then back to Tony. It was as if she was afraid of looking at the jurors.

Tony led her through the courtship, marriage, purchase of the house at Lake in the Woods, vacations and the way they had met in politics.

"Did you resent the way politics began to take over his life?"

"Not back then. It was my dream too." Deb glanced at the jurors, as if to be sure they understood. "I was proud of him in the state senate race. We went to a lot of cookie-and-coffee parties where there weren't more than fifteen people. But he always made a speech, he believed in what he said. He thought he could make a difference and listening to him I believed he would."

"The campaign didn't strain your marriage?"

"No, I wanted it too. I remember an alumni weekend at Miami. I'm not sure what" . . . it was not easy for her to say his name . . . "Buzz did when I went to a luncheon at my old sorority. Anyway, most of my friends from college were there and about half of them had married. Buzz and I had been married . . ." Deb looked up at the recessed lights in the domed ceiling. "It was in our third year. After Buzz got elected state senator. Everyone at the luncheon was sort of bragging about who they had married . . . I remember thinking I didn't have to do that. They knew, or I thought they knew, what Buzz had accomplished, how I was involved in it and what I thought of him . . . And then after lunch and at times during the weekend, my closest friends would tell me their lives weren't really all that good. Most were struggling, they said. I remember driving back to Columbus, not talking or anything, just glad to be with him . . ."

Good so far, Tony thought. A good, involved, loving wife. He next asked about the first campaign and she said that Buzz had been given no chance of winning when he got in the race. He would not have received the nomination if his Republican opponent had not been a four-term incumbent who was considered unbeatable.

Deb described the anniversary dinner, how it had ended with Buzz suggesting they start their family. Tony did not cut her off when she told about the purchase of their house, the nights and weekends they spent decorating it and so forth. Prosaics that further established her care and decency. Never resenting her husband and his ambition, being happy for him . . .

Now Deb was making contact with the jury. And they were encouraging her with their attention. Tony glanced at the clock on the wall above the bailiff's desk. Five after ten. In twenty-five minutes Judge Conklin would declare the morning recess. Tony used the time to bring out the hope Deb had for children, the talk with Buzz in the car, in bed, at meals . . .

"She's doing great," Tony told Kathleen when he and Deb went into the defense cubicle during the morning recess.

"I'm nervous as anything," Deb said. "But this is weird. I feel I'm getting to know those people."

"You are," said Tony. He looked at Kathleen. "Conklin usually takes notes like he's the court stenographer. But after the first half hour he put down his pen and listened."

"What about Bender?" Kathleen suggested. "Is he making objections?"

"Not the first one," Tony said. "Bender has to act like he's interested but he's shifting around in his chair, fiddling with files. He must have looked at the clock a dozen times. I bet the last hour seemed like ten to him."

"It did to me," said Kathleen.

"Kathleen, I ended up on the looking-forward-to-a-family questions. Do you think I should skip some of the background— go straight to the disease and explain Deb's decision to get an abortion if the fetus was positive for HD?"

"I don't know. It's awful being in there, not knowing what's going on."

"I could pick up the rest of the background later. I know the jurors want to hear what went wrong, find out how the disease fits in . . . especially how the disease fits in . . . especially since Deb had all of them when she was telling how much she wanted a child. Deb's made a bond with the jury and it might be a mistake to wait until this afternoon to—"

"What is it, Deb?" Kathleen had been watching Deb as Tony spoke.

Deb shook her head. "I'll be all right," she said.

"But what?"

"Bender's cross-examination," she said. "Will that come to-day?"

"I'm not sure yet," Tony said. "But, Deb, you're going to be fine. That jury is with you. And after last night with Kathleen— Bender will seem easy."

"That may not be true." Kathleen was paying no attention to him and had moved her chair next to Deb's. "Deb," she said, "we keep saying you'll do well. But we don't know any more than you do. We don't know what Bender will ask or how being in the courtroom with a judge and jury will affect you." A dose of reality seemed in order, she thought. Stiffen Deb's spine.

"That's what scares me," Deb said.

"All you have to do is listen carefully to each question and try to give an answer," Kathleen said.

"That's all?" Deb's face had lost color but there was, amaz-ingly, the start of a smile at the corners of her mouth.

"We won't finish direct examination until mid-afternoon at the earliest," said Tony. Over the lunch break he would, he decided, consult Kathleen. Would it be better to let Bender start today or hold him off until tomorrow? In either event Bender would have the daily copy, study it overnight to pick apart everything Deb had said.

It was time to go back in. "You go straight to the witness box," Tony told Deb as they walked into the pit. "Be there when they bring the jury back."

For the rest of the morning Tony asked the questions that would let Deb tell the jury about her mother's suicide attempt, the choices Deb had to make, her struggle with the testing process. As he watched Deb and listened to her answers, Tony also kept an eye on each juror and tried to detect reactions. They were sympathetic, he thought, *except* the schoolteacher in number three and the retired army colonel in number seven. They had looked away from Deb, seemed to be thinking that she had indeed decided to abort the fetus.

Just before the noon break, he decided to risk a question Deb hadn't rehearsed. "Deb," he said, "the doctors told us last week how overjoyed you were when the test showed your baby would be normal. But why did you decide, especially since your husband was against it, to have an abortion *if* the baby had a disease that would not produce symptoms for forty or more years?"

"It was an impossible choice," said Deb. "I thought about it constantly for over a month. A lot of it had to do with what happened between me and Buzz during that time." Deb reached for a tissue but pulled her hand back. "You know," she said, "I've thought about it since it happened and . . ."

"And?"

"And I've asked myself the question you asked me. Lots and lots of times. It felt so awful back then—my marriage seemed to have fallen apart overnight . . . I was seeing what the disease was doing to my mom . . . a child would have to face all that pain. I was resenting that Mom had put me in the position I was in and, I guess, I felt my life had no future. It's hard to understand if you haven't lived with Huntington's disease. But the shock was Buzz and . . ."

Deb stopped talking. She wasn't on the verge of tears, but despite a perfect makeup, her face had broken out in splotches of pink. Her eye sockets were sunken. She tried to find the words that would describe her feeling.

Tony helped her. "Dr. Calder told us that two thirds of the women who have HD and become pregnant decide to abort if the test shows that their fetus also has the gene." It was a leading question, not even a question, really. Bender pushed his chair back but didn't get up.

"No, that wasn't it," said Deb. "I think it was that I just couldn't see how anything could work. I mean, there were times when I wished . . . I thought what Mom tried was wrong but there were times I wished I could go to sleep and not wake up."

"So it was a decision you came to after a painful month. *If* the fetus had the HD gene?"

"No." In a gallery-packed courtroom you could hear Deb's pause to gulp air, the squeak of the judge's high-backed chair and the sound of Bender's pen as he wrote on his yellow pad. "There was everything I've said. But I was also thinking about one of my friends from college. She had three miscarriages, then gave birth to a healthy baby boy. I mean, I still could have children. I wanted to bring a healthy baby into the world. I didn't know for sure when the HD symptoms would hit me. They can't guarantee that. And I didn't think I'd have Buzz . . . He keeps coming into it and this is what I haven't told anyone. I think . . . in fact I'm sure, part of it was that I was fighting for myself. I mean, I reacted against Buzz saying I couldn't."

Tony started to ask a question but Deb shook her head. "I don't know if I could have gone through with it. I knew I'd decided, but I wasn't forced to actually make the choice. It's hard to explain but by then my decision to get a divorce was really firm. So maybe if I'd gotten a bad test I would have *still* had the baby." Good, Tony thought. "I mean, how did I know this wasn't my only chance for a baby?"

She was trying to stay in control, not crying but looking away from Tony and the jury. "You'd have to have been there," she said. "You had to see what was happening between Buzz and me."

"Your Honor," said Tony, "it is twenty past twelve. "The answer leads into the relationship between Deb and Buzz. Those questions will take time and I wonder if this might be a place to take the noon recess?"

"Yes," said the judge. "I lost track of the clock myself."

Tony followed Deb into the defense cubicle. He'd set her off with his question and felt he had lost control of the examination. If he'd tried to stop her, the jury would have been angry. She had said things that Bender could use against her. Had she said anything that would alter the psychiatrist's opinion?

"What would you like to eat?" he asked her. "I'll go down to the cafeteria, bring food back." He thought it would be good to leave Deb and Kathleen by themselves. Later, before court resumed, he would draw Kathleen aside and see what she thought.

"Could you two go somewhere?" Deb asked. "I'm not hungry and I want to be by myself."

Tony looked at Kathleen. Surely she saw Deb's pain, that there was a need to spend time with her. Kathleen got up and opened the door. Tony followed her out.

"Wait," Deb said as he was closing the door. They went back in.

"I've got to use the restroom." Deb looked at Kathleen. "Can you go with me?"

"What did she want?" Tony asked after they came back and Deb had been left alone in the defense cubicle.

"She was afraid of running into someone in the restroom. A reporter or someone who was in the gallery."

"Did she say anything about her testimony?"

Kathleen shook her head. "Only that she now realizes how important it is that she tell her story to the jury."

"You mean this is some kind of therapy for her?"

"I don't know what it is. But she seems stronger than she was before she broke down last night."

"Well, if she keeps spilling out everything that comes into her head . . ."

Tony and Kathleen went through the cafeteria line, got a table in the corner. "What exactly did she say that bothers you?" Kathleen asked.

Tony wasn't sure he remembered it all. He'd been concentrating on the jury as well as Deb.

"I don't think you have a choice," said Kathleen. "We've done everything possible to prepare her. Ask the questions."

It was just after the mid-afternoon recess. Tony had taken Deb back to the bathroom on the night of June 13th. She related how she was at her vanity drying her hair. Buzz had interrupted her. They had had the spat, she had turned the dryer back on.

"Then what happened?" Tony asked.

"He said, 'Don't think you fooled me, I know you want a divorce. I know you didn't want my child and that . . .' This is hard for me to say, and I don't know if I can get through it." Deb glanced at the judge and then seemed to beg pardon from the jury. She wiped her nose with a tissue. "He accused me of killing my baby."

"And then?"

"I had the dryer in my hand, I'd taken a step toward him."

"Then?" At this point during rehearsal Deb had said, "I didn't know. It's all a blur. I'm real confused about what happened next."

In the courtroom her voice could barely be heard. "The dryer didn't slip," she said. "I was so angry I shoved or kind of threw it at him. I was angry, but I didn't . . ."

In the hushed chamber, Bender's voice sounded thunderous, especially in contrast to Deb's. "Mark that place in the official record," he instructed the court stenographer.

"You were saying you didn't what?" Tony asked.

"I don't know . . . I don't know what was in my mind, except I was very hurt and angry . . . But I wasn't trying to kill him." Was she really so sure of that? She had told Tony and Kathleen in the rehearsal about it being more a blur than anything else. Was that really what she still felt? What would she say when Bender cross-examined her?

Judge Conklin held the jury until six-thirty to finish the direct examination by the defense. When it ended, three things seemed clear. Deb had come to be angry to the extent of hating Buzz Garrison, a man she had once been in love with. She had been angry and shoved, rather than dropped, the dryer into the swirling Jacuzzi. And Buzz Garrison was enough of a pluperfect son of a bitch that he had deserved it.

Deb had not lost the jury. All afternoon those in the gallery, as well as Judge Conklin and the jurors, had been riveted to her story. But in her testimony hadn't she confessed to murder, at least as Judge Conklin would be required to define it in his charge to the jury?

The jury would be told: "A defendant is presumed to have

intended the natural and probable consequence of an act purposefully done by the defendant." As, for example, if you intentionally shot someone, it was murder if the victim died—whether or not your purpose had been to kill.

The *only* way out, as Kathleen had seen almost from the beginning, was the defense of temporary insanity. And to succeed there, Dr. Westphal would have to persuade the jury. Kathleen would have to come through strongly in support of Deb's fear of Buzz and her profound and sincere desire for a baby. The jury would have to be brought to the point where they *wanted* to clear Deb and were looking for a *legal* excuse to do it . . .

On the way home from the Hall of Justice, Deb asked if they could stop at a Wendy's drive-through. She wanted to pick up a bowl of chili, a side salad and a small Frosty, take the food to German Village and eat by herself in the guest room. She wanted to be left alone until it was time to go to court in the morning.

"Do you think it was a good idea, leaving her alone?" Tony asked. He and Kathleen had driven to the Thai Village, a restaurant on the fringe of downtown.

"We have to do this her way," said Kathleen. "But God, I've never spent a day like this. That little room feels like a prison cell."

"Maybe tomorrow you should go to the office," Tony suggested.

Kathleen shook her head. "I've got to be there until she gets off the stand. I don't know if she'll need anything. I don't know if it's for me or her. But the feeling is really strong."

After they ate they picked up the daily copy of Deb's direct examination. "I'll study it," said Tony, more as a diversion from the tension rather than a source of enlightenment or revelation.

Deb wore the same navy-blue dress, the same accessories. Judge Conklin reminded her that she was still under oath.

"Mrs. Garrison, I'd like to go over a few of the things you told us yesterday." Bender remained seated at counsel table as he began his cross-examination. In front of him was the daily copy from the day before with yellow slips of paper sticking out to mark the places he would use.

Deb, sitting erect in the box, was looking at Bender, blinking her eyes as he pulled a yellow slip to find the place where he wanted to begin.

"Mrs. Garrison, did you tell us that you said, 'I wanted that baby more than anything I ever wanted in my life'—after the favorable test result?"

Deb nodded.

"Mrs. Garrison," said Judge Conklin. "Our court stenographer can't hear your nods. Please answer with a yes or a no."

"Yes," said Deb.

"No one who was in this room yesterday . . ." Bender paused to glance at the jury ". . . will forget the feeling you described, your hope to make a new life around your baby."

"Yes," said Deb. "I can hardly bear to . . . I may never have a baby."

"I believe you also told us that on the day you found out about your mother's disease you went to see your doctors?"

"Yes."

"At that time you learned of a test which would determine whether your fetus had Huntington's disease?"

"Yes."

"And that night you had a fight with your husband?"

"Yes, I guess you could call it that."

"We don't need to go through it again. I'm sure everyone on the jury remembers the pain you felt, the hurt from his lack of support."

Deb nodded, glanced at the judge, said, "Yes."

"At that time," said Bender, "I mean, within a few hours after seeing your doctors, you were thinking about abortion?"

"I wanted my baby as much as ever, but if it was diseased . . . At that time I just didn't know what I wanted to do. Except I knew I wanted the test."

"If you weren't thinking of abortion, what would be the purpose of the test?"

"Relief," she said. "For me and for Buzz too. We might find out—I was told it was a seventy-five percent chance—that our baby didn't have the gene. I prayed for that . . ."

Tony had been poised to make objections. If Deb's answers seemed to be getting her in serious trouble he would interrupt Bender's flow. Now he relaxed a little. The jurors, at least three of them, had nodded. Deb, he felt, was doing well.

"But your anger . . . I think you said that Buzz seemed to become a different person than the Buzz you knew . . . your anger came because he didn't want to immediately test the fetus?"

"I was hurt for a lot of . . . I just felt he had turned on me, he wasn't supporting me at all. We should have been together in such things . . ."

"Can we agree, Mrs. Garrison, that the urgency of the test was due to your pregnancy? Didn't the doctors tell you that?" Bender was careful not to seem to be attacking her, to avoid a tone of nastiness. He was, he wanted the jury to believe, making matter-of-fact requests for information.

Deb hesitated, seeming to consider how she should answer. "Yes," she said.

"Then can we also agree that you were thinking of aborting your baby within two or three hours after you learned the baby might have a disease that could manifest symptoms after forty-five or fifty years?"

"I think I mentioned my friend who'd had a baby after three miscarriages. Buzz and I could have more children. So I was thinking of a lot of things. But I hadn't made any decision. I certainly didn't *want* an abortion."

"You and Buzz had experienced some difficulty before you got pregnant?"

"It took a little over a year."

"You had no thought back then, I take it, that the baby you were carrying might be—that you might not have another chance to have a baby?"

Deb looked up at the ceiling, then at Bender. "No," she said. "I don't remember thinking that back then."

"You weren't thinking of divorce on the night you found out about the test?"

"No . . . but I was shocked at the way Buzz reacted. It just didn't seem like him. So I was looking back at the last year of our marriage. I was suddenly asking myself questions, about my life, our life. It had *nothing* to do with wanting an abortion . . ."

"You and Buzz had been overjoyed when you learned you were pregnant?"

"Maybe me even more than him."

"Then within a matter of two or three hours you are thinking of aborting the child that meant so much to you and Buzz?"

Bender had not once raised his voice. He had demonstrated no overt disapproval of Deb. *But* he was inviting the jury to reconsider the impression Deb had made the day before. As he kept probing for "information" he was making Deb uncomfortable. She was glancing at the jury during her answers, seeming to apologize for them.

Bender kept asking about a decision to abort. During the voir dire examination Tony had exercised strikes against the most outspoken "right to life" people, but everyone who had a tendency toward that position probably had not been eliminated. Those people would not like Deb's answers. The accumulation of Deb's answers was also calling into question her claim that having a baby was what she wanted more than anything. Tony didn't dare object, fearing he would aggravate the *appearance.*

"Mrs. Garrison," Bender asked, "you decided it would be best to hide the second test from your husband?"

"Yes."

"That was because you'd decided to have an abortion?"

"No. I mean, if my baby had the HD gene . . ."

"During this period you went to campaign events with Buzz?"

"Yes."

"You ate meals together?"

"Yes."

"Slept in the same bed?"

"Yes."

"But you didn't tell him?"

"No."

"And then, if I understood you yesterday"—Bender opened his daily copy—"you called Buzz right after you got the test results?"

"Yes."

"You realized your mistake, that by keeping the test secret you had done something destructive to the marriage?"

Deb looked puzzled.

Before she could answer Bender spoke. "Didn't you tell us you apologized to him for hiding the test?"

"I did, but—"

"Were you telling the truth when you apologized?"

"Not completely, but I didn't want another fight—"

*   *   *

At the morning recess Deb followed Tony into the defense cubicle. "He's making me into a terrible person. A liar. His questions don't give me a chance to explain. It's not fair."

"You're doing fine," Tony said. "It's not that bad." And taking each question and answer by itself, it wasn't. But the feeling in the courtroom had changed. Tony feared it could get worse.

"Bender made it seem like I didn't care about a baby. That all I wanted was a divorce. That's *wrong* . . ."

"That's why I decided months ago that I would have to be a witness," Kathleen said.

Deb stared at Kathleen. "He doesn't badger me like you did. But I know what those jurors are thinking."

"Just keep answering the questions," Tony said. "Between you and Kathleen the jury will believe." Actually he worried that Deb's frustration might erupt in the courtroom. It was another part of Bender's tactic. Bender's brusque appearance belied his subtlety as a cross-examiner. A loss of temper and retaliation in response to Bender's calm, seemingly plodding, very respectful questions would push the jury further away from Deb.

After the break Bender shifted to the night of June 13th. Still seated at counsel table and still making no noticeable attempt to shake Deb, he started by having Deb inventory everything in the bathroom: skylights, plants, vanities, what was on them, screens, towel racks, tanning bed, telephones and television. Seduction by prosaics. Was anything missing on the night of June 13th? Where was everything placed?

"When Buzz asked you to turn off your dryer so you could listen to him, how close to being finished with your hair were you?"

"I'd just started. I knew I'd have to hurry because I wanted to do my nails and give them time to dry."

Bender quizzed her about every step she'd taken toward getting ready that night. Bender had her describe the dress she planned to wear, the jewelry that would go with it. Tony quickly saw what Bender was doing . . . demonstrating out of her own mouth Deb's detailed memory of that night. It was a smart and devastating device to offset claims of I-don't-remember.

"Mrs. Garrison, did you know what happens when you plunge

a live electrical appliance into water when someone is in that water?" The sharper question had come without warning, though Bender's voice had not changed from the flat way he had been asking about hair rinses and lipstick shades.

Deb was stunned, looked at Tony and then at the jury. "I wasn't thinking of that at all."

"You say you weren't thinking of that, but you—don't we all know the danger?"

"I guess . . ."

"You guess?" Bender rubbed his chin as he repeated the answer. "Did you throw the dryer from a standing position?"

"I don't remember, I don't think so."

"Mrs. Garrison, you remember very well. And you know if you had, the cord would have pulled out *before* the dryer hit the water?"

"I didn't know that . . . until I saw the demonstration you did at the beginning of the trial."

"Could we agree, then, that you either stooped or bent over before you"—Bender found the place he wanted in his daily copy —"before you 'shoved or kind of threw' the dryer down on your husband?"

"I don't remember how stooped or bent I was or whether it was one or the other. That part is all blurry."

"Interesting. It's harder to remember than the shade of lipstick you were wearing?"

"Yes . . ."

"Were you careful to let go of the dryer before it hit the water?"

"I wasn't thinking about that."

"Did you experience an electrical shock?"

"I don't remember any."

"Let's assume that Buzz did accuse you of inducing an abortion. Of course, you're the only one who is here to tell us what he said." Bender smiled at Deb.

Deb's hands were quivering on top of the shelf across the front of the witness box. "You're saying I'm a liar, but I'm not. I remember what he said as clearly as . . . Mr. Bender, I'll never get those words out of my head."

"Mrs. Garrison, I didn't say you were lying. In fact I said we'll assume that Buzz said exactly what you say he said."

Deb glared at Bender.

"Well, can we do that and move ahead?"

"Yes, but—"

"All right, we're agreed on that. The question I now ask you to answer is whether you were standing when Buzz said those words to you—or were you bent or stooped over?"

"Object." Tony saw the trap. If she said she was stooped, it would cast some doubt on her claim of what Buzz had said. She was already in the act of throwing the dryer at him. But if she said she was standing—which she must have been—there was a deliberate, almost premeditated character to the subsequent act of taking a step, bending over and shoving the dryer into roiling water. There was a time interval.

But there was no valid objection to the question. Judge Conklin looked at Tony. "On what grounds?" he asked.

"I'll withdraw the objection."

Bender, the judge and the jurors swiveled their heads to await Deb's answer.

"I can't remember," she said.

"You don't remember . . . so it's possible that you could have bent or stooped."

"I don't think so."

"Apparently you do have some memory? You certainly did a few minutes ago."

"I think I was standing." Deb's hands were clenching and unclenching.

Bender, with the help of his bag carrier, pulled the cardboard mock-up of the Garrison bathroom into the center of the courtroom well. The mock-up included the Jacuzzi, Deb's vanity, the floor between them and the electrical outlet into which the dryer had been plugged.

"Mrs. Garrison," said Bender. "Would you step down and show us how it happened?"

"I can't . . ."

Bender looked surprised. "You can't?"

"I just don't remember, I don't know what I was thinking." Which had always been the question for her . . . *had* she meant to do it? What *was* she thinking? She didn't know. And didn't want to know.

"Mrs. Garrison, did you hear me ask what you were thinking?"

Deb stared at him.

"I'm not asking for your thoughts. Just step down here and show us what you did."

Deb kept staring at Bender. She wasn't moving out of the witness box but her body was shaking.

"Mrs. Garrison?"

"I don't remember what I did or how it happened and I'm sure I'd do it wrong."

"You do remember him accusing you?"

"Yes."

"What is your next memory?"

"Just the . . . it was horrible, seeing him in the water and the flashes . . ."

"You had enough presence of mind to disconnect the plug?"

"Yes." Deb dropped her head and nodded to support her answer.

"Was he dead?"

"I think so."

"You *think* so. Did you make any effort to revive him?"

"No."

"Didn't try CPR? Anything like that?"

"No."

Bender glanced at the courtroom clock. It was five minutes before twelve. "No further questions," he said.

Deb didn't want anything to eat. She seemed as much in shock as she said she had been on the night of June 13th. She seemed inside herself as Tony talked to Kathleen about the wisdom of putting her back on the stand for redirect examination.

"I don't think I should," said Tony. "I think the more she explains, the worse it looks."

Kathleen agreed.

"This makes Dr. Westphal's testimony critical," he said.

"It always was."

"And yours." He looked at Kathleen. "It's going to come down to the support you give. You can make them see she wasn't lying. Jesus, you were so right. Our defense wouldn't stand a chance if you hadn't decided to be a witness."

Kathleen only nodded. She needed to hear that.

There was a telephone in the small cubicle assigned to the defendant and the defendant's lawyers. Tony used it to notify Dr. Lance Westphal that he needed to be at the Hall of Justice by 1:30.

Kathleen put her arms around Deb. "I believe you," she said. "I *know* how it happened and it was not your fault."

"I don't want to think about it anymore," Deb said. "But I will. It won't let me alone no matter how long I live."

"Your work in this trial is over. But you have to be in there, Deb, sitting at counsel table . . . And you don't look so hot, honey. Come with me."

Deb got up and went with Kathleen to the restroom.

When they came back Deb had fixed her hair and makeup, but when you looked into her eyes, it seemed no one was there.

As Tony refined the questions he would put to Dr. Westphal, Kathleen sat with her chair pulled next to Deb's, her arm across Deb's shoulders.

When Junior Fultz opened the door to say the judge was calling for the jury to be brought in, Deb got up to follow Tony into the courtroom.

"I'm going back to the office," Kathleen said.

"Okay, I'll call when we recess for the day," Tony told her.

"Let me have yesterday's daily copy. I'll work on our requests for instructions."

He gave her the transcript.

"Good luck with the shrink," she said. "Block out everything else."

Chapter 19

KATHLEEN'S SECRETARY handed her an inch-thick stack of messages. Her mind was back in Courtroom 9A as she flipped through the call-backs. She'd said nothing to Tony, certainly would not in the presence of Deb, but she was feeling the pressure. Tony and Deb were counting on her to overcome the setbacks the defense had suffered.

It didn't help to realize that she'd put herself in this position. Or that she had prevailed on Deb to reject a plea bargain that would have avoided the trial, had Deb out of confinement in April.

One of the call-backs was from her dad. Had something gone wrong with Harrison Donahey's situation?

Dad was probably at lunch but she tried anyway and got him. He hadn't called about Donahey. His concern came from hearing that "there may be a problem with the prosecuting attorney."

"What?"

"Have you eaten?"

"No, but I'm swamped. I can't . . ." She hesitated. What would another hour matter, she could work on the instructions when she got back.

She met him at the Columbus Club, and they were given his table, between the fireplace and the window. "The prosecuting attorney is reading a lot into the fact that you and Tony went to see Harrison Donahey the night before he refused the state's subpoena," he said.

"Dad, Donahey had already told Bender he was going to."

"I know. I think this is Bender's doing, an angry reaction in the heat of trial. But if you don't object I'm going to talk to the prosecuting attorney. Some of us helped get him elected."

"Go ahead." With the trial on her mind, it was hard to get concerned over a threat where she'd done nothing wrong. "Criminal law is a different game," she said. "To tell the truth, neither of us knew exactly what to do when Donahey said he was disobeying the subpoena."

"Well, I admire what you and Tony are doing."

"Whatever else, this has made the rest of my practice seem boring."

As they ate she told him about the trial, that it might turn on her testimony. She confessed her anxiety over pressuring Deb into rejecting a pretty attractive plea bargain.

The waiter served sorbet. "How's Mom?" Kathleen asked.

Dad looked at her strangely, as if she might know something he thought she didn't.

"Is anything wrong?"

"She thinks she might have offended you. Pressing you about Tony . . ."

"What is it, Dad? Come on, you're holding out on me."

"Mother doesn't want you to know—"

"Know *what?*"

"She went into the hospital this morning."

"Hospital? What for?"

"She didn't want to burden you during the trial."

"Dad. What *is* it?"

"She went in to have a cyst removed from her uterus and adhesions broke. It's an old problem, she had some bleeding and went to see Dr. Droak. He thought it should be taken care of. They'll do a laparoscopy, remove the cyst and she should be home on Wednesday."

"What hospital?"

"Kathleen, she's not worried and neither am I."

"I want to see her."

"She's at Columbus General."

Kathleen pushed her chair back. "I'm going right now." She would have to work on jury instructions tonight.

She called Connie, told her she wouldn't be in until later in the afternoon. If Tony had to reach her she could be located by the receptionist at Columbus General.

Adhesions on the uterus. An old problem. It might, as Dad said, not be serious, so why the secrecy, the reluctance to talk to her about it? It wasn't just that she was in the midst of a trial.

Her mother was sitting in a chair beside the window. Kathleen hesitated in the doorway as she looked at her mother—petite, wearing her gray suit with the jacket draped loosely over her shoulders to leave her arms free to hold the magazine she was reading. Dad had gotten her a private corner room on the sixth floor with windows overlooking the river to the east and downtown to the south.

"Kathleen," she said. "What on earth?"

"I got it out of Dad," she said. "Didn't either of you think how I'd feel when I found out?"

Kathleen bent to put her cheek against her mother's powdered face. The scent of lilac was as strong as always.

"What about your trial?" asked Mom.

"Tony's trying the case." She didn't want to talk about the trial right now. She adjusted her chair so they could look at one another.

"I'm glad to see you," she said, as poised and gracious as if she were hosting a tea for the Women's Auxiliary Bar Association. She described the operation, said there was no danger, no risk of cancer and that she should have had it done a year ago. Did she say it too brightly? Kathleen had to wonder.

"I know I shouldn't ask, but is everything all right between you and Tony?" Mom asked quickly, diverting the conversation from herself.

"Let me ask *you* a question. Why are *you* so strong for me to marry Tony?"

Actually Mom had never said it in so many words, but it was increasingly obvious. Now, without any reservation, she said, "I pray for that, Kathleen. I want you to have children, to feel the way I did when I first saw you."

Kathleen looked at her. "You and Dad," she said, "you lead such separate lives . . . sometimes I wonder why you're so strong for marriage . . . for me, I mean."

"You and Tony are different. I think I saw that the first time you brought him to the house. Kathleen, you're sleeping with the man, and believe it or not, that pleases me . . . you can have what Dan and I never had."

Startled, Kathleen said, "How are we different?" Good God, where was this going? It was the frankest exchange she'd ever had with her adoptive mother. She would never have opened this door if she hadn't been drained by two days in that cubicle, two days of wondering if her testimony could carry the impact she'd promised. But she had opened the door and was determined to find out what she'd never know. Mom looked away, out the window.

"Kathleen, I don't *regret* our marriage. No. Dan will probably go first and I can't even imagine life without him." She turned back, looked Kathleen in the eye. There was an intensity that Kathleen couldn't remember seeing. "I love Dan . . . but . . . well, it always made me almost cringe when he touched me."

Kathleen felt herself cringing, and not only for Mom. Her own too-long frozen feelings came back to her. It was Tony who had helped her change that . . . to bring out the womanly needs she had and now could show. "Kathleen, I had to force myself. I hated it but I wanted a baby. And even if I hadn't wanted a baby so badly . . ."

Kathleen hoped she would stop, seeing how hard this was, and yet at the same time she wanted to hear.

"It wasn't Dan's fault. He would have been a wonderful husband . . . for anyone but me, I guess."

"Mom!"

"I know, I should have gotten help. But like a lot of women raised the way I was, I was too embarrassed. All right, that's the way I am. But, Kathleen, you're different. I was, I admit it, sinfully happy when Tony moved in with you. Kathleen, you should get married. You should have a child."

"This cyst. These adhesions. Is that why you and Dad couldn't have children?"

Mom nodded. "Endometriosis is the fancy name for it," she

said. "We tried for four years before we saw a doctor." She said it with no pleasure.

Kathleen scooted her chair closer, reached for Mom's hands, too white and veined, so thin that it seemed she could see through them.

"After that, we moved into separate bedrooms. We couldn't have a child, that was settled. And duty or not, it was too hard to . . ."

"Did Dad blame you?"

"He tried not to, God knows. And he hasn't, not in words. Not the way I've blamed myself. Then it took two years to get you. If those years trying to get pregnant was hard, going through the adoption was almost worse."

Kathleen was crying and hadn't been aware until Mom withdrew her hand, reached to the floor, pulled a handkerchief out of her bag and handed it to her.

"You meant so much to us," she said. "More than any baby could have if I'd gotten pregnant right away."

"God," said Kathleen. She was thinking what it must have been like for them, those six years.

"Dad and I—after the adoption went through—we more or less came to an understanding."

"Mom, I can't help it, this really upsets me. All those years and you and Dad so miserable. Are you saying you did that for me—?"

"Oh, no. Not miserable, honey. No. No. *No.* I know it's a cliché, but there is more to marriage than sex. Didn't I tell you, I don't know what I'll do when Dan is gone."

Kathleen had to look away. She couldn't let Mom see the sadness she felt. Really, it was closer to a kind of horror.

When the nurse came with medication, Mom introduced Kathleen, and after the nurse left, they talked about the details of the operation.

The box that had unexpectedly opened, had been closed. But in its fashion, could it have been Pandora's box? Kathleen had to wonder.

When Kathleen got back to her office she closed her door and pulled the daily copy of Deb's testimony. She had only started reading when Si Wallace knocked and came in.

"I asked the receptionist to let me know when you got back." He closed the door behind him. What now?

He said he wondered why she had not come to him after the stories in the *Post* on Saturday and Sunday. "The firm is behind you and Tony," he said. "I trust nothing I've said—or anything else—has given you another impression?"

"No," she said evenly, "but it's good to hear you confirm it."

"I'd be terribly disappointed if you were unhappy and didn't tell me," he said. "I've taken more pride than I deserve in watching you develop into one of the three or four that the future of the firm depends upon."

"Well, since you ask," she said, "I would like to be on the firm's screening committee."

"I haven't put you on committees because I guessed you wouldn't like the work." Wallace smiled. "Our partners can be tedious."

She nodded with a silent amen. "But the screening committee would be important to me."

"May I ask why?"

"If a case comes to us like the one Tony is trying," she said, "I don't want to turn it down."

She told him she wanted to handle criminal cases, cases where she felt strongly but where it wouldn't be possible to charge her hourly rate. If others had the same option, there might be less burnout.

"The firm will benefit," she said. "We attract business because of our strength in litigation. But great trial lawyers aren't made on insurance company defense work."

He looked interested so she pressed on and told him she wasn't talking about pro bono stuff like representing garden-variety criminals or tenants squabbling with landlords and vice versa. "I mean challenging cases with tough issues."

"I believe you are absolutely right," he said after letting her run down. "You are on the screening committee and I expect your voice to be heard."

Tony did not get back to the office until after six. He had dropped Deb off in German Village, left her at the house with food they had picked up at Wendy's.

"Westphal is no help, a disaster," Tony sounded depressed.

"What now?" She was suddenly angry, blaming Tony, the messenger, for bad news she didn't want to cope with. Probably he was overreacting, she decided, affected by the worries Deb's cross-examination had raised.

"The guy is no match for Ryne Durenberg," Tony said. "Bender will tear him on cross."

"Well, what did he say?"

"To start with, it's his *manner*. Kathleen, I couldn't shut the man up when he was giving his credentials. He told the jury about his grade-point average in college, for God's sake. I couldn't cut him off, that would have looked worse."

You could have and you should have, she was thinking.

"I should have rehearsed him on his qualifications, I guess."

"I wouldn't have done that either," she said quickly. "But has he backed off on anything?"

"No. It's just that . . . he's so *pompous*. Hey, *I'd* love to cross-examine him."

"Did you finish the direct?"

"Yes."

"Did he at least say the magic words?"

"Yes, but that's about all we got—"

"Stop it, Tony. If he said she didn't know the difference between right and wrong at the time, the jury gets instructed on insanity." She was irked, unreasonably, and knew it. She wished she had been in the courtroom . . .

"Let me just give you a for-instance," he said, ignoring her annoyance and even skepticism. Well, damn it, trying this case wasn't his idea or choice. "Bender asks the guy how important dream interpretation is to his conclusions. 'Significant,' Westphal says. The way someone ties their shoes would be significant to this character. So Bender puts on an act, pretends great interest, leads Westphal through a boring treatise on the theory of dream interpretation. Westphal pays no attention to the titters from the jury box and gallery. Then Bender asks about the most revealing dream, the one where Deb wrestled underwater with a sea monster after picnicking on a boat with her husband. 'Suppose I had that dream, only it was me and Judge Conklin out there in the boat?' Bender asks.

"I objected but the judge said he wanted to hear this. 'Now

suppose,' Bender said, 'that I shove a hair dryer down on the judge while he's in the tub. Would that convince you I was insane?' "

Tony threw up his hands. "Westphal should have made a joke out of it. Maybe said that would make Bender very insane indeed. Or he could have said it was only one factor to consider. But guess what Westphal did?"

"How would I know?" she said, half wanting to toss a hair dryer herself.

"He launched his pompous self into another dissertation, into Carl Jung, archetypal psychology, something he calls 'the shadow,' the differences between Freud and Jung and, God, stuff I can't remember. Bender is laughing him out of court and our client into a conviction."

"Tony," she said sharply, "we're wasting time."

He looked at her. "And what's eating you, counselor?"

"I'm *tired*," she said. "You'll get to me tomorrow, won't you?"

"Probably. So you better go with me in the morning and wait. I don't know how long Bender will keep Westphal on cross."

"I need to call the hospital, check on Mom." She picked up the phone. "Then I want you to cross-examine me. Like I did with Deb."

"Is that why you're being a bitch?" Tony grinned. "To get me fired up to rip you?"

She held the phone, not yet dialing. "No," she said, "but I don't want to be up all night. After we're done I've got more work to do on the instructions." But she welcomed him giving her a chance to get off the hook.

She and Tony got to the Hall of Justice at eight, before the judge or bailiff, before Bender, long before the jurors were brought up from the jury lounge.

Tony left her in the cubicle that had been assigned to the defense. He wanted to be in Judge Conklin's chambers when the judge arrived, hand Judge Conklin the three additional requests for instructions that Kathleen had prepared.

After court opened, Kathleen took out one of the files she had brought along. There was a telephone, she could make calls, use the time.

She got no work done. Through the thick door she could hear laughter from the courtroom. She called the hospital. Mom was back in her room after the operation. Mom sounded relieved. At 10:30 Tony came in. It was the morning recess. "Bender is still going strong," he said.

"I heard the laughter."

"It's a circus."

During the noon recess, they ate sandwiches they had brought from home and Tony went to the basement cafeteria for soft drinks. Bender had concluded his devastating cross of Westphal. Then, in chambers, Bender had moved to preclude Kathleen from testifying because of her involvement as an attorney in the case. "The judge gave him short shrift," Tony said. "Reminded him he waived his objection."

"So I'm up?"

Tony nodded. "I'm glad we decided to put you on last."

At 1:10 Tony went out, to be at counsel table when the jury filed in. Five minutes later Junior Fultz opened the door to summon Kathleen.

Standing next to the witness box, she took the oath from Junior Fultz and settled herself in the box. Facing her from across the pit were the twelve jurors and two alternates, the women and men Tony had described to her after the first day of trial. Bender, at his counsel table, was examining notes, paying no attention to her. Deb, seated next to Tony, stared at her with wide brown eyes. To her left and above her, Judge Conklin leaned forward. He was peering down at her like, it suddenly occurred to her, a disapproving nun questioning her excuse for misbehavior. Grow *up,* Kathleen, she instructed herself. Your sister's life depends on it.

Junior Fultz put a glass of water on the shelf in front of her. At counsel table, Tony stood to ask his first question.

Chapter 20

SHE WAS WEARING a midnight-blue suit. Her short-cut hair, wisps across the forehead, framed a quick-eyed, honest face. She spoke in clear, unrushed phrases, looking from one juror to another. Tony had informed Judge Conklin that she would be the last witness called by the defense.

Tony questioned her from the rear corner of the jury box. It gave him an angle. Without being noticed he could check each juror's reaction and keep his eye on Judge Conklin. Tony went directly to the guts of the case and asked about Deb's bruise.

"It was under the left eye. Deb had covered it with makeup but it was the first thing I noticed."

"Where were you?"

"We met on a Saturday morning at Tommy's Diner."

"Did she tell you how she got the bruise?"

"Not until we had talked for about two hours."

Socko Bender had turned in his chair. He seemed more interested in the lawyer who was handing papers to Junior Fultz, the sketch artist in the first row of the gallery who was concentrating on drawing Kathleen, the woman in the back corner who had brought knitting. Studied indifference, which he hoped to communicate to the jury. Pay all this no attention, he was saying.

"You did, however, finally talk about the bruise?"

"Deb said she and her husband had argued," Kathleen said. "He hit her."

Kathleen did not want to bring Judge Roberts into the trial, not unless Bender insisted. He had not in cross-examining Deb.

Bender affected being as bored by the testimony as by the earlier description of how the two sisters got to know one another while talking in the booth at the diner.

"Did Deb say whether she had been struck before?"

"She said she hadn't. But she was afraid of Buzz. 'Buzz had a violent streak,' Deb told me."

"That is unresponsive." Bender rammed his chair back as he got up, belying his feigned lack of interest in the testimony. "I've leaned over backward to be fair, but it is also *hearsay* and improper opinion testimony, as this lawyer-turned-witness very well knows."

"Objection sustained," said Conklin, who had been waiting for Bender's objection. "The jury will disregard everything except that the defendant had not been struck before."

"After Deb told you how she got the bruise, did she exact a promise?" Tony pressed on.

"She made me promise not to tell about getting hit."

"Not anyone?"

"That's right. Not even her father and mother."

Bender was crouched on the edge of his chair, ready to object.

"Did she seem frightened?"

The objection came.

"I think I'll allow that," said Judge Conklin.

"Yes," said Kathleen. "Deb was frightened because she knew Buzz had a violent streak."

Judge Conklin scowled at Kathleen. "The response by the witness was uncalled for," he said. But the jury had the point, emphasized by Bender's outrage and the judge's second instruction to disregard.

Following the mid-morning recess, Tony asked about Deb's decision to conceal the second HD test from Buzz.

"When she didn't do exactly as he wanted," said Kathleen, "he accused her of trying to destroy him and his campaign."

"What was Deb's reaction when she received the results of the second test?"

" 'This is the happiest day of my life,' she said. 'We were all hugging and crying. Even the doctors.' "

"Did Deb change her mind about telling Buzz?"

"Yes. She thought Buzz would be thrilled. She couldn't wait to tell him."

"Did that strike you as odd?"

Tony watched Bender, waiting for the howl. But Bender had, for once, missed the point. He assumed the answer would explain the inconsistency—the earlier testimony that Deb didn't want Buzz to know she was being retested.

"It was more than odd," said Kathleen. "It was chilling. I wondered how Deb could think he would be thrilled when she would be telling him she had an incurable disease that can end in insanity."

Bender's face was flushed. He might have missed his objection, but he was telling Kathleen to prepare for a mauling.

"You and your friend may think what you're doing is cute," Bender told Tony before court convened on Thursday morning. Bender, for the first time, had gotten to the Hall of Justice ahead of him. Overnight, five inches of snow had fallen and Tony and Kathleen had gotten stuck in their drive.

"The truth hurts, doesn't it, Bender?"

"This trial won't be the end for you and her. You two have obstructed the criminal justice system."

Tony just looked at him, shook his head and went into the small conference room where Kathleen was waiting. If Bender chose, he could cause trouble, even if his charge was hyperbolic. Maybe that was his tactic. Send a message, soften Kathleen up for cross-examination.

"Anything new?" Kathleen asked.

"No," Tony said. "I probably won't object much. I'll let the jury see that you can handle Bender and don't need protection."

"Wonderful," she said. "Throw your witness to the lion." But her eyes were bright. Actually the idea seemed to stimulate her.

Still, Tony decided to make a peace offering before the opening of court. "Can we talk a minute?" he asked, approaching Bender's table. Bender got up, walked through the bailiff's door and into the rear corridor.

"Why do you have a hard-on for me?" Tony said without preface.

"Look," said Bender, "I don't like you. I don't like your witness. I don't like the big-deal law firm pulling stunts as if the rules didn't apply to them. Your defendant is guilty as hell. She had to bend over and shove that dryer into the water. Another thing . . . because I knew the defendant's father, I argued my boss into the best deal I've offered a defendant in twenty years. Six months for murder? How did your so-called witness take my act of generosity? It's 'ludicrous,' she said, and turned up her nose."

Bender started back to the courtroom, then turned. "I also don't like it," he said, "when you think I'm too stupid to realize I'm being conned before I cross-examine your *friend* the witness." He didn't wait for a reply.

Kathleen's heels clicked as she walked across the pit to the witness box. The gallery, which had also attracted lawyers, was anticipating the confrontation.

"Tell me, Attorney Sullivan," Bender began, "did the late Buzz Garrison believe the results that showed his baby did not have the HD gene?"

Tony considered an objection. Let Bender call her Attorney Sullivan, he decided. Bender might overdo it.

"That's a good question," said Kathleen. "But I have no way of knowing what was in Mr. Garrison's mind."

"Unlike your client's," said Bender. "You seem to know everything that was in the defendant's mind." As he spoke Bender stalked the witness box.

Kathleen looked puzzled, as if she were trying to remember. "I believe I said Deb seemed frightened by her husband. But I don't think I claimed knowledge of everything in her mind."

"You don't claim to know what she was thinking when she electrocuted her husband?"

"No."

"Tell me, Attorney Sullivan"—Bender turned his back on the

witness box to face the jury—"has the defendant admitted to you that she intended to kill her husband?" Bender turned on Kathleen. "Has not the defendant told you there is no defense to the murder charge?"

Kathleen glanced up at Judge Conklin. She was trying to hide her concern—her fear. Tony objected, requested permission to approach the bench.

Judge Conklin nodded.

"This calls for a violation of attorney-client privilege," said Tony.

"Hasn't that been waived?" asked the judge. "Hasn't the witness already testified to things the defendant said to her?"

"Her testimony related to the time before an attorney-client relationship was formed."

"Mr. Bender?" The judge looked at the prosecutor. Bender argued that no bright line could be drawn, that when the lawyer became a witness the privilege of confidentiality disappeared. "They can't take a shield and use it as a sword," said Bender.

Judge Conklin swiveled in his chair. He seemed to be studying the American flag. He was troubled by the point. This was a gamble Tony hadn't imagined Bender might take. Kathleen could nail him with her answer. But actually it was no gamble . . . Tony knew the answer to Bender's question and that Kathleen, if forced, would not lie.

"I'm not sure on this one," said Judge Conklin. "I'm not going to take the answer at this time. But I assume the cross-examination may last until the noon recess?"

"It will, Your Honor," said Bender.

"That will give me time to do some research." The judge invited counsel to present authorities. "If I decide the question is proper," Conklin told Bender, "you will have the opportunity to pursue it this afternoon."

Bender smiled at the jury as he walked away from the bench. "We'll return to this later," he told Kathleen.

What was the jury thinking? Wouldn't they assume the worst even if Judge Conklin refused to allow the answer?

Bender was firing questions at Kathleen, establishing her various acts as an attorney after receiving the call on the night of Garrison's death. The relevance was to show Kathleen's bias. But now there was a greater danger.

"When did you stop being the attorney and start being the witness?" asked Bender.

"I don't follow," said Kathleen.

"We are having trouble," said Bender, "keeping track of this now-I'm-a-witness, now-I'm-the-attorney routine."

"I have always been a witness," said Kathleen. "I did act on Deb Garrison's behalf when she called me."

"And you still are. You have your associate trying the case, but aren't you here in the courtroom to do what you can to help—?"

"Mr. Biviano has been the attorney since I realized I would have to testify."

"When you saw that the other evidence established her guilt?"

"No."

"Didn't there come a time when you said to yourself, if I don't get in there and testify, my *sister* is going to jail for murder?"

Judge Conklin glanced at Tony. But an objection risked adding to the appearance that they were hiding the truth.

"I have *never* thought Deb Garrison was guilty of murder," said Kathleen quietly but with intensity.

Judge Conklin declared an early recess for lunch, to look at the law. And he still hoped to finish the trial on Friday.

During the mid-morning recess Tony had called Jay Melnik. On the lunch break Tony checked with him.

"A messenger is on his way," Melnik said.

"Jay came through," Tony told Kathleen. Melnik had collared three associates, sent them to the library.

"It's ridiculous," said Kathleen. "Deb isn't capable of judging her state of mind. You don't ask people in that condition to diagnose themselves, to be responsible in their talk."

"That argument won't go." Tony didn't point out the flaws, or that her changed mood indicated the success Bender was having with her. She would realize it soon enough, if she didn't already. He read the Melnik material as he ate his sandwich.

In the end Judge Conklin decided to recognize the attorney-client privilege. "My research supports yours," he told Tony. Tony's, of course, was what Melnik had provided.

Bender took his defeat in stride. The idea had been planted in the jurors' minds, he'd settle for that.

*   *   *

"You say," Bender began the afternoon session, "that the defendant thought Buzz would be thrilled when he heard she had Huntington's disease?" Bender was standing to the side of the witness box, which forced Kathleen to choose between looking at him and looking at the jury. Bender had seen that the choice made her uneasy.

Kathleen looked at the jury. "Deb thought Buzz would be overjoyed that the *fetus* didn't have HD," she said.

"Please, Attorney Sullivan, is it possible to answer the question you are asked?"

"Didn't I?"

"What you told us before is that your sister thought Buzz would be thrilled to hear that his wife had HD."

"That's twisting what I said, Mr. Bender. Deb thought he would be thrilled. To me, Mr. Bender, that means that Buzz cared more about the fetus than about his wife. His joy over the fetus made his wife's condition less important. It meant he would win because she had no reason even to consider an abortion. He might get back in control. But yes, he did care about having a healthy baby. Deb has always said that."

"Is your speech finished?"

"I think that completes the explanation you asked for."

"I wonder why the defendant, when she testified, didn't tell us that Buzz didn't care whether she had HD or not?"

"First, I don't believe that's what I said. Second, since I wasn't here, I don't know what Deb's testimony was."

"You don't?" Bender took a step back, in apparent shock. "Didn't you rehearse the defendant?"

"I don't know what she said in court."

"Unresponsive," said Bender. "Move that the witness be required to answer the question."

"You must answer." Judge Conklin leaned forward from behind his high bench.

"Yes."

Bender pressed for details. "So," Bender said, "you had your sister at a table on the twenty-third floor of your hundred-and-fifty-lawyer office and you worked on her until you were satisfied with her story?"

"The purpose, sir, was to get the truth told so that an injustice would not be done in this courtroom."

"If we are searching for the truth, shouldn't we be told whether your sister admitted her guilt to you?"

Tony's objection was sustained and the jury instructed to disregard the question. How many times and in how many ways, Tony wondered, would Bender make the point?

"Yet even you who are her lawyer, her coach, her spokesperson here in court, her sister, the architect of her defense . . . even you claim that in all of the defendant's married life there was only one time she was struck by her husband?" It was another of Bender's jump-shifts.

"I *claim* nothing," said Kathleen. "I told you what I saw and heard."

"Yes, let's go into that. You like to analyze the defendant's behavior, look for hidden meanings. Do you find it strange that no one besides yourself saw this bruise?"

"I do not. Deb, like many women in her circumstance, was ashamed of it. She also knew how Buzz would react if—"

"Attorney Sullivan, we have your answer. I didn't ask for another speech."

"No, but you've been making a few."

The jury laughed. Judge Conklin, mildly for him, suggested that counsel and the witness limit themselves to questions and answers.

Bender came to the side of the witness box, put his jaw within a foot of Kathleen's face. "What was this so-called argument that led to this so-called bruise?"

"It concerned the campaign."

"Did she tell you what it was about?

"Yes."

"Well," said Bender. "You've testified to everything else she told you. What did she say?"

"She said Buzz would be furious if she appeared in public with a bruise. If anyone found out he had hit her."

"Ms. Attorney." Bender kept his face in front of Kathleen's. "Did you hear the question? Can we agree the argument came before, not after, the so-called bruise?"

"One of the arguments did."

"That argument is the one I am asking about."

"Buzz thought Deb had been discourteous on the telephone."

Several jurors smiled. Bender walked away from the witness box, stopped in the center of the pit and turned. "With whom was she *discourteous?*"

Kathleen looked at Tony. "Object," said Tony. "Hearsay."

"The witness may answer," said Judge Conklin. "It goes to credibility."

"Who?" Bender asked again.

"Judge Sam Roberts."

"Judge Roberts of the Franklin County court of appeals?"

"Yes."

Bender walked to his counsel table. "What was there about the conversation with Judge Roberts that led to a bruise no one but you saw?"

Kathleen left out nothing, told how Roberts was a political crony of Garrison's, how Roberts treated Deb, took liberties in touching her, called to talk about pending cases and got nasty when Buzz was not available. "On this occasion he swore at Deb because Buzz hadn't returned his calls."

"Swore?"

"Do you want the exact conversation?" Kathleen did not blink. Bender turned away and, forcing a smile, faced the jury. He was outside his plan, deviating from what had been, in most ways, a most effective cross-examination of a tough and knowing witness.

"Since you are determined to tell us," said Bender. "Let's hear it."

"I am not determined to tell you anything."

"Spare us," said Bender. "Just give us your story."

"It isn't my story."

Bender went to his counsel table and whispered something to his assistant, who left the courtroom.

"Do you still want the exact words of the conversation?" asked Kathleen.

"Never mind," said Bender. He walked slowly, head down, to the center of the pit. He seemed unsure of what he wanted to ask next. In the exchange he had lost some favor with the jury and was a good enough lawyer to know it. "You'll find a way to work that conversation in," he said. "So let's get it over with." A tactical surrender.

"Judge Roberts told Deb, 'Maybe Buzz is more interested in

being a congressman than representing auto workers.' Deb tried to pacify him. Then Judge Roberts told her, 'Forget it. I'm through screwing with you and Garrison.' Later that night Deb heard Buzz on the phone, groveling, apologizing to the judge."

Bender backed off, went with questions that were intended to show Kathleen's bias in favor of her sister. But they became repetitive, and the jurors seemed less interested. Were they, Tony hoped, seeing Garrison the way Deb had described him, as a man who had to be in control, a man more concerned about being elected than about his wife's eventually fatal disease or the decision his wife faced before she found out her baby did not have the gene?

"Are you the person who hired Dr. Westphal as the defendant's psychiatric testifier?" asked Bender.

"Yes."

"You agreed to pay that man for coming in here and educating us about the shadow, the collective unconscious and archetypal psychology?"

Kathleen smiled. "Yes," she said.

"Tell me," said Bender, "do you want to see your sister get off?"

"Not get off. Declared innocent, because I believe she is innocent."

"I give up. The witness refuses to give a direct answer to a question."

Bender went back to his table. It was a less than strong finish, Tony thought. He decided not to question Kathleen on redirect. "The defense rests its case," he said. It was 3:45.

Judge Conklin declared a recess and assembled the lawyers in his chambers. "Any rebuttal?" he asked Bender.

"Absolutely," said Bender. His assistant had contacted Judge Roberts. "The judge will categorically deny the lies the last witness slandered him with."

Judge Conklin smiled. "This case is not about Judge Roberts," he said. "Who else do you have?"

"Wait a minute," said Bender. "The judge is upset. He wants to talk to you."

"Later," said Judge Conklin. "What other rebuttal do you have?"

"We intend to put Donald LaFarge on the stand."

"For what purpose?" The judge, like everyone at the Hall of Justice, knew LaFarge. LaFarge worked on the board of elections, was vice-chairman of the Franklin County Democratic party. He kept files on everyone in politics, got satisfaction from dreaming up negative, *ad homenem* commercials. He had helped in Garrison's campaign, probably had been a crony. LaFarge was generally liked because of his storytelling knack. "The Teflon hatchet," he was called.

"Mr. LaFarge sat next to the defendant at the Jefferson-Jackson dinner two years ago," said Bender. "He told the defendant about a piece he had read in a Florida newspaper while on vacation. A woman killed her husband by putting a power drill in the water while he was in the bathtub. The testimony, Your Honor, will focus on the defendant's reaction." Tony's stomach knotted. A power drill? Crazy. But not so crazy coming out of LaFarge's mouth. The similarity between it and the hair dryer . . . the comparison could destroy Deb. "That isn't rebuttal evidence," he said.

"It most certainly is. It rebuts the testimony given by the defendant."

"LaFarge was not listed by the state."

"The witness came forward during the trial," said Bender.

"Are you suggesting that Donald LaFarge could keep something like that to himself for seven months?"

"Your Honor, Mr. Biviano's point would be material for cross-examination."

"Where is Donald LaFarge?" asked the judge.

"He's here at the Hall of Justice," said Bender. "Ready to testify."

"This is what we're going to do," said Judge Conklin. "Bring Mr. LaFarge in. I will allow the defense to conduct a voir dire examination. I'll reserve ruling on whether he can be presented to the jury."

"Fine, Your Honor." Bender got up to bring in LaFarge.

"Just a minute," said Judge Conklin. "It is after four and I'm going to send the jury home for the night. But I still expect to finish tomorrow."

"The testimony of Mr. LaFarge will be quite brief," said Bender.

"If I allow him to testify. But in any event," said the judge, "I want counsel in my chambers at seven-thirty sharp tomorrow morning. We'll hear objections to the charge and consider your requests—get that out of the way. Mr. Bender, do you have anything else in rebuttal?"

"Just Mr. LaFarge and Judge Roberts."

"Judge Roberts will not testify. We'll go to closing arguments immediately after Mr. LaFarge testifies. If I don't allow that, we'll being closing arguments when court opens at nine."

How could LaFarge be cross-examined? Tony asked himself. What argument would persuade the judge to keep LaFarge *off* the witness stand? Surely Judge Conklin saw that this was a hoax. Maybe Melnik could find some cases again. An unlisted witness should not be allowed in rebuttal on an issue that had been in the case from the beginning.

"All right." Judge Conklin looked at Junior Fultz. "Bring up the jury so I can send them home for the night."

"Your Honor," said Tony. "I have a motion."

The judge was annoyed, but Tony had to risk that. A worse consequence faced him . . . when the jurors went home they were not supposed to watch television or look at newspapers— but what if one of them did? Judge Roberts would be screaming that he'd been slandered. Bender would leak the LaFarge testimony when reporters asked him if he planned to offer rebuttal evidence. The defense could be mortally damaged even if Conklin didn't let LaFarge testify.

"I move the jury be sequestered," said Tony. "To preclude the possibility of a juror reading or hearing about either Judge Roberts or Mr. LaFarge."

"Any objection?" Judge Conklin looked at Bender.

"I don't think such a drastic step this late in the trial is at all necessary. It will inconvenience those folks and your instructions can cover the point Mr. Biviano is making."

"I'm going to grant that motion," Conklin said. "The jury will be sequestered at the Southern Hotel until a verdict is returned. Junior, you contact the jury commissioner and the county sheriff to make sure the arrangements are made. Items will need to be picked up by each juror at their homes."

It was something, Tony thought. Maybe it meant that Judge Conklin saw through the prosecution's tactic. Maybe the judge realized that LaFarge would be an unreliable witness. Maybe . . .

But the challenge remained. Tony had to shake LaFarge on voir dire. The judge had to be given a legal argument for barring the testimony.

They went into the courtroom to dismiss the jury for the night and to advise them they would be sequestered. Donald LaFarge entered the courtroom as soon as the last juror filed out.

"We'll do this in chambers," said Judge Conklin.

Tony followed the judge, the court stenographer, LaFarge, Bender and Bender's bag carrier into Judge Conklin's chambers. He'd barely had time to tell Deb to wait in the defense cubicle, to warn Deb that she must not talk to anyone. He hadn't been able to call Kathleen or Jay Melnik. How, he asked himself, did you expose a slippery fraud like LaFarge?

Donald LaFarge, of medium height and build, had a soft puffy face and unruly, caramel-colored hair that he styled in the manner of a country-western singer.

Tony's first job was to find out what LaFarge knew.

"Missus LaFarge and I had the pleasure of sitting next to the Garrisons at our traditional Jefferson-Jackson Day dinner two years ago. We were at the head table, myself between the two lovely ladies. At this particular time and occasion Buzz was out making the rounds, going from table to table, shaking hands with those who'd popped a hundred each to be there.

"Now don't hold me to how we got on this subject, but Missus Garrison and I were talking about the Fogle case. Of course I always called her Debbie. As I recollect, the Fogle case was being tried right here in this Hall of Justice at the time and I'm sure the judge and you lawyers all remember that one. The Fogle woman had shot her husband when he came home late at night. She said he was supposed to be out of town on a business trip and when she heard a noise downstairs she thought it was a burglar. In the dark, she shot the man coming up the stairs and it turned out to be her husband. You will recall, the jury didn't buy it . . . they were only out three hours.

"Well, this trial was going on and, just as a matter of conversation, Missus Garrison . . . Debbie if that's all right because she is Debbie to me . . . got talking about ways people kill one another. Now, I happened to mention a story I'd seen in the papers when Missus LaFarge and myself were vacationing in the Tampa Bay area. Woman killed her husband by bringing his power drill up from the basement. Got an extension cord, switched it on, walked it right into the bathroom and zapped him while he was in the tub. I believe I said to Debbie that if you wanted to get rid of someone you could do it that way and make it look like an accident.

"Debbie laughed and made some joke, like how could it be an accident with a power tool? Not exactly standard bathroom equipment." He smiled briefly. "Missus LaFarge wasn't listening to us, by the way. She was blathering to whoever was on the other side of her about her campaign button collection, as was her custom at these political affairs—"

"Mr. LaFarge," Tony broke in, "where did you say Buzz Garrison was when this took place?"

"Making the rounds. Table to table. Winning friends and votes."

"Yes . . . well, Mr. LaFarge, you're a well-known spinner of tales . . . aren't you just inventing this rather colorful yarn?"

"No, sir. It was in the *papers.*"

Tony let that pass. He had to. "Was this the only time you were at a political event with the Garrisons?"

"Lord, no. I hate to count the number."

"Then you must be aware that Deb, or Debbie as you know her, *always* accompanied Buzz when he went around to shake hands with guests. He insisted on it . . . she was such an asset, people loved her. He wanted her at his side at all times . . ."

LaFarge looked stung. He realized that hundreds of people could confirm the way Buzz and Deb worked a crowd together. He moved to recover.

"They *usually* did, that's right, but on this particular occasion I do believe he made the rounds or gone off for some other reason by himself. Now maybe he'd gone to use the restroom . . . all I *know* is he wasn't in on that conversation and *I* was . . ."

Tony eyed him for a beat. "Mr. LaFarge, isn't this whole incident really just something you made up?"

"Certainly not."

"You remember it clearly even though it's been two years?"

"Yes."

"When you read or first heard about the way Buzz Garrison died, did you make a connection to this alleged conversation?"

"I thought about it, yes."

"But you didn't tell Mr. Bender until this week?"

"That's right."

"The incident in Florida has similarities to what the prosecution alleges Mrs. Garrison did? Correct?"

LaFarge nodded. "Seemed that way to me."

"Which makes it hard to believe, with all the publicity, that you didn't mention this to anyone—"

"Now, wait a minute. I didn't say that."

"So you did mention it?"

"Well, sure I probably—"

"Object," said Bender. "The issue is when Mr. LaFarge first came to the prosecutor. He no doubt didn't take the earlier conversation seriously . . . why would he? . . . until he read about the cross-examination of the defendant."

LaFarge was nodding. But Judge Conklin had gotten up from his chair. "Mr. Bender," he said, "I want to hear these answers and you are not to use objections to coach the witness. The court, on the basis of what it has heard so far, has reservations and your attempt to influence the answers of this witness has added to them. Do I make myself clear?"

"Yes, Your Honor."

"Mr. LaFarge," said Tony, "the problem is that it's hard to believe this conversation took place *and* that you didn't mention it to anyone before coming to the prosecutor."

"I didn't say I didn't . . ."

"All right. Whom did you tell?"

"Oh, I can't remember."

"Was it more than one person?"

"It might have been."

"Can you give me a name?"

LaFarge shook his head and the judge told him to say no if that was his answer. Tony wondered if he should push. He had the advantage; LaFarge's story was being attacked as a recent fabrication. But Tony's purpose—as Bender and the judge saw—was to establish that LaFarge did not qualify as a rebuttal witness.

"Not even one name?"

"Well, I'm not exactly certain."

"Could any one of these mysterious, unnamed people have any connection to the prosecuting attorney's office?"

"Well, hell . . . excuse me, Your Honor, that just slipped out. Since I don't recall who I talked to . . . I mean I didn't realize the significance until I read about Debbie's cross-examination . . . I just have no way of knowing the various connections and affiliations those people might have had."

"Did you talk to Ted Gill, the county chairman?"

"It's possible."

"So this story you are telling has been known to a lot of people since Buzz died?"

"Now, look, you've got to make a distinction."

"What would that be?"

"Between what was more or less gossip and the serious conversation I had with Mr. Bender a day ago."

"Your Honor," said Tony, "I believe that the defense has established that Mr. LaFarge is not a proper rebuttal witness and that his testimony is not credible."

"Your Honor," from Bender, "might I ask a few questions?"

"No, I think I have the picture. Mr. LaFarge, would you step outside, please."

"Gentlemen," Judge Conklin said to Tony and Bender, "I'm not sure what I'm going to do. Quite frankly, I have trouble with the credibility of this witness. But that is a question for a jury to decide. I'm disturbed because the conversation between LaFarge and the defendant, if it took place, would be relevant. But if it didn't happen, putting this evidence before the jury could deprive the defendant of a fair trial."

"The jury must determine credibility," said Bender, "as you point out."

"There are also legal issues," the judge said. "Mr. Bender, you didn't lay a foundation. You didn't ask the defendant if this conversation took place."

"I didn't know about it. Your Honor, if you are considering a ruling on that basis, I say I must be permitted to recall the defendant to the stand."

"Any objection to that, Mr. Biviano?"

"Absolutely," said Tony. "To even ask her the questions would suggest that such a conversation took place."

Conklin did not dispute it. He listened.

"Further," said Tony quickly, "the defendant can't be forced back on the stand. Not after both sides have rested."

"Mr. Bender, it appears to me that you could, with reasonable diligence, have discovered the witness."

"Especially since the state called Ted Gill as a witness," put in Tony. "LaFarge talked to him."

"That wasn't specifically admitted," said the judge.

"With respect," said Bender, "I am entitled to question Mr. LaFarge and make a record before you rule."

"All right. Bring the witness back in."

When LaFarge came back the judge put him under oath for the second time. This time, though, the judge added a warning concerning the penalty for perjury.

"Mr. LaFarge," Bender began, "isn't it true that—"

"Mr. Bender." The judge was angry now. "You know better than to lead your witness."

"Mr. LaFarge," Bender began again, "are you certain you discussed this incident with anyone prior to contacting me?" He needed a *yes*.

"Well, probably not in any great detail . . ."

Bender decided to settle for the answer. He needed to offset the notion that the potentially incriminating conversation had somehow been concocted with the prosecution. Without being able to lead, without the chance to talk to LaFarge about what was happening and with the judge giving the witness his maximum-sentence stare, Bender was in danger of hurting his position. LaFarge was confused and his confidence had been shaken. Coloring the facts might be the bread and butter of LaFarge's day-to-day work in politics, but he was not accustomed to being placed under oath in a murder trial and being given a steely-eyed warning that he could be sent to prison for perjury.

"I have no further questions," said Bender. "I just wanted to clear up that one point." Which, of course, he really hadn't. Not the way he wanted to.

LaFarge was again dismissed. "Gentlemen," said Judge Conklin, "it remains a gray question. You will have my ruling when you come to chambers at seven-thirty in the morning. If either side wishes to present case authority, bring that to my residence to-night. But not after eleven."

Deb was still in the cubicle, but she didn't seem bothered by the long delay. "Wasn't Kathleen wonderful," she said. "I can't wait to tell her."

"That's where we're going," Tony said. His expression was not a happy one. Deb picked it up.

"What happened? What went wrong?"

"I'll tell you when we get there. Kathleen and I have a lot to do. We may be up most of the night."

He started out toward the elevators but he had to know, he couldn't wait, not even until they got to his car. He nudged Deb back into the cubicle.

"Deb, do you know a Donald LaFarge?"

"Sure, the vice-chairman of the county party."

"Did you ever talk to him about a woman in Florida who killed her husband by putting a power drill in the bathtub?"

"What? No . . . I don't think so."

"At a Jefferson-Jackson Day dinner two years ago?"

Deb shook her head.

"You are certain you didn't talk with LaFarge about bizarre ways of killing, then mention to him that his wife didn't seem to be interested, wasn't listening. Of course, it was just idle chitchat, but . . ."

Some recognition came into Deb's eyes and Tony's heart sank. "I don't remember anything about a power drill and a bathtub."

Better . . . "What *do* you remember, Deb?"

"I don't *really* remember anything except the kidding. Oh yes, I think we'd been talking about a case that was being tried."

"The Fogle case."

"What's this all about, Tony?"

"I'm not sure, Deb. We've got to get back to the office, though, see Kathleen."

"But, Tony, we didn't talk about a bathtub or a power drill. I'm —well, I'm almost sure we didn't."

"That's fine, Deb. Let's go." He had a throbbing across his temples that felt like hammers trying to pound their way out of his head.

Chapter 21

WHEN KATHLEEN got off the witness stand she went directly to the elevator and left the ninth floor. She thought she had done all right, but being a witness and a lawyer gave one two different perspectives. Until now, she had never quite realized the special vulnerability of a person on that stand and under oath. It was a salutary and chastising experience that more lawyers should experience. In the first-floor lobby of the Hall of Justice she put on her boots. Though bleak, it had warmed and the snow from the night before was melting. She should have driven rather than come with Tony. The sidewalks had been mostly shoveled, but crossing the streets as she walked back to the office she couldn't avoid splattering her hose. A taxi sped by, spraying her coat, making futile the mincing she'd done to pick her way through the slush.

"No calls," she told Connie when she got to the office. Tony had her private number.

"How did it go?" Connie asked.

"Pretty good, I guess. We'll know when the jury tells us."

She went to the bathroom, tried to clean up her coat and hose. Back in her office, she closed the door. What was happening in Courtroom 9A? Tony was still in the pit. Tony. She'd used the trial to postpone her decisions. The trial was nearly over. What about her trial and decision?

She went to the window. Below, the streets were crowded, people struggling through the slush, using the cleared walkways across the statehouse grounds lined up on Broad Street for busses that were delayed. The sky was overcast, a darkening neutral gray with all color washed out. Traffic was snarled and cars had their lights on.

As she looked out at the State Office Tower lights in the judicial chambers, she thought back to her argument in the supreme court when Judge Roberts had sat on the panel. If what had happened was fairly reported, Judge Roberts couldn't blame her. She'd accused him of nothing, only repeated what Deb had said.

On that night a year ago, when she'd stood there an hour before midnight looking down on the deserted streets and statehouse grounds, she'd wondered about her heredity, certain she'd never discover it, not wanting to suffer the complications if she did.

She felt as though, since then, she had been peeling away layers to get to herself. It was like her own personal summing-up for a jury of one. The first layer, peeled for her, had been the mystery about her birth. Then she'd been trapped in her fantasy life, unable to take the risk with Tony. If he hadn't confronted her she'd still be imagining how to seduce him. Now that he was totally with her, had declared how crazy he was about her, how did it make her feel? Scared? She knew that sex had not taken her to trust. She could see Sister Marguerite's disapproving eyes as she said, "I told you so." Instead of answers, sleeping with Tony had exposed the next layer.

Was the obstacle the risk of HD? She had felt she couldn't totally respond to Tony until she knew. Then she remembered her relief on leaving University Hospital. But what had changed? Her choices, her conflicts, were still there. All she'd done was peel away another layer.

She remembered looking out the window, late on the earlier night, how snug and secure her office had felt. She *belonged*. The firm accepted her, protected her. The need to get below that layer had been exposed by Deb's case and the firm politics she'd been sucked into by defending Tony.

Tony. How long would they go on living together? What did

Tony want? Really want? She was afraid to find out, not only because she might in the end be rejected, but because it would force her to face what had been silently waiting for her since she was three and got her first doll. *Children.* Mom thought she should have a child, but Mom didn't know her any better than she knew Mom.

Starting especially with Deb's struggle with the abortion decision, which became moot with the miscarriage, then in meeting the birth mother who had abandoned her, and finally in the trial —she was involved with women who had made choices about children. Now, because of Tony, children were a possibility for her, and *she* had to make the choices.

In her heart she was sure she wanted a baby, a child to feed, clothe, nourish, raise. When she thought of Mom, Dad, even Jill, she couldn't imagine them except as parents. But what did she give up? Her practice took so much of her energy. After her talk with Si Wallace on Tuesday, she had seen exciting possibilities.

Having children, she lectured herself, wasn't like going to the pet store. You didn't just decide it would be nice to have one around. She'd seen the superwomen, her contemporaries who thought they could do it all. They couldn't. At least most of them couldn't. Consciously or not, they made choices. Some sacrificed careers. Some kept children as pets. Some, of course, did manage. Could she be one of them? She doubted it. At least she wasn't confident enough to count on it. The "sacrifice" would mean not becoming the trial lawyer she was sure she could be, not following the career path Si Wallace seemed to have for her. It had never been so clear. To be in her position and to be a woman almost seemed unfair.

Or was she setting up excuses in advance, as a cop-out . . . ? She couldn't blame the firm. The firm would accommodate her. She'd gained enough status to get that. She also felt she could assume Tony would take on his share of the responsibility. No . . . that wasn't the way Tony made her uneasy, even frightened her.

Men *were* different. Obvious, but in today's world a lot of people were blurring the difference. Or trying to. Men still were able to have children as pets. Most could do it without bruising their souls. They did it by being grade-A pet owners. They furnished money, love, advice. They went to Little League games and Blue-bird camp-outs, took thorns out of paws, cradled them when they got hurt. But men could also go to the office, be on the road for a week, work nights and weekends for a month and not feel the way she knew she would when she left her baby at home, when she left her toddler at day care and tried to forget the cries of "Mommy," the reach of tiny arms trying to hold on. She was a modern woman, but old-fashioned too.

She left the window. Her dilemmas followed her. She at least needed to talk to Tony about children. Tony. What was keeping him? It was nearly six. Connie had gone home.

Tony came in at six-thirty with Deb, who ran to her. "You made them see, I watched those jurors, I know they believed you . . ."

"She's right," Tony said. "You were terrific. But . . . we've got ourselves a problem."

Kathleen had seen that in Tony's expression even as Deb was hugging her.

"Deb," Tony said, "Kathleen and I have a night's work to do. How about if we go down to the machines, get some food, then you wait in my office until it's time to go home?"

"Okay." She seemed glad to be left out of it at this point. Especially if there was a problem.

"We may need you later," he said.

Deb nodded. "I feel *much* better," she said. "I'm really glad now that I didn't take a plea. I'm grateful." She looked at Kathleen. "I owe you everything," she said.

"What happened?" Kathleen asked after they'd left Deb in Tony's office and were on their way to hers. He proceeded to fill her in about Donald LaFarge.

She promptly called Jay Melnik at his apartment to line up associates, come down to the library and get the research done.

"I think I can make LaFarge look bad." Tony was in her favored-client chair, she was sitting on the corner of her desk. "But damn, Deb *did* have some kind of exchange with him and probably about that Florida story. What if the judge lets the state recall Deb?"

"They can't."

"They sure can if Judge Conklin says so."

"But you said he wouldn't."

"He hasn't made a final decision on anything. We won't know until tomorrow morning." Tony got up, went over to the window. He turned. "We've got to prepare Deb," he said. "In case . . ."

"Let's at least wait and see what Melnik and his troops find."

"Then we'd better go down to the library and help. In three and a half hours we have to get something persuasive to Judge Conklin."

"No," she said. "I'll go down. You stay here and work on your closing argument."

"I don't know if I'll have to argue LaFarge."

"Be prepared either way."

As she was leaving he said, "I almost forgot. But here's something strange. Bender didn't cross-examine Deb about her conversation with her dad on the night it happened."

She nodded.

"How would you handle that in closing?"

"Be ready, Tony. Bender's going to give it to you right between the eyes. Donahey was protecting his daughter, or thought he was. He lied to do it. The reason Bender didn't touch that on cross is he figured he's better off leaving the jury with the impression Harrison created. Then drive it home in summation."

On the way to the library Kathleen changed her mind and decided to check on Deb. She found her on the telephone. "Mom," Deb whispered, her hand on the mouthpiece. Then back on the phone: "Listen, Mom, Kathleen's here. I've got to hang up."

"Did Tony tell you about the conversation I had with LaFarge?" she now asked Kathleen.

"Yes."

"All I really remember is we were talking about that . . . that crazy Fogle case and LaFarge brought up ways spouses kill each other and I kidded him about his wife, who was sitting next to him. But it wasn't *serious*. My God, I don't remember a thing about a *power drill* and a *bathtub*. Really."

"Good." Leave it alone, Kathleen told herself. It was a mistake to go over this. The more Deb talked the firmer and more dangerous her memory could get.

"But why is Tony asking me? He seems really worried."

"It's the end-of-the-case jitters, Deb. He's thinking about his closing argument."

"Kathleen?"

"Yes."

"I'm okay about what you did to me on Sunday night."

"I've felt awful about that."

"You're the only one who believes me. I mean the only one who can hear everything and *still* believe."

They hugged. But this time Kathleen was the one who couldn't keep from crying.

At ten-thirty she and Tony, with Deb in the back seat, drove to Judge Conklin's house. Their package contained a short brief with copies of eighteen cases attached.

She and Deb stayed in the car.

" 'See you in the morning at seven-thirty' was all he said," Tony reported.

Kathleen went to the Hall of Justice with Deb and Tony in the morning. She would chaperone Deb while Tony, Bender and the judge thrashed out the charge. She had agreed to work with Deb if the state got permission to put Deb back on the stand.

At eight-fifteen Tony came into the small cubicle without knocking. "Conklin sustained my motion," he said. "They can't use LaFarge."

She gave him a thumbs-up.

"I've got to get back," he said. "We're still going over the charge. But that looks pretty good. I think he's going to grant most of our requests."

"The one on reasonable doubt?"

"Yes . . . I've got to cut my summation. Conklin has limited us to an hour a side."

"You were afraid of LaFarge too," Deb said after Tony left.

"Yes, but that had nothing to do with my believing in you. You must believe that."

* * *

At 9:05 Tony came to get Deb and take her to counsel table. "They're bringing the jury up," he said.

"I'll be in my office," said Kathleen. "Call as soon as the jury goes into deliberation."

Chapter 22

Bender spoke first. His red handkerchief protruded neatly from his pocket, his hair was swept back in place. The setbacks he had just suffered from the rulings of Judge Conklin seemed not to have affected him.

He had his hands on the jury box rail and was speaking in a rumbling voice, confiding in the jurors as if they were family. He started by repeating the demonstrations he had performed with the hair dryer during opening statement.

"If the defendant had not acted deliberately, the plug would have pulled."

Bender put down the dryer marked "State Exhibit A" and backed a step away from the jury box. "There is just no escape from the physical facts. The defendant herself admitted that she shoved the dryer into the Jacuzzi. She quibbled but she also admitted she stooped to do it after the argument with her husband. She admitted her violent anger, that she'd even come to the point of hating her husband. So it's murder, and there's no escape." He looked up at the domed ceiling, then turned to face Tony. "Yes," he said, "there is one possible escape and the lawyers think they found it. The escape is called 'insanity.' She didn't know it was wrong, she just happened to *shove* a live dryer in that Jacuzzi without *knowing* what she was doing."

Bender turned back to the jury box. "First, maybe we should talk about another attempted escape. One that backfired. I'm sure you haven't forgotten the defendant's pitiable father. You will have the statement of Harrison Donahey with you in the jury room. Please study it. The defendant's father talked to her that night. *He* recognized murder when he saw it. So he thought the escape was to call it an accident. But as we've seen, there's no way what happened could have been an accident." Bender repeated his demonstration.

"The defendant's lawyers knew they couldn't sell accident," said Bender. "Especially not if they were to claim insanity. And finally the defendant's poor distraught father—no doubt after the defense lawyers talked to him—saw that his accident claim wasn't going to get his daughter off. You saw Harrison Donahey. Is there anyone who doesn't think he is convinced, albeit miserably, that his daughter did indeed intend to kill her husband?"

The jury seemed to be with Bender.

Bender stared again at Tony. "Mr. Biviano and his testifying partner may be many things," he said, "but they are not stupid. To the contrary." Bender kept staring and the jurors did too. Tony tried to keep his expression neutral.

"What did the lawyers do when they saw that the facts proved murder and that accident was out of the question?" Bender kept staring at him. "What the lawyers did was hire themselves a psychiatrist." Bender, shaking his head, turned and put his hands on the jury box rail. "I can only guess," he said, "at how many the attorney Ms. Sullivan tried before she came up with one who would give them the answer they wanted. But we saw who she got. Possibly the sorriest psychiatrist ever to set foot in an American courtroom."

The secretary in number nine allowed the hint of a smile. Bender had used twenty minutes, he had forty to go. To Tony it seemed like he'd been speaking for an hour. Now he was comparing the testimony of Doctors Durenberg and Westphal.

"But even Dr. Westphal wouldn't give the opinion they wanted unless he could assume one critical fact. The critical fact was that Buzz Garrison, just before he was murdered, accused his wife of aborting their baby. Now this presented problems. First, it is absurd. The baby did not have HD. When the defendant heard that news . . . you remember how overjoyed she said she was."

Suddenly almost shouting, Bender said, "Do you think Buzz Garrison didn't know his wife wanted that baby? Why would he think she had induced an abortion? It isn't enough to say she was angry at him, had decided to get a divorce. If you believe the defense, he was the one who perhaps suffered from a form of insanity. Maybe Dr. Westphal would diagnose him as insane. Maybe Dr. Westphal would diagnose you, me and the judge the same way. I don't know. In *his* world everyone is no doubt a little bit crazy.

"But let's overlook absurdity. There are greater problems. One is Harrison Donahey. He talked to his daughter that night. There isn't one word in his statement about Buzz accusing his wife of an abortion—not before he was murdered. *Not at any time.*

"And how about the nurse and patient who were in the hospital after the miscarriage—independent witnesses with no reason to lie. Isn't it clear? This accusation of abortion by Buzz Garrison is an unbelievable story that was made up later to solicit sympathy, even justification, for the defendant. To be used as the underpinnings for her snapping and going insane. A nice try, but clearly preposterous.

"Now, I do believe Buzz and the defendant disagreed on whether to abort their baby if the baby had carried the HD gene. Buzz would never have threatened her, acted as the defense claims. His record of respect for a woman's choice is undisputed. But there was a disagreement. Buzz and his wife each had their points. His was that the baby she was carrying would probably have a normal life until age forty. Why abort it? Why deprive the baby of that life? And yes, the defendant saw it differently. She wanted to kill the fetus and try for a genetically perfect baby."

The jurors were looking at Deb, and Tony didn't like the way they were looking at her. Bender was putting it in the cruelest way . . . making Buzz seem reasonable, Deb a frigid babykiller. Twisting things out of context and perspective. Deb was no such thing. She had never even *decided* on an abortion *if* the fetus was found to have HD.

"But when the test result came," Bender pressed on, "I think the defendant and Buzz were both relieved.

"But then!" Bender slammed his palm on the jury box rail and stepped back. "The defendant had her miscarriage. That upset her. We can understand that. But the miscarriage was not Buzz Garrison's fault!"

Lowering his voice, he went on. "It was a tragedy for Buzz. After all, he had wanted the baby even if the baby wasn't genetically perfect. Yet the defendant blamed Buzz. She resented his opposition to her determination to kill the less-than-perfect baby. She felt *guilty*. She built up a *resentment*. A terrible resentment, with terrible consequences.

"Now, when she has her miscarriage she hasn't gotten over her resentment, so she blames her husband. That is what the facts show, folks. Even the defendant's own testimony, if you study it.

"But this case is *not* about a woman's choice. That argument ended when the baby tested negative. This case is about a woman who, because of her own guilt and resentment, had come to hate her husband." Bender paused. He was looking at each juror individually, going down the line, making sure they got his point.

"So here is what you must decide. This case does not present a question of the defendant's sanity. The question is whether the defendant had a right to commit murder because she had come to hate her husband.

"It comes down to this. Buzz Garrison was deprived of life because the defendant could not get over *her* earlier decision to kill her baby and his refusal to agree with her. Buzz Garrison was killed because her hate festered until it moved her to commit murder on the night of June thirteenth." Bender stood at the box, looking at the jurors. It had been a dramatic finish.

He took a deep breath and glanced at the clock. He was not done. "But," he said, "did plain facts and irrefutable logic stop the defense? Not with Attorney Sullivan waiting in the wings. Attorney Sullivan has the solution. She'll stop being the lawyer and start being the witness. It's like Clark Kent. She steps into the phone booth and out comes Super Testifier, riding to her sister's rescue." Were a few jurors smiling? "And Super Testifier was good at what she set out to do. Very good. I've got to admit that she put me in my place more than once.

"You saw the result, the orchestrated story told by the defendant and supported by no one other than her lawyers. They want you to believe that Buzz Garrison was a monster, a wife beater, a violent man—someone different from the Buzz Garrison who was known by everyone else. If Buzz Garrison was a monster, where are the witnesses? The defendant's friends? Her mother? Her father? Wouldn't there be *someone*—other than Super Testifier—who could provide some evidence of that? They couldn't produce a shred.

"I ask you also to think—think long and hard—about the defendant's most important words. Words spoken before she called Attorney Sullivan, before her lawyers got hold of her and cooked up this preposterous insanity defense; before she sat down with—or got on the couch of—the psychiatrist from outer space and found out what she needed to say if she wanted to avoid responsibility for killing her husband.

"What did she tell the nine-one-one operator? It was no elaborate excuse. Nothing about accident. No mention of being accused of inducing an abortion. "You remember what she said, don't you?"

He made sure they did.

" 'I killed my husband.' *That's* what she said."

When Tony rose he could feel the resistance. Jurors were looking down and to the side, not returning his attempt to make eye contact. "Mr. Bender is impressive," he began. "If I were sitting on your side of the rail, I might even think the defendant was guilty."

It got their attention. *"Unless,"* he said. *"Unless* I thought about what Mr. Bender said. *Unless* I remembered the evidence Mr. Bender left out." The jurors were curious. They would give him a chance, he hoped.

"Let me begin where Mr. Bender ended," he said. "With the words 'I killed my husband.' What that evidence proves is that Deb Garrison was in *shock.* Does being in shock rule out that the killing was accidental? Of course not. Just the opposite.

"There is not the easy solution to this case that Mr. Bender insists there is. The difficult job you are required to do is determine the state of Deb Garrison's mind. That is what the case is about. To determine her state of mind, you have to open up and allow yourselves to *feel* what it was like to live her life. I hope that none of you will ever have to suffer what Deb Garrison endured. But because you are her jury, you must put yourself in her place. You have to let yourselves understand the pressure she was under, the blows her psyche and body had taken. You don't need

Dr. Westphal to understand those things. If you want, you can laugh at some of Dr. Westphal's theories. I did myself. But use your *own* judgment. Is not Dr. Westphal right when he says Deb had been beaten down to the point where she did not know what she was doing?

"Of course Deb agonized over whether to give birth to a baby who would grow up with a disease that ends in insanity and death. It was like no other decision she had ever faced. It was so difficult that she ignored her own disease. How would *you* like to receive that kind of news—when a few months before you didn't even know what Huntington's disease was? And if that wasn't enough, this young woman is watching her own mother go down, get worse every time they visit. Her mother—this disease can be that cruel—had even attempted suicide.

"So does Buzz Garrison support his wife as she faces what might overwhelm any of us? He does not. Those things were insignificant compared to juggling the time slots for political commercials on television. His afflicted wife has to make her decisions alone.

"She considers not giving birth to a child who will inevitably end up diseased and probably insane. Especially after she sees what it would be like to raise a genetically diseased child with an unsupportive husband more concerned about winning elections than about his wife and child.

"Now, I agree with Mr. Bender about one point. The case does not turn on whether you are pro-life or pro-choice. Some of you might not have even considered the decision Deb considered if her fetus had tested positive for the HD gene. Dr. Weingard told you that sixty-five percent of the women who must face that choice approach it as Deb did. *No one knows, including Deb herself, whether she would have gone through with an abortion if the test of the fetus had gone the other way.* But *that* isn't the issue. Deb's baby, as it turned out, did not have the HD gene.

"Thank God, Deb thought, that horrible choice was behind her. From the time of the second test on, Deb Garrison wanted her baby more than she ever wanted anything in her life. She was planning her entire life around her baby.

"And then, tragically, she has the miscarriage. Please, ladies and gentlemen, try to imagine how *that* felt." He pulled his handkerchief, wiped his forehead.

"Let's go to the night of June thirteenth. Put yourself in Deb's mind, standing there at the vanity, getting ready to go out and look good, boost her husband and his political ambitions. You're trying to forget the baby you just lost. You are suffering from a postpartum depression. And *then* you are accused by this husband of killing your baby. Could *anything* be more cruel?" He paused, looked each juror in the eye. They were definitely listening.

"Now Mr. Bender says it is not credible that Buzz accused her of inducing an abortion. Is he correct? Did not Buzz Garrison take it as a *rejection* when Deb did seriously consider having an abortion against his wishes? Did he not convince himself in the rush of his self-centered ambitions that she was determined to ruin his future in politics? Did he not believe she was only waiting until after the election to get away from him and his abuse? Did he not convince himself, however perversely, that she didn't want *his* child? Yes, he thought of it that way. *His.* He even questioned whether she was lying when she gratefully reported that the fetus was healthy. Talk about festering and hate. Buzz Garrison's hate —his anger over his perceived loss of total control over his wife— *that's* what festered and tormented him until he created his own twisted reality. My God, he smashed his wife in the face because he thought she was out to wreck his campaign!

"It's not only credible that he accused Deb of abortion. The evidence *demands* that we believe it.

"So. There Deb is, trying to do everything she can to get Buzz elected because she knows that separation will be easier if he is. She has lost her baby. *And he accuses her of murdering the child she was living for.*

"Is there anyone here who can say that she or he could have withstood the pressure better than Deb?"

The mail carrier in number five winced. Several looked at Deb. Deb was crying now, had her handkerchief in front of her mouth. Tony decided to take the gamble.

"You know what I think," he said. "I think Buzz Garrison caused Deb's miscarriage."

Bender instantly objected and the judge sustained it, but two jurors had nodded, if almost imperceptibly. Or was that his imagination? Tony asked himself.

"Now, Mr. Bender kept repeating the word *absurd,* as if by

giving his opinion he could make it so." Which, of course, was what Tony had just done. "The prosecution says Deb is lying. The prosecution's entire case is based on the assumption that Buzz Garrison is not the person Deb has described. Mr. Bender also says Kathleen Sullivan is lying to you. So you must evaluate both Deb and Kathleen Sullivan. You saw them. Were they telling the truth? Remember how brutally honest Deb was in answering Mr. Bender's questions—even those that seemed to hurt her. Unlike Mr. Bender, I'm not going to tell you who to believe and who not to believe. That is your job and I am confident you will do it conscientiously.

"As you do that job, I want you to ask this question. Was Buzz Garrison, the politician, the same person as Buzz Garrison in his private life with his wife? You have heard witnesses who knew him politically and two strangers who saw him briefly in the hospital. But there is no dispute about Buzz Garrison's *public* image.

"This case is about how he treated his wife when no one was looking. It is about treating his wife so miserably that she was terrified to let anyone know he had hit her. She knew how he reacted to anything that might hurt his political chances. And yes, Deb was afraid of him.

"She did tell one person. She told her sister, Kathleen Sullivan. But she did so only after they had been together for two hours. She did so because makeup wasn't good enough to conceal the bruise she got from being smashed in the face by a six-foot-six ex-athlete. It if hadn't been for that bruise, ladies and gentlemen, there would have been no one to speak for Deb except Deb herself.

"Now it happens that Deb's sister is a lawyer. The prosecution has hammered on that. As though it were somehow something sinister. Coming from Mr. Bender . . . well, the point is, please, use your common sense. Should Kathleen not have testified because she was a lawyer? Should Deb be convicted because her sister happens to be a lawyer? I hope you will agree that Kathleen's testimony should be evaluated on what you saw and heard. Not on the profession that she chose fifteen years ago. Not on Mr. Bender's repeated pandering to a belief that no one should trust lawyers." He turned to Bender. "What is the logic in that? Is he not a lawyer? Does that make everything he has said during the last two weeks subject to automatic disbelief?"

Bender actually seemed to color under the collar. But he . . . and Tony . . . knew that in fact most people did have strong negative feelings about lawyers. His tactic could be derided by Tony, but Bender had felt it was a good one.

Tony paused. He had five minutes remaining. He reminded the jury that Bender would get to speak last, that since Tony could not answer he would rely on the jury to do that for him.

"This case is about two things," he said. "The first we have talked about at length. It is about the state of Deb's mind on June thirteenth. But the second I have not yet mentioned. Nor did Mr. Bender breathe a word about it. Maybe Mr. Bender wants to keep it a secret.

"This is also a case about reasonable doubt." He picked up his copy of the charge Judge Conklin would be giving.

"This is not my idea of what the law should be." He waved his copy of the charge. "This is the law that governs in Ohio and every courtroom in America. The prosecuting attorney takes an oath to uphold the law. And the law he is sworn to uphold includes the fundamental American principle that Deb Garrison must *not* be convicted unless you are convinced beyond a reasonable doubt that she is guilty."

He took Judge Conklin's charge and read slowly the part that placed the burden of proof on the state to prove intent to kill beyond a reasonable doubt.

"When you leave this courtroom and go into deliberation," he said, "you will have Deb Garrison's future, her life, in your hands. When you come back with a decision, make sure it is one *you* can live with for the rest of your lives. If you can say beyond any reasonable doubt that Deb was *not* driven to the point where she didn't know what she was doing—then send her to prison for twenty years. If you can say beyond a reasonable doubt that Deb sat in that witness box and lied to you—send her to prison."

Bender started to rise, reconsidered, sat back without objecting.

"*But* if you have a reasonable doubt, you *cannot* find Deb guilty. Justice will not permit that. The oath you took will not permit it. The law of Ohio will not permit it. Most importantly, your conscience will not permit it. I leave Deb's future in your hands."

Tony sat down at counsel table and wiped his forehead with his handkerchief. He had made the points that he believed had to be made. The jury, at times, *seemed* to be with him. But the case wasn't over. Bender was lumbering toward the jury box rail. He had saved twelve minutes for rebuttal.

"When I was in law school," Bender began, "I had a professor who told us about an old warhorse of a lawyer who had achieved remarkable success in getting defendants acquitted.

"The old warhorse, after he retired, was asked to reveal his secret. 'When the facts are on my side,' he said, 'I pound on the facts. When the law is on my side, I pound the law. When neither the facts nor the law are on my side, I pound the table.' Now, Mr. Biviano has improved that strategy," said Bender. "He doesn't have the law on his side. And he doesn't have the facts. But instead of pounding the table he's been pounding on your emotions. He's been pounding as hard as he can and in every way he can for the last hour.

"Forgive me, ladies and gentlemen, if I bring us back to the law and the facts." Bender paused. He looked, one by one, at each juror. As though challenging them. "You each took an oath to follow the law as Judge Conklin gives it to you," he said. "And to apply that law to the facts of this case. The state—the people of Ohio—rely on you to obey the oath you took.

"That means, folks, that you can't let Mrs. Garrison off just because you might feel sorry for her. Or because her husband didn't *understand* her. Or because they had some arguments. If we were looking for fault in the marriage, I suspect we could find it on both sides. I mean, she is, after all, plotting a divorce but doesn't tell him. She has a test that will determine whether his child lives or dies—she doesn't tell him about that in advance either.

"But this case is not about who caused the marriage to come apart. It is about murder as charged."

Bender walked to his counsel table, picked up a paper, came back to the rail. "This is the charge Judge Conklin will give you," he said. *"The defendant is presumed to have intended the natural and probable consequences of an act purposefully done by the defendant."*

"Your oath requires you to apply that law to the facts you have heard. The facts, folks—that is, the relevant facts—are not even disputed. Here is what they are.

"The defendant on the night of June thirteenth had come to hate her husband.

"The defendant was violently angry and *intended* to hurt her husband.

"The defendant either bent over or stooped to shove a live electrical appliance into the water." Bender stepped back to pick up the transcript. He read Deb's answer, where she said she had thrown or shoved the dryer.

"Now, that brings us to a witness Mr. Biviano didn't mention. A witness of whom Mr. Biviano didn't ask a single question. Let me read you a question I put to the electrical engineer and the answer he gave. 'What would be the natural and probable consequence of putting a live appliance into a Jacuzzi?' This is the answer. 'Death by electrocution.' I think we all know that, even without an expert to tell us. I think Mrs. Garrison knows, though she said, 'I wasn't thinking about that at the time.'

"Let me read you again the law you took an oath to follow: *The defendant is presumed to have intended the natural and probable consequences of an act purposefully done by the defendant.*

"The evidence is that the defendant, in a fit of conscious anger, *purposefully* shoved a live hair dryer into the water. There is no reasonable doubt in this case. There is not even the shadow of a doubt."

Bender glanced at the clock. "I have just three more minutes. Then Judge Conklin will tell you the law you must follow when you make your decision.

"I haven't the time to comment on each of the emotional arguments Mr. Biviano made. They just are not relevant. He made them for one purpose—to divert attention from the *law* and the *facts.*

"As you go into deliberation, let me offer two things to consider.

"First, the insanity defense—the escape that Mr. Biviano and his testifying partner have seized upon—requires the defendant to *prove* that she was so deranged when she shoved the dryer in the water that she was incapable of knowing whether the act was right or wrong. That's the law. Judge Conklin will tell you to follow it.

"As you do, the second thing to consider is the defendant's testimony from the morning I questioned her. I tried very hard not to badger her or accuse her. I hope you'll agree that I didn't. I only asked for the facts. The facts came out clear and undisputed. The defendant remembers almost everything about that night. In detail. She remembers the necklace she was going to wear, the color of her lipstick and where everything was placed in the bathroom. She remembers shoving the dryer into the water. She remembers being angry at the time and wanting to hurt Buzz. There is no evidence that she was disoriented or confused. The lawyers and her psychiatrist, I'm sure, have scoured her history. There is no evidence of anything remotely resembling a mental disorder.

"The only vagueness came in response to questions that asked about her intentions. 'I don't remember,' she kept saying. Well, what else could she say?

"Insanity? Excuse me for being blunt—don't let the defense play you for suckers. In Ohio, ladies and gentlemen, what this defendant did is called murder.

"One last word. It is not your fault that the defendant is on trial. You are not punishing her. She is punished because of what she did—not what you are going to do. I am confident that each of you will follow the oath you took when you became members of this jury. If you do, there is only one verdict you can return: Guilty of murder as charged."

Chapter 23

Tony's call came at twelve-fifteen.

"How does it look?" Kathleen asked.

"I don't know. Bender was strong in rebuttal."

"Is Deb all right?"

"She's nervous, naturally. But she wants us to get away for lunch. How soon can you be here?"

"Give me fifteen minutes."

"I'll get a sandwich for Deb, be waiting for you out front."

They went to Lindey's in German Village. Tony told her that the jury was having lunch brought in. "With all the instructions and verdict forms," he said, "they won't reach a verdict before late this afternoon at the earliest." In addition to Guilty and Not Guilty by Reason of Insanity, Judge Conklin had given them verdict forms and instructions on Involuntary Manslaughter, and Not Guilty—outright acquittal.

"We're in a hurry," Tony told the waiter. The idea of getting away for a meal had seemed appealing, but it was also a burden. It felt as though things were happening in the courtroom. Tony gave her the highlights of the summations.

"Tony," she said. "Nobody could have tried this case better than you. I mean it." And she did.

When they got back to the ninth floor Junior Fultz told them nothing had happened. Tony was trying to get a reading on Junior's reaction to the summations. Kathleen went to check on Deb.

She found Jill in the defense cubicle with her daughter. Deb had used the phone to call Jill, and Jill wanted to be there during the wait for a verdict. Deb and Jill had chairs pushed together at the end of the table. Deb was holding Jill's hand, stroking her forearm.

"Tony is back," Kathleen told them. "I'll leave you two. We'll be in the courtroom."

"Wait. Don't leave," Jill said as Kathleen was about to close the door.

Kathleen pulled a chair, sat at the other end of the table. The windowless room smelled familiar with its musty residue from the smokers and bodies who had made it headquarters during trials. The scent of barbecue sauce came from the wastebasket in the corner. It was a small room with the table centered under a tray of fluorescent lights. The table, like the four chairs, was coated in a milky shellac that was blistered and peeling.

"What's Mr. Biviano doing?" Jill asked. She was having trouble talking. She swallowed between words. "Why did he leave Debbie here alone?"

"It's all right, Mom," Deb said. "I told him to go."

"It's not all right. You have questions."

"I'll find Tony," Kathleen said, and slid her chair back, glad for an excuse to leave. She was remembering the day and a half she had spent in this room while Deb was testifying; the morning she had waited to be called as a witness.

"No," said Jill. "Don't you leave us too."

Jill's upper body started shaking. She withdrew her hand from Deb and clasped her arms in front of her chest. Deb got up and wrapped her arms around her mother.

"What questions do you have?" Kathleen asked Deb.

Deb had been looking at the jury all through the trial. "There was a difference," Deb said. "They seemed to be with me when you testified. But during Mr. Bender's last argument—after Tony's—I could see it in their eyes. They're going to find me guilty. When do I go to jail?"

"Wait a minute," said Kathleen. "Tony thinks we've got a good chance. He was watching the jury too."

"You don't know what it was like," said Deb. "It was like being the freak in a carnival. Those people stare at you as if they can figure out by looking if you're a murderer or lying or whatever. They never stop looking. It's horrible."

Kathleen nodded. What could she say?

"Will there be a verdict today?" Deb asked.

"Probably not."

"But what happens tonight if they find me guilty?"

"Deb, please, there's no point in torturing yourself—"

"No . . . I want to know. *Tell* me."

Kathleen sighed. "Well, you might spend a night in detention before we get you released on bond pending your appeal. During the appeal you'd be as free as you've been while waiting for trial—"

"What if they find me insane?"

"Like I've said, you'd go to the Columbus Psychiatric Hospital until we get you released."

"But would I go tonight?"

Kathleen didn't think so but she wasn't sure. "The jury isn't likely to reach a verdict today," she said. "I'll do some checking on the procedures." She slid her chair back again.

"Then can I stay with Mom and Dad? This could be my last night."

"Yes," said Kathleen, hating even to have to consider all this. "But you have to be here before the jury goes into deliberation tomorrow morning. You have to be here when they break for the night. They have to see you at counsel table each time they come out of the deliberation room."

Jill wasn't helping. "This could be our last time together. By the time Debbie serves her time I'll be gone or in an institution . . ."

And now they were crying, holding each other. Above, on the beige wall, a reproduction of Gilbert Stuart's George Washington seemed to be looking down his powdered nose at them.

"If they somehow don't convict me," Deb said after wiping her tears with her wrist, "I'm going to live with Mom and Dad when I get released from that awful hospital."

Kathleen badly wanted to be out of the room. The way Jill was affecting Deb made her angry. Jill was making the wait impossible for Deb—God knew what they had talked about while she and Tony were at Lindey's. Still, who was she to be critical?

"I have to see Tony," Kathleen said. "I'll check on the post-verdict procedures too."

Deb and Jill nodded, as though already resigned.

The afternoon passed, supper was taken in to the jury; Kathleen, Tony, Deb and Jill looked at but didn't eat sandwiches in the cubicle. There was nothing to do but wait. No one wanted to talk. Actually Kathleen and Tony had spent most of the time out in the courtroom where it was less oppressive, taking turns checking on Deb and Jill.

The courtroom at night, with half the lights turned off, was an eerie place to wait. Missing was the excitement of a trial before the jury and a packed gallery. All that remained was the tension of not knowing the outcome.

Judge Conklin had gone home. When he was needed the bailiff would call him. When the judge came back to dismiss the jury for the night, Tony would try to get answers to Deb's procedural questions. Bender had gone down to the prosecuting attorney's office on the fourth floor. His bag carrier was holding the fort, sitting on the state's counsel table, listening to Junior Fultz tell war stories about the length of past deliberations.

Kathleen killed time telling Tony the sadness she had felt that afternoon in the small room with Jill and Deb. In a way it made her feel closer to her natural mother, guilty about not spending more time with her. And guilty about her initial irritation with Jill.

You couldn't wait in the near-empty courtroom without keeping your eye on the light over the door to the jury room. It was red. Except for the request to have supper brought in, it had been red since Kathleen and Tony had come back from lunch. The green light would come on when the jury reached a verdict, wanted to recess for the night, needed something or had a question.

At ten the green light came on. Junior Fultz went to the door, unlocked it and disappeared. He came right out. "They have a question," he said. "I'll ring up the judge." He left the note on his desk so that counsel could look at it while he was making his call.

The note read: "What is the effect of provocation and passion? Do we consider insanity if we find the defendant acted with provocation and passion?"

Was this a good sign? It looked as if the jury—or some of them —might be hung up between insanity and involuntary manslaughter. But you couldn't trust a question. It might only be the problem of one juror.

Kathleen and Tony went back to counsel table so they could talk as they waited for the judge. "In my closing I went all out for not guilty by reason of insanity," Tony said. "I didn't argue provocation and passion," he added, knowing that a finding of provocation would only reduce the charge from murder to manslaughter. "I didn't want the jury to compromise on involuntary manslaughter," he said. "Maybe it was a mistake . . ."

"Well, it's what I would have done," Kathleen said. She dreaded the thought of a compromise verdict. Involuntary manslaughter would mean prison for Deb.

Judge Conklin arrived half an hour later. He decided to bring the jury back into the courtroom to reread the charge on the elements of murder and involuntary manslaughter. He would define provocation and passion. At Tony's request he agreed to reread his instruction on insanity and the one on reasonable doubt. It was better than they had a right to expect. Kathleen ran into the small room to make Deb presentable for sitting at counsel table and being seen by the jurors when they came out.

That done, she left Deb with Tony and waited in the ninth-floor lobby. She did not want to be seen by the jurors, not after hearing what Bender had said during closing argument.

Tony came out as soon as the jury returned to their deliberations. "I didn't much like what I saw," he said. "Two of them leaned forward to listen closely when the judge read that part about mere words not being sufficient to establish a provocation." Despite the hour, the jury had elected to keep deliberating. "If they're close to a verdict, that isn't good."

Ellen Sharkey, a reporter who had been covering the trial, came by on her way to call in her story. "I just wanted to tell you," she said to Tony, "I've been covering the courthouse for eight years and I don't think I ever heard a better closing argument than the one you made."

"Do you think it will do any good?"

"Who knows?" Sharkey said, and went on to the press room.

At one A.M. the green light came on again. The jury wanted to break for the night. Deb went with Jill.

When Kathleen and Tony got home, the light on her answering machine was flashing. One of the callers had been Si Wallace. "Call no matter how late," was the message.

She awakened Wallace. "Kathleen," he said, cutting short her apology. "Judge Roberts called me. He's threatening the firm. Roberts reminded me that we have important cases in his court."

"Si, I didn't—"

"Never mind. I know you didn't do anything wrong. We're not going to stand for this from Roberts. I intend to file a complaint with the board of grievances on Monday morning."

"Wallace is treating this like the most important matter in the office," she told Tony. "He's spoiling for a fight."

"Wallace runs the firm well, doesn't he," said Tony.

"He holds us together." She smiled. "It does surprise me," she said. "I never thought securities lawyers could get that steamed."

Saturday was a day of waiting. The jury sent out two more questions. At one-thirty they asked to have the 911 operator's testimony read to them. At five they asked to have the instruction on reasonable doubt reread.

At eleven P.M. they wanted a break. The judge instructed Junior Fultz to offer them the option of continuing deliberations on Sunday or waiting until Monday morning to resume.

"They say they aren't close to a verdict," Fultz reported. "They want to break until Monday morning."

Several wanted to attend church. The jury commissioner would handle arrangements, make sure there was no exposure to the media, that no contacts were made.

Tony said the jurors looked tired when they came out to be dismissed. Some had red, swollen eyes. Two stared at the floor. "They've been fighting," he said.

* * *

On Sunday morning Kathleen and Tony sat at their kitchen table looking out at a silver wonderland. The bare limbs of the maple in the backyard and the trees beyond the stockade fence were sheathed in ice. She had bran and sliced banana, he a Danish hot from the microwave.

"We've never talked about children," she said abruptly. Now or never. "I mean, I don't know what you think. Do you ever think about having kids, or want them, or what? I'd like to know, Tony." I need to know, she added silently.

He was looking at her with adoring eyes. Like when they'd been at Hunan Gardens celebrating after her argument in the supreme court; like he'd looked at her so many times since. She didn't want to give up having him across the table, looking at her like that. Yet she was risking it—

"I *want* kids." He grinned. "Maybe that's because I'm from a family of nine."

His answer surprised her, not that he wanted children, but she had expected he would answer with a question, find out how *she* felt before committing himself.

He went on . . . he couldn't wait to teach a little boy how to swing a bat. "A little girl would be just as good," he said quickly.

She laughed, left well enough alone. Whatever she decided, the question of Tony and children was off the table.

They decided to go to the office, take their mind off the wait by catching up on work that had been put aside for the trial. Deb was with Harrison and Jill. After the trial, Kathleen thought, she could deal with the frayed feelings left over from her time with Deb and Jill in the grubby cubicle at the Hall of Justice.

On the drive to the office, Tony's mood improved. He had been thinking about the jury's questions. The break for Sunday, with some of them going to church, was good, he decided. "They couldn't have gone this long—they couldn't have gotten into such a draining fight," he said, "unless at least some of them have bought not guilty by reason of insanity." He looked at Kathleen for support in this.

"Or murder," she said. She feared the deadlock. She was trying not to think about it, but the divided jury increased the likelihood of a compromise on involuntary manslaughter.

Tony said he was going down to his office, wanted to dictate correspondence so it could be typed on Monday. She filled her coffeemaker and got it started, then called to check on Deb. Harrison answered.

"We've been talking about the news," said Harrison. "They've discovered the Huntington gene—"

"What?" Except for the stories about the trial, she hadn't been reading the newspapers.

"The Huntington disease gene. They've located it."

"What does that mean?"

"It's a step." Harrison sounded excited. He was hopeful for Jill and Deb, though he cautioned that a cure hadn't been found. "The first result may be a simpler and more accurate test," he said. "But they don't even have that yet. Still, this could open the door to a new era in HD research."

"How is Deb doing?"

"Well, I'm more excited than Debbie or Jill," he said. "But just think . . . suppose they find the cure."

Harrison promised to have Deb at the Hall of Justice by eight in the morning and said that Jill would be with her.

Kathleen left the office to get copies of the *Post* and the Sunday New York *Times*. The *Times* had a long story about HD but nothing more definite than Harrison had reported.

It was good news but, thinking on it, frustrating too. Somehow the hope raised by discovery of the HD gene made it harder to bear the lack of a cure or the assurance there would be one. She wondered if the news and Harrison's excitement—for clearly he had seized on it to ease his remorse over damaging Deb's case— was making the day intolerable for Deb and Jill. For Kathleen, the day was proving to be harder than the wait in the courtroom with the red light staring at her.

In the late afternoon she refilled her coffee mug and went to the window. Once again she found herself questioning the decision to reject a plea bargain. Though she believed in Deb's defense, she would not even have considered aborting a pregnancy because her baby had HD. She certainly would not have stayed with Buzz Garrison. It was odd. Her views were the same as his. She was pro-choice but couldn't personally imagine aborting a child. How would she feel if she were the man? The woman, because she carried the baby, had control of the decision. What could a man who disagreed do? Was the jury thinking the same way and forgetting or overlooking Buzz's abuse of Deb?

The discovery of the HD gene made her realize how little control anyone had. What if it had been discovered a year ago? Would her own birth records have been opened? Would Deb have considered aborting her fetus? There was no end to the would-haves.

It was nearly dark outside. The city streets and sidewalks were almost deserted. Tony came in at seven, and it was a great relief to see him. She told him about the HD discovery—and the feelings it had produced.

"Maybe it's a good sign," he said. Was he clutching at straws?

"Did you get any work done?" she asked. His forced optimism was only adding to her anxiety.

"A lot," he said. "What say we take our week in Bermuda right after the trial? We'll leave on Tuesday."

"Oh, Tony, that's a lovely fantasy, but—"

"Wait," he said. "Don't say anything until you hear the deal." He had spent the afternoon on the telephone. He had the airline reservations. He had called the people at the inn where he'd worked. "They'll go all out for us." He'd gotten Chip Drucker's blessing.

"You told Chip Drucker we're taking off on Tuesday for Bermuda?"

"Not you. What would I tell him if you turn stubborn?"

"Go on."

He had called Marty and Jay Melnik. "I did tell them," he said. "But they're okay. Melnik is a super guy."

"And Marty?"

"We've made up. We've had a couple of long talks."

Melnik and Marty, he said, would cover her practice, watch her mail, make sure nothing went wrong. "They think it's about time you got out of this place."

Tony argued they both deserved it . . . the trial, the Judge Roberts fuss, and, of course, themselves. It sounded like overkill on a jury summation.

"How do you know we'll get a verdict before Tuesday afternoon?" she asked.

"I've got a backup. There's space on the Wednesday flight."

"And if there's no verdict by then?"

"I'm a gambler."

Monday morning. No verdict. Judge Conklin started another trial in Courtroom 9B. He would, he told them, come back as needed. Tony thought the jurors looked better going into deliberation after a day's rest. He hoped for a quick verdict.

Neither Deb nor Jill talked about the discovery of the HD gene. Kathleen left them in the small room. Talking to them would make everyone, herself especially, feel worse. Everything had to be suspended until the jury reached a verdict.

At lunchtime, food was taken in to the jury. At 3:30 the green light came on. Junior Fultz unlocked the jury room door.

"They have a verdict," he said when he came out, and left to advise Judge Conklin.

Kathleen went to get Deb and Jill from the cubicle, started to follow Deb into the courtroom. Now that a verdict had been reached, it no longer mattered if the jurors saw her.

"Wait," said Jill. Deb went on, to stand behind the counsel table, next to Tony.

"I'm sorry about Friday afternoon," Jill said. "I know I get cranky, I meant to say something all day Saturday but this waiting has been such an awful time . . ."

"It's okay." Kathleen was thinking about the verdict. She could scarcely breathe.

"I have to tell you this—"

"We'll talk later, Jill."

"I can't go in that courtroom and maybe hear Debbie get sentenced until I've told you."

There wasn't time for Kathleen to explain that no sentence would be passed until after a pre-sentence investigation. She wanted to be in the courtroom, standing at the rail, right behind Tony and Deb when the jury came in.

"Kathleen . . . I've been living with a terrible ache since I gave you up. Well, I don't feel that now, and having the world know I have HD has helped me get through this trial."

"I know something about aches," Kathleen said. She was guiding Jill into the courtroom, getting her seated. "We'll talk later . . ."

The jury came in. You couldn't tell. They were avoiding eye contact with everyone. The forelady handed the forms to Junior Fultz, who took them to the bench and handed them up to Judge Conklin. The judge read them, checked for signatures and handed one of them back to Junior Fultz. "You may announce the verdict." Judge Conklin's voice gave no hint.

"In the case of *The State of Ohio* vs. *Debora Garrison,*" Junior Fultz began in the theatrical, distinct voice he had developed over fifty years for this duty, "we, the jury, do unanimously find the defendant Debora Garrison not guilty."

A mistake, Kathleen thought. Surely they meant not guilty by reason of insanity.

"Is this your verdict?" asked Judge Conklin.

The jurors nodded. They were looking at Deb as the forelady stood. "It is," she said. Bender had the jury polled and each juror affirmed the verdict.

Tony held Deb, letting her cry into his shoulder, sheltering her from the newspeople and from spectators who had crowded forward along the gallery rail to congratulate her. Deb wrapped her arms around Tony.

Kathleen stayed behind the rail, her disbelief in the verdict having changed to joy and then to the realization that the moment belonged to Tony and Deb. She had played her part, but this was Tony's triumph. She stared at them, separated by the gallery rail and the crowd who had wedged into the pit, filling the space between the rail and counsel table.

Tony looked up as if someone had whispered to him that she was standing outside the rail, wanting his arms and body as much as the acquittal for Deb. Kathleen smiled at him. He raised an arm, motioning to her. She worked her way to the gate in the rail, into the pit and through the crowd to reach him.

Jurors wanted to talk. News people wanted interviews. It was still hard for Kathleen to trust the verdict—even after talking to the jurors. "We just didn't think she knew what she was doing," the retired army colonel told them. He had been the most articulate, and though not the foreman, he had been a strong voice in the deliberation.

"We thought . . . at least most of us did . . . that she wanted to hurt him," said the colonel. "But she wasn't thinking about *electrocuting* him. She was just mad, real mad. On Saturday we got into some fights about the instructions the judge gave us. Now if you want my opinion, the law on insanity or temporary insanity . . . whatever you lawyers call it . . . doesn't make much sense. The young lady wasn't insane. Like the other lawyer said, she wasn't disoriented at all. But you see, I don't think that proves she wanted to kill him. I don't mind admitting that I told those people about my experience in 'Nam. There are times you do things without knowing what you're doing, without thinking."

"So we all had these different theories. But when we came back after the day off we tried to fit them together and still follow the law. Well, it came down to this. The prosecution didn't prove she meant to do it." The colonel eyed Tony. "That young lady has been punished enough already," he said.

So the defense strategy had worked. The one they had formulated on the Sunday afternoon following the indictment. They'd combined the three theories: insanity, battered wife, provocation and passion. They had known the challenge would be to make the jury *want* to let Deb off. That had to be done to have a chance with the insanity defense. They'd succeeded to a degree beyond their hope. The jury, in spite of the instruction Bender read twice during summation, had not been convinced on intent to kill.

The law on that was confusing, Kathleen had to admit. Intent was a critical element and the state had to prove it. The insanity defense also probed the defendant's state of mind, but the defense had to prove that. The jury had gotten tangled, but they were right. Deb wasn't insane and if you accepted the defense *evidence,* she should not be convicted of murder.

"I think it was your testimony," said Tony on the way home from the Hall of Justice. "You made them see the relationship between Deb and Buzz."

She smiled and kissed him. *"I* think it was Deb's honesty," she said. "Her willingness to answer Bender's questions, even when her answers seemed to destroy her."

They picked up lo mein from the Chinese carry-out and blew a hundred dollars on a bottle of Dom Perignon. They went home to

German Village to begin their private celebration, to pack for Bermuda. But the calls didn't stop. The Eyewitness News crew came by from Channel Ten to tape an interview. Si Wallace called, wanting to have lunch with Tony tomorrow, then insisting on breakfast when Tony explained that he'd be gone for ten days. An instructor in the school of journalism at Ohio State wanted Tony to represent her in a Title Ten sex discrimination case and failed to see why Tony couldn't see her that night since he was going to be out of town for so long.

Tony offered to take the phone off the hook. "No," said Kathleen. "This is your night. Make the most of it. Our time starts at three-fifteen tomorrow afternoon."

When Harrison Donahey called, Kathleen went to the bedroom to pack. She was uneasy again, as unsure of herself as of what she would need to take to Bermuda. She had to smile at that . . . equating the two dilemmas. She could hear Tony on the telephone detailing for Harrison what he'd been told by the jurors.

"Some of them had trouble with the instructions," Tony was saying. "That's what tied them up so long. What it came down to was they finally decided to stop arguing about the law and do the fair thing. Bender's been calling it a runaway jury, and in a way he's not so far from the truth. They ran away from technicalities alone and got to the *justice* of the case. Maybe that's what people mean when they talk about the genius of the jury system, combining the law with common sense to get justice . . ."

While Kathleen waited for him, she worried that her decisions were coming unraveled. When she got on that plane tomorrow she would be leaving a place that wouldn't be there when she returned. The verdict had changed Tony. No longer would he need her to make his way in the firm. It had changed her. It was foolish to think about children and career as some sort of trade. It wasn't that neat. It wasn't a law case, for God's sake. And yes, she'd been genuinely elated for Tony but, face it, also shamelessly jealous—would she ever stand in the pit after a verdict, mobbed and admired for winning an acquittal in a murder trial?

Could it really work out? The old bond between them was gone . . . they no longer had the trial and Tony's struggle to make partner . . .

Tony was saying goodbye to Harrison, promising to meet for

lunch when he got back from Bermuda. Meanwhile, she had put nothing in her bag, which lay open on the bed. Itself a question mark.

She heard him whistling as he came into the bedroom. He had no idea what had happened, what she was going through.

"Hey, Kathleen," he said, looking at the empty suitcase. "I thought you'd be packed."

"Tony, I just don't know . . ."

"Throw in the basics," he said. "A skirt, a couple pairs of jeans, a few sweaters. We'll shop when we get there. I can't wait to help you pick out clothes. In fact, lady, there isn't anything I won't love doing with you." He pushed her onto the bed and fell on top of her. "Oh God, Kathleen, this is scary . . . can it really be this good?"

He shoved the empty suitcase off the bed. She let him roll her on her back and unbutton her blouse. He was on top of her, his arms propping his head and chest up from the bed, his eyes devouring her. And looking into them, she finally began to understand that she had gone past the point of choices. There just would be no future for her without Tony. Of that she felt suddenly certain.

Maybe there would be pain. Maybe? Surely there would be. But this person, this man Tony was who she wanted to live through it with. When they got to Bermuda there were things she wanted to tell him, things she had told no one. She wanted him to know the scared little girl still inside, the little girl who, if they got married, was sure to cause trouble. Even Tony couldn't quick-fix that. It would take time . . .

It was as surprising as the verdict announced in court that afternoon by Junior Fultz. She relaxed. She no longer felt as if she were facing a trial and that the trial was about to begin, though she knew in a profound way that that was happening. In coming to the place where there were no choices, she had come to the place of trust.

She looked up at him and she trusted him. Not him so much as what she was doing. She felt his lips on hers, his hands pressing life into her body. This was a trip she had to take.